D0341367

7-15

DELCROIX
ACADEMY

THE CANDIDATES

DELCROIX
ACADEMY

THE CANDIDATES

BY INARA SCOTT

HYPERION
NEW YORK

First Edition

1 3 5 7 9 10 8 6 4 2

This book is set in Miller Text.

Printed in the United States of America
V567-9638-5-10166

Library of Congress Cataloging-in-Publication Data on file.

ISBN 978-1-4231-1636-3

Reinforced binding
Visit www.hyperionteens.com

SUSTAINABLE FORESTRY INITIATIVE
Certified Fiber Sourcing
www.sfiprogram.org

THIS LABEL APPLIES TO TEXT STOCK

To Kraig, Leo, and Annija, whose love makes it all worthwhile; and to Susan, who believes in me so much I can't help but believe in myself.

With grateful thanks to Jennifer Besser, who is surely a superhero disguised as an editor.

PROLOGUE

HE HAD greasy shoulder-length hair and a stained white T-shirt stretched tightly across his full, round belly. As he approached the nurses' station near one end of the crowded waiting area, the odor of rotting fruit preceded him. Something about the wildness in his eyes and the trembling of his chin made me nervous. I looked over at Grandma, but she was engrossed in conversation with a man almost as old and blind as she was.

"You killed her. You all killed her." The man's voice started low, nervous, and then grew in strength. He opened a grimy backpack and pulled out a gun.

I froze. Grandma left off midsentence and gaped at the shiny weapon now pointed in our direction. The whoosh began in my ears, drowning out any other sound. As I jumped to my feet, a familiar tingle shot from my toes to my fingertips. . . .

CHAPTER 1

"DANCIA!"

I pulled off my headphones and waited, hoping I was hearing the TV and not Grandma calling. I checked the clock: ten fifteen, which meant *The Price is Right* was on and Grandma should have been occupied.

It came again, this time from the hall outside my room. "Dancia, can you come out, please? There's someone here to see you."

Music blared through the headphones, and I leaned over to turn down my ancient silver CD player. Surely I had misheard Grandma. Someone to see *me*? Dancia Lewis, the incredible invisible girl? No way.

I threw open my bedroom door, expecting to see my four-foot-tall grandmother entertaining a neighbor's cat in our living room. Instead, a pair of well-dressed strangers sitting on the couch turned toward me in unison, got to their feet, and smiled.

I restrained the urge to slam my door. On the right stood a teenage guy with thick chestnut hair, chocolaty brown eyes, and the kind of perfectly square jaw I thought only existed on models. He wore khaki pants and a white shirt—classic preppy gear, though on him it looked incredibly hot.

3

The man on the left had black hair with wings of pure white at the temples, and unbelievable blue eyes the color of the Caribbean Sea. Not that I've ever seen the Caribbean, but I swear you could have cut and pasted his eyes right into an ad for the Bahamas.

Meanwhile, I looked like I didn't know how to operate a washing machine. My gym shorts had a glob of strawberry jelly on them from breakfast, my wrinkled gray T-shirt looked like it had been slept in (which it had), and my Seattle Mariners baseball hat had a dark ring around the brim.

Grandma practically winced as her gaze traveled up and down my outfit. Her taste runs toward matching velour tracksuits, so I don't usually worry about her opinion much. Still, this time I think she was right.

She moved quickly, snatching the hat off my head, and I felt my curls spring instantly back into place. Without thinking, I tried to flatten them back down with my hands. I should have known it was a lost cause. I work pretty hard at being unremarkable, but there's nothing I can do about my hair. It's light blond and super curly. Very hard to miss. White-girl 'fro, if you know what I mean. I tried to dye it once, but you cannot imagine what happens to dry, frizzy hair when you dye it. It's not pretty.

Grandma dragged me the ten feet from my bedroom to the couch. "This is my granddaughter, Dancia Lewis," she said proudly.

"Miss Lewis, so nice to meet you. I'm Richard Judan, chief recruiter for Delcroix Academy." The older man stepped forward and shook my hand. His voice was deep and smooth, like a politician's or TV newscaster's.

"Delcroix?" I repeated, like some idiotic parrot.

Delcroix Academy is this ritzy private school on the

outskirts of Danville, where Grandma and I live. It's about eighty miles from Seattle; too far to commute for work, but I've heard some people buy houses between Seattle and Danville just so they can send their kids to Delcroix and keep jobs in Seattle. Because, really, who would live in Danville if they didn't have to?

The school sits on a hill overlooking our town. An iron fence surrounds endless lawns, which are green even in the middle of summer, when the rest of Danville's grass withers and dies. Enormous front gates open only for the buses that bring kids to and from school each day. People have to leave their cars in a special parking lot at the bottom of the hill and take the buses up, even the teachers. I guess it's a security thing. Half the kids are probably royalty from some foreign country. They definitely don't hang out in town. The kids at my school make fun of them the way you make fun of a movie star, or the president. Famous people you see from a distance, but never expect to meet.

"Yes, Delcroix." Caribbean Blue Eyes gave me a smile so white it gleamed, then gestured toward his sidekick. "This is Cameron Sanders. He'll be a junior at Delcroix this fall, and he's one of our student recruiters. He works with me over the summer to identify potential new freshman and tell them about the school."

"Call me Cam." The boy stuck out his hand for me to shake. He was tall, way taller than me, and I'm a good five foot nine. In middle school I really had to slouch to hide the fact that I was the tallest girl in my class. Naturally, Grandma is always on me to stand up straight.

"Hi, Cam." I tried to wipe my hand surreptitiously on my shorts, because it had suddenly become damp, and the last thing I wanted was for him to think I was one of those people who always had sweaty palms. I couldn't avoid meeting his eyes, so I looked, and instantly I got this fluttery feeling in my chest. Even though I knew it was impossible for a guy that attractive to ever notice a girl like me, his gaze felt warm and inviting. He had an air of athletic outdoorsyness, like he could run a marathon or climb a mountain and look gorgeous doing it.

Reluctantly, I extended my hand.

"Great to finally meet you, Dancia." He closed his palm over mine, and I could barely keep from jumping when an electric shock rippled through my arm.

It sounds weird, but I seriously felt something, like when I was five and accidentally put my finger in a socket. Static electricity from the carpet, I guess, except it felt stronger than that. I knew I couldn't be imagining it, because it wasn't exactly a good feeling, and if I'd imagined touching Cam, it would have felt good.

Startled, I jerked my hand away and dropped my eyes, but not before I caught him smiling at me. It was a comforting smile, like he felt the shock too, and he wanted to tell me it was all right.

Mr. Judan smiled as well. But his smile wasn't comforting. It was triumphant. Like he'd won the lottery or something.

We all stood there for a minute, me shifting uneasily on my feet and absently rubbing my hands together before I realized everyone was waiting for me to sit down. I grabbed a wooden chair from the dining room table—we call it that even though we don't have a dining room, and the table sits in a space between the hall and the living room—and sat down beside Cam.

"Now, what can we do for you?" Grandma asked the strangers. Her denture-bright smile flashed across the room, and I knew these men had gotten the poor thing's hopes up. Recruiter . . . Delcroix . . . I could see her putting the pieces together. She was probably already having visions of me riding that bus up the road to the magic gates, which was insane because 1) we're not rich, 2) I'm not particularly smart, and 3) we're *so* not rich.

Grandma's been taking care of me since I was four, when my parents died, and we pretty much live on her social security. Grandma owns this house, which isn't too far from my school, and we've got enough to eat. I babysit some kids from church when I want to buy new music or a book the library doesn't have. I can't afford a cell phone, but it's not like I have friends to text, so it doesn't really matter.

Anyway, we definitely could not afford to pay private-school tuition.

"We're here to talk to you and Dancia about Delcroix, Mrs. Lewis."

"Why?" I asked, trying not to sound as suspicious as I felt. Despite my best efforts to keep my gaze planted on Mr. Judan, I kept stealing little glances at Cam from the corner of my eye. Even sitting down he was impressive. His hands, which were resting on his knees, looked strong and tanned. I tried to ignore it, but something about him radiated ultra-sweet and encouraging signals, like he wouldn't be at all bothered if I jumped into his lap.

Mr. Judan spread his hands as he spoke. "Dancia, I'm sure this is unexpected, but the decision of the board of directors was unanimous. We'd like you to join the incoming freshman class at Delcroix." His voice practically purred with warmth.

Grandma sucked in her breath. "Really? But we can't . . . How could we . . ." She gestured around the room, and a blush spread over her papery smooth cheeks.

That was when I started to get mad. Not at Grandma, of course, but at Mr. Judan. Because it was obvious we couldn't afford Delcroix, and it wasn't fair to make Grandma embarrassed like that. I mean, who were they kidding? The kids who went to Delcroix lived in mansions and had servants. They weren't like Grandma and me.

"Cost is not an issue, Mrs. Lewis. Many of the Delcroix students attend under a full scholarship. Cameron is one of our scholarship students, in fact. Dancia would have all her expenses paid in full."

"You'll even get to live on campus," Cam said to me. When Grandma's blush deepened, he turned to her and added, "Not that there's anything wrong with your house, of course. But on campus, Dancia can use the library or computer lab any time she wants."

Nice recovery, I thought. Truth is, our house isn't much to look at. Two tiny bedrooms, a little kitchen, bathroom, and living room. You can vacuum the entire house from the plug in the hall outside my door. I know because I do most of the cleaning around here. Grandma's got arthritis and can't push the vacuum, or scrub the counters, or clean out the fridge, or much of anything that requires physical exertion.

"I see." Grandma dabbed at her eyes and settled back in her chair as Cam spoke. Grandma has foggy blue eyes that water all the time, so she's constantly wiping their corners. Still, she's a stickler for appearances. Even when she's wearing her tracksuits—a pink one today, with purple trim—her hair is perfectly curled and she always wears makeup.

It's a little unnerving to know your grandma spends more time on her appearance than you do.

"What if I don't want to live there?" I asked. It wasn't as

though I could just ditch Grandma. She could barely carry grocery bags in from the car.

"We ask all students to live on campus during the week," Mr. Judan replied. "It's an important part of the Delcroix experience, and a time to bond with your schoolmates. But you're free to go home over the weekend."

"I was worried about it too, when I was a freshman," Cam said. "But you'll love it. You'll get to know everyone really well because you spend so much time together. The food is great, and the library is perfect for studying. My dad lives in Seattle, and I didn't even realize how loud our apartment was until I came to Delcroix. I go home for vacations and long weekends. It's perfect, and my scholarship covers it all. Yours will too."

I had to admit to being impressed by the offhanded way he conveyed this information, like he wasn't the least bit embarrassed about being on scholarship at a rich kids' school.

"Why me?"

"Delcroix is what we call an invitation-only program, Dancia," Mr. Judan said, smoothing an invisible wrinkle in his pants. "We select each student individually because of the special gifts he or she will bring to our campus. We look for a very diverse student body. Some of our students are dancers, some are gifted mathematicians, others are poets. They all have different talents, but they have one thing in common: after they graduate, we expect them to do amazing things to better humanity, and they do. Our students go on to be senators, CEOs, principal ballerinas, and Nobel laureates. And we'd like you to be a part of our school."

"We think you're something special, Dancia," Cam said, leaning forward as if he intended to use his entire body to convince me of his sincerity. "We wouldn't be here otherwise."

I snorted. Unattractive, sure, but I couldn't help myself. The whole thing was absurd.

"Special?" I said, keeping my voice calm. "I think perhaps you've mistaken me for someone else. I'm the one with the B average and mediocre ball-handling skills."

Grandma glared at me, but I held my ground and raised my eyebrows at Mr. Judan. No one was less exceptional than Dancia Lewis. I had made sure of that. Unless somehow they knew about . . .

Mr. Judan interrupted my thoughts with a voice that could have soothed an angry pit bull. "You *are* special, Dancia."

He was good. I found my shoulders relaxing even though I wanted to keep them tense.

"To be honest," he continued, "we might not have found out about you if the *Danville Chronicle* hadn't run a story about what happened at the hospital. Once we heard that, we started talking to your teachers at the middle school. It wasn't long before we knew that you would be perfect for Delcroix."

My heart started racing as I let myself complete the thought: unless somehow they knew about . . . my power.

CHAPTER 2

I TOOK a slow breath. Cam tried to make eye contact with me, but I pinned my eyes on Mr. Judan and the perfect white wings of hair at his temples. He couldn't really know, I told myself. I mean, sometimes I don't even know what I've done until it's over, and even then it's not always clear.

"You saw the article!" Grandma's face practically split with the size of her smile. "Wasn't that just remarkable? I don't know what would have happened if Dancia hadn't been there. There were children in that room. That man could have done something terrible."

"We were just lucky he tripped," I said. "I didn't really do anything."

"You threw yourself at a man with a gun who was threatening a room full of people. I'd say that was doing something," Mr. Judan said.

"It really wasn't a big deal." I turned away so they wouldn't see the blush I could feel crawling across my cheeks.

It happened about a month ago, and I can't say I regret going after the guy. After all, he could have hurt Grandma. She may be a hundred years old, and I may sometimes cringe when we're out in public because she lacks control of certain bodily functions, but she's *Grandma*. She's all I've got, and I wasn't going to let anyone hurt her.

Still, it was pretty horrible.

We were at the hospital, waiting for Grandma to get her cataracts checked—even though it's totally illegal, she lets me drive her home after they mess with her eyes. It's pretty cool, if I do say so myself. How many fourteen-year-olds get to drive? Anyway, we were in the waiting room, flipping through old *Highlights* magazines, when this guy came in. He started swearing about how the hospital killed his wife and how we were all going to pay. His words slurred together like one long painful thought. The only thing I could think was to make sure he didn't hit Grandma.

So I went after him. Next thing I knew, he was sprawled on his back, not moving. Grandma said I rushed toward him, and before I even touched him, he fell backward and hit his head. Last I heard he was in a coma. They said I must have startled him and he tripped. Of course, they didn't see the way he looked at me as he flew through the air—terrified, the whites of his eyes glowing against the red veins that snaked through them.

I think he mouthed "Stop," or "Please."

Maybe both.

I picture him every night now as I fall asleep, the stubble on his cheeks and dark circles under his eyes. When he first started talking, his voice sounded thick and muffled, as if he might start crying.

"It's quite rare for a child your age to do something like that," Mr. Judan said. "We understand from your teachers that it was not the first time you've gone out of your way to protect someone. That's a talent in itself, Dancia. A talent for courage."

And I thought I had been doing such a good job blending in. Stupid, nosy teachers.

"What's that supposed to mean?" I asked. "It's not like teenagers don't ever help other people."

"No, of course not," he said, his voice a low rumble. "But when you are young, your self-protective instincts are very strong. Stronger than almost anything else. When a child is able to overcome those instincts and put her own safety in jeopardy to help someone else, it's truly exceptional."

I didn't like his use of the word "child." I was turning fifteen in November, after all. And it wasn't like I wanted to risk my life. I never planned to do anything to that guy. But for some reason when I see someone in trouble, my body takes over and crazy things happen.

"Seriously, it's amazing what you did," Cam said.

When I let myself look at him, a little pool of warmth formed in my stomach. He was staring right at me, and I couldn't contain the mindless little smile that sprung up in response.

"You were some kind of hero," he added.

I basked for a moment in his appreciative gaze, and thought about what he and Mr. Judan had said. They didn't think I was a freak with magic powers. They thought I was a hero.

Being a hero was definitely better than being a freak. Unless they wanted me to keep doing heroic things. That was absolutely out of the question.

See, the problem is, I can't control my power. Or I should say, in certain situations, like where people are hurt or threatened, I can't seem to stop myself from using it. It's a reflex, like throwing your hands in front of your face when someone hurls a ball at you. Thoughts just appear in my brain. I get scared, or mad, or overwhelmed, and think of something, and somehow, magically, it happens. Like when I imagined the guy at the hospital falling and knocking his head on the corner of an end table, or when I imagined a lifeguard chair landing on this jerk at the water park who was teasing a chubby girl about her swimsuit.

It might sound cool, but it's actually terrifying. Because when I use my power, even when I don't mean for it to happen, people get hurt. Now, maybe those people did bad things and deserved what they got, but who am I to make that call? Maybe some people out there would be willing to take the responsibility for putting someone in a coma, but I'm sure not.

I decided a long time ago to try my best not to use it. The consequences are just too great, and the mistakes, well . . . I don't like to think about the mistakes. I've organized my life around this, and most of the time I'm successful. But then there are those times, like the hospital, where I can't avoid it. The reflex takes over.

"I'd probably flunk out after the first week," I said, pushing aside thoughts of the hospital. "I'm only doing basic algebra, and I did terribly in chemistry. Don't all the Delcroix kids take AP classes? I don't see how I could keep up."

"No one flunks out of Delcroix," Cam said. "Once you're asked to attend, your grades don't matter." He sent an apologetic look at Mr. Judan, who raised an eyebrow. "I mean, they matter to colleges, and you have to apply yourself, but they won't kick you out for your grades. Not everyone is good at regular schoolwork. Like Mr. Judan said, the other kids are artists, or dancers, or computer geeks. You'll see. You'll fit in somewhere."

Yeah, right. They had no idea who they were dealing

with. Dancia Lewis *blended* in, she didn't *fit* in. There's a big difference.

"We do have one rule at Delcroix," Mr. Judan interrupted, "and we take it very seriously. We require all incoming students to sign the Delcroix Pledge. You must promise to use your talents only to advance the common good and to achieve the betterment of humanity. It's simple, but very important. Delcroix will give you incredible tools and will groom your talents in ways you could never learn on your own. But those skills bring power, and that power must not be abused."

My mouth dropped open. A pledge? Are you kidding me?

"A kid was expelled for hacking into a government computer system," Cam said, no trace of a smile on his face. "He tried to sell the information he found there. We had to kick him out. He spent some time in jail as well."

The room was silent for a moment as everyone contemplated this story. My head was spinning. A part of me already desperately wanted to go to Delcroix, if only to be near Cam, while the other part wanted to run screaming from the room.

"What are you good at?" I asked Cam. When I focused on him, I couldn't think about anything else.

"I'm good at communicating," he said. "I've never gotten the best grades, but I'm always class president. People seem to like me." He leaned back against our mangy couch and managed not to sound conceited at all.

"You're the president of your class?" I had no trouble believing that. He looked like he should be president of something.

"I was last year. We'll have new elections this fall. You could run, you know. The freshman elections are wide open because everyone's still getting to know each other."

I couldn't help it: I snorted again. "Me? Run for student government? I don't think so."

"You can be anything you want at Delcroix." As Cam leaned forward, his knee bumped against mine. I jumped about four feet into the air.

Very cool, Dancia, I thought. Do you want Cam to think you're a complete idiot?

Grandma cleared her throat. "I'm going to get some lemonade," she said. "Would you care for a glass, Mr. Judan? Cameron?"

They both nodded and stood up when she did.

"That sounds lovely, Mrs. Lewis," Mr. Judan reached down to open his briefcase and pulled out some papers. "We can work on the enrollment forms while Dancia and Cameron talk."

"Wait!" I jumped up, shaking myself from my Cam-induced stupor. "I need to think about it a little."

Grandma gave me her best *What, are you insane?* look. "Dancia, what is there to think about?"

The panicked words tumbled out of me. "I'm not sure if I want . . . I mean, I was really looking forward to going to Danville High and . . . my friends are all there and . . . what about the soccer team?"

Grandma crossed her arms over her chest. I think she knew everything I said was a lie—except for the part about not being sure what I wanted. That was definitely true. But it was all happening too fast. Danville High might not hold any promise of friends, interesting classes, or good times, but at least I knew what it would be like. I knew how to control it, how to blend in.

I knew none of those things about Delcroix.

Mr. Judan's mouth tightened and his eyes went cold. But then he smiled at me like that's what everyone says when they're offered a place in Delcroix's freshman class with a full scholarship. "I have a good idea: why don't you and Cameron have lunch tomorrow? You can think things over tonight and ask Cameron any questions that might come up."

Grandma practically seared me with her stare, so I turned to Cam and reluctantly said, "All right. How about noon at Bev's?"

Cam nodded. "Sounds perfect."

Mr. Judan gave an apologetic shrug. "After that we really will need you to make a decision. I hate to rush you, but we'll need to do some placement tests and evaluate you so we can design the best possible curriculum. Freshman orientation starts in a week, and we'll need to get some of this paper-work processed before then."

I swallowed hard.

At that moment, all I could think of were those cartoons where Goofy gets stuck in front of a snowball rolling down a hill, and the snowball hits him, and he's smushed into the side of it, and you can see him spread-eagled on the snowball as it keeps rolling down the hill.

Because that's exactly what I felt like.

CHAPTER 3

ABOUT A half hour later, Mr. Judan flashed his ultrawhite teeth at Grandma and me one last time before he ushered Cam into a black Mercedes-Benz. They roared away the second the doors closed.

As soon as they disappeared from view, Grandma rounded on me and shook a gnarled, arthritic finger in my direction. "What are you thinking? You don't want to go to Delcroix? Do you have any idea how important that school is? What an honor it is to be chosen to attend? What possible reason could you have for not wanting to go? The money won't be a problem because they're going to pay for everything. And don't give me that story about missing your friends and looking forward to high school. Last week you were telling me that you wished summer would go on forever. And what's this nonsense about soccer? You said you'd never make the varsity team at Danville High."

Nice move, Dancia. Tell Grandma everything, why don't you.

Problem was, Grandma was one hundred percent right. I loved soccer but didn't have the skills to make the varsity team. And I didn't have friends, or classes, or anything to look forward to. It's a sign of just how depressed I was about the whole thing that I had confided all this to Grandma.

But while Danville High sounded depressing, Delcroix sounded terrifying. How could I blend in there? Being invisible and staying unattached were the only ways I knew to avoid triggering my power. The more emotionally attached I got to someone, the more likely I was to use my power to protect them. I had stopped making friends in the sixth grade after my best friend, Aileen, got teased by a bully and I dropped a tree branch on his head.

He went to the hospital. Twenty stitches and a concussion.

While staying unattached kept me from acting on behalf of someone else, being invisible kept me from using my power to defend myself. I made sure I didn't fit into any of the school cliques so I wouldn't develop enemies. I wasn't too smart, too pretty, too nerdy, or too preppy. I was just Dancia Lewis, the girl who everyone recognized but no one knew.

The trick to this was the Dancia two-step, which I'd developed over the years and found to work in most social situations. Step one, act bored and impatient, like you're waiting for someone. This tends to keep people from approaching, but also makes you look reasonably cool. Step two, if they do approach, ask them questions about themselves. People love to answer questions like that. You can find an excuse to slip away later, and they'll have a pleasant memory of talking to you, but no idea who you are. Step two was dangerous because sometimes I would forget I wasn't supposed to be making friends, and end up in a real conversation. But I'd remember later, and the next time I saw the person, I'd start again with step one.

What if the two-step didn't work at Delcroix? What if I

couldn't blend in there? Would I start dropping tree branches on everyone? How many people could I send to the hospital before someone started to wonder?

"You heard them talking about that pledge," I said, trying to sound pitiful. At this point, sympathy was my only hope. "It's weird, right? I mean, how could you pledge never to do anything that wasn't good, or wasn't going to advance humanity, or whatever he said?" As I spoke, actual tears began welling up in my eyes, which was embarrassing because I never liked crying in front of Grandma.

Her face softened. "My dear girl," she said, coming over to give me a hug, "what's this really about, anyway?"

Hugging Grandma is sort of like hugging a kid, because she's so much shorter than I am. Sometimes I wish she were a few feet taller so I could feel like she was taking care of me, instead of the other way around. But still, it was nice, and I started to cry even harder. She held me for a minute and then pulled me over to the couch. She grabbed some Kleenex from the coffee table—we've always got Kleenex around because of Grandma's eyes—and handed them to me. I blew my nose and started to feel a little more in control.

"You're a good girl, Dancia. You could make that pledge, even though I agree, it does seem a little silly. After all, if you were going to do something bad, you wouldn't stop at breaking a pledge, now would you?"

She smiled at me, and I laughed a little. Then she got serious again. "Is there something more going on? Something else I should know about?"

This was the question I dreaded. Whenever something happened with my power, I'd get really depressed, and even though I tried to hide it, Grandma always knew. She'd ask all these deep, probing questions, which only made me feel worse. Eventually she'd give up, but not before looking at me with her droopy, worried eyes and saying, "If there's ever anything you want to tell me about—anything at all—you know I'm here."

I wished I could explain my situation to her, but Grandma has enough problems. She's got diabetes, high blood pressure, cataracts, and a bunch of other things I can't even pronounce. I know because I go to her doctor's appointments with her. She's got handfuls of pills to take every day. I couldn't add my problems to her list. It was already long enough. She shouldn't have been saddled with raising a kid at her age, and I knew she didn't get help from any of my other relatives. I guess they figured I had someone to take care of me, so why should they bother getting involved?

"I don't like being singled out," I said. "They want to make a big deal about what happened in the hospital, and I hate that."

She nodded. "I know that's how you are now, Danny, but you weren't always that way. When you were a little girl, you loved being in the spotlight."

"I did?"

"You did. Dance recitals, school concerts, you name it. Your mother was like that too. She loved being onstage. I wish . . ." Grandma's eyes filled, and this time it looked like real tears. I get nervous whenever Grandma starts talking about my mom, because then she starts crying, which makes me want to cry, and it's all just too much.

My parents died in a car accident when I was four. They got run off the road by some guy who was probably drunk. We were living in Seattle at the time, but it happened here in Danville. I think Grandma feels guilty about it because we were visiting her. She says sorry to me sometimes, as if it were her fault my mom died.

I don't really remember my mom, but Grandma has lots of pictures of her in photo albums. She pulls them out every now and then, after I've gone to bed, and looks at them and cries. I've seen her do it when I get up to go to the bathroom. I pretend I don't notice. My mom was her only kid, so I guess she took it pretty hard when she died. She even changed my last name so it would be the same as my mom's maiden name. Grandma told me once that she's determined to keep my mom's memory alive. As if we could ever forget.

It's hard to believe I used to like being in the spotlight. I vaguely remember school concerts before I learned about my power. But once I realized all those strange things that happened around me weren't coincidences, life changed.

"Grandma, don't make me go to Delcroix." I struggled to clear my throat.

She shook her head. "I would never force you, Danny. But I wish you'd consider attending. Your mother would have been so proud of you, being chosen this way. She always wanted the best for you." Before she could catch it, a tear traced a line through her baby pink blush. "She dreamed about going there herself, you know." Her mouth wobbled a little as she tried to smile.

"Really?" It hadn't even occurred to me that Delcroix had been around when my mom was a kid.

"She wanted to be a singer," Grandma said. "She was a determined little thing, your mother. She practiced and practiced, sang every chance she had at school and at church, hoping someone would notice and offer her a place at Delcroix."

"Was she good?" It seemed amazing, somehow, that I had never known this about my mother. I'd seen pictures of her singing, but I had no idea it had been a big deal to her. I figured it was like my playing soccer—fun, but not something you take seriously.

Grandma laughed a little sadly. "She was good enough for Danville. Not good enough for Delcroix. She finally sent them a letter asking if they would let her audition, and they sent her a polite 'no, thank you.' She didn't sing much after high school."

I paused, imagining the girl I'd seen in pictures. She had wide-set eyes, like mine, but she had straight hair and a big smile. She looked like someone you'd want for a friend. "And you think after that she would still want me to go to Delcroix?" I asked.

I really hoped she would say no.

Grandma didn't hesitate. "Oh yes, I'm sure of it. It would be like her own dream coming true. I know the teachers at your middle school weren't the best, and if I'd had some way to send you to private school before now, I would have. Danville High isn't any better than your junior high. I know you'll be bored there. You would be challenged at Delcroix. Imagine how it would feel to be surrounded by people who are so talented, so intelligent!"

Grandma, bless her heart, thought the reason I got straight B's was because I was bored. She was convinced I was some sort of genius who wasn't being challenged.

Okay, it's true that I probably could have gotten A's if I'd wanted to, but everyone picks on the smart kids, like they pick on the stupid kids. So I get B's. It was safer that way.

"Grandma, what if I do something wrong and they kick me out?" I searched desperately for some reason to explain why I was prepared to break her heart and the heart of my dead mother by not attending Delcroix. "It would be too horrible, don't you think?"

"So you think it would be better not to try?" She gave me one of those hard, square looks that make me feel like I'm five and have been caught stealing a pack of gum from the grocery store. "That's not the Dancia I know and love. The Dancia I know isn't a coward. She's a fighter. She's the bravest person I know."

Great. Now she was using psychology on me. And it totally worked, because I immediately started feeling guilty about disappointing my mother, and my grandmother, and not even being willing to try.

"But, Grandma, I can't leave you alone. You need me."

She frowned. "Dear girl, I know you do a lot of work around here, but that's exactly the problem. You spend too much time taking care of an old woman. A girl your age should be playing with her friends, or going to the mall, or whatever children do these days. You need more than life in this house, and you're never going to get it as long as you're stuck here with me."

She looked upset, and I felt terrible because I never thought she'd blame herself for my being such a loner. I wanted to tell her it wasn't her fault, that it was my stupid power that wrecked everything, but I couldn't.

"It's up to you, Danny. I'm not going to force you to go." As she studied my miserable expression, her face softened. "Why don't you go out to lunch with that boy tomorrow and see what he thinks. Maybe he can help."

Cam. Oh my goodness, I had forgotten about Cam.

Lunch, tomorrow, with Cam.

A rush of fear and anticipation made me so dizzy, I had to sit down.

"Okay, Grandma," I managed to spit out. "That's a good idea. I'll have lunch with Cam. And then I'll decide if I want to go to Delcroix."

How I would survive there—*if* I decided to go—remained a mystery.

CHAPTER 4

BY ELEVEN the next morning I had worked myself into a complete panic. As part of my invisibility routine I'd made a point of accumulating a wardrobe of completely nondescript clothing. This had never particularly bothered me before because I'd never been invited to lunch with an incredibly hot guy. Now I realized with painful clarity that none of my clothes really fit—everything had come from a clearance rack at Walmart or the Goodwill—and the colors ranged from black to brown to tan. So basically, I'd be cleaner than yesterday, but not much more attractive.

I locked my bike to a "No Parking" sign and walked into Bev's Café—the only decent restaurant in Danville—right at noon. Some annoying oldies music blared from a jukebox across the room. Grandma loves Bev's. It's got black-and-white floor tiles, white tabletops, and red leather booths. She thinks it's adorable. I just like the hamburgers.

Cam had already grabbed a corner booth, and he waved at me. Pure terror swept over me.

He was even cuter than I remembered.

I took a deep breath and wandered over, trying to act as if I did this sort of thing every day.

"Hey, Dancia. Glad you could meet me." He lounged

against the booth, his shaggy hair falling into dark eyes.

"Yeah, hi." The words stuck in my throat like I'd just swallowed a huge mouthful of peanut butter. Of course I knew he had only agreed to meet me because it was his job. But a girl could dream, right?

I sat across from him, and a waitress bustled over. She brightened as soon as she saw me. "Dancia, sweetie, how are you? How's your grandma?"

"She's fine, thanks, Patty." I hoped Cam didn't think it was hopelessly geeky to talk to the waitress. Grandma and I came in here a couple times a month, and it was impossible not to know everyone. "How's Ella?" Ella was her cat, and Patty doted on her the way most people doted on their kids.

"What a sweet thing to ask! Actually, she did the cutest thing the other day . . ." As she handed us menus and filled our water glasses, Patty droned on about Ella's latest adorable antics, which included shredding the living room curtains. Then she aimed a curious look at Cam. "Are you new to town? I don't recognize you from the high school."

Cam held out his hand. "I'm Cameron Sanders. I go to school up at Delcroix."

"Oh." Patty took a step back. She focused on his hand for a moment, and then wiped her own on her apron. "Delcroix? Really? You folks don't come in here much." She shook his hand with a quick, nervous jerk.

"A terrible mistake." He gave her a wide smile. "This place is great. From now on, I know where I'll be coming on my days off."

Patty stared at him silently for a moment and twisted her hands together. I couldn't tell if she was horrified or appreciative. I guess I hadn't thought about how other people in town might view Delcroix. I mean, the kids in my middle school thought the Delcroix kids were rich weirdos, but we didn't pay them much attention. Grandma, on the other hand, talked about Delcroix like you'd have to be some kind of god to go there.

"Does one of your teachers really write speeches for the president?" Patty asked, the words coming out in a rush. "My sister said it wasn't true, but I heard it was. And they said he might come for a visit this year."

Cam nodded. "They talked about him stopping by. But we don't know for sure."

"Well, that would be nice." She twisted her lips into an awkward grimace that I think was meant to be a smile. "I sure would like to see the president." With that, Patty gave Cam a little nod that was almost a bow, and then she scurried away.

I grabbed my glass and drank down about half. Maybe Delcroix was even more out of my league than I'd thought.

With Patty gone, silence stretched out between us. Ask a question, I told myself. That always works.

"So I guess you like Delcroix a lot, huh?"

He paused and studied me with those big dark eyes. "I love it. I think you would too."

"What do you like about it?"

"Well"—he gazed directly at me as he spoke—"I know a lot of kids who feel like they can't be themselves at their school. They think they have to change themselves to fit into a group or feel accepted. That doesn't happen at Delcroix. Everyone just *is*. Hard to believe, I know, but it's the truth. You don't have to pretend at Delcroix."

His voice dropped, and even though he couldn't have planned it, his words traveled straight to my heart. Not have to pretend? What would that even feel like?

"You can just be yourself, Dancia. Wouldn't that be amazing?"

Something about Cam's voice was hypnotic. The restaurant, Patty, even the cheesy music faded away. I closed my eyes for a second and imagined walking down the hall of a new school, people passing by and saying hello, friends waiting for me as I got to class. I swallowed hard as tears pricked the backs of my eyes.

When my eyes opened, Cam was studying me. His forehead wrinkled a little, like he was concerned. "I know it sounds strange," he said softly, "but you aren't the only one who feels that way."

How did he know what I was thinking?

I waved my hand and struggled to sound nonchalant. "Actually, my middle school was fine. Really. I mean, there's all the usual stuff with the geeks and the cool kids, but in general, everyone gets along."

"Of course." He nodded and picked up the menu. The magic string connecting us snapped and dissolved. "So what's good here?"

"You've really never eaten at Bev's?" I couldn't hide my surprise. "Didn't you say you started at Delcroix two years ago?"

He looked a little embarrassed. "I stay pretty busy at school."

I thought about what Patty had said, how the people from Delcroix never came down here, and I realized with a start that before Cam, I'd never met any kids from there. Sure, we made up stories about them, but we'd never actually talked to one. Which made them seem odd, all of a sudden, or maybe just snooty. But not Cam. Cam would never be snooty. I could tell.

"Oh, I didn't mean anything by it," I said. "I just thought everyone in Danville ate here. They have really good hamburgers and fries. But stay away from the clam chowder."

He grinned. "Thanks for the tip."

When I got home two hours later, I marched straight up to Grandma and scowled.

She didn't even close her magazine. "How was lunch?"

"Great," I snapped. Amazing. Incredible. And I was now completely in love with a guy I'd probably never speak to again.

"What did you and Cameron talk about?"

"Nothing. School. Delcroix."

Everything. We talked about soccer and how the girls' team needed a new forward. We talked about the cool electives Delcroix offered, like popular music, poetry, and independent study, where you could make up your own class. He told me about his dad, how he missed him during the school year but how fun it was to live on campus. I played it cool, pretended like I had lots of friends I'd be leaving behind, but I had the feeling he knew the truth. He wasn't mean about it. He was . . . sweet. Caring. Understanding. He told me about amazing things they did, like getting to visit Cape Canaveral. One of the space shuttle pilots had gone to Delcroix, and does a tour for the advanced astronomy classes. Not to mention all the musicians who do guest lectures there. Not just classical musicians, either. Cool people. People I'd heard of.

"And did you make a decision?"

I set my jaw. "I'll go to Delcroix, but if I don't like it by Christmas break, I'm transferring back to Danville High."

She flipped through a few more pages. "That sounds lovely, dear. An excellent plan."

"Aren't you going to say anything else?" I snapped. "Like, I told you so?"

"Why would I do something like that?" Grandma said, closing the magazine. "Now, what should we have for dinner?"

I stomped off to my room, thoroughly annoyed by the knowledge that, as usual, Grandma had gotten exactly what she wanted.

CHAPTER 5

I WOKE early the next morning after a night of very little sleep, and stumbled into the bathroom. Through puffy eyes I took in my usual attractive early-morning hairdo—half frizz, half ringlets—and a crease across my cheek from my lumpy pillow.

I picked halfheartedly at a few blackheads. My whole body felt out of sorts. I'd spent the night fantasizing about Cam, imagining us as boyfriend and girlfriend, walking down the hall arm in arm. It was painfully delicious, even in my mind, and definitely not conducive to a good night's sleep.

But he was just being nice, I kept reminding myself; just doing his job.

As if that could keep me from developing the crush of the century.

I decided to go for a jog. Running usually helped clear my head. And now that I knew Cam, I had a figure to maintain.

I dug through my hamper and found an old pair of running shorts and a relatively clean T-shirt with a picture of Danville Central Hospital on it.

Grandma's not much for doing laundry, and unfortunately, neither am I.

Grandma's door was closed, which was a relief because

I had a suspicion she would want to talk about Delcroix as soon as she woke up. I tiptoed past her bedroom and through the living room, locked the door behind me, and started off at a decent pace down the street.

According to Grandma, people in Danville used to make good money working at the mill or logging in the forests. But they stopped logging before I was born, and closed the mill, so now there's just a lot of rundown houses and people without work. People like Grandma and me, who are just getting by.

The bright side is that the forests nearby are young and thick, and there are trails within a few miles of my house. When I was a kid, Grandma would take me on picnics and nature walks, and I always loved it, even when I pretended not to. I feel better in the woods, like my problems aren't so overwhelming.

We're close to Mount Rainier, which has always worried me a little because they say it's only a matter of time before it erupts again, and it would be just my luck to get caught in a freak lava flow. But this morning all I could see was the peak off in the distance, covered with snow. It looked peaceful, and the air was damp and still. The slap of my sneakers against the road was the only sound I could hear, and I calmed down a little as I ran.

Maybe things would be different at Delcroix, just like Cam said. Maybe I wouldn't feel threatened. Maybe I wouldn't have to try so hard to make myself invisible. Danville Middle School wasn't exactly a good place to stand out, but with all the amazing kids at Delcroix, no one would be paying the least bit of attention to me, right?

Even though I hated the idea of leaving Grandma alone, I had to admit that living at Delcroix sounded pretty amazing.

No doctor appointments, no cooking or cleaning, a computer, a library I could use whenever I wanted. . . . And then there was Cam. Living at Delcroix meant I'd get to see Cam *every day*.

Images of Cam seemed to block out all rational thought, so I didn't see the kid running toward me until we were about to collide. He was looking over his shoulder and scowling at the road behind him, eyebrows knit together like a dark smear across his forehead. He had long legs and arms, black hair, and pale skin. I thought I saw the scrawl of a tattoo across one bicep.

"Hey!" I yelled, ducking out of the way just in time to avoid being flattened.

He stopped and spun around. His gaze darted wildly from my face to the road and back. Sweat beaded on his forehead. He brushed it off with an impatient, trembling hand.

I saw panic in his eyes, and fear in the rigid, jerky way he kept moving, as if he couldn't afford to stand still.

"Are you okay?" I asked.

He looked over his shoulder again, and then took a step closer to me. Grabbing my shoulders, he peered right into my face. "If a man asks if you've seen me, say no, okay?"

Beautiful silvery-gray eyes stared out from spiky black eyelashes. I froze, unable to tear my gaze from his.

"Okay?" he repeated, shaking my shoulders. His voice cracked.

I gulped, my heart pounding in my chest. Suddenly I had a taste of the fear that seemed to consume him. "Should I call the police?"

"No!" His voice cracked again. "No," he repeated. "Just say you haven't seen me."

He let me go and started running down the block. When he got to the corner, he took a right and headed in the direction of the open space on the edge of town.

Just as the boy disappeared from view, a beige sedan appeared at the head of the street, several blocks away. It moved slowly, deliberately.

As the car approached, I could see the driver looking carefully from side to side. He was blond and clean shaven, and mirrored sunglasses covered half his face. When he saw me, he pulled over and rolled down the passenger-side window, the seat belt pulling tight against his shoulder as he leaned to the side.

He pushed up the sunglasses and arranged his face in a semblance of concern. "Excuse me, miss, but did you see a boy run by here? He would have been about your age, tall, with a tattoo around his arm."

My heart thumped hard, paused, and thumped again. The whoosh of a windstorm filled my ears. "No," I said, trying to sound calm. "I haven't seen anyone."

His mouth tightened, and then he manufactured a worried grimace. "Are you sure? See, my son and I had a fight, and he stormed off. I'm really worried about him. You're absolutely sure you didn't see him?"

Now I knew something was up. Unless this guy fathered that kid when he was in elementary school, he was lying. And the kid had looked terrified. Why?

"Look, I already told you no. Now, I'm right in the middle of a workout, so if you don't mind . . ." With an annoyed look, I backed away and started running again. It took all my willpower to set a steady rhythm and keep my shoulders loose, as if I had no idea something unusual was going on. Behind me, I heard the car engine rev and the tires squeal. I shot a glance over my shoulder just in time to see the car turn in the direction of the open space.

The same direction the kid had run, just a minute before.

He was in danger. I couldn't ignore it. And I was the only one who could help him.

Helplessly, I fixated on the car as an image appeared in my head. A second later, both front tires blew out with a sound like a shotgun. The car began fishtailing wildly. There was a sickening sound of screeching tires and then crashing steel as the sedan slammed into a huge red pickup parked on the side of the road.

I sucked in a deep breath, spun around, and sprinted toward the car, my heart beating so fast I couldn't hear where one heartbeat stopped and the next began.

A huge lump stuck in my throat.

I hadn't thought he would crash like that.

Please, let him be okay. Please don't let me have hurt him.

A woman in a bathrobe ran out of the house behind the pickup with a phone in her hand. I got close enough to look over her shoulder as she peered into the car window.

Thank you, oh thank you.

He must have hit the steering wheel, because a crack ran down one lens of his sunglasses, and a thin line of blood connected his eyebrows. But he was alive. He swore loudly and pulled the glasses from his face. The seat belt I noticed earlier held him pinned to the seat, and he jerked it loose.

The woman with the phone began asking him questions. "Are you all right? Can you hear me? Do you know what day it is?"

The man barked something at her, but I couldn't hear what he said. The rushing still clogged my ears, though it sounded muted now, like the distant roar of the ocean. He grabbed a cell phone and held it up, glaring at the woman until she backed away from the car. As soon as she gave him room, he leaned over his cell as if wanting privacy, and began to speak in a low voice. A few seconds later he flipped his phone closed and pushed against the car door. It didn't budge, and he swore again.

I eased my way toward the sidewalk when I saw a couple of other people coming out of their houses. Clearly the situation was under control. The lady in the bathrobe started calling the police or a hospital while the man with the sunglasses pulled himself out of the car window, *Dukes of Hazzard* style. He paced back and forth, muttering nasty phrases and looking furious. Once again I started running—nice and slow so it didn't look like I was running away.

Relief rolled off my shoulders in waves, along with a strange, unfamiliar sense of triumph.

Usually after something triggers my power, I feel horrible. I tell myself I shouldn't have gotten involved, that I should have fought the instinct to throw my power at someone like a ten-ton truck. Invariably, I seem to end up hurting someone, and I worry about the person I hurt—if I did the right thing or not, and if I had the right to be making that decision at all. And this time I could have seriously hurt that guy. If he hadn't had his seat belt on . . . Well, the very thought of it made me cringe.

Despite that, I had the oddest sensation of wanting to laugh in Sunglasses Guy's face. All because he'd been following a tough-looking kid with a tattoo who I didn't even know.

This was precisely why I needed to keep myself separate from normal human beings. Clearly I was deranged. I should have been feeling guilty, and here I was enjoying the memory of that guy pulling himself out through the window of his car.

I turned the corner and headed toward the open space, following the kid's path without even thinking. Of course he was gone. When I got about three-quarters of the way down the block, the noise of the accident began to fade, and the quiet of early morning resumed. I glanced at my watch: barely six a.m. It always amazes me that so much can happen in such a short period of time.

That's when I heard the sound of footsteps.

I slowed down. I tried to breathe shallowly so I could hear better, but my heart was beating too fast. A few blocks away, the open meadow stood empty and quiet.

Had Sunglasses Guy come after me? The footsteps continued, and I darted a look over my shoulder.

Nothing.

I slowed down further, and the sound grew softer, barely audible. Too scared not to look, I stopped and spun around.

The street was empty.

I wiped the sweat from my forehead and forced myself to smile. Tattoo Kid must have really gotten to me. Now I was imagining that *I* was being followed. How ridiculous was that?

I started walking, my gaze darting back and forth across the street. When I heard a noise again, I yelled, "Who's there?"

A woman opened the front door of a tiny bungalow with peeling yellow paint. She looked up and down the block and then stared at me, obviously thinking I must be crazy, yelling at myself like that. I laughed nervously and started running.

A few houses down, a fat orange-and-white tabby cat padded down a driveway to sit in the middle of the sidewalk. It sat there, licking one paw and staring at me.

I stuck out my tongue and picked up the pace. This time I didn't stop until I got home.

CHAPTER 6

A WEEK later, as Grandma and I pulled into the Delcroix Academy parking lot, I was filled with confidence and optimism about the year to come. I emerged from the car ready for the first day of school, smiling at everyone I saw, knowing I would be a success at anything I tried. . . .

Ha! Actually, as I unbuckled my seat belt and prepared to haul myself out of our old Volvo station wagon, I decided that agreeing to go to Delcroix was the worst decision I had ever made.

Because the more I'd thought about crashing that car, the worse I felt. They used the accident on the news that night as an excuse to talk about the importance of seat belts, and to show gory pictures of what can happen if you aren't properly buckled. They showed pictures of one guy who'd hit his head on the windshield and died two days later from a brain injury. I could have done that. Killed someone.

I couldn't blend in at Delcroix. I crashed cars on a whim and dropped branches on kids' heads. Within a week of starting school I'd probably send an anvil crashing down on some Delcroix genius and end up the subject of a top-secret government investigation.

"I'm so proud of you, Dancia, for deciding to give Delcroix

a try. I'm sure it seems a little intimidating now, but I know you're going to love it here." Grandma beamed at me, happiness radiating from her watery eyes.

I mustered a half smile. "Yeah, right. Well, I guess I'll see you on Friday." I leaned over to give her a kiss on the cheek, and then jumped out of the car before she could say anything else.

I walked around to the back of the Volvo and whacked the trunk panel right next to the latch three times, hard, so the door would open. When it finally did, I scooted my hideous, second-hand silver-and-black trunk back and forth until I could haul it out and let it fall to the ground with a thud. They said we were each allowed to bring one trunkful of stuff, and that it would be collected from the parking lot and taken to our room while we were at orientation.

With my belongings settled, I took a look around. Rows of parking spaces lined the narrow lot. A lone oak tree sat at one end, about twenty feet outside the edge of the iron fence that encircled the bright green, perfectly manicured Delcroix grass. The tree had spreading, scraggly branches and an uneven crown. On one side, the dark green leaves dipped low enough to touch, while on the other, the stump of a branch fifteen feet high sprouted thick bunches of new twigs.

The uneven branches were soothing, for some reason, and the tree looked almost big enough to hide behind.

Always good to know you've got options.

I stood for a minute looking at Grandma through the window. She waved and then slipped on the enormous plastic sunglasses she wore over her regular glasses. She was ready for a morning of mall walking in matching blue-and-white velour and bright pink lipstick. Being close to the car made me feel a little better, and I thought for a minute about asking her to stay, at least until the bus pulled up.

But no one in high school waits with their grandma for the bus. I'd made a huge fuss that morning about her leaving as soon as I unloaded my trunk, and she'd agreed that she would. I guess she figured she'd already won the war by getting me to try Delcroix, so she'd let me win this one battle. Now part of me wished she'd fought a little harder.

Reluctantly, I waved back, and she slowly drove away. I didn't have any choice then, so I turned around and started checking out the kids who would be there to witness my doom.

I mean, my freshman year.

They arrived in a line off Highway 78 in big SUVs and fancy new Subarus, tires crunching on the gravel. I wondered if I would be the only kid who didn't have a trust fund. Okay, to be honest, everyone around here drives Subarus, and some of the kids looked downright normal, but I didn't waste time looking at them. I focused on the super-rich ones. Isn't that what anyone would do?

A small group began forming on one end of the parking lot: girls wearing ultralow shorts and tight T-shirts that showed off their perfect boobs and flat stomachs, and boys standing a few feet from them wearing jeans or lowrider shorts, pretending that they weren't checking out the girls. Their trunks were scattered around beside them, lots of shiny black boxes with silver rivets at the corners, and overstuffed duffle bags that looked ready to burst. Some trunks were painted bright colors, or decorated with team logos or skateboard stickers. None looked quite as old and dingy as mine.

As I looked around, I realized the crowd was different from what I used to see at my middle school. Other than the rich kids, the groups I was familiar with—the jocks, the nerds, the brains, the goths—weren't there. I mean, there were kids you could probably throw into those categories, but they were hanging out in cliques of two and three, while all these other types of kids kept arriving. There were long-haired girls in leotards, boys with dreadlocks, a girl holding a pair of drumsticks, kids with lots of piercings in unusual places, and nerdy-looking guys with button-down shirts tucked into pants that practically came to their armpits. They were all different ethnicities too, whereas Danville was mostly white.

A few guys started throwing a Frisbee back and forth, and a sporty-looking girl wearing Adidas soccer shorts and running shoes joined the game. She was the kind of girl I hate on sight—long straight brown hair in a perky ponytail, perfect body, tanned skin, and seemingly no fear of dropping the Frisbee or making a fool of herself.

"Do you play?"

I was focusing so hard on the girl I had decided to hate (her name would have to be something sweet and charming, like Beth or Sarah), the voice at my side startled me.

"Huh?" I tore my eyes from Perfect Girl to examine the much more normal specimen at my side. This girl, I was relieved to see, was short and had hair almost as curly as mine. Only she apparently hadn't learned not to comb it, so it surrounded her face like a black cloud at least two feet in diameter. She wore a white button-down shirt and jeans, despite the fact that the sun was August-hot even at nine o'clock in the morning, and they'd told us to wear comfortable clothes because we'd be doing some of our orientation activities outside.

"Frisbee. Do you play Frisbee?" She had a cheerful voice and broad smile.

I shrugged and tried to look standoffish. "Not really."

"Me neither! I'm hopeless at Frisbee. I aim one way and it goes the other. My name is Esther, what's yours?" She seemed oblivious to my attitude, and grinned as she dropped a backpack on the ground beside us. It was made of soft brown leather and probably cost as much as my grandma's Volvo. There was a trunk a few feet from us that matched perfectly. I figured it probably cost as much as our house.

"Dancia."

"Wow, that's a really cool name. What does it mean?"

"I dunno. I guess my mom made it up."

Esther laughed. "Well, it sounds cool. So, are you as nervous as I am? I think I slept about thirty minutes last night."

Unwittingly, I smiled. "I think you have me beat. I slept at least an hour."

She sighed dramatically, her dark eyes twinkling. "I'm jealous. Will you poke me if I fall asleep during something important? With my luck, I'll end up in detention before school even starts."

Esther, I suspected, had never spent a day of her life in detention.

We chatted for a few minutes. Esther asked all sorts of questions—where I was from, what my middle school was like, what I was looking forward to at Delcroix. It took me that long to realize that she had used my own tactic against me. It was impressive, actually, the way she drew me out. The difference was that Esther alternated between asking questions and telling me all about herself. Before I knew it, we were talking like old friends.

Except, I wasn't supposed to be making friends.

Just as I was realizing I needed to put the brakes on the conversation, a bus pulled through the huge black gates at the far end of the parking lot, and both our mouths snapped shut. The bus was shaped like the old yellow cheese that had picked me up every day for middle school, but this one had been painted steel gray. It ground to a stop by the gates, so I hitched my backpack over my shoulder, grabbed the end of my trunk, and started dragging it in that direction. Even though I should have ditched Esther then and there, I guess I was just too nervous at the thought of handling this all by myself.

I turned back around to her. "Are you coming?"

She nodded quickly and picked up her backpack. Her trunk had a handle on one end and wheels, and she started pulling it behind her. She grinned at me, and I reluctantly smiled back. Esther had an air of confidence, like she assumed we were now best friends, and it was strangely magnetic.

She started talking again right away. "Do you think we'll all fit on one bus? Or maybe they make two trips? I can't believe they don't let you drive up to the school yourself. My dad says that's a good safety precaution, but I think it's a little much, don't you?"

I gave her a nod, but didn't speak. I focused on dragging my trunk and not letting it whack me on the back of my heels with every step. She barely seemed to notice, talking about how her mother was a lawyer who worked in the district attorney's office, and how her dad had driven her to orientation, which was a really long drive because they lived outside Seattle, but he said he'd take her because it would be such an incredible experience. According to Esther, six people in the United States House of Representatives and two in the Senate had gone to Delcroix, not to mention the guy who'd just become the new Supreme Court justice. Naturally, I had known nothing about this, but Esther actually seemed to know and care about politics.

Besides that, Esther clearly liked to talk. I mean really, *really* liked to talk.

I decided that was okay, because if she kept talking, I wouldn't have to.

We joined the group of kids milling around in front of the bus. The door opened with a hiss, and two guys jumped out. I stopped and stared. It was Cam and another guy I didn't know. Just looking at Cam erased all my doubts and fears, and brought back that hopeful feeling I'd been left with at Bev's.

Cam shook his shaggy hair from his eyes and held up his arms. His biceps bulged impressively from under a dark green T-shirt. A gold dragon hovered over the word DELCROIX on the front, and the word STAFF was sprawled across the back in matching gold letters.

"Hey, everyone, could I get your attention for a minute? Trevor and I have a few things to tell you before we board the bus."

The girls began to whisper to each other as soon as they got a look at him.

"You can have my attention any time you want, Mr. Gorgeous," Esther said under her breath.

"I'm Cam Sanders. I'm a junior at Delcroix. I'm one of the orientation staff here on campus early to help get you settled. With me is Trevor Anderly." He motioned toward the other boy, who also wore a STAFF T-shirt. Trevor was a few inches shorter than Cam, with close-cut blond hair and light blue eyes that seemed to take in every person in the crowd at once. When he locked his gaze on me, something about that stare made me shiver.

"Trevor's also part of the orientation staff and one of the team leaders. He'll be giving you a tour of the buildings and grounds. The rest of the upperclassmen arrive next week. For now, you have Delcroix all to yourselves."

There was scattered clapping, which Cam acknowledged with a smile, even as he raised his hands for quiet. "As you probably know from the packet you received in the mail, the next couple of days will be dedicated to orienting you to Delcroix and getting you settled into the Residence Hall—or the Res, as we like to call it. Today we have some welcome activities planned, and you'll have time to get unpacked and meet your roommates. Tomorrow you'll get your class schedules, meet with your advisers, and get to know your teachers. Wednesday you'll break into your freshman teams. Your classes start on Thursday, but don't worry, we'll keep you busy until then."

A murmur started in the crowd, and a few people raised their hands.

Cam shook his head. "I'm sure you have lots of questions, but let's save them until we're up at the school." He turned to the bus and patted the door fondly. "This is the old Silver Bullet," he said. "She'll take you to and from school, and today she'll be running extra trips to get your gear up to the Res as well. If you go home for the weekends, you must be back in the parking lot ready to catch the bus at seven thirty a.m. on Mondays."

"Classes start at seven forty-five, and if you miss the seven thirty bus, you'll be late," Trevor said. He shoved a casual hand into his pocket, but nothing about the tone of his voice matched the pose. "I wouldn't miss the bus if I were you. They don't appreciate it when you're late."

"Yeesh," Esther said. "Does that guy think he's the Grim Reaper or something?"

I hid a smile. I had a feeling Trevor wouldn't appreciate a freshman making fun of him.

"Now," Cam continued, "you can leave your trunks over by the grass, and everyone file onto the Silver Bullet. We've got a lot to cover today, so let's get started."

The crowd bunched into a rough line and started up the steps. No one said much. I guess we were all a little nervous. Even Perfect Girl, who I saw a few feet ahead, plucked nervously at the waistband of her shorts.

Cam stood by the door, smiling at all the kids as they went by. Trevor glowered at us from the back of the line. When I walked by Cam, I started to drop my eyes, but he waved and threw an arm around my shoulders like we were old friends.

"Dancia, great to see you," he said, giving me a squeeze. "Let me know if you need anything, okay?"

I think I might have nodded, but to be honest, at that moment everything got a little fuzzy. Once he put his arm around me, the entire world went dark and quiet, and all I could see or hear was Cam. He was warm and smelled a little woodsy, like a pine forest in the hot sun. Close up, his eyes drew me in, soft and inviting.

Then his arm was gone and he was waving at someone else in the crowd. But the message had been sent, and the other kids nearby looked at me with a kind of respect.

"You know him?" Esther hissed as soon as we were on the bus, her forehead wrinkling with amazement.

"He was my recruiter," I said, trying to sound nonchalant.

"Your recruiter?" Esther repeated. "What do you mean?"

"He came to my house with Mr. Judan to get me to go to Delcroix. Didn't they come to your house?"

She shook her head. "No, I just got a letter in the mail. I think someone might have called my mom. But why would they need to recruit anyone? Everyone knows how amazing the school is."

"Oh, yeah, right." A little ping of discomfort colored my voice as I tried to imagine why they would have sent someone to my house and not to hers. "Well, it's probably because I live in Danville. They must visit the people who are really close by." I didn't mention going out to lunch, which now seemed downright odd.

"Yeah," she echoed. "Well, whatever. I can't believe he touched you." Her smile told me she didn't care about the recruiting thing, and I breathed a sigh of relief.

"Esther!" A girl waved at Esther from the back of the bus.

Esther squealed in reply, "Hennie?"

The girl had long dark hair and olive skin. Her eyes were dusky brown, and a little dimple stood out in her cheek. Indian, I guessed. Even though she was prettier than Perfect Girl, something about her nervous expression made it impossible to hate her. Her gaze kept darting around the bus, and when she'd waved at Esther, she'd looked hesitant, as if unsure she'd be welcome.

Esther dragged me down the aisle until we came to a stop in front of Hennie. "Dancia, this is Hennie. She and I went to camp together for years. We were best friends until she moved to L.A." She leaned over and gave Hennie a sideways hug. "What are you doing here?"

Hennie's face brightened, and she giggled. It was a delicate, musical sound, the kind I dreamed about making every time I opened my mouth and a snort came out. "What do you think? We moved back to Seattle. My dad found a new job when I got the invitation to come to Delcroix. Can you sit with me?" She patted the seat next to her, then froze, her hand covering her mouth in shock. "Oh, I'm sorry, how rude! You're probably sitting with your friend. I didn't mean to . . ."

"No, no." I waved my hand at them. "Don't worry about it."

"Yeah, don't worry about it. Dancia's sitting with me."

I spun around, not recognizing the voice behind me. Then my mouth dropped open. It was the dark-haired kid I had crashed a car to protect. Except now he looked anything but scared.

CHAPTER 7

IT TOOK me a second to shake off my shock.

"Who are you?" I asked.

Esther, the traitor, ditched me as quickly as she had befriended me. She was now sitting next to Hennie and chattering at a frenzied pace. They were holding hands like long-lost lovers, with huge smiles on their faces. If they weren't so happy it might have smarted a little that I was so easily forgotten and left to the sharks.

Er . . . the shark. Wow. Once I focused on him, I realized the shark was way better looking than I'd remembered. He must not have showered that morning, or been sick or something, because he looked totally different now. He had thick black hair that covered his forehead and partially covered his steel-gray eyes. Spiky lines from a tattoo peeked out from the edge of his shirt. His face was all angles, with high cheekbones and hollows underneath and a sharp chin. He wore a dark T-shirt that hugged his wiry torso.

He rolled his eyes. "Come on, you know me," he said. "In fact, I owe you a favor."

"What do you mean?" I tried not to stare at the tattoo, but it kept catching my eye, like something was crawling on his arm.

"You got that guy off my tail. So I'm forever at your service." He bent over in an awkward half bow.

"Forget it." I surreptitiously scoped the bus for another open seat. The last thing I wanted was to think about that day and what I'd almost done to Sunglasses Guy. Just the memory of the car crashing, and the look of fear on the boy's face when he'd grabbed my shoulders, was enough to make me sick all over again.

"Can everyone sit down so we can get going?" Cam called from the front of the bus.

The boy patted the seat beside him. "I don't bite, I swear." When I continued to hesitate, he gave me a tiny, almost apologetic smile. "I suppose I should introduce myself. My name's Jack, and regardless of what you might be thinking, I'm a very nice person."

"Really?" I said suspiciously. "Why was that guy following you?"

Jack waved away the question. "Oh, it was a misunderstanding. No big deal."

"A misunderstanding? It didn't look that way. You looked scared."

He shifted in his seat, the smile fading. "Yeah, well, I don't like being followed." He peered out the window and popped a few knuckles. A second later he turned back to me again. "I think they're waiting for you," he said, nodding toward the front of the bus.

I realized with horror that I was the last person standing, and Cam was looking expectantly at me.

"Oh. Right." I slunk into the seat and forced a laugh. "So you're just Jack, huh? No last name?"

He grinned, shifting his long legs and moving his backpack so we had more room. "Jack Landry."

The bus seats were dark green pleather, enough room for two but just barely. I tried to make sure our legs didn't touch as we rearranged our positions on the seat and the bus started rumbling across the parking lot. But Jack didn't seem to have the same concern. Every time he leaned against me I had to stop myself from lurching out of the seat.

The problem was, I could have been sitting next to an alien for all the experience I had with guys like Jack. My middle school wasn't exactly chock-full of dangerous-looking guys with tattoos. Not that I'd spent much time scoping out the boys at Danville Middle. Since I figured boyfriends were right up there with best friends for having the potential to set off my power, I didn't bother. I ignored them, and for the most part they ignored me.

"I do appreciate it," he said. "Not everyone would go out of their way to help a stranger."

"No problem." I glanced away, hoping he'd drop the subject.

"What did you say to him? I thought he was right behind me."

"I told him I hadn't seen you, like you said."

"That's it? You must be convincing." A note of skepticism seemed to underlie his words.

Was he skeptical of me? What could he possibly think I had done?

I shrugged, trying to look unconcerned. "Well, you're the one who told me to say it. You must have thought it would work."

"I guess." He stared at me as if he were waiting for some sort of explanation.

As I was thinking of something to say that might distract him, the bus stopped and everyone got quiet. A cloud of dust drifted through our open window. The big iron gates that circled the school loomed in front of us. The driver held something up to a square, black-armed device that stood just to the left of the road leading up to the school. It issued a loud beep, and then, with a sound like a roller coaster going up the first big hill, the gate slowly began to retract.

When the gate had opened wide enough for the bus, we pulled forward. I lost sight of the gate after we cleared the opening, but you couldn't miss the mechanical voice calling out loudly, "Caution, the gates are closing! Caution, the gates are closing!"

A second later the clang of heavy metal bars slamming together echoed through the bus.

Jack jumped and whipped his head around, as if expecting someone to sneak up behind him.

The bus fell silent. Everyone seemed to watch, fixated, as the gate disappeared from view. Then someone broke the quiet with a burp, and you could almost hear the relief in people's voices as they laughed and restarted their conversations.

"I guess some kids think they're still in middle school." I tried to smile, but it was hard when Jack's face looked so pale. He didn't respond.

I studied my fingernails. Jack's hands were in his lap, his knuckles white. When I looked up, I saw his throat moving as he swallowed. He craned his neck around to look at the road behind us.

"They must be serious about the whole security thing," I offered.

"Security?" Jack asked.

"You know, protect the students and visitors." I gestured toward the rest of the bus. "Keep the bad guys out?"

"Keep the bad guys out, or us in?"

He said it under his breath, and I wasn't sure if he meant for me to hear. But his words settled between us, heavy and impossible to ignore. When I looked down, I realized I had clenched my hand into a fist. Deliberately, I released each finger, one by one.

"You're kidding, right?"

He snorted. "Yeah, I'm kidding. Why would they want to keep us in? We're just kids, right? Just a bunch of kids."

He turned away to stare out the window, a little smirk playing around his lips. I considered saying something else, but Jack's eyes didn't look quite right, and I couldn't tell if he was joking or not. I turned back to the aisle, where Cam stood next to the driver.

"Now that we're here," Cam said, "I'd like to tell you a bit more about the place where you'll spend the best four years of your life. Or at least, the best four years thus far." A group in the back of the bus hooted and clapped, and the noise drowned out whatever Cam said next.

Hugely relieved by Cam's somehow comforting presence, I turned my face toward his and tried to erase the memory of the gates slamming shut behind us.

Cam started describing the history of Delcroix: It had been established almost sixty years ago by a couple who wanted to make sure that kids with special gifts were nurtured and challenged. Their names were Peter and Cindy Delcroix, and they died in the late eighties. They left the school a huge endowment to keep it going.

What followed was more detail about Delcroix than any student could ever want to know—except maybe Esther. I'm sure she was fascinated. I wouldn't have thought it possible for Cam to be boring, yet I found myself losing interest and sneaking glances at Jack. With one finger he tapped out a rhythm on his chest a few inches below his collarbone, not even pretending to listen. He'd regained some of his color—though his skin was still incredibly pale—and his eyes had lost the wildness I'd seen earlier.

"You okay?" I finally asked.

"Sure," he said. "I'm fine." His voice cracked and he cleared his throat. "I'm fine," he repeated.

I hesitated and then said, "I'm nervous too, if that makes you feel any better."

Jack laid his head back against the seat. "I haven't gotten much sleep lately," he admitted.

"Me either."

"I wish we didn't have to live on campus," he said. "I don't like the idea of being surrounded at night by a bunch of teachers. Gives me the creeps."

"They said we could go home on the weekends. Are your folks nearby?"

He shook his head. "I'm from Portland. But I can crash with a friend. What about you? You live in Danville?"

I nodded. "I live with my grandma. She's pretty old. I need to go home over the weekends to help her with housework."

"Your grandma, huh? What's she like?" he asked.

"Grandma?" The question caught me by surprise. No one ever asked about my grandmother. "She's okay. My parents died when I was little, so she's like my mom, I guess. What about you? Are your grandparents around?"

Jack shook his head. "I don't really know," he said. "No one ever introduced us."

I laughed uneasily. "Isn't that something parents usually do?"

"Not my parents."

"Oh." I knew plenty of other kids at school with screwed-up parents. In fact, sometimes I wondered who those kids were, on all those TV shows, who had moms who stayed home and helped them with their homework, and dads who put on ties and drove off to work in shiny black cars. I mean, I'm not saying those kids don't exist. I just wondered if I'd ever meet any.

It occurred to me that Esther was probably one of those kids. And Hennie. Maybe Delcroix was full of them, and I was the only one with a screwed-up family.

Me and Jack, maybe.

"So . . . how does it feel to be invited to the great Delcroix Academy?" Jack asked.

I laughed. "If it's so great, I'm not sure why they want me around."

Jack nudged me with his elbow. "Come on, you must have some special talent. World-class mathlete? You don't look like a computer geek. Maybe spelling bee queen?"

"Hardly. I'm not sure why I'm here, actually. I'm pretty much mediocre at everything. What about you?"

"I'm their token poor kid. Economic diversity and all that."

"No way." I shook my head and started to relax for the first time that morning. "They've already got me."

Ten minutes later, after a tour of the grounds that I barely heard because Jack and I were busy comparing our lack of talents, the bus came to a halt in front of the school building—what I think Cam called the Main Hall. Jack abruptly stopped talking, and we both gaped at our first full view of the school.

A pair of stone dragons guarded the outside of the building—I think Cam mentioned something about their being the school mascot just before I spaced out. A set of marble steps led into the dark interior of the school, with a pair of white columns framing the doors. Lush green vegetation surrounded the red brick building, a far cry from my weather-beaten middle school with its straggly rhododendrons and dead grass.

A path ran around the side of the building, and you could see the corner of another red brick structure tucked behind the Main Hall. It must have been the Res. A third building, a square white house with shutters on the windows and a wide front porch, stood just to the left of the Main Hall. I assumed this was the house where about half the teachers lived during the week, the ones that didn't drive to work in the morning. Cam called it the Bly. Apparently someone named Bly had died and given the school money to build it. A giant rosebush crawled up the side of the Bly, and even though it had been a hot summer, the leaves were still green, and several red roses bloomed up around the second story of the house.

Our rosebushes at home had yellow spotty leaves and one or two dying blooms.

Everything at Delcroix was different, even the flowers.

Jack and I waited, both quiet, as the bus emptied out around us. The buildings looked so serious, like a fancy college or prep school, reminding me once again that I was way out of my league. What I'd told Jack was painfully true. I wasn't some supersmart, gifted-and-talented genius. I was a fraud, a girl they thought was a hero but was really a coward, and it was only a matter of time before they figured that out.

I got off the bus in front of Jack. He followed me down the steps, but when I turned around he had wandered off. His hands were thrust deep in his pockets, his jaw clenched as he stared up at those huge columns. He looked back and forth between the crowd and the school, glaring at everyone who walked too close. I guessed he was nervous, but he did look genuinely intimidating, so I stayed away.

It was a little disappointing, because I'd felt so comfortable with him, and it had been a relief to find someone who felt the same way I did about Delcroix. But it was for the best.

After all, I wasn't here to make friends.

I walked up the white steps, trying not to look like a tourist as I checked everything out. Inside, the school resembled Danville High, only smaller. The walls displayed bulletin boards, glass trophy cases, and pictures of past principals. But unlike Danville, incredible paintings hung everywhere, alongside black-and-white photographs matted in silvery metallic frames. Blown-up newspaper clippings showed a new ballet company opening in Texas, a guy in an army uniform shaking the president's hand, and a doctor cutting a ribbon by the doors of a hospital. Former students, I guessed.

Everyone seemed to walk off the bus with a crowd of friends, and even though I wanted to be alone, it was hard to watch everyone else laughing and hanging out together. I guess that's why, when Esther and Hennie ran up to me a few seconds later, I couldn't muster a bored look.

Hennie was even cuter standing up than she had been sitting down, but a few feet away she tripped over her shoelace, and if Esther hadn't caught her, she would have done a spectacular face plant right in the middle of the front hall. Esther whooped with laughter. Hennie, her gorgeous skin two shades darker, tried to look nonchalant as she regained her balance. But then she turned to Esther and broke into uncontrollable giggles.

"Hennie, you're as clumsy as ever!" Esther teased.

"Dancia, you would not believe how many times I've saved Hennie from total disaster. I swear, she is the most uncoordinated person you will ever meet."

"Thanks a lot," Hennie exclaimed. "At least I don't sound like a hyena when I laugh."

For some reason this set Esther off again, and they laughed together until they were both wiping tears from their faces. The two of them were infectious, and I couldn't help but smile.

"Now Dancia is going to think we're completely insane," Esther said.

"I don't know about insane," I said. "But not normal. Which is cool, if you ask me."

Hennie nodded gravely. "I had a feeling you'd understand."

Esther grinned and looped her arm through mine. She spun around slowly in the hall. "Isn't the school amazing? Look at all these pictures! It's like an art gallery in here."

"My mom said she heard they had to have a security system just for the art. And I heard Kofi Annan came to visit last year. Can you imagine?" Hennie asked.

I had no idea who she was talking about, but I tried to look knowledgeable. "Yeah, it's amazing."

Esther poked her in the ribs. "You're so serious, Hennie! Let's talk about something much more important—did you see all the cute guys on the bus? And who were you sitting with, Dancia? What's his story?"

I nonchalantly perused the crowd to see if Jack was lurking nearby. He was, still standing at the edge of the crowd with a scowl on his face. I steered Hennie and Esther farther away and whispered, "He had just seen me around. We don't really know each other."

"Well, he's hot, so you'd better introduce us," Esther said in a stern tone.

"You think so?" I looked at him again out of the corner of my eyes. Jack's face looked older than the other guys', but his body looked like a kid's—with skinny arms and legs.

"Esther likes dark, tormented boys," Hennie observed.

"And you like blond, happy ones?" Esther asked. "That's new."

Hennie looked around and then gave a nod toward a tall, lanky boy with a pierced nose, eyebrow, and lip, and long dreadlocks.

"Him?" I said, surprised. Despite what Esther said, I had a hard time picturing sweet, clumsy Hennie going for Nose Ring Guy. "You like him?"

"He's an artist," Hennie said dreamily. "I saw him sketching while we were waiting for the bus."

"Oh, Dancia, we're in trouble now," Esther groaned. "Once Hennie sets her mind on someone, she talks about him non-stop. But she's so shy, she'll never talk *to* him."

Hennie giggled, which set off Esther, and before I knew it, the two of them were laughing again. I started laughing too, a warm feeling spreading through me.

I'm not sure what brought me back to my senses. Maybe it was Jack, who walked past us, his hands deep in his pockets and a contemptuous look on his face as he surveyed the crowd. Maybe it was the drug of the laughter wearing off, or the crush of the crowd as Cam and Trevor and a few others wearing STAFF T-shirts started herding us into a group at the end of the hall. Whatever sparked it, a dull ache slowly drowned out the good feeling Esther and Hennie had inspired. Friends make you vulnerable, I reminded myself. They make you prone to do stupid things and send people to the hospital. No friends and no attachments was the Dancia Lewis way. It had to be.

"Please head into the auditorium, everyone," Cam shouted above the din. "Principal Solom will be giving you all your official welcome."

CHAPTER 8

I CAN sum up Principal Solom's speech in four words: Welcome to boot camp.

Of course, there was a lot more. They showed a movie with pictures of rockets built by Delcroix scientists, and hospitals with kids being cured of horrible diseases by Delcroix doctors. There were scenes of students playing sports, doing plays, and dancing.

But then the movie was over and Principal Solom started talking. She was a tiny woman, maybe five feet tall, so she couldn't use a podium or she probably would have disappeared completely. She must have been almost as old as Grandma, but instead of having that soft, helpless look to her, she looked like she wouldn't think twice about putting you in a headlock and elbowing you in the stomach if you talked back. I was sitting halfway back in the audience, but I still wanted to shudder at the look in her eyes as she marched up and down the stage and barked rules at us for an hour.

The school day started at seven forty-five and ended at three thirty. There were mandatory study hours between seven thirty and nine thirty, when you had to stay in your room or go to the library. Lights-out was at ten thirty. There were rules about when you could visit the opposite sex, when you could use your computer, and how loud you could play your music. They even had rules for when you could use your cell phone. That part didn't bother me, of course, because I didn't have one.

The Res, Principal Solom told us, was a four-story U-shaped brick building just behind the school. On each floor, the girls' rooms were on one side, and the boys' were on the other. The middle of the U was a big common room. There was a phone in the commons, but you could only use it if you reserved a time slot in advance.

I doubted I'd have too much competition for the common phone. If Delcroix was anything like my middle school, I'd be the only kid without a cell. Still, this sucked because there were only a few hours a day they would let us use the phone. We weren't allowed in the common room during school hours, or study hours, or after lights-out.

Boot camp, I tell you. Boot camp.

I went to find my room right after the lecture, while the other freshmen were still milling around chatting. I figured that was my only way to avoid talking to Hennie and Esther. I managed to lose them in the crowd as we left the auditorium, and ran out of the building and across the grass to the Residence Hall. Like the Main Hall, the Res was an imposing, red brick structure. But whereas the Main Hall seemed built to intimidate, with its big white columns and marble lions, the Res was trying to masquerade as someone's home, with curtains in the windows, and pink and purple pansies outside.

But no one could really mistake it for a home. You had to use an ID badge, which they'd given us first thing this morning, to open an electronic lock on the outside door.

Each room had a keypad at the door, where you punched in another security code. They said it was so we didn't have to carry keys around, but it made me feel like I was living in a bank, always pushing buttons and waiting for green lights before I could go anywhere.

Trevor and two other staff people were standing in the hallway laughing when I walked in. They looked surprised to see me.

"That was fast," Trevor said. "Did you run over or something? Principal Solom scare you that bad?"

"I'd just like to go to my room, if that's okay," I said. I wasn't really in the mood to have Trevor make fun of me.

For a second, Trevor actually looked concerned. "Is everything all right?"

"Fine. Can you just tell me what room to go to?"

He stared at me with those disconcertingly light blue eyes, and I had the uneasy feeling that he could somehow see into my brain. "Sure." He grabbed a box and pulled out an envelope. "Room 422. The pass code to the door is on the sheet inside. Don't lose it. You're rooming with Catherine Arkane. Go up the stairs and take a left. It's near the end."

I nodded and started to leave. Just as I reached the base of the stairs, I felt a hand on my sleeve. Trevor had followed me. I swallowed hard, expecting a lecture about being respectful to upperclass students, but instead I got a serious look.

"If anyone gives you a hard time, you let me know, okay?"

"Uh . . . okay. Thanks."

As if I'd ever initiate a conversation with Trevor.

I ran up the stairs and found my room, without any trouble. The card inside the envelope gave me a six-number code.

I punched it into the keypad until I heard the click of the door, and peered inside. Two trunks sat in the middle of the floor in a tiny, sterile-looking room: my junky one, and an elegant, unmarred black-and-silver version with a printed label on the end that read "Catherine Arkane." The far side of the room had a sloped ceiling, with one bed tucked in a window dormer. Another bed was pushed into a corner. Matching desks and dressers lined the other walls.

I closed the door behind me and threw myself onto the striped mattress of the bed under the window. Closing my eyes, I pictured Cam putting his arm around my shoulders. It was a lovely image, but for some reason it disappeared a second later and was replaced by the image of Jack, his face pale as he leaned against the bus seat, eyes closed. What had he said? *Keep the bad guys out, or us in?*

What a weirdo. I pictured the first time I saw him, eyes wild, Sunglasses Guy close behind. Jack was bad news, no matter that he was someone at Delcroix I actually felt like I could talk to. I couldn't afford to get mixed up with someone like Jack. Not when I was teetering on the edge of complete freakdom all by myself.

I got on my knees and looked out the window, but the only thing I could see was the thick evergreen forest that surrounded the school. I looked for a latch, but the window didn't open. The building was cold even though it was at least ninety degrees outside. I figured they had central air and that was why they didn't want us opening the windows.

Hard to believe that in a few minutes, Jack would be right down the hall from me, unpacking his trunk just like I should be unpacking mine. I wondered what kind of things a guy like Jack would bring to school. He didn't seem the sort to have pictures and knickknacks.

Cam's room would be on the second floor with the other juniors. I imagined his room as warm and friendly. He'd have lots of photos on his walls. Trevor would probably be in some of the pictures, along with Cam's other friends. I bet he had a lot of friends. And a girlfriend. Probably a gorgeous girlfriend.

That was a depressing thought, so I decided to focus on unpacking.

It didn't take long. I set my CD player on the dresser next to the bed by the window, put away my clothes, threw some pens and notebooks into a desk drawer, and put my sheets and comforter on the bed. I set a picture of Grandma and me on the window ledge.

That was all I had.

I heard a few noises down the hall and then some giggling and yelling outside my room. The others were starting to arrive. I lay back down on the bed and picked up the picture of Grandma. It was crazy, but it suddenly hit me that tonight would be the first time I'd been away from her overnight. I hadn't had friends to do sleepovers with, and my soccer camps had only been for the day. An achy feeling started in my chest as I thought about her. What if she needed help cooking dinner? Who would load the dishwasher, or stir the soup while she puttered around and forgot what she was doing?

I lay there for another minute or two as the sounds in the hall got louder. Then I heard the door click, and someone thrust it open so hard it slammed against the wall and bounced back a few inches.

A thin, dour-faced girl wearing knee-length navy shorts and a white button-down shirt stood in the doorway. She had long black hair pulled back from her face with a red headband. She wasn't unattractive, but her thin lips were pressed together, her hands on her hips as she surveyed the room. I jumped to my feet.

"Hi, I'm Dancia—"

"I see you took the good bed," she snapped.

I recoiled. "I'm sorry, I didn't realize you might—"

"Sure, whatever. Keep it. I'm Catherine. Nice to meet you." She spoke in short clipped tones, and her gaze flicked up and down my clothes and then around the room, landing on the picture of Grandma and me.

"So," she said, "where are you from?"

"Danville."

"Really?" She sounded horrified. "Where did you do middle school?"

I blinked. "At Danville Middle."

"What do your parents do?"

"My parents are dead. I live with my grandma. She doesn't do anything, really, except go to doctor visits and watch *The Price Is Right*."

I had a horrible, childish urge to stick out my tongue.

"I see."

Catherine flounced over to her trunk, paused to rearrange her position so I couldn't watch, and then flicked a combination lock. She opened the trunk and pulled out a picture in a large silver frame. It was her, wearing a school uniform of a navy pleated skirt, white shirt, and tie. She was shaking hands with Mr. Judan.

"I was personally recruited by Mr. Judan," she said, placing the picture on her desk and giving it a loving pat. "He came to my boarding school. I attended Saint Mary's School for Girls in San Francisco. It's a very prestigious school that only accepts forty students per class, and I was at the top of my class every year. I took the SAT last year and got a perfect score on the math section. Mr. Judan said I'm a math wizard. That's why he wanted me here at Delcroix."

"Oh." I was pretty sure I was supposed to be impressed by all this information, and since I'd already pissed her off by taking the bed under the window, being from Danville, and having dead parents, I decided not to tell her that Judan had come to recruit me as well, and told me they wanted me here for my unusual courage. "That's great."

I sat back down on my bed and plucked at the hem of my pants.

It was going to be hard not to hate Catherine Arkane.

I thought about what Esther had said on the bus when Cam hugged me: no one had recruited her at all, or maybe they had called her mom at work. It made me wonder again why the school had sent Cam and Mr. Judan to meet with Grandma and me.

"What was it like?" I tried to sound impressed. "When he recruited you, I mean. Did he meet with you by himself?"

"Well, my dad was there too," she said. "He flew all the way from D.C. to be there."

"But that was it? No one else from Delcroix?"

She sniffed. "As if the chief recruiter isn't enough?"

I kept my eyes on my pants. So Cam hadn't visited her? This information was both thrilling and unnerving. I loved the idea that Cam and I had some special connection, but I couldn't escape the inevitable conclusion that he and Mr. Judan must have visited me by mistake. They must have gotten my name wrong, or transposed two numbers on an IQ test somewhere. Catherine Arkane obviously belonged at Delcroix; I did not.

Catherine pulled another picture out of her trunk, this

one of her and a man in a suit and tie. "That's my dad. He went to Delcroix. He works at the White House."

I squinted at the picture. Catherine's father looked a lot like her—tall, thin, and grumpy.

"That's cool."

Catherine placed the picture on the desk. "Right. Cool."

She pulled three more frames out of her trunk: two displayed pictures of her in a school uniform standing beside men wearing suits, and one showed her awkwardly hugging a woman wearing a suit. I wondered if anyone in her family ever wore jeans.

"Is that your mom?" I asked.

She nodded. I had the feeling she had lost interest in talking to me. I was officially beneath her.

She unpacked with smooth, efficient motions, like someone who had done this many times before. She seemed to know exactly where each picture should go on her desk, and where all the clothes would fit in her drawers. I put on my headphones, turned on a CD, and pretended not to watch her.

When she was finished, she sat down on the edge of her bed and cleared her throat. I sat up warily.

"Time for ground rules," she said, and fixed her dark eyes on me.

"Ground rules?" I removed my earphones.

"Look, I started boarding school when I was in fifth grade, so I know a little bit about how to deal with roommates. Here's the story. You don't touch my stuff, you don't make noise when it's time to study, and you don't leave the lights on after ten. Got it?"

I nodded. What could I say? Somehow I'd managed to get a complete psycho for a roommate. It only seemed fitting.

"I'm here to study and learn. I consider it the highest possible honor to have been chosen to attend Delcroix, and I hope you do too. I intend to make Mr. Judan and my father and all the other people who came before me proud. And I don't intend to let anything stand in the way of my success. Do you understand?"

"Absolutely," I said. "You're absolutely right. Those rules sound perfect. I only wish I had thought of them myself."

She narrowed her eyes at me, as if trying to decide if I was joking. I kept my face impassive. Catherine Arkane, I decided, was like a young Principal Solom. Intense, motivated, and unafraid to throw an elbow if necessary. Luckily, I had dealt with people like Catherine before, and found the thing to do with them was simple: bow in their general direction, agree with everything they said, and then stay the hell out of their way.

Of course, I'd never had to *live* with someone like her before.

That might make things a bit more difficult.

CHAPTER 9

"ALL RIGHT, everyone, gather 'round." Trevor gestured for us to come closer.

I swallowed hard, and like everyone around me, obeyed without question. Tall Douglas firs and spindly vine maples surrounded us, creating pools of shade from the morning sun.

"Look around you. These ten people will be your freshman team. Each team shares an adviser, a homeroom, ethics seminar, and study hall. You'll see each other every day, and hopefully you'll end up supporting each other through the year. Even though you'll only officially be in a team for your freshman year, the friendships you make now will stay with you throughout your time at Delcroix. I know everyone on the team I started with are still good friends, even two years later."

I looked around the circle to assess the damage. Perfect Girl stood to my left, wavy ringlets framing her face like a golden-brown halo. Perfect Girl's name, I had learned the day before, was Allie. It figured—cute and perky, just like her.

Jack stood to my right. That also didn't surprise me, because fate seemed determined to stick us together ever since we'd arrived at Delcroix two days before. Jack had shown up next to me in the auditorium our second morning at school, when they introduced us to all our teachers and handed out our schedules, and it turned out we had a lot of the same classes. We spent most of the day wandering around together, getting lost as we tried to find our classrooms, and talking about how weird everyone else was. That worked for me because, other than Esther and Hennie, who I kept trying to avoid, it seemed like every other freshman at Delcroix was some ultrasmart, ultracool, and ultratalented kid who made me intensely uncomfortable. It made me feel infinitely better to know that Jack was as unsure about why he was here at Delcroix as I was.

The amazing thing about Jack was that he really didn't seem to care what anyone thought about him. Once, during an assembly, a teacher came over to shush him, and he just stared at her, as if daring her to say something else. She didn't.

This morning after breakfast the team leaders had split us into groups and walked us out to the forest. Jack appeared at my side moments after they announced the groups. Even though the trail into the woods narrowed in spots, and we had to walk single file, Jack managed to stay close to me. A few of the other girls, including Allie, gave him come-hither looks, but for some reason, he only talked to me.

Now Jack hung back a few feet from the circle, looking bored. He rolled his eyes as Trevor spoke, which was particularly bold because Trevor was staring right at him.

"Mr. Landry, why don't you go around the circle and say everyone's name?" Trevor said. "I'm sure you remember them from roll call."

The faces of our group held a mix of nervous smiles and

studied boredom. I kept my own expression blank.

"Dancia, Allie, Alessandro, Paul, Emma, Hector, Marika, Gideon, and Yashir," Jack said, pointing at each person as he spoke.

Everyone looked amazed. I couldn't remember more than one or two names in the group. Trevor narrowed his brow, clearly irritated that he hadn't managed to embarrass Jack. We went around the circle a few more times, practicing all the names. Alessandro was a short, dark-skinned kid with longish black hair. Paul, Emma, and Gideon looked like your basic middle-class white kids, nothing too special. Hector was tall and buff, the kind of guy who would never notice me if we passed in the hall. Marika had long dark hair in braids down her back. She was cute in a wholesome sort of way. Yashir was the guy that Hennie liked. He seemed serious but friendly. He wore silver rings on several of his fingers, and he fiddled with his dreadlocks when he spoke.

"Okay, now that you're all acquainted, let's get down to business." Trevor led us over to an enormous wall in the middle of the forest. It was about twelve feet high and at least that long, made of smooth, dark wood planks.

"This is the wall. On the back of it is a ladder that leads to a platform a few feet from the top. Follow me—this will be your only chance to see it before we begin." He led us around the backside. The platform looked frighteningly high off the ground. Nervous laughter trickled off into silence.

Jack snorted under his breath. "You've got to be kidding me."

Trevor glared at him. "Your job as a group is to get over the wall. After I explain the rules, you will have thirty minutes to complete your task. Not a second more."

"You want us to climb that thing?" Gideon asked doubtfully, as we returned to the front.

Trevor smiled. Not a nice smile. More of a smirk. "You can get over the wall any way you choose. There are only a few rules. You can't go around the wall or touch the sides. You can have up to two people stand on the platform. While they are on the platform, they can help those coming over, but they must come down in the order they went up. Once someone gets over the wall and comes down from the platform, they can come back around and help as spotters for people going up, but they can't touch them."

Everyone groaned. Trevor silenced us with one of his icy-blue stares. He showed us a few basic safety moves, telling us to push the person into the wall if they started to fall, which sounded more sadistic than safe. We practiced with him for a minute or two, then he held up his hands for quiet.

"You know the rules. I'll be watching to make sure you obey them. The clock starts now." Trevor pushed a button on his watch and stepped back to lean against one of the trees.

We looked at each other silently. Hector walked over to the wall and reached his hand up as high as he could. It went about two-thirds of the way to the top. He motioned to Paul, the skinniest kid. "Why don't you stand on my shoulders?"

They flailed around for a few minutes, trying to get Paul onto Hector's shoulders. Once they did, Hector leaned against the wall for support, but he could barely stay upright when Paul tried to stand up. Paul, meanwhile, got so scared when he tried to straighten his legs that his entire body shook, and he couldn't reach up to grab the top of the wall.

"It's high up here," he said, his voice wavering as he tried to get his legs to stay still.

Allie said, "He needs more support from below."

Hector frowned. "What's that supposed to mean?"

She put a French-manicured hand on his arm and patted comfortingly. "It's hard to stand up straight on someone's shoulders. I was a cheerleader, so I know. It takes forever to learn to do that. A pyramid is easier and more stable."

Why was I not surprised that she was a cheerleader?

Allie guided the group into forming a pyramid at the base of the wall, with her at the apex. She ended up an easy foot or two from the top.

"Wait!" Marika interrupted, as Allie started to pull herself over. "Shouldn't we plan this out? I mean, once Allie goes over the wall and comes down from the platform, she can't be part of the pyramid anymore. Shouldn't we think about the order?"

A few scattered groans greeted her questions. After a pause, Allie called down, "Good point, Marika." She climbed down from the top set of shoulders and jumped lightly to the ground. The rest of the pyramid dissolved around her.

"You mean we're going to have to do that again?" Hector asked, rubbing his shoulders.

"Cheerleading isn't as easy as it looks, is it?" Allie said with a wink. Everyone laughed.

Great, I thought. Perfect Girl is cute *and* funny.

After milling around a while longer, people started throwing out ideas for the order. Everyone, that is, except Jack and me. I had no intention of offering stupid suggestions that would bring attention to myself. Jack seemed to have the same plan, except his also involved following me around and whispering comments under his breath, like: "Do you think this is actually a test to see if we're stupid enough to throw ourselves over a twelve-foot wall simply because Trevor told us to?"

A good point, when you thought about it.

Finally they decided to send Gideon up first, and then alternate girls and boys. My rude awakening came when I heard the group discussing who should go last.

"It will have to be someone skinny. I'll hang down the wall and they can hold on to my ankles. The people on the platform can pull us both up," Yashir said.

"They'll have to be tall," Marika added. "To catch your ankles. And strong enough to pull themselves up the wall if necessary."

"What about Dancia? She's tall and thin." Jack and I stood a few feet from the crowd, and Yashir motioned for us to come closer. "Dancia, can you do a pull-up?"

I admit I was so flattered by him calling me thin that I didn't hesitate before responding. "Yeah, one or two." A second later, it occurred to me I probably should have kept my mouth shut. Before I had time to retract my statement, Yashir and Marika—the apparent decision-makers of the group—nodded.

"That's it, then. Dancia goes last."

I made a halfhearted protest, but no one was listening. They were already focused on making the pyramid and getting Gideon to the top. It's harder than you'd think to pull yourself up and over the top of a wall, and as I watched Gideon struggle, my stomach began to roll. I might have to do that by myself? What were they thinking?

Panic started to set in, so I decided to throw myself into the fray. Even though I force myself to stay on the sidelines a lot, doing nothing drives me absolutely crazy. I guess that's why I like running so much. It gives me something to do when I get stressed out. After about twenty minutes of struggling in the heat and getting stepped on, climbed over, and kicked in the head countless times, my face burned and sweat soaked my T-shirt. But everyone—except Jack, of course—was completely absorbed in the task. Marika almost ripped her pants trying to get her leg over the top, and Yashir smashed his knee getting Hector off the ground. The giggles and cheers when Yashir made it up were infectious. Jack spent some time in the pyramid, and when his turn came, pulled himself up and over the top of the wall with surprising strength. But he did it all with a lazy, uncaring air that would have made me crazy if I had stopped long enough to pay attention.

Then came my turn. Emma and Alessandro were standing on the wall, and Yashir was hanging off the wall by his arms.

"I'm supposed to do what?" I asked, squinting up at Yashir.

"Just grab his ankles," Alessandro called down. "We'll pull you both up."

Emma didn't look like she could pull up a toddler, let alone two teenagers. Still, I nodded. Alessandro sounded as if he actually believed this was possible.

"You'd better do it fast," Yashir said. "This hurts like hell."

"Okay, okay!" I screwed up my courage and jumped. His ankles were higher than they looked, and the first few times, I missed. Then I caught his ankle for a second before falling back to the ground.

"Dancia, Dancia," Allie started chanting softly. A few others joined in. Their attempt at encouragement fell somewhere between inspiring and nauseating, though the nausea probably came more from my fear of failing than from anything else. My hands turned slick with sweat, and I had to keep wiping them on my pants before I jumped. On the fourth try,

I managed to get a hold of both ankles, and they started to pull us toward the top.

The pain hit immediately, shooting from my elbows to my shoulders. I thought my arms were going to be ripped from their sockets. Somehow in the midst of the agony, I tried to lock my hands tight.

Though I had wanted not to care, I realized at that moment that I did. I wanted to get over the wall. I might not have friends, and the entire school might one day remember me as that girl no one really knew, but by God I was going to get over that wall.

Except . . . I was slipping. Slowly but surely, I was falling back toward the ground. Alessandro and Emma pulled Yashir high enough to get his torso over the wall just as one of my hands slipped down to his shoe. Alessandro reached over to try to grab me, but he couldn't get more than a handful of my ponytail. I would have willingly given up every curl on my head to have gotten over the wall at that moment, I swear.

"Two minutes left!" Trevor roused himself from his position by the tree long enough to shout at us, and the cheers got even louder. I think Allie might have actually done a jumping jack or two in my honor.

I clutched tighter at Yashir's shoe and willed my fingers not to let go. But at that moment my fingers didn't appear to be taking orders from my brain.

I looked down, pleading really, as if I could convince the ground to move away from my feet. That was when I saw Jack looking up at me, hands in perfect spotter-form, a tiny furrow in his brow. When our eyes met, he nodded.

"No problem," he mouthed.

I turned my attention back to Yashir's shoe—an enormous bigger-than-my-head concoction of black leather and hard sole—and my fingers slipped another fraction of an inch. My mind spun furiously. Had I asked Jack a question? Why did he nod? Did he think I wanted his help?

Even as the questions shot through my brain, something amazing happened: the air under me suddenly felt solid. I pushed against it and was able to shift my hold on Yashir's shoe to grab his ankle, and then his calf. One more push against that wall of air and I threw my other hand up, where Alessandro caught it. He hauled me up with a one-handed death grip I will never forget, and I was there, stomach on the top of the wall, ready to throw myself onto that platform on the other side.

Our team went crazy. Yashir shouted for Emma and Alessandro to get down so we could jump onto the platform, and they did. Everyone whistling and shouting like we had just won the lottery. Yashir tumbled onto the platform and practically hauled me the rest of the way over. When my nerves and shaking hands calmed down enough to move, I stood and looked over the wall, an enormous smile decorating my face.

The team smiled and cheered, but it was Jack's gaze that caught mine. He shrugged as he looked around our group, as if to say, "What a bunch of idiots."

Then he winked at me.

My smile dissolved. Had Jack helped me over the wall? Was that what his nod had meant?

But I knew that when I'd looked down he hadn't been touching me. Anyway, the rules were clear—once you went over, you couldn't help except to spot. If Jack had pushed against my foot, everyone would have noticed, and Trevor would have busted him for sure. But there had been something solid under me, I couldn't deny that.

Could it be that somehow, without touching me, Jack had given me a push?

I went down the ladder in a daze, my euphoria quickly evaporating. When I reached the ground, Allie ran over to give me a hug. I wasn't trying to be rude, but I didn't really hug her back. I just couldn't look into the eyes of Perfect Girl and pretend I was happy. Not with a lead weight suddenly hanging on my shoulders. Allie didn't seem to notice, bouncing away a second later and high-fiving Hector, then linking arms with Emma.

"Congratulations," Trevor said, motioning for us to circle around him. "I didn't think you were going to do it. I saw some excellent teamwork out there. I was impressed."

Jack stood next to me, and I could feel waves of something—satisfaction? pleasure?—radiating from him. He alternated between a bored stare at Trevor and a sideways glance at me. I had to restrain myself from grabbing his shirt and spinning him around and demanding to know what he had done.

Was it possible? I could hardly dare to voice the thought in my head. The signs seemed to point to one conclusion, but I refused to believe it could be true. Because if it was, Jack had special powers just like me. And unlike me, he wasn't scared to use them.

CHAPTER 10

THE REST of the week went by in a blur. We started classes and settled into the school routine. Everyone seemed excited about different subjects—the dancers hung out in the studios, the science kids were practically drooling over the lab, and Yashir and his friends were always sitting around in the commons, drawing.

Everyone, of course, but me, who had no subject to look forward to, and nothing to excel at. I swear, I was the only kid, other than Jack, of course, who was in all the remedial classes.

I saw Cam a bunch of times during the week, but it was only for a second or two between activities. He wasn't a team leader, like Trevor, so he didn't eat in the cafeteria with the freshmen. Usually I saw him walking the halls with Mr. Judan or one of the other teachers. He always waved to me and smiled. Sometimes he'd even stop and say hello, or ask how my day was going. He said he was working for Mr. Judan, doing boring office stuff. I could barely pull myself together enough to speak to him. I think the problem was that it took me about ten minutes to become accustomed to his gorgeousness, so the quick stops in the hall always left me incoherent.

I passed Hennie once, speaking to a girl in Chinese, and then another time with a boy speaking Spanish. Both times she tried to get me to stay and talk, but I said I had to get to class. Every time I saw Esther, she was hanging out with a different group of boys and laughing that big laugh of hers. Kids always looked happy when they were with Esther. She did these imitations of people—teachers, even Principal Solom—that were hilarious. She could somehow make herself completely change to fit whoever she was impersonating. I swear, when she would do Principal Solom, she would actually shrink.

I tried to duck and hide whenever I saw Hennie and Esther, but it was hard. It wasn't that I didn't like them. It was that I liked them too much. I was generally able to avoid them during the day without being rude—for this first week, they had us doing activities each afternoon with our teams, and sitting with them at meals—but at night, after study hours, it was impossible to avoid them completely. We just fit together so well, the three of us. Like we were meant to be friends.

Catherine came in pretty handy in all this. She shut the door to our room at exactly ten o'clock, and didn't allow visitors. And I wasn't lying when I told Esther and Hennie that I needed all my free time to study. Our teachers had actually assigned homework for the first day of class, and then once classes started, I was swamped. I wasn't even taking hard classes. Some of the others were taking higher-level stuff, like calculus and physics. They were doing review work until the upperclassmen arrived on Monday. I was just reading books and doing basic math problems, and I was still overwhelmed. Let's just say Danville Middle hadn't exactly prepared me for Delcroix.

Meanwhile, Jack had become my constant companion, dropping notes over my shoulder in class and making snide comments in my ear when Trevor led us through another group activity. There was no repeat of what had happened at the wall, and the further away from it we got, the more I started to doubt my own conclusions about what had happened. Maybe I was stronger than I thought. Maybe I had just imagined that cushion of air suddenly supporting my weight. Maybe Jack was nothing more than a clever cheater who had somehow managed to escape Trevor's eagle eye.

Besides, I was missing Grandma. I was also trying as hard as I could not to bond with the two nicest people I'd ever met, and I was living with a psychotic dictator who had measured the space in our closet and marked the halfway point with masking tape to make sure I didn't cross the line. So I guess I just wasn't tough enough to push Jack away too. Before I knew it we were trading music and talking about our old schools. He figured out right away how horrible Catherine was, and he endlessly made fun of her for being so in love with Delcroix and sucking up to all the teachers. He even came up with the perfect nickname for her: Buttondown, because she always wore white button-down shirts and navy pants or skirts. They were probably part of her old school uniform. Even though I knew I shouldn't, I couldn't help but laugh every time he said it.

It wasn't until Friday afternoon, when we were waiting for the Silver Bullet to take us back to the parking lot to go home for the weekend, that I realized the Dancia Lewis way was going to have to change. We were outside the Main Hall, dragging bags of dirty laundry and backpacks full of homework. Everyone was excited to see their parents, though there were some drama queens who were already complaining about how much they'd miss their friends.

Esther gave me a back-cracking hug. "Dancia, I've barely seen you all week," she wailed. "Where have you been? I mean, you've been in your room, of course, studying, which is good, and I can't really blame you. After all, my dad will kill me—and I mean kill me—if I don't keep my grades up. But we missed you last night. We were in my room listening to music. You should have come down."

I hung my head. "It's algebra. You start mixing letters and numbers, and my eyes cross. And you wouldn't believe the essay I've got to write for English. I figured I had to get a start on it before I went home."

Hennie gave me a gentle squeeze and a deep assessing look. "Everything okay?" she asked. "How's your team? Are you getting along with everyone?"

"I guess so." I shifted from foot to foot. "I mean, well, Jack and I have been hanging out a lot."

"Jack? You mean the guy with the tattoo?" Hennie grinned. "Are you sure you're just friends?"

"Definitely." I nodded vigorously. "Just friends."

Esther snorted. "That's how it starts, Dancia. Trust me, it always starts that way. Then when you least expect it, everything changes."

"Not us." I took a quick look around to make sure Jack wasn't right behind me. "No way."

Esther cleared her throat and adjusted a pair of imaginary glasses on her forehead, just like our World Civ teacher, Mrs. Paskett. "Yes of course, dear, of course. You're right, of course. How could I ever doubt you." Her voice rose two octaves and quavered, just like Mrs. Paskett's. Hennie and I burst out laughing.

When I could speak again, I elbowed Hennie in the ribs. "So when are you going to talk to Yashir, Hennie? He's on my team, you know. He seems really nice."

Hennie threw her hands in the air. "As if I could talk to him! He's in my Spanish class, but he hardly says anything. Tell me more about him. I need details!"

I thought back, relieved I'd managed to change the subject. "He's usually one of the leaders of our group. Not too bossy, but everyone seems to listen to him. He loves to draw and paint, of course. He's from California, and his mom does all his piercings." I was surprised by how much I already knew about him. I guess some of the "get to know you" games Trevor had made us play had actually worked.

"He's perfect for you, Hennie," Esther said. "And if you're feeling shy, Dancia can help."

Hennie bit her lip. "I don't know, Esther. You know my dad. He won't like the piercings."

"We're at *boarding school*, silly. Your dad won't even know."

"But I've barely talked to him," I said. "What makes you think I can help Hennie?"

Esther patted my hand. "Don't worry. Boys are simple creatures. I can teach you both what you need to know."

Hennie straightened her already perfectly straight skirt and sighed. "It's true. Esther's like a walking encyclopedia on the male species."

Esther nodded sagely. "You know what I always say: they're just like girls, only different. Now, Dancia, he's on your team, so aren't you friends already?"

"Well, I guess . . . I mean, I can talk to him. It's not like we're strangers. But I wouldn't say we're friends either."

Esther waved aside my protest. "By Thanksgiving you'll

be best friends with everyone at this school. It's just a matter of time."

On that chilling note, I changed the subject to our classes. The only ones we had together were World Civ and chemistry. All of the freshmen had to take an ethics class, but Esther and Hennie were in the other section. My ethics class was taught by this goofy little guy named Mr. Fritz. He had a puff of long white hair on top of his head, and really big ears, which made him resemble something between Albert Einstein and a troll doll. We all had math, but different levels—I was in algebra, the ninth grade course at my high school. Esther and Hennie were already starting calculus.

In the afternoons I had a two-hour block of classes that my adviser, Mrs. Dade, said would change throughout the year. I was starting with a self-defense class and a public speaking workshop. Mrs. Dade didn't tell me why they'd put me in these classes, just said every student had concentrated "focus time" after lunch.

The only problem was, unlike everyone else at Delcroix, I had no focus. Esther was really into theater; for her focus periods she had an acting class and a famous playwrights class, where they were studying Shakespeare and some Greek guys I'd never heard of. Hennie was taking all sorts of different languages—Hindi-Urdu, Chinese, and French literature instead of English.

"You're taking Spanish too? What are you, some kind of genius with languages?" I asked.

Hennie lowered her eyes. "I speak five now, but my dad speaks ten. I want to know at least that many someday so I can work for the UN. My dad knows two ambassadors who went to Delcroix, and they said it was an amazing place for languages."

It wasn't hard to see what her "focus" was.

"Someday I'd like to learn Spanish," I said wistfully. They used to have real Spanish classes at our middle school, but they'd cut them when I was still in elementary school. Something about budget problems. By the time I started there, they just had this video they played once a week. It was ridiculous. I knew my colors and how to count to ten. That was about it.

"I can teach you," Hennie said.

"Really?"

"It's easy. You just have to practice speaking with someone. We'll do it at night. Just a few minutes a day." Hennie gave me one of her gentle smiles, and I had to turn away because I thought for a second I might cry.

The bell sounded, and we started up the steps onto the Silver Bullet. I passed Catherine, who glared at me through narrowed eyes. Then I walked by Jack. He had on his headphones, and his eyes were closed. I wasn't surprised. Jack tuned out whenever he got in a crowd. He hated crowds. He wasn't much of a people person in general—he hadn't made many friends since we'd started school—but he really hated crowds.

I thought about how certain I'd been, just five days ago, that he was trouble and to be avoided at all costs, and then how I'd just told Hennie that we'd been hanging out all week.

I slipped past him and headed for the back of the bus. Hennie and Esther had saved me room beside them. Esther patted the edge of the seat and grinned. I stole a look back toward Jack, and then Catherine, before I fell into the seat. There wasn't quite room for three, so I balanced on the edge with my feet in the aisle.

"You'll have to give me your phone number," Esther said. "So we can talk this weekend."

Hennie pulled her backpack onto her lap. "Give me your number. We can have a three-way call."

The bus started abruptly just as Hennie was pulling on the zipper, and her fingers slipped. She knocked herself in the nose, and Esther giggled. Hennie glared at Esther and then laughed when, a second later, the bus jerked again and I fell into the aisle. The bus driver hollered at me to get back in my seat, and I did, practically hoisting myself onto Esther's lap.

It was then, laughing as the bus pulled away from the Main Hall, with the green lawns of Delcroix stretched out on either side of us, and all the other freshman shouting and calling to each other, that something inside of me unwound.

I had friends. Esther and Hennie were my friends. Jack, troublemaker or not, was my friend. And, as hard as it was to believe, even Cam was becoming a friend. No one knew better than me how dangerous this state of affairs could be, but it seemed silly to keep fighting the inevitable. I'd have to make myself into a jerk or a pariah to keep it from happening, and I just didn't have it in me to do either of those things.

Life was changing. I wasn't sure where it was taking me, but I had a feeling things would never be the same.

CHAPTER 11

THE UPPERCLASSMEN started school on Monday, and the Res and the Main Hall felt more like a regular school as they filled with students and teachers. I started eating meals with Esther and Hennie. Jack said he didn't like the cafeteria because Trevor was always hanging around staring at him, and I had to admit, it did seem that way. Even after he didn't have to eat with our team anymore, Trevor still made time to look for each of us at every meal.

I tried to tell Jack that Trevor was just being nice, making sure none of us got lost in the crowd, but Jack had it in his head that Trevor didn't like him. So after checking in, Jack would scarf down some food and head for the library, or go outside somewhere on the playing fields to eat. We still hung out between classes and during free time, and we started studying together too, because we had all the same assignments. It turned out Jack was really smart, and when he bothered to finish his homework, he got good marks.

Of course, he usually didn't bother.

On Thursday they had tryouts for cross-country. Actually, tryouts isn't really the right word. They let everyone join the team who would agree to attend practices. The school was so small it wasn't like the turnout was overwhelming.

Esther and Hennie decided they would join the team with me. Esther's mom thought it would be good for her to do some sports, and Esther thought she'd be able to chat more while she was running than while playing volleyball or swimming. I thought this was rather naive on her part, or maybe she just didn't pant as much as I did when I ran. Hennie said she needed to do a sport that didn't require too much coordination, which was wise. I had never seen someone trip quite so often, with so little reason, as Hennie.

I nervously adjusted my shorts as we walked up to the practice fields where the coach had told us to gather. It had poured the night before, so the field was soft and damp, but the sun had been out for a few hours, and tiny tendrils of steam were actually rising from the ground. Soccer season wasn't until the spring, but a bunch of guys were playing a pickup game. The fields were tucked into the far corner of the grassy area that surrounded the school, bordered on one side by tall evergreens. The sun hovered right above the trees, bright and hot.

I bent over and retied my shoelaces. Although I liked to run on my own, I'd never tried it with a team, and I had a horrible feeling I wasn't going to be able to keep up.

"So, is this the new Delcroix cross-country team?"

I froze. Cam had walked up directly behind Hennie. She turned around, eyes wide, and then backed up so he could stand next to me. I struggled to remain calm, with him only a few feet away.

How did he get better looking every day? He was wearing black-and-white-striped soccer shoes and shin guards, and with the sun beating down on him, I swear he looked like a superhero—even taller and stronger than I remembered. The light caught red and gold highlights in his hair, and sparkled on the gold Delcroix crest on his T-shirt.

Esther responded first, naturally, flipping her hair back with a grin. "I don't know about that. Someone might need to call 911 if I have a heart attack halfway through the run."

Cam smiled, and the corners of his eyes crinkled in the most adorable way. "You shouldn't worry. I bet Dancia can give you some pointers."

I swallowed hard. Did Cam really remember that I liked to run? "Um, I guess."

Brilliant. Sparkling conversation.

Hennie and Esther looked at Cam, then at me, then back at Cam.

"How far do you think they'll make us run today?" Hennie asked, her voice barely above a whisper. She twisted her hands as she spoke.

Esther hadn't been kidding when she said Hennie was shy around boys. Just yesterday I'd tried to get her and Yashir to talk when we were studying in the commons together, and she'd actually snapped her pencil in half, she was so freaked out.

"Maybe a couple of miles," Cam said. "They start the freshmen out pretty easy. You can jog at first, to get used to it. I don't think they do speed work for a week or two."

Esther looked horrified. "A couple of miles? As in, actual *miles*?"

I had to laugh. "What did you expect when they said the average course length was five kilometers, Esther? That you'd be running inches?"

Esther threw a hand across her forehead. "That's it. I'm definitely going to die out there. You might as well call my mom now. Or maybe call a helicopter. Does Delcroix have a helicopter? I'm going to need immediate transportation to a hospital. You should put them on standby."

"I'm sure Dancia will get you out. Just make sure you don't get stuck on the wrong side of the wall, Dancia. I'm not sure Esther would make it over in her weakened condition." Cam gave me a knowing look, like we were sharing a private joke, and I nearly choked.

Cam must have talked to Trevor about me. Or at least about our team. That's the only way he would have known that we did the wall.

"What wall?" Esther asked. "You mean the wall Dancia's team climbed during orientation? I heard about that. It sounded awful. Why does the school have all those things out there in the woods anyway? Poor Hennie's team had to jump off a platform from thirty feet in the air." Esther's nose wrinkled with distaste. "Tell the truth: is it all just an elaborate system for punishing incoming freshmen?"

"It's mostly for that," Cam said, deadpan. "We tried other ways of punishing the freshmen, but the police kept showing up."

We all laughed appreciatively, even Hennie, who was apparently still trying to recover from actually speaking to Cam.

"No, seriously, it's called a challenge course, and everyone in the school uses it, even after orientation," Cam said. "We see it as a way to develop and test leadership skills. You don't get much of an opportunity to meet challenges like that wall in everyday life, and we believe it's good for you to learn how you'll react when pushed. Will you rise to meet the challenge? Will you give up? Will you cheat?"

Even though he smiled as he spoke, I got the feeling he was saying something very important. I swallowed hard at the wave of guilt that followed, as memories of the wall, and the nudge I'd felt from Jack, replayed in my mind. I hadn't wanted to cheat, but had I? Had an invisible hand helped me climb the wall?

"Good afternoon, Cameron, ladies."

The voice sounded familiar. I turned around to see Mr. Judan walking in our direction, his white teeth gleaming and thick hair swooping back from his forehead in elegant waves. Once again I was struck by the feeling that he was way, way too attractive and well dressed to be working at a high school. Even out here, in the middle of a field, surrounded by kids in shorts and T-shirts, he looked ready to go have dinner with the president, with his fancy suit, red silk tie, and expensive-looking leather loafers.

He smiled at each of us, but instead of making me relax, his anchorman voice made me dig my nails into my palm. "I know Dancia, and I recognize Esther. You must be Henrietta. How lovely to see you all."

We smiled politely. No one looked particularly comfortable, even Cam. Silence fell over the group.

"How is everyone enjoying school thus far?" His white teeth sparkled through a broad smile. He didn't seem to notice that he'd managed to make us all profoundly uncomfortable.

Even Esther struggled to respond, her mouth flopping open and closed several times. Surprisingly, it was Hennie who spoke up for the group.

"It's been wonderful, sir, but we were just discussing the challenge course. I had no idea Delcroix utilized stress-induced leadership scenarios. Why is that?"

Delivered in Hennie's sweet, breathy tone, you could almost miss the underlying bite in her question.

Mr. Judan raised one black brow. "What do you mean, my dear?"

Oh my. From his direct tone, I gathered he hadn't missed the bite.

"Cam explained that the school directs us toward challenges in order to see how we react in times of stress. I find this fascinating, and couldn't help but wonder—is there some sort of test involved here? And if so, what happens if we fail?"

Yeesh. I hadn't thought about it that way. I looked at Hennie with newfound respect. Listening to her quietly confident voice, I had a sudden vision of Hennie sitting across the table from her brilliant father, debating foreign policy in one of the five languages she spoke.

Note to self: don't mess with Hennie.

Mr. Judan shot Cam a look I couldn't read. Was he pissed? Was the whole challenge thing supposed to be a secret? Cam's tanned skin developed an underlying hint of pink.

"No, no." Mr. Judan chuckled, and an easy smile spread across his face. "No test at all. I think Cameron may have misstated the purpose of our challenges. You see, research tells us the best teams come out of shared experiences. We want you to have a highly supportive and successful freshman team, so it makes sense to give you opportunities to take part in one of those experiences."

He locked eyes for a moment with Cam, who seemed to get some silent message, because he nodded a second later.

"Now, I really must be going. It was a pleasure to meet you all. Please, join me in my office when you are finished with your game, Cameron. I have something I need to discuss with you." He waved to the cross-country coach, Mr. Yerkinly, who was walking up from the Main Hall.

An uncomfortable silence followed. Then one of the

soccer players waved to Cam. He glanced down at his watch. "Looks like it's time for our game. I'd better go." He paused. "Dancia, do you have a second?"

My heart stopped. "Um, what?"

"I just wanted to catch you alone for a second."

I shot Esther a quick, semi-hysterical glance. "Sure."

We walked a few paces away, to the edge of the field. My heart was beating so fast I thought I might faint. When we were out of earshot from Esther and Hennie, Cam gave me one of his slow smiles. "Listen, I just wanted to say that I know Trevor encouraged you to spend a lot of time with your team, especially during the first week, but I don't want you to think that you have to keep hanging out with them now that orientation is over."

I blinked and tried to focus on what he had just said. My heart slowed abruptly. Apparently he hadn't pulled me aside to ask me to be his one true love.

"What do you mean?" I asked.

"I just mean, there may be people on your team that aren't as good for you as other people. That's all. Esther and . . . what's her name? Hennie? Esther and Hennie seem like nice girls, Dancia. I can see that you three are already great friends."

Still unsure of what mysterious code Cam was using, I cocked my head and stared at him. "Yeah, Esther and Hennie are super," I said uneasily. "We have a lot of fun together."

Cam looked pleased. "I thought so. I just wanted to make sure you knew that was okay. To hang out with them, I mean, instead of people from your team all the time. And you should come find me at lunch sometime. I'd like to introduce you to some of my friends too."

If he was trying to confuse me, he had absolutely

succeeded. First he was talking about my team, then Esther and Hennie, and now he wanted me to meet his friends? Why me? Why not Esther, who could actually talk to him and make him laugh; or Hennie, who was like a picture from a magazine? As baffled as I was, I still felt a rush of pleasure.

"Okay," I said. "That would be great."

He walked me back over to Hennie and Esther, and gave each of us one of his blinding smiles, starting with me. "Remember, whatever you need, Dancia, or any of you, let me know. I'd love to help."

The second he was out of earshot, Esther hit me with her notebook.

"'Whatever you need, I'd love to help'?" she repeated. "What's going on with you and Cam?! Are you, like, going out or something?"

"What do you mean?" I asked, my voice cracking. I swallowed and tried to regain my composure. "I told you, he was my recruiter. They probably have a rule that they have to be extra nice to the people they recruit. Besides, he said 'any of you.' He wasn't just talking to me."

Esther snorted. "I don't think so." She and Hennie exchanged meaningful looks. "He didn't even notice us. He only had eyes for you. What did he say over there, anyway?"

I threw my head back and closed my eyes, retying my hair into a massive ponytail. "I have no idea. Something about how he thinks I should be friends with you, and that I shouldn't worry about spending all my time with my team. I couldn't follow him."

"You mean, he doesn't want you to spend all your time with Jack," Hennie said knowingly.

My mouth dropped open. I hadn't even thought about it,

but the only person on my team I had become friends with was Jack. Was he trying to say something to me about Jack?

Esther giggled. "Oh, Hennie, that's brilliant! He's jealous! He's been watching Dancia hanging around with Jack these last two weeks, and he's horribly jealous!"

"You're crazy, Esther," I said, not wanting to think about the possibility, even though somewhere in my brain it was as if a rainbow had broken across the sky. "And you too, Hennie. He only said that because he likes the two of you. Esther totally made him laugh just now. And, Hennie, you're a hundred times prettier than I am. He could not stop staring at you. Did you see that?"

"Yeah, right," Hennie said. "He was staring at me because I practically threw up on myself, I was so nervous."

That made me laugh. "I guess he is pretty cute, huh?"

"No, not pretty cute," Hennie said. "Try drop-dead gorgeous."

"And so not interested in either of us, Dancia," Esther said. "Seriously, what do I have to do to convince you that he was totally checking you out? And he must have been asking about you to his buddy Trevor. Which is definitely a good thing."

"This is all crazy. Honestly, I wouldn't know what to do if he *was* interested. I've never even had a boyfriend." I don't know what possessed me to say that, but the words exploded out of me. It was like I'd been hiding a dirty secret and had finally come clean and told the truth.

My words provoked a sympathetic sigh from Hennie. "Me neither. My parents won't let me. Don't worry, though. Esther's had lots of boyfriends. She can give you advice."

Esther actually blushed. "It's just that I've got lots of friends who are boys," she explained. "And for some reason they always end up liking me. But it's not cool at all because then when I have to break up with them, I lose a friend *and* a boyfriend."

Hennie rolled her eyes. "I feel sooo sorry for you."

I elbowed her and mimicked playing a violin, so relieved that they weren't making fun of me for being such a dork that I felt a little giddy. "Yeah, poor, poor Esther."

"I swear, Hennie, it's just like we're back at camp," Esther said. "Except, of course, that we've got Dancia now. So there are two of you to make fun of me."

Hennie saluted. "The two musketeers, reporting for duty, sir."

At that moment, Mr. Yerkinly held up a clipboard and blew his whistle. "Anyone here for cross-country?"

Esther stumbled backward theatrically. "Get the cell phones ready! Alert the helicopter! Esther Racowitz is ready to start running."

She started at a slow jog toward Mr. Yerkinly. Hennie and I grinned at each other and followed a few paces behind.

CHAPTER 12

ABOUT HALF the freshmen at Delcroix were from California, and they kept asking those of us from Washington and Oregon when it would start raining. They had heard stories, of course, about how it rains all the time, so they had been amazed that the month of September was dry and hot, with just a few days of rain here and there to break up the sunshine. I tried to tell them to relax and enjoy the warm weather, because the rain would be here soon enough.

And right around October fifth, it came.

I actually like the rain. I know people complain about it, but I think it's soothing. I like to run in it because it keeps my face cool, and I like to hear the slap of mud and wet pavement under my feet. I like to watch the clouds moving across the sky. I like listening to the rain on the roof at night, and seeing the drops slide across windows while I'm at school. People don't understand that here in Washington it doesn't just rain all the time. Sometimes it rains, sometimes it drizzles, and sometimes it pours. There's a big difference between those things.

Really.

Anyway, once the rain started, it seemed like the teachers got really serious about homework. It was as if they decided we weren't outside anyway, so we might as well be studying. I barely had time to breathe between cross-country practice and all the algebra and English homework. And don't get me started on chemistry. I completely failed to see the value in memorizing the stupid periodic table of elements.

They also mixed up our afternoon focus periods. I ended my public speaking workshop (which had been a nightmare—I will never, ever pursue a career as a politician) and started a pottery class.

Why pottery? I have no idea. They told me where to go, and I went.

The pottery class was a mix of people like me, who had little or no artistic talent, and people like Cara. Cara had thick glasses, a round face, and short dark hair with bangs. She was in my English class. She spoke with a heavy accent; English was apparently not her first language. I would sit and watch her at the pottery wheel, trying not to gawk as she effortlessly spun the wheel with her foot, dipped her fingers into a plastic container of water, and coaxed a perfect vase to form from a lump of clay.

My lump usually remained pretty much like it started—a lump.

Later, after our masterpieces had been fired, my "mug" looked like something a kindergartner would have made for her mom in art class, whereas Cara's vase looked like something you'd sell for thousands of dollars in an art gallery.

It was like that in all my classes. There were always one or two kids who were geniuses at the subject, and as the year progressed, you got to know what each person was amazing at: Hennie with her languages, Esther with her acting, Catherine with her math, and Cara with her pots. There was this kid Amir who ran for freshman class president, and no one even bothered to run against him. He was like Cam—everyone just seemed to believe he'd be the best one for the job.

Nothing much changed for me in the boy department. Esther still thought Jack and I might end up together, in that friends-blending-into-more sort of thing that happened to her all the time. On alternate days, though, she thought Cam and I were meant to be.

I was just thrilled for any scrap of attention Cam gave me. Which happened fairly regularly, but not regularly enough to justify any fairy-tale fantasies. He and I had developed a pretty decent friendship—nothing more than that.

Jack and I, meanwhile, had gotten closer. There was no one else at Delcroix—not even Hennie or Esther—who understood me like Jack. But we were friends.

Only friends.

At this point in the year, cliques had formed, but they were still pretty fluid. People started by hanging out with people from their teams, and then with their roommates. Now they were starting to gravitate toward people who had their same focus. But that was harder to figure out, and there just weren't enough people to limit yourself to only the other actors, or dancers, or musicians, or whatever.

I, of course, remained the girl without a focus. I tried not to think about it, and brushed aside the casual questions that people started to ask. They clearly wanted to know why I was there, but were too polite to ask me outright. It was midway through October when the weirdness came to a head. We were in pottery class, and I was sitting at a table with Cara, Marika, Allie, and Catherine. We were painting our latest creations, and they were raving about how much they loved Delcroix and how great it was to finally feel like they fit in somewhere. Even Catherine, who never smiled, looked less angry than usual.

"This is so nice, you know?" Marika said. "I never really had a chance to make very many friends before, because I was always in the advanced classes. The older kids ignored me, and the kids my age thought I was a total freak."

Catherine nodded. "I started reading when I was three, so they put me with the second graders when I was in kindergarten. Even at my boarding school I had to have special tutors. How was I supposed to make friends that way?"

You probably had to start by not being such a creep, I thought to myself.

Catherine had her own little clique of Button-downs, who, like her, had recycled their school uniforms to wear at Delcroix, and insisted on ironing their white shirts and navy bottoms before they went to class each morning. I liked to think they were the least popular kids in the school. The truth was, everyone at Delcroix seemed to have some friends, and the team thing had actually worked to get everyone hooked in with a group.

Still, it was nice to imagine that everyone at Delcroix disliked Catherine as much as I did.

"I never had time to make friends," Allie said. "I had cheerleading or gymnastics practice every day after school, and I was taking advanced classes on top of that, so I couldn't hang out like other kids. Then they thought I was stuck-up, but it wasn't that. I was just busy."

Marika looked at me. "Dancia, didn't you go to school here in Danville? What was it like?"

"What was Danville Middle like?" I paused and searched for something interesting to share. Nothing came to mind. "It was okay, I guess. The usual sorts of things—annoying teachers, cliques . . ." I trailed off, not sure what else to add.

"Did they pull you out for gifted classes? That's what they did at my school, which sucked because then everyone would make fun of you," Cara said.

I cleared my throat. "Not really. I mean, no."

"They didn't pull you out?" Cara asked.

"No, I wasn't gifted."

Cara's mouth dropped open. Slowly, her face turned bright red. "I didn't mean . . . I'm sorry . . ."

"What does that mean anyway, that they say you're gifted?" Allie rushed in, obviously trying to save me from looking like an idiot. "Those programs are so stupid. There were tons of smart kids at my school that weren't in our classes. I don't know how they selected people for it. It must have been totally random."

Everyone looked uncomfortable. Catherine gave me a withering look.

"So, what did you . . . er . . . *do* at your school?" asked Cara.

She was obviously trying to be nice and give me a chance to tell them what I *was* gifted at. I guess she just assumed if I was at Delcroix, I must be amazing at something. But I wasn't. Truth was, I didn't *do* anything, except occasionally crash cars and drop branches on people.

I groped around for an excuse. "I wasn't able to participate in a lot of activities. I live with my grandma, and she needed me at home."

Allie nodded with relief. "Of course. That was really nice of you."

"It wasn't a big deal." There was another uncomfortable pause, and I looked down at my pitiful excuse for a bowl, and then at the paint tray in front of me. "Wow, I need a lot more paint if I'm going to make this look decent." I backed away from the table. "I better go refill the red."

It was the lamest excuse ever, and I'm sure they all knew it, but they smiled and continued talking, as if they hadn't just exposed my complete and utter failure as a Delcroix student. Sometimes I wished I could use my power, just once, and show them all that I wasn't just a pitiful lump of clay, a badly formed bowl that wouldn't even hold water. But what good would that do? I'd use my power and something horrible would happen. Marika would end up in the hospital, or Catherine would lose a limb.

That wouldn't be so bad, though. I squirted a bottleful of red paint into my tray and imagined the scene. Catherine didn't need both her arms. She was just a big old brain in a grumpy body anyway.

I suffered through the end of the class, gathered my backpack, and ran out the door the second the bell rang. I didn't have cross-country for an hour, but figured I might as well get started early. I needed the run. I had gotten halfway to the Res when I remembered that I'd forgotten to wash out my paintbrushes. Our teacher was an absolute fanatic about her brushes, and had threatened to drop our grade by a full letter if we didn't clean them up after class. So I turned around and ran back to the art room.

I was a few feet away when I heard Catherine's voice, still inside the room. I hesitated, hoping she might be coming out so I could avoid talking to her, but then I heard her speak my name.

"Why *is* Dancia here, anyway?" she said.

I pressed myself against the wall, heart beating fast. Catherine had been harsh to my face, but I hadn't imagined she would say things behind my back too.

"What do you mean?" It sounded like Marika.

"I mean she's just a poor kid from Danville," Catherine said. "What possible reason could they have for accepting her?"

"Everyone here is different," Allie said. "Maybe she's got something going on we don't know about."

"Right." Catherine snorted.

I recoiled at the disgust in her voice.

"I mean, come on. You heard her yourself. She doesn't do anything," Catherine continued. "You should try living with her. It's ridiculous. I knew girls in fifth grade who were smarter than that. I keep expecting her to bring back some papier-mâché art project, like a kindergartner." There were rounds of giggles after that. "They probably needed to accept a kid from Danville to keep the town happy, and she was the smartest one they had. Which isn't saying much for Danville, let me tell you."

She went on, but I couldn't listen to any more. Dirty paintbrushes or not, I turned around and ran down the stairs to the Res.

The common room was empty when I got there, so I went right to the phone and dialed home. It rang fifteen times before I hung up, scowling. My throat was tight and my eyes were prickling. I had to keep swallowing hard and telling myself not to cry. How stupid to cry about someone like Catherine, who I already knew was a jerk. Besides, it wasn't like she hadn't said anything I didn't already know. I didn't belong at Delcroix. It was that simple.

"Everything okay?"

I spun around, not surprised to see Jack sitting at one of the tables, his chemistry book open in front of him. He always seemed to appear when I needed him. I rubbed my hand across my eyes. "I suppose."

"Let me guess—Button-down giving you a hard time?"

I laughed shakily. "How did you know?"

"She's a soulless nightmare, a robot who can't think for herself except to attack other people, because in the end, she's horribly jealous that they have the capacity for free will."

Jack's rages against Catherine always made me feel better. We shared a smile. I could feel the tension slipping out of my body.

"Were you trying to call Grandma?" he asked.

"Yeah, but she must have her hearing aid turned off. She does that sometimes in the afternoon." I indicated his book. "You doing homework already? We've got three hours before study time. I'm not sure that's allowed."

"Yashir's got a bunch of other guys in our room listening to music. It's pretty loud. I needed some space."

Yashir and Jack were roommates. They didn't hate each other, like Catherine and I did, but they weren't exactly best friends. For one, Yashir liked to play music all the time, and it drove Jack crazy. Then again, having a roommate at all drove Jack crazy. He didn't like to have people around when he slept. He said he missed his privacy at night more than anything.

"You always need space. They could build you your own separate house out back and you'd still complain that you needed more space."

Jack grinned and tipped his chair onto its back legs. "Hey, I found two spots in my room today that would be perfect for a hidden camera. Did you check yours?"

I laughed. We had a little game we played, where we pretended we were under surveillance and looked for ways the school could be watching us. Jack had started it when Trevor began watching him every day at lunch. He would bring it up every time we had to use our ID badges to get in or out of a building, and whenever we keyed a code into a lock on a door. Naturally, he also brought up the fact that the windows in the Res didn't open, while they did in the Main Hall and the Bly. And then there were the gates. Jack hated the gates. He didn't believe there was any good reason to keep us locked up behind giant iron bars.

"I'll be sure to do that when I get back." I sat down at the table with him and flipped the book around so I could look at it. "Boyle's law? We aren't covering that until next semester."

He shrugged. "It looked interesting."

"I didn't think anything in a textbook could be interesting. Especially not a chemistry textbook."

"Yeah, I must be desperate."

"Any chance you actually want to do some studying? I wouldn't mind working on that problem set we have due on Friday."

"Sounds good."

I ran back to my room and got my book. Jack and I worked together for almost an hour. Luckily for me, he already seemed to know most of what we were studying. I asked him why he hadn't signed up for one of the AP classes, and he said he didn't want to have to work that hard.

Typical.

We did our chemistry and talked about our ethics homework as well. As always, it was a huge relief to hang out with the only person at school I didn't have to worry about disappointing. We were just finishing up when Esther and Hennie entered the room. Hennie tripped over the doorjamb and gave a little shriek, barely regaining her balance in time to keep herself from falling into our table. Esther caught her arm, and they both gave me apologetic smiles as they stopped in front of us.

"You ready to run?" Esther asked. She leaned forward and rested her hands on one knee and stretched her calf. "I'm going to do a whole mile today. Seriously."

I sighed. "Any chance I can skip?"

I'd burned up my hour of free time studying with Jack, and in that time the gray clouds that had covered the sky when I came over from the Main Hall had opened up, and buckets of rain were now dropping from the sky. Besides, Allie ran with the cross-country team, and I wasn't sure I could look her in the face after what I'd heard.

Hennie's eyes got wide. "Are you kidding? You'd be in so much trouble. Mr. Yerkinly said you can't skip unless you're in the nurse's office puking. And even then he wants you to run when you're finished."

"I should go," Jack said.

"No, no," Esther said. "We shouldn't have interrupted." She gave me a huge fake wink. "Dancia, if you're not feeling well, you shouldn't run."

"No, you're right," I said. I closed my book and stood. "I can't skip practice."

"I should get back to the room anyway," Jack replied. "Yashir wanted to sketch my tattoo for some project."

"Yashir?" Hennie repeated, failing to sound casual.

"Maybe we'll stop by later," I suggested. I couldn't believe it hadn't occurred to me before to try to get Hennie and Yashir together through Jack. I guess because Jack and Yashir were barely ever in the same room, except after lights-out.

Jack nodded. "Sure. Stop by." He sauntered off, books under his arm.

"He seems nicer today than usual," Esther observed.

"He is nice," I said. "Well, maybe not exactly *nice*, but he's a good person."

Hennie studied the empty doorway he had just walked through. "There's something sad about him," she observed. "I bet he's relieved to have a friend like you, Dancia."

"How do you know that?" I asked in surprise.

"Hennie can always tell that sort of thing about people," Esther said. "She's practically a mind reader."

Hennie flushed. "I just get a feeling sometimes when I talk to someone. Like they're speaking with a second voice. I can hear the things they want to say but can't. But it doesn't always happen. And I'm not always right. My mom says I'm just good at reading people's faces. She says my dad's the same way, and that's what makes him a good negotiator."

This revelation shouldn't have surprised me. I had already sensed that Hennie understood me far better than I would have liked. But suddenly it raised a strange and frightening new suspicion.

"Esther, you're into acting, right?" I asked. "There isn't anything weird about that, is there? Nothing unusual, no strange coincidences after you act out a scene?"

Esther looked at me as if I were losing my mind. "Weird about acting?" she asked. "I don't think so. I mean, sometimes when I impersonate someone, I actually feel like I'm getting inside of them. Like, the other day I did Mr. Yerkinly, and I swear, my pants got looser." She giggled. "I guess that's weird good, though. Not weird bad."

I had to close my eyes because a wave of dizziness passed over me. For the first time I wondered if maybe I'd been thinking about Delcroix all wrong. I'd been assuming everyone else at the school was different from me because I was the one without a talent. But I had a talent, didn't I? I hid it, suppressed it, and tried to ignore it, hoping it would go away. But it was still there, inside of me. I had a talent to make things happen. Strange, unbelievable things. It wasn't a talent for math or science; it was a different sort of talent.

And it suddenly occurred to me: what if everyone else at Delcroix had a talent like that too?

CHAPTER 13

WHEN I got to practice, I avoided looking at Allie, but she made a point of coming over and asking if we could run together. Hennie and Esther usually ended up jogging and walking for half the workout, so I rarely stayed with them, but Allie and I had never run together. I said okay—what else could I do? Luckily, we were doing a speed workout, and running sprints had us both panting so hard we could barely talk. We were a good match, though, and if I didn't hear her laughter at Catherine's horrible words ringing in my ears, I would have enjoyed it.

Or I should say, I would have enjoyed it if I hadn't been gnawing on my new fear, like Mrs. Burker's dog on one of Grandma's soup bones. Eventually I convinced myself I must have been wrong. After all, if other people at Delcroix had talents like mine, surely someone would have figured it out by now. It wasn't like they could cover up something like that. Not these days. It would be on the Internet before you knew it. The kids would brag about it, and the parents would try to make money off it somehow. That's just how things worked.

But even after I dismissed the idea as silly, the unease and fear lingered, like a cold stone in the pit of my stomach, and I kept looking around me at all the other students, wondering what their secret powers might be.

After practice I hit the showers and then collected my books and went to the library, skipping dinner altogether. The Delcroix library was pretty much like my middle school library, except three times as big, and instead of a grumpy part-time volunteer, there was a very helpful librarian.

In the center of the room there were two rows of long tables, and around them, individual desk cubicles. If you wanted to do serious studying, you tried to get a cube. The long tables were good for working in groups, or screwing around when you were supposed to be studying.

I couldn't deal with the possibility that I'd have to see Catherine or any of the other girls from pottery at dinner, so I took a cube and pulled out my algebra.

Study hours had begun, and the library had filled in around me, by the time I closed my math book and pulled out my English. A shadow fell over my cube as I started turning the pages of a story that I didn't even have to read until next week. I looked up, expecting to see Catherine scowling at me, or even Jack.

It was Cam.

I straightened in my chair. "Hey, how are you?" I said casually. Catherine might think I was as stupid as a fifth grader, but for once I was going to act like I was in high school.

"How are *you*?" he asked. A little wrinkle formed across his forehead. "Trevor and I looked for you at dinner. Is everything okay?"

I squirmed with pleasure at the thought of him looking for me. "Yeah, I just wasn't hungry tonight."

He grabbed a chair from the long table nearby and sat down next to me. "Not hungry? I can't believe that. How are you going to keep up your strength for practice tomorrow if you don't eat?"

I shrugged. "I'll be okay. I had a lot of studying to do."

Cam shook his head, sending his hair into his eyes. He leaned forward. "Are you done now?"

My heart fluttered when he got close enough for his shirt to brush against my arm, but I shook off the surge of excitement. I'd been excited before by Cam seeming to want to get close to me. I should have known by now not to take it too seriously. "Just about. Why?"

He stood up and indicated with his head toward the back door of the library. "You want to find something to eat?"

I narrowed my gaze. "It's study hours, Cam. Besides, the kitchen is closed."

Cam held out his hand. "Come with me."

We made our way out of the library, my hand tucked inside Cam's. I ran through a hundred different reasons why he might be holding my hand, none of which involved his everlasting love and devotion. He could have felt sorry for me. I could have looked so pathetic, as I sat there in the library all by myself, that he felt compelled to intervene. He could have somehow found out what Catherine had said. This seemed far-fetched, but then again, he was holding my hand, so clearly miracles were possible. He could have been trying to make some other girl jealous. This seemed similarly far-fetched, because I had a feeling Cam could get any girl he wanted. But still, it was possible.

He could also be the sweetest guy in the world, and he thought I needed something to eat and was just holding my hand to be nice.

Unfortunately, this very simple explanation was likely the truth.

He led me through a corridor on the first floor and around the back of the cafeteria. We stopped at a big steel door with a window on the top that looked into what I assumed was the kitchen. Then, to my utter dismay, he let go of me and punched a code into the keypad.

I stepped back, hesitant, as he pulled the door open. "Won't they catch us?" I asked.

"It's okay, I have special permission," Cam said, "because I work for Mr. Judan."

I nodded. "Right. Of course." Cam wouldn't have done anything that was against the rules. He was practically a teacher. What was I thinking?

He gave me an encouraging smile. "That's good, that you're worried about it. They are really serious here about the rules. But you don't have to worry about it when you're with me."

Cam hit a switch just inside the door, and the room filled with light. There was a rectangular table, a stainless-steel freezer, and two standing refrigerators. A row of sinks stood at the far end of the room, next to a huge stove with eight burners.

Cam opened the fridge and grabbed a carton of eggs. Then he reached under the counter and pulled out a large bowl.

"You like eggs?" he asked.

As if I would have said no. "Are you sure this is okay?"

He waved off my concern. "No problem. As long as I clean up after myself, they're cool with it." He cracked three eggs into the bowl and pulled a gallon of milk from the fridge and added a splash. He pulled out a fork from a drawer behind him, and mixed the whole thing.

"You do this sort of thing often?"

"Not during the school year. But I lived here over part of the summer, and they didn't have a chef then. I got to know the kitchen pretty well."

"Can I help?" I asked.

"Sure. There's bread in the pantry to the left. Can you grab a few pieces and throw them into the toaster?"

I nodded. When the bread was toasting and the eggs were in a pan, I shook my head. "I can't believe you're cooking for me. I didn't know guys cooked."

He scrambled the eggs perfectly, leaving not a trace of the brown stuff on the bottom, which Grandma always served. "My dad wasn't around much in the evenings. I had to learn to cook or I would have starved."

"He left you by yourself?" I said. "When you were in middle school?"

Cam buttered the toast and then handed me the pan. He flashed a smile. "Sorry, no plates back here. They keep those in the other room. Besides, it's less to clean. Do you mind?"

I shook my head and set the pan down on the counter in front of me. The smell of the warm toast and eggs was so good, my mouth watered. I dug in, forgetting I was supposed to be pretending I wasn't hungry.

"Anyway, to answer your question," Cam continued, "he didn't have a choice. My folks split when I was little; my mom moved to Florida, got remarried, and had other kids. We never had any other family in Seattle, and my dad never made enough money to send me to any after-school programs. We lived in an apartment building, so there were always people around if I had an emergency. It was okay.

But I got tired of eating cereal and peanut-butter-and-jelly sandwiches for dinner."

Somehow I'd forgotten that Cam was on scholarship at Delcroix, like me. "I had the opposite experience," I said. "Grandma was always home. It drove me crazy. I used to dream about having the house to myself, just for an afternoon. Just so I could prove that I could handle it."

"Everyone wants what they don't have, right?" Cam said.

"I guess."

I slowed down my eating, realizing I had to prolong this moment as much as I could, because Cam and I were actually hanging out together, just the two of us, and who knew if this time would ever come around again.

"Coach Yerkinly says you're doing great on the cross-country team."

"The first meet pretty much sucked," I admitted. "I had no idea that hill at the end would be so hard. I had nothing left for the finish. I practically had to walk it."

"My freshman year on the soccer team was a disaster. I don't think I scored a single goal," he said. "But I got better. It just took some time. Have you run with Anna? I bet she'd take you out sometime and give you pointers. If you wanted a little extra coaching, I mean."

Anna was the captain of the girls' team. She had long brown hair and huge eyes surrounded by thick lashes. Her hairline came to a little point in the front, so her face was shaped like a heart. I knew Cam and Anna were friends, but I tried not to think about it. She was gorgeous, super fast, and ate lunch every day with Cam. In short, she was everything I aspired to be.

"That would be great." I bit my lip. I was dying to ask him why he'd asked the coach about me, but I didn't. I couldn't get the words out of my mouth. I guess I didn't want him to say that Mr. Judan had asked him, for some recruiting thing, so he'd had to find out. I wanted to believe that he liked me.

We stayed in the kitchen for about an hour, just talking. Cam decided my eggs looked so good, he had to have some too, so he made himself a meal as well. Then we stood by the counter, drinking glasses of milk and talking about running, our friends at Delcroix, and how we liked our classes. I almost told him what had happened that afternoon with Catherine, but I didn't. I just said that I didn't love my roommate, and he nodded. He said he hadn't gotten along with his freshman roommate either.

I wasn't sure, but I had the feeling when he said it, he knew what a jerk Catherine was, and he was telling me that he sympathized with me and what I was going through.

He didn't hold my hand again, but he did touch me on the shoulder as we walked back to the Res in the dark, and I had a moment of panic as the thought occurred to me that maybe, just maybe, he would actually try to kiss me.

When we got to the door we stopped and faced each other. My breath caught in my chest, and my vision blurred a little, even as I fought to remain calm.

He's not going to kiss you, I told myself sternly. Stop getting so excited. It's not going to happen.

After an interminable, painful pause, Cam said quietly, "I'm sure it's hard sometimes, but I'm looking out for you. You know that, right?"

I didn't, or hadn't. I couldn't speak or even believe what I'd heard. But I nodded, dumbstruck.

"Good. I want you to tell me if there's ever anything that's bothering you. I'm here for you, Dancia. I don't want you to forget that."

I stood there for another moment, barely breathing, before I realized that I was supposed to acknowledge what he'd said. "Um . . . that's really . . . nice of you. Thanks. And thanks again for the eggs."

Cursing myself for not being able to think of anything even slightly more interesting to say, I waved good-bye and ran up the stairs to my room. Catherine, who was leaning over her calculus book and frowning at a page of symbols and numbers, sniffed when I walked in.

"You missed dinner," she said. "And I found some of your clothes on my side of the closet. I put them over there to get them out of my way." She pointed to a clump of fabric she had wadded into a ball in the corner of the room, under my desk. "Don't let it happen again."

At that moment I knew exactly how Jack felt about having a roommate.

But it didn't matter. I was glowing. Catherine and all her mean, nasty words didn't matter.

Cam and I had a connection, a real connection. He was looking out for me. I didn't know why, and I hardly dared to hope for what it might mean. But there it was. Amazing.

Who cared about old Catherine Arkane anyway?

CHAPTER 14

"FROM THE time of Plato and Aristotle, human beings have been fascinated by the study of ethics. In this class we have been discussing the questions people have struggled with for centuries. For example, when is an action right or wrong? How can we tell good from bad? Can we judge the rightness of our actions based on the number of people who are affected?"

Mr. Fritz, the puffy-haired troll doll of a teacher, leaped up from his desk and began to pace in front of the room, his hands an animated blur.

"My goodness, he does love his subject, doesn't he?" Jack murmured. His seat was next to mine at the back of the class.

I ignored him and turned more squarely toward Mr. Fritz.

"He is rather cute, though," Jack mused, rubbing his chin thoughtfully.

"Quiet!" I hissed. Now that I knew Cam was watching out for me, I wanted more than ever to do the right thing and stay out of trouble. But it was hard to turn around and tell that to Jack when he and I had been sitting in the back for weeks, making fun of Mr. Fritz and the other kids in the class.

"All right, all right." Jack held up one hand in mock surrender. He sat up straighter at his desk and poised his pen above his paper as if about to take notes.

Mr. Fritz continued to ramble about Kant and John Stuart Mill, who we were supposed to be studying. My attention began to wander, and I slid into a pleasant daydream about Cam making me eggs and holding my hand. It was pitiful, but I'd been in a semi-comatose state ever since he'd said those incredible things to me the night before. It only heightened my euphoria that my dinner with Cam was my delicious little secret. It wasn't that I didn't want to tell Esther or Hennie, but it felt as if something magic had happened between us, and sharing it might make it go away.

I'm not sure how much time passed, but when I slid a glance at Jack a little while later, he was actually listening to Mr. Fritz, nodding occasionally and taking notes. I looked down at my own blank paper with a surge of embarrassment. If Jack could pay attention, surely I could do the same.

"Now, we're going to play a little game. Class, everyone on your feet and push your desks against the wall. We're going to need some room."

With a few groans, everyone stood up. Twenty sets of chairs and desks scraped against the linoleum floor. They had combined my team with another one for the class, and we'd spent enough time together over the past month and a half that I knew everyone pretty well, even the ones who weren't on my team. Catherine wasn't in the class, thank goodness, but Cara was. I'd been ignoring her since the pottery-class incident, though she hadn't seemed to notice.

I moved my stuff like everyone else, hoping no one could tell I hadn't paid a bit of attention to the lecture and had no idea what was going on.

When we were done, Mr. Fritz dragged a large wooden platform from behind his desk and dropped it in the center of the room with a loud thud. It was about a foot high and three feet wide. "My dear astronauts, you have been visiting a foreign planet, finding a life-saving cure for an epidemic that is sweeping Earth. Your mission is complete. But there has been an accident, and the body of your ship has been damaged. This is the emergency travel pod, and it only has enough gas for one trip back to Earth. Anyone left behind will die. To take off, you must get everyone on the travel pod, for three full seconds."

He beamed at us and ran his fingers through his white hair, fluffing it to a soft cloud. "Oh yes, and you've got fifteen minutes before the oxygen runs out in your space suits. Better get going."

Kurt, a skinny kid with limp hair, pushed a thick pair of glasses up his nose with a pencil. "Mr. Fritz, with all due respect, there are twenty of us. There's no way we can all fit on that piece of wood at the same time."

Several people, including Gideon and Hector, nodded in agreement.

"It's your spaceship," Mr. Fritz said. "And your crew. You must find a way."

More groans. I was instantly reminded of our trip up the wall. What was it about this school and its obsession with group activities? I tried to force myself to hang back from the crowd, but I couldn't help throwing out a suggestion here and there as we tried various positions on the platform. We put some of the group on shoulders, stood on each other's feet, and held on to each other. I'm tall, so everyone thought I should be on the outside of the circle. This left the short, cute girls, like Allie, to stand on my feet, which I did not appreciate. But everyone was groaning and laughing, so I put aside my irritation. We got close to success, but someone slipped off the platform before we could count to three.

"Is this some kind of lesson in futility?" Alessandro snickered. "Is it ethical to say we quit?"

"This is stupid," a dark-haired girl named Morah said, not quite under her breath.

The momentum in the group slowly fizzled out, and before long we were reduced to aimless attempts at the same things we'd done before. Ten minutes passed. I didn't like the idea of giving up, but I was out of ideas and starting to get frustrated.

Jack, who had been reclining against one of the desks, raised his voice above the mumbled conversations. "We're going to have to sacrifice some of the group."

"Are you kidding me?" Yashir looked horrified. "Sacrifice some of our group? As in, leave some of us behind?"

"Right. It's the only way to get the cure back to Earth." Jack spoke casually, his hands thrust deep into his pockets.

The room exploded into conversation. "What?"

"I'm not staying behind."

"We can't divide the group."

"You're sick, man. Truly sick."

A smile played around Jack's mouth as he watched them. For some reason, this ticked me off. We had been having a good time. Sure, we weren't succeeding, but it had been fun trying. Everyone was in a good mood. Why did Jack have to go and ruin it?

"Let's leave him behind."

"Yeah, if you think we should leave someone behind, how about you?"

Jack sat down in one of the discarded chairs. He laced his fingers together behind his head and leaned back. "I was simply pointing out an option. You can leave me behind if you want."

"You have three minutes left," Mr. Fritz called from behind his desk. I could have sworn he was trying not to smile. That's when I realized he must have known the platform was too small. This whole thing was nothing more than a setup to get us to realize we were going to have to do something drastic if we wanted our "mission" to succeed.

Everyone panicked. Yashir and Marika and a couple from the other team started barking orders at everyone, telling them to jump up on the platform and hold hands like we had tried once before. I stood there and watched, getting angrier by the second. A few people called me to jump on, but I waved them off. My hands clenched into fists.

They assembled on the platform, strangely serious now. Little clumps of people fell off every few seconds and then scrambled to get back in the group.

"One minute!" Mr. Fritz held up his watch.

Jack stood and ambled over to me. "What a bunch of morons," he whispered. "You would think they're really trying to save the earth. What do you say we knock them over?"

"No way, Jack," I said. "I want them to do it."

Cam would want them to do it, I thought. Cam wouldn't like the way Jack was trying to mess things up. Cam would want them to do it, and he'd want me to help.

"Come on, it would be fun," Jack said. "Just a little nudge and they'd all fall down, like a human domino chain. You have to admit you'd like to see that."

"No, I wouldn't, Jack."

Okay, I wouldn't have minded seeing Allie fall down, or Marika, or Cara. I stared at them, happily clutching each other as they stood on the platform, and for a minute I was back in that hallway, hearing them talking about me ... laughing about me. ...

"Tell you what, I'll knock them over, and you can watch." Jack took a purposeful step toward the group. He winked at me over his shoulder and started to raise his hands.

I shook my head to try to erase those horrible feelings. I wasn't going to allow Jack to do something mean.

Looking back, I don't know what I thought I could do— hold the whole group up on the platform? Drop something heavy on Jack? Whatever it was, the desire to do *something* was overpowering. The need rose inside me, almost a physical thing, and then I felt the familiar tingle and heard the whoosh in my ears.

It was the power. When I realized what was happening, I shut my eyes tightly and clenched my fists. No, I begged. Not now. What if I hurt one of my classmates? What if the whole school found out about me?

I would be in so much trouble if the power took over. I wouldn't be able to stay. I didn't know what they'd do with me, but they wouldn't let me stay and pretend that I was a normal kid.

I forced myself to take a deep breath and think before I did anything stupid. I knew whatever popped into my mind was going to happen, but what if the thing I imagined was that nothing happened?

Sounded crazy, but worth a try.

I opened my eyes and stared at the platform, refusing to look away even when Jack whispered my name. I focused on

the wood, trying desperately to keep my mind fixed on everything as it existed right at that moment. Surely if I filled my
thoughts that way, nothing bad could happen.

The desire to look away was so strong, my hands began
to shake. I set my jaw, determined not to let go. I told myself
it was just like being in a staring match with Grandma. The
vision of the wood wavered but did not disappear.

Jack leaned forward, his face close to mine. I ignored
him as deliberately as I shut out the power. A second later,
the tingle faded. The tight grip I had on my body relaxed so
suddenly I stumbled backward and almost fell to the ground.
At the same time, I heard the group chant, "One, two, three!"

They exploded into cheers. They must have done it,
I realized dimly. The taste of bile unexpectedly filled my
throat.

I raised my hand. "I need to go to the bathroom, Mr.
Fritz," I managed to croak out as my stomach lurched.

Without waiting for a response, I ran down the hall to
the girls' room and made it into a stall just in time to bring
up the foul remnants of the frosted flakes I had eaten for
breakfast.

Again and again I retched until I had emptied my stomach and the stuff I was bringing up burned my mouth and
my nose. When I could see clearly, I leaned back against the
bathroom stall and raised a shaking hand to wipe the sweat
off my forehead. I was hot and cold at the same time, and so
tired, I thought I might pass out.

Was this the price to be paid for refusing to use my
power? My stomach roiled and cramped, and my limbs
were like limp white noodles on the floor of the bathroom.
A tear dribbled out of the corner of my eye and slid down

my cheek. I was too tired to wipe it away.

Someone knocked on the stall door. "Dancia, are you all right?"

Great. That's all I needed. A rescue party.

"Yeah, thanks." I tried not to groan the words.

"Are you sure? Mr. Fritz wanted me to check on you."

I looked at the bottom of the stall door, where I could see a pair of cute brown boots with stacked heels. It was Allie.

"No, I'm feeling better. I must have had eaten something funny at breakfast." I tried to make my voice sound strong, but I don't think it worked.

"Okay." She sounded doubtful. "If you're sure."

"I'm sure."

I watched the boots pause for a moment, then clomp out of the bathroom. When I heard the door swing closed, I pushed my hair back from my face and tried to stand. My legs felt decidedly unsteady, so I stopped halfway and sat on the toilet.

I didn't seem to be feeling any better, but I also didn't seem to be getting worse. I decided to try to walk back to class. My head spun as I got to my feet and started to pull open the door.

My legs started to shake. Just before they buckled, I leaned against the wall. My body slid against the cold metal like a jellyfish. When I reached the ground, I dropped my head onto my knees.

Damn, damn, damn. A sob of rage and frustration built deep in my throat. I refused to let it escape. Not here, not when Mr. Fritz could burst in at any second.

My brief triumph at having squelched my power faded as the colors swirled behind my closed eyes. I might have discovered the ability to stop the power, but clearly this was no alternative. I couldn't spend my life throwing up, passing out, or huddling in a bathroom, unable to walk. Apparently, my power was a part of me, and trying to stop it was like trying to cut off my arm.

But what was the alternative? Going back to the way things had been in middle school? Hiding and making myself invisible? Blowing off Cam, Jack, even Hennie and Esther, and making myself into a pariah? That no longer sounded like much of an option. For one, it hadn't really worked in the past. I'd been doing it since I was ten, after all, and I hadn't been able to stop myself from wreaking havoc. If anything, I was using my power more as I got older, not less.

For another . . . well . . . I thought about the feeling of Cam's hand covering mine, and the way my heart skipped when he'd said, "I'm looking out for you, Dancia." I couldn't hide from Cam—or if I could, I sure didn't want to try. And Esther and Hennie were the best friends I'd ever had. When they were around, I forgot how different I was, and felt like someone who could fit in. Someone who belonged.

In an odd way, Delcroix was giving me my first chance to be a regular kid, and I didn't want to give it up. No, I refused to give it up. The fact was, in the short time since Mr. Judan and Cam had first come to my house, I had changed. Hiding and trying to be invisible weren't enough for me.

Not anymore.

CHAPTER 15

BY THE time I came out of the bathroom, the bell had rung and people were headed down to lunch. I waited for the crowds to thin out before I tried to move down the hall. I limped along slowly, still dizzy and weak enough that I had to stop every few feet and take a deep breath. I wasn't sure how I was going to make it back to my locker, which was all the way in the basement. Then I heard a familiar voice behind me.

"You look horrible."

"Jack, I don't want to talk to you right now." I tried to ignore him, but he reached over and grabbed my backpack and slung it over one shoulder, and then took my elbow and supported my weight as we hobbled along.

"Because I made some comment in ethics class?" He was incredulous. "I don't get it. What's wrong with you?"

"Look," I snapped. "It's been a long day. I'd really rather not end it by fighting with you."

He frowned, a look of concern crossing his face. "Sorry. Anything you want to talk about?"

I had to grit my teeth at the sting of tears in the back of my eyes. Though I'd gone years without anyone to confide in, now it seemed I couldn't get enough of it. And I was so used to confiding in Jack, it was odd to remember that there was something huge and horrible in my life I could never tell him about.

"No."

"Well, don't pull any punches on my account."

The corners of my mouth turned up just a hair. "Sorry, I'm not trying to be rude. It's just . . ." We reached the top of the staircase and peered over. There was a long line of kids waiting to get into the cafeteria. It was loud, people were laughing and yelling at each other, and I spotted Hennie and Esther a few feet away.

I imagined facing Hennie and having her hear that "second voice" she had told us about the day before. A groan escaped from my throat. "I don't think I can handle this right now."

Jack nodded. "You look pretty green. I'm not sure the cafeteria is the best place for you. Why don't we skip lunch? I want to show you something anyway."

"Show me what?"

"It's hard to describe. You'll have to follow me."

Hennie and Esther were, of course, engaged in conversation, so they hadn't seen us yet. If they saw me, I would have no excuse not to sit with them. I looked back at Jack.

Too much had happened that morning, and the last thing I wanted was Hennie figuring it out with her weird way of sensing things. And I definitely couldn't take Esther's bubbly confidence right now.

"Come on," Jack said, a mischievous look in his gray eyes. "I won't get us in trouble, I promise."

I shook my head. "You have a way of saying 'I promise' that is entirely unconvincing."

He laughed. "You're a smart cookie, Dancia Lewis. Now come with me."

He turned and headed up the stairs while I followed a pace or two behind. We were on the second floor, where most of the classrooms were, but Jack led me up to the third. I hadn't been to the third floor since orientation. Trevor had briefly walked us around up there, mainly to show us a couple of dance studios and practice rooms for the orchestra students. I think they said the honors seminars, like Cam's class, met up there as well.

"We're going to walk around the building, and as we do, I want you to picture what it looks like from the outside."

"What do you mean?"

"The shape of the building," he said patiently. "From the outside."

I pictured it, three stories of red brick, tall windows on every side. "Okay, I've got the picture. Now what do you have in mind?"

"Come on." We walked past a bunch of studios and smaller classrooms with chairs arranged in a circle. The halls were deserted, and the squeak of my sneakers reverberated in the silent air.

The school was shaped like a square doughnut, with the auditorium filling the middle. Jack opened a few doors, pointing out that each outside room had windows overlooking the grounds, and all the inside rooms looked over the auditorium roof. They all appeared to be about the same size and shape. We turned two corners and walked down two sides of the square, then got to the back of the building.

"Now these are the practice rooms." Jack pushed open the door to a gleaming white studio with scattered chairs and a dry-erase board along one wall, with a staff for writing music. "They're rectangles, right? And unlike the other outside rooms, they don't have windows."

I shifted uneasily on my feet. "That's because they have special acoustic panels on the walls." I took a few hesitant steps through the door. "They told us that. I heard that guy Tony who plays guitar raving about how great it was to practice in here."

"Sure," he agreed. "But humor me for a minute and let's try something." He carefully walked from the door to the back wall, placing the heel of each foot next to the toe of the other as he did. "Thirty paces," he said, a note of triumph in his voice. "I walked the rooms on the other side of the building this morning. They were forty-five paces. Now granted, I was doing it fast because we were supposed to be meeting with our advisers, but still. That's a considerable difference, yet the building is a square, and the cutout in the middle is a square, so the front and back rooms should match, right?"

I backed out of the doorway and into the hall. "You must have measured wrong. I think we ought to be getting back downstairs. I'm feeling much better now. We can still get lunch if we hurry."

He paced back to me. I couldn't help but count along. Thirty paces.

"They didn't tell us we couldn't come in here." He flipped a lock of black hair out of his eyes as he stared down at his shoes. "And lunch just started. Trevor won't even know we aren't there yet. It usually takes him ten minutes to come find me. We need to go to the front rooms now. You can watch me pace it."

I bit my lip. Something about this felt wrong, like we were doing something we shouldn't. But we were just looking at classrooms, right? Not stealing or anything. And it would be weird, wouldn't it? If the rooms were different sizes?

"Okay, but let's be quick."

We ran back along the silent hallways, our feet slapping against the smooth wood floors. The front of the school flooded with a blaze of yellow light as gray clouds slipped past the sun. The classrooms had tall windows divided by dozens of individual glass panes, all sparkling with reflections from the sun's glare.

Jack paced carefully from the door to the windows. Forty-five steps. He paced back again. Forty-five steps.

"Someone's going to be pissed at the architect," I joked weakly. "His square isn't exactly square."

Jack spun around, facing the window. "There's something weird about this place. I knew it from the first time Judan showed up at my house. I bet there's a secret corridor on the back of the school. They didn't have any excuse to put it on the first or second floors, so they've got it up here. I wonder what it's for? How do you get to it?"

His words caught me by surprise. I hadn't thought about Mr. Judan, or recruiting, since the first day of cross-country. So he had visited Jack? He hadn't visited Esther, but had he visited Jack?

"You mean he came to recruit you?" I asked. "He came to your house?"

"Of course. Along with Pretty Boy."

"Pretty Boy?" I asked, though I suspected I knew exactly who he meant.

"You know, *Cameron*," he said with an exaggerated air of importance.

Cam had gone with Mr. Judan to visit Jack, but not Esther or Catherine? Jack didn't even live in Danville, which

133

blew apart my theory that he only visited people in town.

What did that mean?

"I'm going downstairs," I said. "This is crazy. The hall must be a different width on the other side, or the inner classrooms must be different."

"Wanna bet?"

I shook my head. "No. I don't."

"What about the gates, and the keys, and codes, and all the places for cameras. What about all that, Dancia?"

"That was a joke, Jack."

"Maybe for you."

"You're crazy. They're into security, that's all. If I knew you were taking any of this seriously I would have stopped it a long time ago." I turned and headed back toward the stairs. A moment later I heard Jack's footsteps behind me.

"Maybe you can ignore it all, but I can't. Not anymore." He got in front of me. "Cam nearly killed me with that electric handshake of his, and Judan would make a snake nervous. And now this? The whole building's probably rigged so they can spy on us. Who knows what's in the secret corridor up here."

I stared up at him, wide-eyed. Cam had given him a shock?

He picked up on it immediately. "He shocked you too, didn't he?" Jack crowed. "I knew it. They handpicked us, Dancia. You and me. But why? What for?"

"They're recruiters," I snapped. "That's what they do. They find kids with special talents and try to get them to come to Delcroix. No mystery."

"Okay, so tell me why I'm here. You and I both know I don't fit in. Delcroix students are dancers and debaters, and they've got parents who sent them to special camps and enrichment programs starting when they were two. They're lab rats and Button-downs, like your friend Catherine. I barely made it through eighth grade." He started to tick off items on his fingers. "I don't do sports, dance, draw, or sing. I can't add numbers in my head. My penmanship is lousy. So you tell me, what am I doing here? What's so special about me?"

I grabbed the banister for support as I started down the stairs. "How should I know why you're here? Maybe they need poor kids." I hated myself for sounding like Catherine, but the words just came out. I couldn't help it.

Jack stopped me halfway down. "If they had just wanted a poor kid, they could have picked one a whole lot nicer and smarter than me. I'm a delinquent. Ask anyone. I'm barely getting by. And what about you? How many times since school started have you told me that you don't know why you're here? You're mediocre at everything. So what's really going on?"

With that, my patience ran out. Even though I didn't think I belonged at Delcroix, the last thing I needed was Jack acting like horrible Catherine and all her friends. "Look," I said, poking my finger into his chest. "If you think the school is so weird, why are you still here? Why not go back to whatever place takes delinquents like you? I'm sure everyone would breathe a sigh of relief if you decided to take the bus all the way back to Portland."

He stared at me. He was so close, I could see his nostrils flare. I thought I had gone too far, and he would get pissed and stomp away from me, but he didn't. He just kept staring.

Noise from the stairwell below filtered up to us.

Jack pushed his hair back from his eyes. "I've got nowhere else to go," he said flatly. "They told me I could start over here. They said things would be different, and I believed

135

them. I have no idea why, but for some reason, when Pretty Boy told me that, I believed him. I must have been crazy."

I pictured my conversation with Cam at Bev's Café, and the night before in the kitchen. He had convinced me too. Sometimes I thought he could say anything and I'd believe him. My thoughts flew to that moment at my door when he'd told me he was looking out for me.

I'd believed that too.

"He's right," I said, more confidently than I felt. "Delcroix *is* different. Look, I know it seems odd, and I feel weird here too sometimes, but we've got to give it a try. It could be our only chance."

"I did try," he said. "But it isn't working. The whole roommate thing doesn't work for me, and those gates. Well, you know how I feel about the gates. And I think they follow me when I leave school on the weekend." He leaned back against the wall, looking defeated. "Sometimes I want to just take off and not come back."

I stared at him, astonished. I had no idea things had gotten so bad for Jack. Then I started to get a little panicky at the thought of him leaving. Even if he was trouble, there were times when he was the only person I could talk to. What would I do without him?

"I promised Grandma I'd stay until Christmas. You have to give it that long before you really know, one way or the other. You can't leave now. It's not even Thanksgiving yet. You have to stay at least that long," I babbled.

"Maybe." He didn't sound convinced.

"There are things about the school I don't like either, but we've got to keep trying. We'll never know if we don't try." I wasn't sure if I was talking to him or to myself, but it was suddenly vitally important that he agree.

Jack stared at the wall in front of him. After an interminable pause, he let out a loud sigh and turned to me. "All right. As long as you're with me. No more blowing me off when you're upset, okay?"

With a huge feeling of relief, I knocked against him. "Okay, you got me. But you can't kill off any more of our classmates. Agreed?"

He grinned. "Sometimes you've got to save the Earth, Dancia."

We laughed and walked down the steps together, our shoulders almost touching. I turned at the bottom of the landing and barreled right into a broad, masculine chest. When my eyes hit shaggy brown hair and a pair of concerned eyes, I sucked in my breath in horror.

"Cam?"

"Dancia? What were you doing upstairs?" He put his hands on my shoulders and examined my face.

I tried to school my thoughts into a semblance of coherence. Had they told us not to go upstairs? Had I forgotten a rule? Were we in huge trouble? "I . . . we . . ." Cam's hands burned my shoulders, making it impossible to think straight.

"Dancia thought she left a book in her adviser's classroom," Jack interjected.

Cam dropped his hands and looked over at Jack. "Landry, what are you doing here?" He turned back to me. "Don't you usually have lunch with Esther and Hennie?"

I nodded vigorously. It suddenly occurred to me that Jack and I had been walking way too close together when I'd bumped into Cam. Oh Lord, what if he thought we were . . . The last thing in the world I wanted was for Cam to think Jack and I were . . .

"Yeah," I agreed, somewhat breathless with panic. "I realized my book was missing just as the bell rang for lunch. Jack happened to be around when I was heading upstairs."

"Right. I happened to be around." Jack leaned against the wall by the stairwell and exhaled a bored sigh. "Anything good for lunch today?"

A wave of gratitude passed over me.

Cam crossed his arms over his chest as he looked back and forth between us. "I didn't notice," he said sternly. "Why don't you go take a look?"

Jack shrugged. "Fine by me." He ambled away with his deceptively easy stride.

As soon as he was out of earshot, Cam dropped his arms, his eyes dark with concern. "I don't mean to sound like a parent here, but are you sure you know what you're doing? With Landry, I mean?"

Oh no! He did think we were together. "I just bumped into him, Cam," I stuttered. "He's on my team. We're friends. But I'm not *doing* anything with him."

Cam ran his fingers through his hair. "I didn't mean to imply anything. He just strikes me as a tough kid. I don't want to see you get into trouble."

"Don't worry," I said, emphasizing the words. "It wasn't a big deal." I gave him the most sincere, believable, and earnest look of which I was capable. "We went into a couple of classrooms looking for my book. I got confused as to where I had left it."

It seemed to work, because his shoulders relaxed and his voice loosened. "It's easy to get confused up there. The school is a big square, you know, so the rooms all look the same."

"Except the practice rooms, right?"

He laughed. "Well, they don't have windows. I guess that's different."

I hesitated, dying to ask about what Jack and I had discovered. But asking Cam would have meant admitting that Jack and I had lied about the lost book. And even though I had the sense that Cam would have been happy to blame the lie on Jack, that didn't seem right. I had already let Jack lie for me.

Besides, it seemed like such a stupid question. I'm sure there was a simple reason why the rooms were different sizes.

"Anyway," he continued, "I'm just a little worried about you hanging out with Jack." He put his hand on my shoulder and looked intently at me. "It isn't that he's done anything wrong, but you know how you get a sense from people? Well, I get the sense that Jack is bad news. I hate to see you going down the wrong road because of someone like him."

I nodded, my entire body wilting at his touch. "You don't have to worry about me, Cam. I won't do anything stupid."

He laughed, and we headed down the stairs together.

I had the feeling he was waiting for me to say something more, like promising I would stay away from Jack, but I just couldn't do it.

I thought about what Hennie had said, that Jack seemed sad. I felt that in him too, today more than ever.

How was I supposed to stay away from him when my heart said that, like me, Jack really needed a friend?

Cam went down to lunch, and I headed for the pay phone by the office so I could call Grandma. With all my confusion, I needed to hear her voice, even if it was only for a second. As

I picked up the receiver, I heard voices coming from inside the office.

"So I missed my adviser appointment this morning," Jack said. "What's the big deal?"

It was horrible of me, but when I heard Jack's voice I leaned closer to the window.

"The big deal is that we expect our students to follow the schedules we give them. This isn't a voluntary program, Mr. Landry, and you don't get to choose which appointments you attend." It was Mr. Judan.

"Fine, whatever."

I cringed. Jack was using his cold, I-don't-give-a-crap voice, the one I'd heard him use on Trevor and teachers who tried to get him to behave in class. I couldn't imagine Mr. Judan would appreciate that.

Mr. Judan dropped his voice, and I had to strain to hear. "Mr. Landry, I took you from whatever bridge you were living under and offered to pay your way to Delcroix. In return, you promised that you'd live by our rules. You do intend to keep up your end of the bargain, don't you?"

There was silence from Jack. I wondered what he was doing, where he was looking. I sent a silent plea to him to look down, to nod, not to pick a fight.

"If I were you," Mr Judan continued, "I would drop that tough-guy attitude and start thinking about how you're going to make it here at Delcroix. Something needs to change, and it better be you. I would start by apologizing to me and to Mrs. Harbiner."

That voice gave me a shiver, deep in my bones. There was a muffled sound that I hoped was Jack apologizing, and then nothing. I hurriedly dropped my change into the phone and pushed the numbers. The phone was just starting to ring when Jack came out of the office.

He stopped outside the door and let his backpack fall to the ground at his feet. I assumed he didn't see me, because he let out a deep breath, and his shoulders seemed to collapse. He looked so dejected, I took a step toward him without realizing what I was doing. The phone cord snapped me back. Jack's head shot up, and he stared at me just as Grandma answered the phone.

"Hello? Is that you, Dancia?"

"Yes, Grandma." I gave Jack an apologetic look. With an abrupt shake, he threw back his hair and assumed his old uncaring stance. He picked up his backpack, gave me a nonchalant salute, and then strolled toward the front door.

CHAPTER 16

THE NEXT two weeks were exhausting, as I tried to juggle my desire to please Cam and my worry about Jack's increasingly despondent looks. Cam started showing up regularly at my cube at the library, and we'd go for little walks around campus before cross-country practice or after dinner. It took us forever to walk anywhere, because everyone in the school knew him and stopped to say hello. They treated him like a combination of hero, kid next door, and best friend. He was too unassuming to be intimidating, yet too perfect to be normal. I figured it was only a matter of time before he became the leader of the free world.

He introduced me to everyone and made a point of calling me his friend. I figured this was both good and bad. Good, because the entire school now knew that Cam liked me. Bad, because it sounded like he was serious about the "friend" thing. I never did tell Esther and Hennie about the eggs and the "I'm looking out for you" comment. I knew they'd make a big deal about it, and since nothing really happened with him, I didn't want to sound stupid because I'd gotten my hopes up about the whole thing.

Then there was Jack, in all my classes, with increasingly dark circles under his eyes and a wary look about him. He was acting out more, getting in trouble, and not turning in homework. I was worried about him, but I didn't know what I could do to help without losing my chance to be with Cam. I started avoiding him around the cafeteria, and trying to talk to him less during class, but then he'd drop me a note and make me laugh, or I'd need his help with a chemistry problem, and we'd end up studying together and talking all evening long.

The weekends became a kind of salvation. At least then I didn't have to worry about who I was talking to or who might be watching.

Halloween fell on a Sunday, so half the class was wearing costumes that Friday when we rode the Silver Bullet to the parking lot. Allie and Marika wore fairy costumes, which naturally required tiny bodysuits and see-through gauze skirts. Yashir and some of his friends dressed like guys in a band I didn't know. They wore leather pants and ripped shirts, but they didn't look very different from usual, so I thought the costumes were pretty lame. Esther and Hennie and I were matching witches. It was fun doing makeup together and fixing our hair, but my heart wasn't really in it. Cam and Trevor and some of their friends got football uniforms, and Anna and her friends dressed like cheerleaders.

Jack didn't dress up at all.

Neither did Catherine.

Grandma was waiting when we pulled into the parking lot. It was raining, so I sprinted from the bus to her car, gave Jack and Hennie and Esther a wave, and then dove inside.

I gave her a peck on her baby powder–scented cheek, and settled with relief into the seat. The bus ride had been painful, and it felt good to be going home. Jack had ridden up in the front, barely acknowledging me when I got on with

Esther and Hennie. I could practically feel the frustration and anger spilling out of him, even though he tried to hide it behind an uncaring facade.

I forced myself to think about Cam instead of Jack, but that didn't make things easier. Cam had given me a hug before I'd left that afternoon, but then disappeared with Anna and his other friends. Most of the upperclassmen stayed at school over the weekends, and they were having a Halloween party. I had horrible visions of him hooking up with Anna at the party, as would be fitting for the quarterback and the head cheerleader.

"How was your week?" Grandma asked as she inched the old Volvo into traffic.

Driving with Grandma was always a bit of an adventure. Half the time she drove so slowly, people honked at her and shook their fists as they passed. The other half of the time she raced through stop signs and intersections like she didn't even notice they were there.

Which, of course, she didn't.

I struggled to find something unexciting yet true to say to Grandma. "It was okay. We're starting a new unit in algebra. Something about vectors. And Esther and Hennie and I are doing a project together for World Civ. We're doing a report on the Mayan ruins."

"Did you see that boy that you like—what was his name? Christopher?"

Weird as it sounds, I think Grandma really wanted me to find a boyfriend. It was the one thing she always asked me about when we were going home for the weekend. Of course, she forgot what I had said the minute I said it, and asked me the exact same questions the next week, but it was nice. At least she cared enough to ask.

"Cam. His name is Cam. And yeah, we hang out some-times. But we're just friends."

Grandma and I did not talk about boys—not that there had ever been anything to discuss. Even though I wouldn't have minded talking about my problems with Cam and Jack, I figured that was one line I should never cross. If I told her how much I liked Cam, but how I liked Jack too, and didn't know how to choose between them, I'd have to tell her every-thing. It was the classic slippery slope.

She waited a minute for me to say something more, but I managed to keep my mouth shut. "I see. And what about the others? What about that boy that you waved good-bye to in the parking lot? What's his name?"

Trust Grandma to push all the right buttons.

"His name is Jack. We're in most of the same classes. We're friends too, but I'm not sure he's someone I should hang out with. He gets into trouble a lot."

Grandma turned back to the road. "Trust your instincts, dear. You'll be meeting a lot of new people at Delcroix, and they will be very different from the people you've met before. Don't let yourself be taken in by appearances."

"What does that mean?"

Grandma flicked on her blinker, even though our street was six blocks away. "You must be tired after such a long day. I made meatballs and spaghetti for dinner." She ignored my question, which either meant she had already forgotten what she had said, or didn't feel like answering. She did that some-times. It was infuriating.

"Fine."

The incessant clicking of the blinker filled the silent car. Finally, Grandma turned down our street.

"Grandma, how do you know what your instincts are? I

mean, what if you have two different instincts? What do you do then?"

I suppose I threw out the question because I didn't think she'd respond, and because I was annoyed that she'd brought up trusting your instincts and then dropped it. But as soon as I spoke the words, I realized I really needed to know the answer.

Cam obviously thought Jack was trouble, and part of me believed him. But another part of me wondered if Jack was just saying what I felt. When I was at school and we were busy studying and doing after-school activities and home-work, and behaving like normal teenagers, Jack's sugges-tions about Delcroix seemed ridiculous. But in the car on the way home, I couldn't shake the feeling that maybe Jack was right. Something seemed odd about Delcroix, with all its gates, and keys, and locks, and all the students with their crazy talents. Not to mention creepy Mr. Judan, who hap-pened to recruit both me and Jack, and the uneven sizes of the rooms on the third floor.

And if Jack was right about all that, could Cam be wrong about Jack?

It was all so confusing, it made my head hurt.

Grandma slowly pulled the car into our driveway, ran over the hose and an empty pop bottle I'd left outside the week before, and stopped inches from the garage door. She turned off the car and we sat there, neither of us moving. We sat there so long, I had almost forgotten my own question when Grandma finally spoke up.

"I suppose there's no good answer to that, Danny. I wish there was. But if you take the wrong path, something deep inside you will feel twisted. There are times when that will be the only way to know the right from the wrong."

Her words sat heavy in my chest. "You mean I won't know until after I've done something if it was the wrong thing?"

"I didn't say that."

I threw up my hands. Sometimes it felt like Grandma spoke in a code only she understood. "How do you know, anyway?" I asked. "Did you ever do anything wrong?"

"Of course," she replied, a little tear running down her cheek. "We've all done things we regret. But I left the meatballs on the stove. We should get inside before they burn."

CHAPTER 17

GRANDMA LEFT me alone all day Saturday, except for a quick trip to Goodwill to look for a new blanket to cover the holes in our couch, and a visit to the hospital to pick up some new prescriptions.

On Sunday afternoon we went to Walmart to get a couple of bags of Halloween candy. Grandma asked if I needed any new clothes for school, so I wandered around aimlessly, watching other girls shriek and coo as they held up outfits for their friends. They made it look so easy. I lingered over the shirts, rubbing the smooth cotton of a snug-fitting pink hoodie between my fingers, and wondering whether Cam liked bright colors. He probably didn't like brown, gray, and more brown, which pretty much described my wardrobe.

Grandma raised her eyebrows when she saw what I was doing. "Pink?" she said with surprise. "Now that's a change. It would certainly be nice to see you in a pretty color."

She rifled through the rack and pulled out a large. "Looks like it's made to fit a third grader," she sniffed. "Well, try it on. Can't hurt." We walked over to the fitting room, and Grandma grabbed a few more shirts on the way. Another pink one, then a blue V-neck, and a purple-striped button-down. She was all business, grabbing shirts from the racks and handing them to me, shushing me with an impatient hand when I started to argue. I finally got to the dressing room with about six shirts, not a single one of them brown.

I tried on the pink hoodie first. It clung to me in a way that none of my other clothes did, but I can't say it looked bad. All that running had been good for me, I guess. I walked out to where Grandma was waiting. She had a strict rule about approving any clothes she bought for me.

"Good Lord, child, are you sure they let you wear things like that at Delcroix?"

I wasn't committed to the pink anyway. "Probably not. I'll go take it off."

"No, no, no, I was only asking." She pursed her lips. "Turn around, let me see the whole thing."

I spun around slowly, hoping no one I knew was within a ten-mile radius to see me modeling clothes for my grandmother, like a six-year-old.

"It's fine. We'll get it."

"But, Grandma, I don't think . . ."

She shook her head. "I'm tired of seeing you in brown."

I was too, I had to admit. There was something beguiling about the color, the way it made my cheeks look creamy instead of washed out. Besides, I was starting to wonder if dressing the way I did was a little silly. Was I really less likely to get into trouble just because I didn't wear bright colors?

The purple-striped number was a disaster, but the blue one made my eyes stand out. We took it, along with a new pair of jeans that weren't quite as baggy as the ones I usually wore. Grandma seemed happy. I knew she had always hated my wardrobe.

We picked up a few more things—some notebooks for me, a trashy tabloid and some denture cleaner for Grandma—and headed to the checkout. The woman in front of us had just begun to unload a full cart, so I looked around for a magazine to flip through while we waited.

I turned toward the rack behind me, then stepped back.

Jack was lounging behind the racks of candy and gum, hair falling into his eyes, hands deep in the pockets of his cut-off khaki shorts, pushing a cart almost filled with ramen noodles.

"Are you sure you want that pink one?" he said. "It looks a little flimsy. Might get ripped if they make us go back over the wall."

Seeing Jack at Walmart was so unexpected, I found myself gaping at him. In my mind, Delcroix was hundreds of miles away—completely separate from my life in Danville. But here was Jack, wearing the same ripped shorts he'd been wearing a couple of days ago at school.

"Eh? Who's this, Danny?" Grandma thrust her glasses higher on her nose and pushed me aside to take a closer look at Jack. "What's your name? You look familiar."

"Jack Landry." He straightened and extended his hand. "But I'm not sure how we would have met. I only came to town a couple of months ago, just before school started."

"Where from?" Grandma demanded, shuffling over to shake his hand.

"Portland. I moved here to go to school at Delcroix." Jack gestured in my direction. "Dancia and I are on the same team."

"You never lived in Danville?" Grandma asked.

"For a little while," he admitted. "I moved when I was five."

Grandma considered him for another moment, then her face lit up. "Aha!" she said triumphantly. "You must be Tom

Landry's son. I knew you looked familiar."

The smile froze on Jack's face. "You knew my father?"

Grandma snorted. "He lived a few blocks away from us. Never saw you or your mother much." She poked me in the side. "You remember Tom, don't you? Teacher at the high school. He moved to California a year or two ago. How is he doing?"

"We don't see him," Jack said, his lips curling as if the words left a sour taste in his mouth.

The woman in front of us was arguing with the clerk, insisting that the nightgown she had picked out was on the clearance rack and should be fifty percent off.

"Did you move up here with your mother?" Grandma asked.

I threw her a black look. Didn't she know it was rude to bring up such personal issues in the Walmart checkout line? I'd tried to talk to Jack a few times about his parents, but he didn't like to talk about them much. He had something against his mother, and he always changed the subject.

"I'm staying with a friend," he responded.

I'd heard all about his friend, who was really just the older brother of someone Jack knew in Portland. The guy didn't have a job, and as far as Jack could tell, he spent most of his time doing drugs and crashing out in his house, which his parents had left him when they died.

It didn't sound like a good arrangement.

The woman in front of us got fed up. She threw the nightgown at the clerk and stomped out. Grandma moved forward and started fumbling through her enormous purse as the cashier rang up our items.

"Are you ready for Halloween?" I asked Jack. "I don't see any candy in your cart."

"Nah. I'm just going to turn off the lights. I wouldn't want any little kids coming to my place."

"You should come over for dinner," Grandma said as she took our bag from the clerk and tucked the receipt into her purse. She examined the contents of Jack's shopping cart, her cloudy blue eyes soft. "You look like you could use a good meal."

Jack looked from Grandma to me and raised his brows a notch. I could feel the question in his expression.

I couldn't muster a decent protest. Even though I wasn't sure what to do about him, the thought of Jack sitting alone on Halloween, eating ramen noodles in the dark, didn't seem right.

"Sure," I said. "Come on over."

Despite my fears that Grandma would do something horribly embarrassing, or Jack would say something weird about Delcroix, dinner proved surprisingly pleasant. Jack turned out to be one of those kids who could charm adults until they were putty in his hands. He entertained Grandma with stories about his childhood, like how he hadn't learned to ride a bike until he was ten because he was so clumsy, and how he failed kindergarten because he wouldn't share his toys. She seemed to find this hilarious. He asked her scores of questions, even got her to talk about how she had moved to Danville with my grandpa fifty years ago, when they were young and just starting out.

Grandpa had been a logger. He died before I was born.

Jack praised Grandma's homemade chicken soup so much you would have thought she was Emeril, and he really seemed to like it, because he ate three bowls. I guess he was awfully hungry. Then Grandma broke out the sherbet, and we all had big bowls.

"Mrs. Lewis, that was the best meal I've had in years," Jack said, sounding sincere.

Grandma smiled, but something underneath her smile was serious. "You come here for dinner anytime you want, Jack. You shouldn't be eating those noodle things. You need protein, a growing boy like you."

"I appreciate that. I'm not much of a cook. But you know they feed us pretty well at school."

Grandma leaned over and patted his hand. "It isn't home cooking. You come here when you want some real food."

I'd never seen her fawn over someone like that before. It was embarrassing.

I stood and started gathering our bowls. Grandma pushed back from the table and took them from my hands. "Why don't you and Jack go sit outside and watch for the trick-or-treaters. I'll clean this up."

Now this *was* disturbing. Was Grandma, with that innocent gleam in her drippy eyes, trying to set Jack and me up? That was definitely not on the menu for the evening. Jack and I were friends. Nothing more.

"I don't think—"

"I'll need to be getting home soon," Jack said.

"Go." Grandma pushed me toward the front door. "You've got a few minutes to talk before Jack heads home."

We walked out onto the porch, where an old wooden bench was slowly decaying by the front door. I sat down on one end, Jack sat next to me. Closer, I thought, than was absolutely necessary. It had been warm and sunny all day, one of our rare Halloweens where we got a last taste of summer weather, and I ran my hands over my bare arms nervously. Somehow things felt different at my house than they did at school. At school we'd sat next to each other hundreds of times while we studied or ate dinner. And it felt like there was always someone watching. Here, it felt too private. Like anything could happen.

"My grandma's a little pushy," I said apologetically.

"She's great. I wish I had someone like her."

"Were you serious when you said you didn't know if you had grandparents?" I looked straight ahead, focusing on the fact that we were outside, in plain view of the entire street. There were little kids in costumes starting down the block with their parents. It wasn't like Jack was going to jump me right then and there. And it wasn't as if a little part of me was curious to know what that would be like, if he did.

"Yeah. I guess they're dead. My mom and I don't talk much. She never really mentioned them."

"Is your mom in Portland?" I asked.

"I don't know where she is. I haven't seen her since the spring."

I pulled back, puzzled. "Really? Then who did you live with?"

He shot me a sideways look. "I don't mean to shock you, Dancia, but some kids don't have a cozy little house to live in. I bummed around. There are lots of places to go."

I turned to him, unable to hide my shock. "You mean you were homeless?"

He shrugged. "I usually had a friend I could crash with. I'd rather be on my own anyway."

"Isn't that illegal? For you to be on your own, I mean. Don't they put you in a foster home or something?"

"They didn't know about me," Jack said. "They thought I lived with my mom."

I leaned back on the bench. Jack usually had a friend to crash with? What did he do the rest of the time? I thought about what I'd overhead Mr. Judan say—something about Jack living under a bridge. Was that what homeless kids did in Portland? Lived under bridges?

Jack scowled when he saw the expression on my face. "Look, it's not so bizarre. Lots of kids do it. I still went to school. I made money doing odd jobs for people. I did okay."

"But how . . . I mean, was it scary?"

He turned that half smile on me, the one that he'd used so effectively on Grandma. "I'm telling you, it wasn't a big deal. Anyway, I don't want to talk about me. How's cross-country going? You haven't mentioned it for a while."

"It's fine." I tried to shake the image of Jack sleeping on the street, or under a bridge. I wondered what kind of "odd jobs" he had done to make enough money to support himself. "We run a lot more than I did on my own. It feels good. It helps me clear my head."

"I'm not much of an athlete, myself. I doubt I could run to the end of the block." Jack leaned back and laid one arm on the bench behind him. He practically touched my shoulders as he did, and goose bumps broke out on my arms. I scooted a few inches to the side.

"I'm sure you've got a lot to do," I said. "You probably want to get back home."

"I guess so." Jack stared at the street. "I do like it here." There was something wistful in his voice, and a little part of me felt like reaching out and grabbing his hand.

He must have read my mind, because he turned his head

and looked down at me. There was no smile now, just a serious expression no boy had ever aimed at me before.

I swallowed hard, hoping he would look away, but he didn't.

He was going to kiss me. I knew it. It would be my first kiss.

But this wasn't right. I fought the invisible fingers that seemed to hold me in place. I didn't like Jack. Not like *that.* I liked Cam. Cam was the guy for me. Not Jack.

My mind was screaming for me to move, to get out of the way before he leaned closer and touched his lips to mine, but my body seemed determined to stay put.

A million questions ran through my mind. Would his lips be warm? Soft? Wet or dry? Did you tilt your head like they do in the movies? What if I wasn't good at this—

In the midst of my panic, the shrill sound of the phone ringing cut through the silence.

A second later, Grandma called, "Dancia! Phone for you."

I jumped up and practically flung myself across the porch. "I'll be right back." I bolted into the house; my heart was thumping as if I had just gone running.

Grandma handed me the phone. "It's Esther."

I took a few deep breaths before holding the phone to my ear.

"Hello?"

Esther's voice bubbled through the receiver. "Dancia! Do you have your costume on? Are you ready for Halloween? I couldn't believe it when I got home—my little sister is going to be a pumpkin and she looks so cute, I can't stop pinching her cheeks. It's driving her crazy!"

"Esther, can I call you back? I have a friend over."

Jack stood in the doorway. The sun was setting behind

him, so I could only see a dark outline, not his face. He said something to Grandma as Esther continued to chatter in my ear. Then he grabbed his Walmart bag from the couch. He waved at me from the doorway and turned to leave.

"Esther, hang on a sec." I covered the receiver with one hand, walked as far toward the door as the cord would stretch, and yelled, "I'll see you Monday."

He looked back and smiled, then threw his bag over his shoulder and kept walking. I watched him go, with only an ounce of regret and a pound of relief.

CHAPTER 18

I FOUND myself glancing repeatedly in the side mirror as we drove to Delcroix early Monday morning. It was dark and cold outside, and I had that creepy feeling you sometimes get when you think someone's watching you. For a few blocks I thought a beige sedan was on our tail, but then it turned off the road, and I cursed Jack for getting me so wound up.

We arrived at the parking lot fifteen minutes early, but there were already half a dozen cars sitting in the lot. I went to stand under the foggy glow of one of the streetlights. Paul and Alessandro were the first from my team to arrive, and they joined me. We exchanged halfhearted waves, but didn't say much. I liked them both, but we hadn't spent much time together since orientation. Marika got there next. I still couldn't look at her the same way, after the incident in pottery class. In her defense, I don't think she liked Catherine that much either. She mostly hung out with Allie and Emma.

I was wearing the pink hoodie and an old pair of jeans that hung low on my hips. When we'd talked the night before, Esther had persuaded me to leave my hair loose. This seemed like a huge mistake to me, but she was always complaining about how it drove her crazy that I kept my hair locked up in a ponytail. She believed in being natural and loving yourself the way you were, and she kept telling me how beautiful my hair was.

I thought this was complete nonsense, but it seemed to work for Esther. Besides, she was persistent, and I couldn't help but wonder what Cam would think. So there I was, in a tight pink shirt with crazy blond curls spiraling out from my head in every direction. The real Dancia, exposed for all the world to see.

The crowd got bigger and the sky turned pale gray as the Silver Bullet appeared up the road, making its way toward the parking lot. I looked around for Esther or Hennie but didn't see them. More people had gone home this weekend than usual, I guess for Halloween, and there were lots of cars and parents milling around. The iron gates creaked open to let the bus through. I suppressed a shudder as Jack's words rang in my ears again.

Keep the bad guys out, or us in?

He's paranoid, Dancia, I reminded myself. Of course he's going to think weird things about the gates.

The Silver Bullet rolled to a stop, and Cam jumped out. They always sent an older student to make sure that all the freshmen who had left school over the weekend were accounted for Monday morning. I don't know what they'd do if you weren't there. Sound the alarm and call your parents, I guess. No one had missed the bus yet.

My heart did that little flip-flop Cam always inspired. Everyone seemed to want to get on the Silver Bullet at once, so I hung back and let them find their places. I joined the line at the very end. Esther and Hennie waved from the front. There was no sign of Jack.

When I passed Cam, he looked up from a list in his hand. His mouth was tight. He ran his fingers through his hair and said, "Hey, Dancia, you haven't seen Landry, have you?"

It was the first time I'd seen Cam in days. I was freezing in my pink hoodie and my hair was down, and all he could do was ask about Jack?

"No. Haven't seen him."

From the way he shook his head, I could tell he was irritated. He pressed his lips together, then shook his head and gave me one of those blindingly adorable smiles. "I guess some people have to learn the hard way," he said. "Trevor wasn't kidding about them being pissed if you miss the bus."

"Yeah, well, I guess I'd better get on, then."

Cam nodded, still scanning the parking lot for signs of Jack. Esther and Hennie were sitting together at the back of the bus, but all the seats near them were full. I took the first empty spot near the front, and slid over to the window.

Cam jumped on and nodded to the driver, who tugged on the handle to close the doors. As we pulled away, I caught sight of a black car crossing the parking lot. I was pretty sure it was someone dropping off Jack.

I felt horrible, watching that car speed across the lot. I thought about how mad Mr. Judan had been when Jack missed his adviser appointment a couple of weeks ago, and how he'd told Jack something needed to change.

This was not the kind of change Mr. Judan had in mind.

The bus made a slow circle around the lot and stopped at the gate. Cam and the driver were looking at each other and laughing about something as the driver opened his window and held out his security card. I didn't mean to do it, I swear, but I had this feeling, this crazy feeling that Jack needed me. It was just like when I saw him being chased by

Sunglasses Guy. I had no choice. I had to do something.

I stared at the card and pictured it flying into the air even as the whoosh filled my head. The strange thing was, instead of the card doing just what I pictured, it only moved a couple of inches. And then, as I watched, it shimmered and seemed to lengthen. I'd never seen anything like it—the whole thing turned pale and foggy, almost as if the card were made of smoke. The edges that had once fit squarely in the guard's hand curled like a snake several inches above and below.

And then it disappeared.

I sucked in my breath. I hadn't pictured *that*. I'd never made anything disappear before.

Cam flinched, then spun around in the aisle as if looking for something. His eyes found mine, and then moved past, searching. He whipped his head around and looked behind him, out the door, toward the parking lot.

The driver swore under his breath. "What the—that damn thing jumped right out of my hand!" He peered out the window, then pulled his head in and swore again.

Cam stepped back. "I'll get it," he said grimly.

"No, it's my fault. It must have fallen under the bus." The driver stomped off the bus, leaving the doors open. The black car flew past my window toward the exit, kicking up gravel as it went. The minute it disappeared, Jack's black hair appeared in the doorway.

"I hope I'm not late," he said to Cam.

Cam stared at him, his eyes slowly narrowing from surprise to suspicion. "When did you get here?"

"Just now."

Jack and Cam faced off. They were almost the same height, but Cam had a good twenty pounds of muscle on Jack.

"That means you're late. Next time there won't be a convenient *accident* to slow us down." Cam spoke quietly, his eyes locked on Jack. The rest of the bus was filled with laughter and the rumble of thirty conversations all happening at the same time. I doubted if the others even noticed we had stopped.

Jack shrugged and tried to push past. Cam put one hand on either seat and blocked the aisle. "I mean it, Landry."

"Sure, whatever." Jack turned his shoulder and barreled into Cam's arm. Cam lifted it, shaking his head as he watched Jack make his way down the aisle.

I sank deeper in my seat, hoping Jack wouldn't look at me. He scowled and slipped into a seat next to Allie.

Still swearing under his breath, the driver took the steps two at a time and slammed into his seat. "Had to crawl under the damn bus," he muttered. "And now I'm off schedule."

As the gates retracted, Cam sat down next to me. I should have been thrilled, but I couldn't stop picturing that card rising like a curl of smoke out of the guard's hand. The whoosh and the power had left me. It had come and gone so quickly, I never really had time to get worked up about it. But what had happened? Had *I* done that to the card? Had Jack? What kind of power did he have, anyway?

Needless to say, however confused I had been earlier that morning, I was infinitely more so now.

Cam sighed and pushed his hair away from his eyes. His brows were drawn together in a look of concern, or maybe sadness. I couldn't tell. "Hey, Dancia," he said.

All the noise in my brain stopped as I lost myself in Cam's nearness. "Hey."

"You okay?" The concern deepened. Those incredible eyes connected with mine, and he turned his body so his shoulders blocked the rest of the bus from my sight. "You look freaked out. Not because of that, I hope." He jerked one thumb in Jack's direction but kept his gaze pinned on me.

It was amazing, but somehow as he spoke, my nerves started to dissolve. "No, I'm okay," I said. "Just out of it. It is Monday, after all."

The worried line between his eyes eased, and he gave me a slow smile. "Good. I wouldn't want you worrying about Landry."

Landry? I thought fuzzily, my brain turning to goop as Cam's smile radiated through my body. Who was that? "How was your Halloween?"

He leaned closer and knocked his shoulder against mine. "It was okay. But I missed you. You should have stayed for the party."

Was he trying to send me into heart failure? I looked out the window, hoping to catch my breath. The sun was just starting to break over the trees, and the gray-green lawns rushed past as the red brick of the school drew closer.

"Did you get in a workout this weekend?" I asked, once I'd regained enough composure to look at him again.

"Yeah, I went to the gym and lifted, and then played a few games of soccer with Trevor and the guys. We played pickup against Anna and her girls. They almost crushed us— but they really need a new forward. I can't wait for you to start playing soccer this spring. They'll be psyched to have you."

I stifled the surge of jealousy and forced myself to sound casual. "I guess I'll have to see how things go. I'm getting nervous about report cards. Grandma won't let me play unless I get at least B's. I got an English paper back last week, and I swear, there was more red ink than black."

"You and me both. I turned in a physics lab Monday, and I don't think I got a single thing right. Not even my name."

I giggled. "I don't believe it."

"I'm not kidding." He shook his head solemnly. "If Trevor didn't let me copy his homework, I'd never make it to soccer practice."

We chatted for a few more minutes before the bus rolled to a stop. Cam slid out of his seat. "You should find me at lunch today," he said. "I keep inviting you and you keep ignoring me. I'm starting to think you don't like me."

A huge grin spread across my face. "Right. As if."

"Well then . . . ?"

"Okay, okay, I will!"

"Good."

The driver opened the door and said good-bye to Cam as he jumped down the steps. I let the crowd fill the aisle and flow out of the bus.

I stared at the green back of the seat. Cam really seemed to want to eat lunch with me. He wasn't just saying it to be nice. He truly wanted it.

This could not be explained by the fact that he was my recruiter. I'd been downplaying things for weeks, but the fact was, he kept seeking me out. He was definitely paying more attention to me than to anyone else, and now he was going to introduce me to his friends? Could Esther be right? Could he really be interested in me? Was it possible that something could go so absolutely, wondrously, perfectly right in my life?

A sense of terror mixed with my initial jolt of delight. What in the world would I have to say to a bunch of juniors? What if I said something stupid, and he changed his mind and decided I was a complete loser and he never wanted to speak to me again?

Esther grabbed my arm and practically hauled me out of my seat. "What did he say to you? Does he like the new hairdo? You have five minutes to spill the beans, or else."

"Esther's being a bit dramatic," Hennie breathed, a wicked gleam in her eyes. "We'll let you tell us over lunch, if you prefer."

We walked off the bus. I made sure Cam was otherwise occupied before I casually said, "Actually, I told Cam I would meet him at lunch."

Esther squealed. Loudly.

I looked around, desperately hoping he wasn't within earshot. "Shhh!" I said. "He's going to think we're a bunch of idiots."

"I don't care!" she said gleefully. "That's it—you *are* getting together! I knew it!"

I glared at her. "Keep your voice down."

She didn't look the least bit repentant, but she did give me a whispered, "I'm sorry. Now, tell us what's going on!"

I pulled her and Hennie up the stairs and into the Main Hall. Once we were in a relatively secluded spot next to the office, I sighed with relief. The words spilled out of me like a flood. "I wish I knew. The truth is, I have no idea what's going on."

Hennie pursed her lips. "You don't know what's going on, or you can't tell us?"

"I don't know," I insisted. "Honestly, I can't believe he could possibly like me. I mean, I'm just a freshman, right? And hardly a beauty queen."

"Don't be ridiculous. You're tall and you have a great

body. And boys love that blond-hair-blue-eyes thing," Hennie sighed. "I'm just a short little Indian girl. Yashir will never notice me."

Esther waved a dismissive hand. "That's ridiculous. You're gorgeous, and boys go for the sweet, quiet types. It's a well-known fact."

"He didn't even look at me on the bus this morning," she said.

"That's because you never talk to him," Esther said logically. "Which we are planning to change as soon as possible." She pinned me with her gaze. "Now, Dancia, let's get real. You're smart, you're funny, you're tough, you don't let anyone push you around—basically, you're hot, regardless of whether you're a freshman, and Cam knows it. He's been watching you since school started, you guys hang out after school, and now he asks you to have lunch with him . . ." She let her voice trail off suggestively. "I think it's obvious what's going on here."

"Well, it's not obvious to me," I wailed. "Half the time he looks at me like I'm his little sister, and the other half I feel like we're just friends. And you know he and Anna spend tons of time together. What if they're going out? I don't even know!"

That was the truth. I'd never really figured out exactly what his relationship with Anna was. I knew they were close friends, but I didn't know exactly what that meant.

A bell rang and we all jumped.

"I still need to go to my locker," Hennie said, looking nervously at the crowds now streaming around us. "We'll have to catch up later. Tell you what, Dancia. We'll do some research and get back to you, okay?"

I nodded gratefully. Was high school always so complicated?

Our lockers were in the basement, spread in narrow rows around white support pillars. We weren't allowed to go to our dorm rooms during the school day, so we had lockers to stow our books in between classes. Hennie and Esther and I had each been assigned a locker in a different area, so after quick hugs, we split up and promised to find each other whenever we had a break that afternoon.

With visions of melting brown eyes dancing in front of me, I blinked furiously and tried to focus on my combination lock. Classes. I did have classes today. But what were they?

"Where'd Prince Charming go?"

I froze at the sound of Jack's voice floating over my shoulder. I jerked the lock open, grabbed a book from my locker, and threw it into my backpack. The Cam-induced haze abruptly melted away.

What was I supposed to say to him? I was jolted back to my utter confusion of the morning and the terrifying realization that once again, I'd used my powers to protect him. Or at least I'd tried. The scary thing was, Jack inspired some kind of protective instinct in me that I couldn't ignore. He seemed determined to get into trouble, and I seemed just as determined to get him out.

And then there was the whole scene on my porch the night before, and the maybe-almost kiss. Or had I imagined that too?

I turned around and tried to play it cool and friendly. "Hey, Jack, what's up? Sleep through the alarm this morning?"

"Forgot to set it." He had one hand looped around a

couple of books, the other deep in his pocket, and he slouched in a lazy, relaxed way against the bank of lockers behind me. He was wearing dark, baggy jeans and a snug black T-shirt.

"That's ridiculous. How could you forget to set your alarm? Are you trying to get yourself in trouble?"

He flipped his hair out of his eyes and walked over to my side. "What are they going to do? Suspend me? I don't think so. Then Prince Charming and the rest of them couldn't keep an eye on me."

I nibbled my lip uneasily. "What do you mean?"

"You know, holding us here—behind those gates—makes it awfully easy to keep an eye on us." He held up his ID card. "They track our every move, Dancia. Trust me, they're not going to suspend me."

I sighed. "We've been through this before, Jack. They have to do that. It's for security."

"They keep saying that, but what's the big danger they're securing us from? Most kids seem to survive just fine without being kept behind a locked iron gate."

"How should I know? Terrorism? Weird people who try to abduct kids?"

"If you say so."

"What do you think Cam has to do with it?" I wasn't sure what "it" might be, but when I talked to Jack, it seemed hard to pretend that things at Delcroix were business as usual.

"Have you seen the way he looks at me? You'd think he's expecting me to plant a bomb or something."

I threw my backpack over my shoulders. Truth was, Cam did look at him funny. Cam didn't trust him. If Jack knew half the things Cam had said to me, he'd be even more convinced that they were plotting against him.

"Whatever. You're crazy. Can we just go to class, please?"

He shrugged. "Sure. By the way, thanks for dinner. It was nice to have actual food for once. And someone other than my stoner roommate to eat it with."

I made a face, relieved that he'd accepted the change of subject. "Grandma thinks you're sweet."

"Oh no, really? She called me sweet?" He laughed. "After the cold shoulder I get from her granddaughter, I was beginning to think I'd lost my touch."

I winced. Jack *had* been trying to kiss me last night. I had hoped we could forget all about that awkward sitting-on-the-porch moment. Even if a tiny part of me had been curious as to what that might have been like, the bigger part of me wanted Cam. I couldn't let Jack think something might develop between us. I steeled myself to be frank.

"Jack, it's not that I don't . . . I mean, it's not that I don't like you, it's just . . . well, you know Cam and . . . well . . ."

He laughed as he shifted his books and put one arm around my shoulders. "What?" he said in a dramatic voice as he pulled me closer. "You mean Cinderella has already found her prince? And it isn't me? I am crushed. Truly, deeply crushed."

"Jack!" I shrugged out of his grasp and tried to ignore the fact that he smelled good, like cinnamon and coffee, and that it felt rather nice to have his arm around me. I tried to focus instead on his reaction. What I said didn't seem to bother him. Maybe I had misinterpreted him after all.

"You don't really think I'm going to let that pretty boy stand in my way, do you?" He winked at me and kept smiling. "Darling, you and I were meant to be. That's all there is to it."

What was that supposed to mean? He sounded like he was kidding, but was he serious? Every word out of his mouth just confused me more.

"Jack—"

"Forget about it, Danny. Don't worry that curly little head of yours." He gave me another squeeze and raised his hand at Hector on the stairs.

"Wassup, Jack. Dancia." Hector nodded at us, raising his eyebrows a little as he passed. I hung my head. Damn! Now Hector was going to think Jack and I were going out.

We started up the stairs together, and my eyes landed on the cover of the book Jack was holding under his arm: *Essays in Ethics.*

"Oh no!" I whacked myself on the forehead. "I forgot my ethics book in my locker."

"No problem." He grinned and handed me his. "You know who's really got your back around here."

CHAPTER 19

THE CAFETERIA at Delcroix was similar to my middle school's. Long tables filled most of the space, and a lunch line with hot and cold food snaked along the back wall. Kids yelled at each other across the room, and irritated-looking teachers who were unlucky enough to be on lunch patrol leaned against the walls, trying to tune them out. Unlike my old cafeteria, though, Delcroix's had huge windows overlooking green rolling hills and a thick forest in the distance. Of course, no one paid any attention to the view. The wildlife inside was much more interesting.

I'd been eating in the cafeteria for almost two months now, and I'd long since tuned out the incredible view. But today everything was going to change.

Today I was eating lunch with Cam.

The minute I walked through the doors, I started to feel light-headed as I considered having to approach Cam and Trevor and Anna by myself. My knees actually trembled, and I looked around anxiously for a table to sit at before I collapsed.

"Dancia, there you are! You aren't getting away this time. Come on over here and I'll introduce you around."

It was Cam, looking gorgeous, as usual, as he made his

way through the crowd toward me. I watched him take hold of my elbow.

With the touch of his hand, my throat momentarily swelled shut, but I swallowed hard and gave myself a stiff internal shake. I decided not to risk speaking, and simply nodded.

We crossed the room toward a table where five other beautiful people were seated. Trevor was there. I had to admit he was handsome in an austere, frightening sort of way.

"You know Trevor and Anna, and this is David, Claire, and Molly." Anna jumped up and landed at my side the instant Cam and I reached the table.

From the look on her face, it became clear to me that Cam might think he was just friends with Anna, but Anna did not feel the same way.

"Dancia, how sweet of you to join us for lunch. Why don't you come sit over by me? We can talk about strategy for this week's meet." She practically dragged me away from Cam and plopped me down in a chair.

"Thanks," I managed to spit out.

"No problem." She turned a sunny smile back to Cam. "You probably can't stay long, anyway, can you? Didn't you say you had to check in with Mr. Judan before Ethics this afternoon?"

"I've got time to eat," Cam said. He shrugged apologetically at me. "I do have to leave a little early. But we've got time to hang out first."

Cam sat down next to me. I nudged my chair closer to his and farther from Anna's.

Anna narrowed her baby-doll eyes. "Super."

"Hey, you've got Mr. Fritz for Ethics, don't you?" Cam gestured around the table as he spoke. "We were all in his

172

class our freshman year. He's pretty cool, isn't he?"

"Yeah, he's okay. He sure does love Kant, though."

Trevor groaned from the other side of the table. "You aren't kidding. Too bad you can't understand anything he's talking about."

It was the most human thing Trevor had ever said, and I found myself actually smiling at him. "I spent twenty minutes just trying to read one sentence the other day," I agreed. "It's like the guy was speaking in another language half the time."

Anna sniffed. "I didn't think it was that complicated."

Trevor laughed. "Even for you, that's insane, Anna. No one understands Mr. Fritz's class. Especially not Kant."

"At least the activities are cool," Molly said. "Like that spaceship thing—did you do that?"

"You mean the one where we all had to get on a little platform with some medicine to save the planet Earth?" I tried not to think about how I had ended that day in the bathroom, vomiting. "Yeah, we did that one."

"I remember that," Cam said. "Anna and Claire nearly broke my toes when we tried it."

Anna gazed at Cam with an air of fond remembrance. "I loved that game."

Trevor rolled his eyes. "You loved anything that required standing on Cam, Anna."

Claire and Molly giggled. They spent a few minutes reminiscing about how they had tried to get all the girls up on piggyback, but everyone ended up falling down, and none of them managed to get back to Earth with the cure.

"How did your group end up, Dancia?" David asked.

I froze. I didn't want to tell them how I'd gotten sick, or draw unnecessary attention to Jack. "Someone in the class suggested we leave certain members of our group behind. Once we did that, everyone else fit on the platform."

"Who did that?" Cam asked.

"Jack," I said reluctantly.

"Landry did what?" Trevor asked.

Why did they insist on calling him Landry? Like he wasn't worthy of being called Jack? For some reason it bothered me.

"We tried a bunch of different things, but eventually realized we couldn't get everyone to fit. Jack said we should leave some people behind rather than giving up our mission and letting everyone on Earth die. I guess it made sense."

It did make sense, in a twisted sort of way. I hadn't wanted to see it at the time, but looking back I could. It was the ease with which Jack had made the suggestion—like it was no big deal to let members of our team die—that had been so disturbing. But it was a game, right? Just a game. I couldn't remember now why it had seemed so incredibly serious.

A worried crease appeared on Cam's brow. He and Trevor exchanged significant looks. The more I hung around them, the more it seemed that Jack was right. They did have something against him.

I shook my head. Now I knew I was paranoid. I was starting to think like Jack.

Cam pointed to the tray in front of him. "Do you want anything to eat?"

His plate of french fries and a huge hamburger did not look appealing. "No thanks. I had a big breakfast. I'll probably get hungry as soon as lunch is over."

Anna had a little bowl of salad on her tray, and she picked at the contents. "You should really eat something," she said sweetly. "I don't want you missing practice."

I tried not to laugh as I contemplated her ten-calorie salad. "Thanks, Anna. I appreciate the concern."

Cam picked up his burger and took a big bite. I looked around the room and saw Esther and Hennie a few tables away. Esther winked and gave me a thumbs-up, which I hoped no one at our table witnessed. On the other side of the room, sitting at a long table with a bunch of people from our team, was Jack. He was cozied up next to Allie, who gazed at him with the same adoring expression that I probably wore around Cam.

That was new. Jack and Allie were friends, of course, and had been since orientation, but I'd never seen them eat lunch together. And I'd never seen that particular look on Allie's face before. Like she was staring at Superman.

Jack didn't seem bothered by it. In fact, he had a genuine grin on his face, not even his usual ironic half smile.

Jack could talk to anyone he wanted, I told myself sternly.

Allie draped her arm over his. He leaned over and said something in her ear. I forced myself to look away, and as I did, I caught Anna watching me. Her eyes flicked back and forth between Jack and me, and a coldly assessing look crossed her face. Then her lip curled into an approximation of a smile. She picked up her fork and stabbed a piece of lettuce.

"Anything new with the student council?" I forced myself to say cheerfully to Cam, trying to erase the image of Allie touching Jack's arm. "Aren't you planning a big dance right before Christmas break?"

"Random Flashes of Genius is playing." He spoke between enormous bites of meat. "It's going to be amazing."

The desire to look back at Jack and Allie was almost

overwhelming. I bit my lip and resisted. "Where will it be held?"

Cam dunked a handful of french fries in ketchup. "Here in the cafeteria. But we decorate it. Anna's in charge of the decorating committee, actually."

Figured. I nodded as if I cared, and permitted myself a brief fantasy of slow dancing with Cam. Meanwhile, Trevor kept throwing suspicious glances in Jack's direction, and then whispering to David, the guy sitting next to him. I wanted to lean closer to hear what they were saying, but Anna seemed to be watching, so I gave her a sunny smile instead and relaxed against the back of my chair.

"Where do you race this week, Anna?" Cam asked.

"Saint Mark's. It's a tough course. Lots of standing water around the back end. Tons of freshmen didn't even finish last year." Anna smirked at me, though she covered it up quickly to smile at Cam.

"Maybe you and Dancia could run together sometime, Anna."

Anna picked up a cucumber and nibbled at the edges. "I usually run in the morning, on top of our regular practices. I wouldn't mind giving you a private lesson, Dancia, if you want to come with me sometime. Maybe next week."

I floundered, unable to think of a single excuse. "Wow, uh, thanks."

"No problem." She fluttered her lashes at Cam, even though she was supposedly talking to me.

Cam looked pleased. "That's nice of you, Anna."

Nice? Granted, I barely knew her, but I had the feeling "nice" wasn't a particularly fitting word.

Cam finished his meal and apologized for having to leave early. I waved him off and then told the rest of the group I had some homework I needed to talk to Esther and Hennie about. Not that they cared, but I figured I had to come up with something.

When I got to their table, Esther could barely contain herself. She was convinced Cam wouldn't have invited me to lunch if he didn't like me. She thought this was the beginning of something big. Hennie told me that she'd heard Cam and Anna used to go out, but they'd broken up this summer, and no one really knew why. Esther said that meant the perfect amount of time had elapsed for Cam to find someone new. He wasn't pining over Anna, because they were clearly still friends, and that was good, but he was definitely single, which was also a plus.

I just had to shake my head in wonder. The junior class president, most gorgeous guy in the school, and he wanted to spend time with me? I just couldn't believe it. Something was seriously amiss. I couldn't stop smiling and looking down at the pink shirt like it was some kind of magical talisman.

CHAPTER 20

IT WAS a few days later that I realized things really had changed between me and Cam. I was finishing up my longest run yet—six miles—and I was completely exhausted. Rain was falling in a light drizzle high above the trees, though little drops made their way through the canopy of evergreen branches to fall on the path below. Sweat soaked my T-shirt, rolled down my back, and dampened the waistband of my leggings. My legs were trembling, but I had that post-run euphoric feeling.

That was when I saw Cam walking toward me. He was wearing his soccer shoes and had on track pants and a T-shirt. He had an expression I'd never really seen on him before— fury. Sure, I'd seen him annoyed, even downright pissed like on the day Jack was late for school. But this was something different. His whole body was stiff, and he was walking with a brutal efficiency, like he had somewhere to go and something serious to do when he got there.

I was almost scared to say hello, but he saw me first and held up his hand in acknowledgment. "How was your run?" he asked.

"Fine." I was still breathing hard, so I sucked in a lungful of air before I continued. "You okay?"

We stopped when we reached each other in the trail.

"Yes. No . . ." He ran his fingers through his hair. "I guess."

"That doesn't sound okay," I said, surprising myself with my own courage. "Do you want to talk about it?"

He hesitated, and then said, "I was just headed somewhere private. Want to come?"

Private sounded good, though I had a feeling in his current state he wasn't thinking about me at all. "Sure. We don't have to be back for dinner for another twenty minutes, right?"

He nodded. I turned, and we started walking in the direction he had been headed. For a while we were quiet, and I listened to the sound of the rain and wondered if I should say something.

Esther would know what to say. She'd probably be able to make him laugh.

Hennie would know what he was feeling. She'd look in his eyes and say exactly the right thing to make him feel better.

I was clueless.

"I got a call from my dad," Cam finally said. "He's working double shifts over Thanksgiving, so he suggested I stay at Delcroix for the holiday."

I digested the information. "That sucks."

"I should be used to it by now," he said. "He's been doing it forever. I can't remember the last time he ever *has* been around for a holiday." He picked up a stick that had fallen in the path and hurled it into the woods. With him angry like this, his broad shoulders seemed even bigger than usual, and his body seemed capable of doing a lot of damage.

"Did you stay here last year for Thanksgiving?"

He nodded. "It was okay. There were a few of us that stayed, and they made us a turkey and everything. The rest of the teachers left, but Mr. Judan stayed. I swear, I see more of him than my own dad." He stopped where a narrow trail split off from the main one. "Follow me."

The trail was barely wide enough to walk down; wet leaves brushed against our legs and soaked my pants. The farther we got from the trail, the denser the forest became, with blackberry brambles filling the undergrowth, and ivy crawling up the trunks of some of the trees.

We finally came to an old log stretched like a bridge across a spot in the trail. Yards below, a tiny stream flowed at the bottom of a steep ravine. The log was old and decaying, covered with bright green moss. Cam walked across the log and then turned around to extend his hand.

"Are you coming?"

"Um, I'm not sure I'm crazy about walking across wet, slippery logs," I said, only half joking.

Cam's shoulders relaxed just a hair, and he gave me a tiny smile. "Dancia the brave, scared to walk across a little log? No way."

I put my hands on my hips. "Are you making fun of me?"

He nodded soberly. "Absolutely."

"Well, in that case." I walked closer to the log and extended my arm, wiggling my fingers imperiously. "You'd better hold my hand, tough guy."

He took a step toward me and then started to lose his balance. He wobbled, caught himself, and flashed a genuine grin. "Maybe I spoke too soon. It is a bit wetter than usual."

Giggling, I stepped forward and grabbed his hand. We made our way, unsteadily, until we were almost across the log. But then he hit the same slippery spot he had hit before, and tipped to the left and then to the right. This knocked me off balance, and with a shriek, I pitched forward, right into his arms.

He took two quick steps back, lost his footing, and slid into a puddle of mud at the other end. I landed on top of him. We burst out laughing.

He held me in his arms for a minute, and we lay there in the mud puddle, smiling. Part of me was desperately hoping something more might happen—I mean, if he did like me, wasn't this the absolute perfect place to kiss?—but the other part just hoped the moment would never end. His body was warm and strong, with big muscles and arms that enfolded me. I realized I'd never been hugged by someone quite so much bigger than me before, and it made me feel safe and protected.

"Is this where you were headed?" I asked.

"Not exactly," Cam said ruefully.

"Not that it isn't nice," I said. "I mean, it's a great mud puddle and all."

Cam laughed. "You're a good sport, Dancia. I'm sorry for dragging you out here."

"It's okay," I said. I could feel his heart beating under my cheek, and wanted to bury my face in his chest. "That's what friends are for, right?"

Cam was silent, and I started to panic, thinking maybe I'd said the wrong thing by calling us friends. But then he put his hands underneath him and raised his body to a sitting position. Reluctantly, I did the same, and we separated, untangling our bodies so we were sitting in the mud, a few feet apart.

Cam looked at me intently. "It's funny, you know? When

I got that call from my dad, the first person I wanted to talk to about it was you."

"Really? Me?"

He punched me on the shoulder. "Yes, you. You're so honest, Dancia. I feel like I don't have to pretend when I'm with you. I can just be myself. Everyone else around here expects so much from me. But you—well, I feel like you just want me to be me."

"Cam, you're an amazing guy. How could anyone except you to be more than that?"

He looked away, a muscle twitching in his cheek. "It's complicated. I can't really explain."

"Try."

"Well, Mr. Judan, for one. I owe him so much, but sometimes . . ." He extended his hands helplessly.

"Mr. Judan?" I was having a hard time following him, but I had the feeling he needed to talk.

"Yeah. He's always there for me. He gives me a job over the summers, he lets me stay at school for vacations. And he's there to talk to. I know some people think he's weird, but he's actually really great when you need to unload."

I couldn't imagine talking to Mr. Judan, but I figured Cam didn't need to hear that right now. "But he expects a lot from you?"

"He just always expects me to do the right thing. You know, the Delcroix Pledge and all that."

"He takes that seriously?"

Cam nodded. "You can't imagine."

"Wow," I said slowly. "I had no idea."

He stood up and laughed, though it sounded forced. "Enough of that. Are you getting cold? We can go back to school if you want."

I would jump into the Arctic Ocean with ice cubes strapped between my toes if Cam were with me.

"No, I'm fine."

"Then let's go."

Cam's "spot" in the woods was an old evergreen with low branches that you could easily climb. I followed Cam fifteen or twenty feet up the tree before I got freaked out and had to stop. He kept climbing another ten feet above me to a branch that looked barely thick enough to support his weight. He said it gave him a great view of the school and Mount Rainier on a sunny day. We sat there in the tree, not talking, and let the rain mist on our foreheads as we looked up at the sky. It was peaceful and quiet, and when we climbed back down, Cam seemed to have lost his anger. We joked and laughed as we walked back to school.

Meanwhile, I had lost whatever objectivity and control I once had.

I was now totally and completely in love.

CHAPTER 21

FROM THERE on out, my infatuation with Cam eclipsed all rational thought. I forgot about Jack, Delcroix's weirdness, talents, and gates. All I could think of was Cam.

I figured out his schedule and "happened" to be walking by his classes when they got out. I found his locker and hovered around the corner in the morning, hoping I'd see him before first period. I even found myself hanging around the second-floor stairwell in the Res, in the hope that he might appear on the way to breakfast or dinner. And when he touched me? Even if it was a casual hug or accidental bump with his arm, forget about being able to concentrate for the rest of the day.

The frustrating thing was, nothing seemed to change. We got to be great friends, but there was always something separating us. I knew I was special to him, and I knew he cared about me. But I had the painful, horrible feeling that it was only as a friend.

"Well, TGIF, right?" Esther said as we filed onto the Silver Bullet. It was the middle of November, and we were bundled up in thick fleece coats and rain gear. The windows of the bus fogged as we drove down from the school, and we had to wipe them clear to see the cold, gray landscape outside. Parents waved at their kids as soon as they saw them, and ushered them into waiting cars.

I nodded. "Yeah. Thank goodness we can finally sleep in for a couple of days. Though Grandma said there was some early morning sale at the mall Saturday, and she's determined to drag me along."

Esther and Hennie groaned sympathetically.

Hennie perked up as a beautiful dark-haired woman waved from across the parking lot. "There's my mom. I better go. See you guys later!" She gave Esther and me hugs, then ran off toward an enormous silver SUV.

Esther spotted her dad's car. "Listen, you should call me tonight. We can talk about the next step in getting Hennie and Yashir together. I think the holiday dance is our best bet."

So far we'd managed to introduce them and even get them in the same room together a few times, but that's about as far as it went. Hennie still could barely put two sentences together when Yashir talked to her. For a girl who could practically read minds, Hennie seemed to have no idea how cute Yashir thought she was.

"Sure, I'll call you." I tried to muster a convincing smile. Leaving Delcroix for the weekend was always a little depressing. Even though I missed Grandma during the week, and worried about her being by herself, my days at Delcroix were such an intense mix of good and bad that it felt weird to just spend the weekend sitting around the house, studying and listening to music. I also couldn't shake the nagging fear that one of these weekends, Jack was going to leave school and never come back.

Most of all, I hated being away from Cam, even for a couple of days.

"Are you okay?" Esther cocked her head to one side and studied my face. "Can we give you a ride somewhere?"

"Grandma will be here in a little bit. She had an errand she needed to run. I'll be fine."

This was a blatant lie. Actually, Grandma had left a message with the office that I would have to take the bus home, because her doctor had rescheduled her appointment. But I hated to always be asking for favors from Esther. She already lent me her cell phone on a regular basis so I could call Grandma.

"Okay, if you're sure." Esther looked between me and her father's car.

"I'm sure. You should go." I pushed her gently in the direction of her dad. She looked reluctant, so I pushed a little harder. "Esther! I've lived in Danville all my life, you know. We're barely three miles away from my house."

An arm emerged from the car and motioned toward Esther. "My dad wants to take off, otherwise I would stay, I swear," she said.

"Esther, you're being ridiculous. I'll see you on Monday!" I gave her my biggest smile, and she finally ran away.

The parking lot emptied one car at a time. I hitched my backpack higher on my shoulder and started to walk toward the opening in the fence that led to the highway. I kicked a few stones as I walked, hoping everyone would be gone before I went to stand by the bus stop, which was about a hundred yards down the road.

It was a stupid thought, but I couldn't help wondering what it would be like to have parents to pick me up. Would I tell them about my power? Would I talk to them about Cam?

A few cars lingered in the parking lot, but my gaze landed on an old black one with a dent in the door and a tall kid standing next to it. Jack, of course. He was talking to Alessandro and Allie.

He leaned against the car with his usual lazy posture. He looked up and caught my eye. I gave a quick wave and then kept walking.

Two more cars entered the parking lot as the last few stragglers emptied out. They drove past me toward the kids at the back of the lot. A minute later I heard Alessandro and Allie greeting their parents, then saying their good-byes to each other.

"Call me later?" Allie said, more as a statement than a question. Even her voice was cute. No one answered, but I had a feeling Jack was nodding. The car doors slammed, and then the wheels crunched slowly. The cars pulled alongside me as I neared the mouth of the parking lot.

Allie leaned out of her window. "Do you need a ride somewhere?"

"No, thanks." I waved. "I'm meeting someone in a few minutes."

"Okay, see you Monday." Allie gave me one of her cheerleader smiles. Her mom, who shared Allie's thick brown hair and blue eyes, shot me the same smile.

They pulled out a second later, followed by Alessandro. I took a quick look around to confirm that I was alone. Or, almost alone. The black car cruised to the mouth of the lot, stopped, and then backed up to my side.

Jack leaned across the passenger seat and rolled down the window. "Hey, where you headed? Out for a hot date?"

"Right. Me and Friday night are a crazy combination."

"I figured. Where's your Prince Charming?"

"He's not my Prince Charming, and how should I know where he is?" Lately, Jack had taken to making fun of how much time I spent with Cam. It bothered me because I felt guilty for avoiding him when Cam was around. But part of me also liked it, because I figured if Jack noticed and thought we were together, then other people—like Anna—might have as well.

"If you say so."

I kept walking. Jack's car trailed slowly behind me.

"What are you doing driving?" I asked. "You aren't sixteen."

"I have a license that says I am."

I shook my head. "You really are a delinquent."

"It's not a big deal. My friend was headed out to Seattle for the weekend with some of his buddies, and he knew I'd appreciate the wheels, so he dropped off the car for me to use."

"And the license?"

"Where's Grandma?" He avoided my question.

"She's got a doctor's appointment."

"Why don't you let me give you a ride home? I don't think there's a bus for another twenty minutes, and those clouds look nasty."

I had to admit the thought of standing by the road in a downpour wasn't appealing. Highway 78 was the truck route through Danville—not exactly a scenic place to spend a Friday afternoon, and a veritable wind tunnel when the trucks came through. "I probably shouldn't."

"Grandma wouldn't want me to leave you here. Not a sweet boy like me." He threw a handful of fast food wrappers and newspapers into the back of the car and gestured toward the passenger seat. "It's only a couple of miles. Come on."

"Well, I guess if you put it that way." I walked up to the door and pulled on the handle. I had to give it a hard jerk before it opened. The seat was shiny black plastic with a few rips. There was an impressive amount of garbage on the floor and around the seats. I cleared a spot for myself and my backpack, and sat down gingerly. "Nice car."

"Thanks," he drawled.

I stared at his profile. There were times when I looked in Jack's eyes and saw something dark and bleak hidden there. Maybe it was the same thing Hennie saw. It made him look lost and sad, and every time I saw it I got angry at his mom and all the people who should have been around to take care of him but weren't.

I laid my head against the headrest and closed my eyes. Suddenly I couldn't wait to be home.

"So do you think I'll ever get invited over for dinner again? Or have you decided Prince Charming wouldn't like that, just like he doesn't want you to talk to me at school anymore?"

The attack caught me off guard. I kept my eyes closed and fought a wave of panic. "What do you mean?"

"Look, I'd have to be an idiot not to see how you try to avoid me, Dancia. At least when other people are around. And it's not hard to figure out why."

"I don't know what you're talking about. I just get busy. You're not my only friend, you know."

"Don't lie to me," he said, waving a tired hand. "It's way too obvious."

"I'm not lying," I insisted.

"Danny." His voice was quiet. "I thought we were better than that. I thought we weren't like the rest of them."

I guess I was feeling a little defensive, or guilty, or both, because what came out of my mouth next was totally unexpected. "What happened at the wall, then? If we're so honest with each other, why don't you tell me what happened at the wall?"

I regretted the words instantly. I was past that. Nothing happened at the wall. Nothing special, anyway.

He glanced into the rearview mirror. "I helped you over."

"I figured that—"

"Have you noticed that tan car, two blocks back?"

I sat up straighter in the seat and started to turn around. He shook his head quickly. "No, don't turn around. Look in your mirror. See the tan car?"

There was a nondescript sedan, maybe a Buick, at a stop sign two blocks behind us. "Sure, I see it."

"Watch this." Jack slammed on the accelerator and turned a quick left. After sailing through the next two intersections, he dropped down to a crawl. Seconds later, the Buick's tires squealed as it rounded the same corner. It slowed abruptly and remained a safe distance behind.

Jack repeated the move several more times—speeding up to take a turn, then crawling slowly down the next couple of blocks. Each time he did, the tan car would appear a minute later, fast then slow, lingering at intersections and never getting too close. I doubt I would have noticed if Jack hadn't pointed it out.

"What's going on?" I asked, my knuckles white around the door handle. Though I tried not to think about it, I couldn't help but notice that the tan Buick looked like the car I thought I had seen following Grandma and me after Halloween.

Jack roared through the next two stop signs like they weren't there, pulled two quick rights and then a U-turn, and sped down a one-way street. We ended up a few blocks from my house. He pulled the car to a stop and ran his fingers through his hair. His hands were shaking.

"Are you all right?" I asked.

He blew out a breath and knocked the steering wheel with a fist. "I hate when they follow me."

The barely restrained violence rolled off him in waves.

"Maybe it was a coincidence," I said.

He laughed—a flat sound that had no hint of amusement. "Right." He paused and then said, "I should take you home. They'll be waiting for us there anyway. I don't know why I bother."

We drove the last few blocks in silence. I looked up and down the street apprehensively, but didn't see any tan Buicks. Jack threw his car into park and gazed straight ahead.

"Do you want to hang out for a minute?" I was crazy to ask, but there was a white line around his lips, and his hands kept shaking as he clenched and unclenched them on the steering wheel.

He blew out another breath. "Are you sure you want me to?" His eyes had turned from gray to silver.

I wasn't sure, but didn't think I could back down now. "Grandma will be home soon. We can sit on the porch until she gets here." I tried to make it sound like that was Grandma's rule and not just me being terrified to let him in the house.

He nodded.

We walked up to the porch. I sat on the bench, but Jack paced in front of me. Every now and again he punched a clenched fist into his open palm. The silence between us grew, and I didn't know how to break it. Jack looked as though he were wrestling with something—something he either wanted to say or didn't want to say. Something serious.

Finally he spun around and fixed me with a silvery stare. "I was in jail. A couple of years ago."

"Oh," I whispered.

"It was a juvenile detention center. I was thirteen, running with a gang in Portland that stole cars. They put me in for a few months, and then I did a year's probation. My mom showed up for the trial and pretended like we were living together. She never wanted to go through the hassle of putting me in foster care. I knew she didn't want me around, so I didn't go home much. When I was on probation I had to check in with her and my probation officer all the time, keep up my attendance at their stupid school. It sucked. I couldn't go anywhere without someone knowing where I was."

He paced up and down the porch, and I watched, barely breathing, not wanting to interrupt the flow of his words. "Is that why you hate being followed so much?"

"I suppose." He dropped onto the bench beside me. "When I was really little, it was my dad who was following us. I'm not sure which is worse—the guys from Delcroix or him."

My stomach dropped. "Why was your dad following you?"

"He wasn't a very nice guy. My mom tried to avoid him for years, but he always found us."

"Oh." From what I remembered, Tom Landry had always seemed nice enough. Kind of quiet. They always said those were the ones you had to look out for.

"Shit." Jack ran his fingers through his hair. "It just pisses me off, that's all."

"Do you still . . ." I tried to picture thirteen-year-old Jack stealing a car. "I mean, how could you steal things? Weren't you scared you'd get caught? Didn't it seem wrong?"

"I did get caught." He stood up and shoved his hands into his pockets. "And no, it didn't seem wrong. It still doesn't. The way I figure it, I got a bum deal in life. I got a shitty dad

192

who beat me up, a junkie for a mom, and some weird powers that make them both hate me. If I have to help myself to a little of what other people have, I figure I deserve it."

I should have been prepared, but the mention of "powers" sucked the air from my lungs. I struggled to think logically, which required ignoring the word I couldn't quite process. "Jack," I managed to say, "are you in trouble?"

He barked a laugh. "Besides with your boyfriend? No. I'm not in trouble."

I couldn't suppress a tiny shudder of pleasure at the thought of Cam being my boyfriend. "I didn't mean at school. I meant, with the guy who loaned you his car, or whoever you're living with."

He shook his head. "It's the Delcroix people. I know it is. They've been on my tail ever since I got to town. I try to lose them when I leave school, but they're good at what they do. I don't always see them until it's too late. Like today."

"Like Sunglasses Guy?"

Jack cocked his head. "Who the heck is Sunglasses Guy?"

I flushed. "The guy who was following you the day we first met."

"Oh. Yeah, he was one of them."

"I don't believe they're from Delcroix," I said, crossing my arms over my chest. "That doesn't make any sense."

Jack took a few steps toward me. "Dancia," he said, "haven't you figured it out by now? Delcroix's not just some ordinary private school on a hill. They're searching out kids like you and me. I don't know what they want to do with us; I haven't figured that out yet. But they don't have any intention of letting us slip through their fingers. Ever since school started I've tried damn hard to lose myself in crowds, and it's impossible. They're always there."

I focused on the front door, dreading what would come next. "What do you mean, kids like you and me?"

He knelt down in front of me and grabbed my hand. "It's time to come clean. Tell the truth. Both of us. I can feel it whenever you get upset. Like that morning—I don't know what you did to Sunglasses Guy, but you practically set my hair on end. And then in Mr. Fritz's class. You wanted to do something then, I know you did. And you made yourself sick when you tried to stop it. And the wall. Do you really want to talk about the wall? Because I helped you there, and you know it. So we're alike, you and I. We're not normal. Neither of us. Let's just admit it, okay?"

Tears flooded my eyes. Suddenly all I could think of was to run. I didn't want to talk to Jack about powers, or Delcroix, or guys in tan Buicks. I just wanted to be left alone.

I jumped off the bench and ran toward the front door, fumbling with trembling hands for the key in my pocket. After several tries I managed to get it in the lock. Ignoring Jack's insistent voice behind me, I threw open the door and tried to rush in, but something blocked my path. I threw up my hands but couldn't find an edge.

Either air had turned solid, or there was something blocking the door.

Something invisible.

CHAPTER 22

I SPUN around. "Did you do this?" I slammed my fist into the invisible wall between me and my house. It rippled a little, like heat waves rolling off the blacktop in summer. "Is this how you use your power? To bully people? Let me go, Jack. I don't want to talk about it."

Jack leaned against the porch rail, his body once again a relaxed slouch. His voice was soft, coaxing. "How can you say that? I'm no bully."

The wall didn't move, so I hurried down the porch steps and started for the backyard. A tangle of emotions curdled my brain—shock, mostly, mixed with fury. But as my mind tried to sort through the tumult of feelings, my body took over. It had no doubt what it wanted to do. It wanted to run.

"Come on, why don't you want to talk about it?" Jack called. "It's not like it's a secret anymore. At least, not from me. And I'll be straight with you too. Don't you want to know what really happened at the wall?"

"No." I pushed open the gate in the chain-link fence. It swung into the mass of weeds that was our backyard. Jack followed, a few paces behind. A narrow, overgrown, concrete path led to the back step, and I started down it, only to have my foot smack into another barrier of solid air. I kicked it, which did nothing but leave me with a sore foot.

"Cut it out," I yelled.

The familiar tingle started in my fingers. I knew what was happening, but for once I had no desire to stop it. I turned around and looked at Jack, smugly standing just inside the backyard, the open gate to his right. Usually in these situations I lashed out, the instinct overwhelming me before I had time to consider my options. But now, with an invisible wall in front of me and Jack's smirk behind, I looked around with a calculating eye.

A second later, the gate swung back, catching Jack in the chest and pushing him out of the yard.

"Oof." He stumbled backward. The barrier in front of me dissipated, and I rushed farther into the backyard. Jack rubbed his stomach and smiled weakly. "That was a good one. I should have seen that coming."

"Leave me alone!"

Inside, I exulted. For once I had used my power on someone who had the ability to fight back, and it felt incredible. No guilt, no second-guessing. The crackling energy still rushed through me, and I relished the force of it. The awareness that usually left me terrified suddenly felt right—like I was in control of it, instead of the other way around.

Jack threw open the gate. "What's wrong with you? I thought we were friends."

"So? That doesn't mean you can push me around whenever you want."

"This is because of Prince Charming, isn't it? What did he tell you about me?"

I scowled at him. "This is about you being a jerk. You can't blame that on Cam."

"I'm a jerk? All I want to do is talk. That's all." He raised his hands in a gesture of supplication. "Come on, you can't stay mad at me, Danny. You know you can't."

I stared at him, and slowly my anger deflated. He was right. Besides, I wasn't really mad at Jack. I was mad at life—at fate, I guess. You would think it would be a relief to find another person like me, but in that moment it just made it worse. Because if Jack was like me, then I was like Jack, and the two of us were somehow bound together.

And I was no longer going to be able to pretend that side of me didn't exist.

"No more invisible walls?" I asked.

"No more flying gates?" he countered.

I pursed my lips. "Fine."

I turned and stomped up the path to the back door, not looking to see if Jack followed.

With her usual crackerjack attention to detail, Grandma had left the door unlocked. Inside, the house was dark and cool, with the curtains drawn tightly in front of the large window that overlooked the street. I marched to the refrigerator, taking off my coat as I went.

"Do you want something to drink?" I said over my shoulder.

"Sure."

As I jerked open the door of our ancient, dented fridge, I could feel Jack's presence fill the room. Still twitching with the power, I had a hard time keeping my body from shaking. I grabbed two cans of pop and threw one at Jack. He caught it with a grin, and we went into the living room.

I sat down on Grandma's armchair. Jack pulled off his jacket, assumed a comfortable position on the sofa, and threw his feet up on the coffee table.

"Grandma doesn't like feet on the furniture," I said.

He thumped his feet on the floor. "I wouldn't want to make Grandma mad." He opened his can and watched it fizz, then took a sip.

I clenched my fists, trying to decide whether I liked or hated him. It was a tough call. "So . . . what do you want to talk about?"

"What exactly can you do?" he asked, setting the soda down. "My power has to do with changing the properties of things. I can make air solid, or turn a solid into a liquid." He smiled drily. "I'm not sure about all the ramifications of what I'm doing. I've studied a little chemistry on my own, just to make sure I don't end up doing something dangerous, but I still don't know how it all works."

As much as I didn't want to be having this conversation, I leaned forward, captured by what he had said so casually. "Could you . . . vaporize someone?" I asked.

"Probably. I haven't tried. The idea freaks me out, to be honest. Things seem to keep their essence, they just change form. I'm not sure what that would do to a person." He pointed to a tall wooden lamp with a broad white shade. "Watch this."

It was like watching a candle melt on fast-forward. The gold knob on the top slumped and poured down. Then the white shade wilted, drew into itself, and turned into a thick gas that hovered a few feet in the air. Finally the wooden base liquefied, and the whole thing merged into a yellowish cloud.

"Wow," I breathed. "You can do that whenever you want?"

"Sure." He nodded and the lamp reassembled itself, base, shade, then bulb. "It's not always the most useful thing in the world. It's great for self-defense—I can turn the air solid and knock weapons out of people's hands, or hold them in place if need be—but it doesn't help pay the bills."

I pictured the day Jack was late to school, when I'd tried to help him and then the security card turned into smoke. I knew he'd had something to do with it. "When did you start using it?"

"When I was a kid. Two or three maybe. My mom and dad lived together then. One time Dad tried to hit my mom, and I wrapped the air around him like a chain. He went crazy." Jack's body tightened as he spoke, and he began to thump one fist against his knee. "He drank a lot, so at first he thought he was imagining it. After a while he realized it was me, and, man, was he ever pissed. When I was four I told him if he ever hurt my mom again I'd make him disappear. I don't think he really believed I could do it, but it freaked him out enough that he told us to leave."

I rolled my pop can back and forth between my palms. "Did your mom know about it? About your powers?"

He laughed, an ugly, hurt sound that I think would have made me cry if I hadn't been staring so hard at that can. "She thought I was some kind of freak. I think she would have turned me over to child services if she wasn't scared they'd take her meth away or make her take care of me."

"Why did your dad come after you if he had kicked you out?"

Jack took another drink of soda and contemplated the lamp for a minute before he continued. Under his gaze the bulb turned gassy, then solid, then gassy again. "I don't really know. He always said he felt bad and wanted to make sure we were taken care of, but then my mom would say something to piss him off, and we'd be right back where we started. She moved to Portland to get away from him, but she was pretty much gone by then. Total meth-head. By the time I was ten I was on my own. I found other kids to hang out with, and I didn't tell them about my powers. But I practiced them in secret, so I could get out of trouble."

He balled the soda can in one hand, strode over to the kitchen, and pitched it toward the garbage. It hit the rim and bounced off. He picked it up with a wry smile. "Told you I wasn't much of an athlete." Once the can had made it into the garbage, he leaned against the doorway. "And what about you? When did you realize you had your power?"

"I don't know." I spoke slowly, unsure of how to explain what had been in my mind for so many years. This whole scene with Jack had become surreal, like it wasn't really happening. Part of me suspected it was just a dream.

"I always thought it was a coincidence that the exact things I pictured in my mind actually happened. But then these weird things started happening. Things that weren't impossible, but were unusual, hard to explain." I described the incident at the water park, when I tipped the chair onto the bully, and the time I dropped a branch on the kids messing with Aileen.

"I finally realized that I was the one doing those things. They only happened around me, you know? And they were too odd, too unusual to be happening by chance. And I always got this feeling right before they happened . . . It was like . . ." I struggled to find the right words. "It was like I needed to do something; like an energy was building inside of me that I had to get rid of. It was almost like my body was channeling some kind of force. Something that was inside me but came from all around."

I'd never tried to articulate it before, and saying the words out loud gave me the oddest feeling, as though a knot inside me had begun to unravel.

Jack sat back down on the sofa. "Your power is different than mine. I'm not sure what you're doing, but it sounds amazing."

"I suppose," I said, "but it's also dangerous. I always seem to end up hurting people. I put a guy in a coma when he threatened to kill my grandmother. Sunglasses Guy could have died if he hadn't been wearing his seat belt. I try not to use it, because it scares me. *I* scare me."

"Interesting." He leaned back and threw his arms over his head. I was stuck for a minute by the odd comparison between how comfortable he looked and the way Cam and Mr. Judan had been so out of place in my living room. "Has it always been that way? I mean, when you were little, what did you do?"

I shrugged. "I don't remember anything specific before the water park. Like I said, I thought they were coincidences, so I didn't pay much attention. All the things I remember are bad."

He thought for a minute. "I bet you used your power more when you were a kid, and it was only after you identified it that you started seeing all the things you say are bad. Thing is, they really aren't bad. They're just the other side of the coin. Saving people's lives is good. Helping me escape from Sunglasses Guy was very good. Putting someone in a coma? Tough to say, I suppose, but it seems to me saving Grandma's life was worth it. In any case, yours isn't an evil power. It simply is what it is, neither good nor bad. It's all in the way you use it."

I pushed against the armrests and raised myself out of the chair. "Easy for you to say. You don't send people to the hospital on a regular basis."

"I also don't go around saving people's lives," he said softly. "You take risks to protect other people. You just don't want the responsibility that goes along with it."

"Of course I don't want the responsibility," I cried. "I just want to be a normal teenager."

"You think normal teenagers don't have to make choices? You think their choices never hurt people? There's a bit of evil in everyone, Dancia," he said, seeming much older than fifteen. "No one's pure. You've got a gift, and I think you'd be crazy not to use it. Just think of all the people you could help, if you only tried."

I walked past him into the kitchen. There was a pile of dirty dishes in the sink. I dropped open the dishwasher door and started to load the cups, my body on autopilot while I stared through the kitchen window.

"You say that like it's something I can control, but that's just it. I can't. When I'm mad or scared, my power takes over. It isn't like yours."

"I don't believe that." He came up beside me and leaned against the counter. "You did a pretty good job of slamming that gate on me. You call that an accident?"

"No, it's not an accident. It's . . ." What was it again? Somehow my own explanations didn't make sense the way they usually did. "It's a reflex."

Jack snorted. "A reflex? I don't think so. Your *reflex* seems a little too well thought out to me. I think you've been controlling your power all along. You keep it suppressed and hidden away until something big happens. Something you can't ignore. And then you tell yourself it's just an instinct so you don't have to feel responsible for it."

He was so close, my stomach tightened. I focused on his words, which had a painful sort of resonance. Could he possibly be right? "That can't be true," I said. "You don't know how it feels. It's like a tidal wave. How could I control that?"

He grabbed my hand and pulled me to face him. "Let's try it," he said, looking into my eyes. "Let's see what you can do."

I froze. My hands were wet and slippery from the dishes, and he felt warm and rough. I tried to free myself, but he wouldn't loosen his grip.

"What are you doing, Jack?"

He chuckled. "I'm taking you outside, what do you think I'm doing?"

"But we aren't moving," I said in a strangled voice.

"Oh, right." He still didn't move.

My pulse fluttered like the wings of a hummingbird. Jack's eyes locked on mine, and it was like that time on the porch, when I thought he was going to kiss me.

Then, for some unknown reason, I took a step forward, a step toward him. He laughed and dropped my hand, then picked up his coat and ran out the door, leaving me to stare at his back.

What had I been thinking? I couldn't let Jack kiss me. I was into Cam. CAM. Not Jack, CAM.

Argg! I grabbed my coat and followed him.

We walked into the backyard. A few old cans and some plastic bottles that should have made it into the recycling bin littered the weedy grass. Near the back of our yard was an old stump that sat in the shade of a gnarled apple tree. Jack picked up a few of the cans and set them on the edge of the stump.

He walked over to me and crossed his arms. "Push them off."

"What?"

"Use your power. Push them off. Like the branch, or the gate. Remember the feeling of the power coming over you, and channel it. And this time try to figure out what you're doing. Focus on that force you described, and try to understand how you're using it."

I raised one eyebrow. "Who are you, Obi-Wan Kenobi?"

He laughed. "We're in trouble if I am, because then you're Darth Vader."

"Or Luke Skywalker," I said indignantly. I leaned my head back and shook my hair from my face. "I guess no one would ever mistake me for Princess Leia, huh?"

The smile dropped from his face. "You know you're gorgeous, right?"

My heart did a funny little dance that made it difficult to breath. "Shut up."

"I mean it." He reached out to touch a long curl, his hand brushing my cheek.

I panicked. I can't describe it any other way. One long look from those gray eyes, which had gone unaccountably soft, and I got so nervous I could feel the individual beads of sweat forming on my forehead.

I pulled away. Jack opened his mouth to say something, and because I was suddenly desperate to stop him, I turned my eyes to the cans and the log and tried for the first time in my life to summon the familiar tingle of power.

Nothing happened. I tried again, thinking hard about the cans moving, just like Jack had said.

Still nothing.

I pictured the lamp that Jack had melted, and the card

I'd seen him turn to smoke. If Jack could control his power, why couldn't I?

A bird chirped, and across the street, someone started their car.

The cans did not move.

I started to get mad. I'd been living with this darn power for all these years, arranging my whole life around it, and Jack comes along and, poof! I'm supposed to be able to control it?

I threw up my hands. "I'm sorry, Jack. I can't do it. You're wrong."

"Try again," he said, his voice gentle. Caring. "You're fighting with yourself. The power's inside you. Let it out."

I turned back to the log, and this time, instead of trying so hard, I forced myself to relax. Instead of thinking about the cans, I thought about the force inside me. I listened, if that makes any sense, to the noises that I usually tune out.

And then, with an explosion like a gas stove lighting, a surge of prickling heat swallowed me whole, more intense than anything I had felt before. My fingers popped and sparked as I moved them, and Jack faded into a blur. I flicked my fingers, and a feeling of pain and pleasure moved through me.

I stared at the cans and imagined them, one by one, flying from the stump.

The cans stayed put.

I focused on the force and tried to figure out how to use it. I realized that the energy in my body was nothing more than a small amount of the energy all around me. I looked at the weeds and the tree, and for the first time saw sparkles and ripples of energy in everything, from the sky to the earth. The cans had forces working upon them and energy inside them, and they were all in balance. Deliberately, I stretched out a finger and pushed at those forces, knocking them momentarily out of balance.

The cans exploded into the sky like they'd been shot from a gun. It took them a long time to fall back down.

I looked at the stump and then looked at Jack, my body still tingling with the flow of power.

"That was incredible," he said, almost reverently. "*You* are incredible."

And before I knew what was happening, his lips touched mine.

CHAPTER 23

I ADMIT I didn't move. Not right away. I knew I should, but I didn't. Jack was right—I *could* control my power. It was amazing, incredible. And for some reason it felt natural to channel all that emotion into a kiss.

So I didn't push him away even though I knew I'd regret it later. It was thrilling and terrifying all at once. His lips were gentle but searching for something I didn't quite know how to give. At first it was like we were two pieces of a puzzle that didn't quite fit together. His teeth bumped against mine, I didn't know where to put my arms, and I wondered if maybe kissing wasn't all it was cracked up to be. But then something between us clicked, and everything else faded away. I forgot about my power, forgot to worry about whether Jack and I were meant to be, and let myself enjoy being kissed for the very first time.

I'm not sure how long it took me to come to my senses. I must have been pretty into it, because when I finally pulled myself together enough to move, I realized we had fallen to our knees, and my jeans were damp from the ground. With strangely weak hands, I pushed against his shoulders and drew in a breath.

"We have to stop, Jack."

He didn't protest. His arms loosened as soon as I drew back and untangled myself from his embrace. He fell back on the grass, looking at me and not saying a word.

I sucked in a deep breath and pulled my hair back from my face. My whole body prickled with heat. As I stood I kept my eyes on the imprint our knees had made in the grass.

"We shouldn't have done that." It was the only thing I could think of to say.

"What? We shouldn't have kissed each other? It had to happen sooner or later. I'm not the only one who felt that. I know I'm not." His voice held a hint of anger.

"But it's not right, Jack. It was just an emotional day, that's all. Neither of us really wants this." I gestured help-lessly toward the ground where the weeds had begun to spring back into place. My lips felt soft, and the skin around my mouth stung a little from where it had been rubbed by the tiny hairs above his lip.

I was fairly certain what I said was true. Not one hundred percent certain, but close.

He jumped to his feet. Jack had this way of moving that was like a cat—graceful but nonchalant, as if he refused to expend too much energy on his movements.

"You don't mean that."

"I do mean that. I think we should just be friends." I spit out the words fast, mustering all the confidence I had.

"Friends?" he drawled. He looked at me, his eyes difficult to read. "Didn't seem that way a few minutes ago."

"I know. I should never have kissed you. I really just want to be friends, Jack. That's all." I tried to speak firmly. Jack had been through a lot, and part of me wanted to be the girl who understood him and cared for him when no one else did. But at the same time I knew I couldn't take that on. Jack needed something from me, something I didn't think I could give. I couldn't make up for his dad, or his horrible childhood. I had to concentrate on getting my own head straight, and figuring out what to do with my power.

My power.

I had controlled my power. I had taken some part of the energy around me and used it to send those cans flying. The power didn't have to control me. I could control it!

A thrill raced through me, momentarily drowning out my horror over what I'd done with Jack—and what Cam would think if he ever found out.

Jack's mouth flattened into a thin, angry line. "You know Prince Charming doesn't really like you, right?"

I froze. "What's that supposed to mean?"

"He's working for them, Danny. He's only being nice so he can keep an eye on you."

"That's ridiculous." A knot of fear formed in my stomach. That was exactly what I had thought about Cam. That the whole thing didn't really add up. That there had to be something else going on.

"Think about it. Why is he paying so much attention to you, a freshman? I mean, you're cute and all, but look at the girls surrounding him." In a second, Jack had changed from a cat to a snake, complete with hooded eyes and an evil, forked tongue.

"Why do you think he's always warning you to stay away from me?" he continued. "They know I'm on to them. They don't want me to lead you astray. Prince Charming's just the bait they're holding out to keep you deaf, dumb, and blind."

Tears sprung to my eyes, and I had to stop to catch my breath. "You're a horrible person, Jack Landry," I cried. "I can't believe I ever felt sorry for you, or let you kiss me!"

I marched over and grabbed his arm, suddenly filled with righteous energy. "Get out of here. I don't want to ever speak to you again."

Jack didn't move. When I touched him, he stared at me with eyes so full of anger and pain that I stopped, transfixed. Silence fell over us.

"What are you kids doing?"

The voice of a stranger startled us both. Jack jumped. I dropped his arm and whirled around in surprise.

It was Shelly Burker, my next door neighbor. Mrs. Burker was a solid woman of at least three hundred pounds, with an uncanny ability to move silently. Over the years I had learned the hard way not to underestimate her ability for stealth, or the enjoyment she took out of getting me into trouble. It was entirely possible that she had been watching us the whole time.

"Um, what do you mean, Mrs. Burker?" I asked warily.

She put her hands on her hips and fixed me with a cold stare. "You shooting off bottle rockets or something? I saw those cans go flying in the air."

"I'm trying out for the football team," Jack said. "I was working on my throwing arm. I guess I've got a lot to learn, huh?"

Mrs. Burker's small piggish eyes examined Jack carefully. "Who are you, boy? You Tom Landry's kid?"

I cringed when Jack's normally pale skin turn even whiter. "Why do you ask?" he said tightly.

"I knew the man, that's all. And you look like a carbon copy of him." She turned back to me. "Does your grandma know you've got this boy at the house while she's away, Dancia?"

I shifted from foot to foot as I tried to meet her gaze. "He was just leaving," I said, glancing over at Jack.

Even though I wanted to stay mad at him, I was struck by a pang of sympathy. Jack must hate hearing people talk about his father. After spending his life running away from Tom Landry and the hurt he had caused, it would be devastating to walk right back to where he once lived—where everyone recognized Jack as his son.

Jack started to say something else, but the roar of Grandma's Volvo drowned out his words. She pulled slowly into the driveway, barely missing Mrs. Burker's wide bulk.

"Is that you, Shelly?" Grandma called.

"Yes, I was just talking to Dancia and her little friend." She looked at me with a triumphant gleam in her eye.

"What's that?" Grandma shoved the door open and got out leg by leg. With a great sigh, she heaved herself out of the seat. A scarf with blue and red flowers covered her white curls, and she wore a matching American flag sweatshirt and pants and her old purple rain parka. "Oh, Jack!" Her watery blue eyes turned up in a smile. "How nice to see you again. Are you staying for supper?"

He gave Grandma a little bow. "Thanks, Mrs. Lewis. It's nice to see you too. But I think I better go. Lots of homework, you know." He extended his hand to Mrs. Burker. "Lovely to meet you, ma'am."

Her eyes narrowed suspiciously. "If you say so."

They shook hands, and he raised hers up to kiss the back of it. She jerked it away, but a little gleam of pleasure shone in her eyes.

She watched as he walked down the driveway. "Impudent boy," she said, "but I think I like him." She put her hands back on her prodigious hips. "That doesn't mean I believe a word he said."

I wiped my hands nervously on my jeans, then appealed directly to Grandma. "Jack and I were messing around in the backyard. He threw some cans in the air. Mrs. Burker thought we were setting off firecrackers. But we weren't, I promise."

"Hmm." Grandma turned to Mrs. Burker. "They weren't bothering you, were they, Shelly?"

"I suppose not," she admitted.

"Well, not much more to say, is there?"

Mrs. Burker sniffed but didn't argue. "I'll be getting along home, then."

Grandma gave me a sharp look as Mrs. Burker sauntered away. "You two weren't in the house alone, were you? I may like the boy, but I never said you could be taking up together when I wasn't here."

"Taking up together?" I played indignant, hoping my lips didn't somehow give away what had been going on only minutes before. "Grandma, he gave me a ride home and I gave him a soda. I am almost fifteen, you know. Old enough to be in a house with a boy."

She didn't fall for my wounded-innocence routine. "I don't care if he gave you a diamond ring. No boys in the house when I'm not around."

I rolled my eyes and huffed, though I was just as happy to have an excuse never to let Jack in the house again. My lips felt swollen and tender when I ran my tongue over them. Grandma stared at me with a vaguely suspicious expression as I started inching toward the back door.

"I better get started on my homework." I gave a forced laugh. "They really laid it on thick this week."

Grandma studied me over the top of her glasses. "I'm sorry I couldn't pick you up from school. Is everything okay? You look like something's bothering you."

I took a few steps back. "School was fine. Nothing's bothering me."

She chuckled. "You would say that if they had jabbed needles under your fingernails."

"That's ridiculous." I had to suppress a smile. "It really is fine."

"If you say so." She shuffled over to the car and opened the trunk. "How does chicken sound for dinner?"

"Great." My shoulders dropped with relief at the change of subject, and I hurried around the back of the car to pull out the grocery bags.

A tiny part of me actually wanted to tell Grandma what had happened, just so I could figure out if I had done the right thing by pushing Jack away. I was still smarting from the things he'd said about Cam, but I knew I'd hurt him as well, and that made it hard to stay mad.

I just couldn't get my head around how quickly things between us had changed. I thought Jack knew how I felt about Cam, so I was safe. I thought we could just be friends, and not worry about all that boyfriend-girlfriend stuff. But now I'd done something I couldn't undo. And I had a horrible feeling I'd regret it for a long time.

"You and Jack didn't get into a fight, did you?" Grandma asked. "He looked a bit odd when I drove up."

"Jack and I are pretty different," I said, throwing the bags onto the counter as we entered the kitchen. "He's had a hard life, Grandma. I'm not sure what to think about him."

She sighed. "I wondered what had happened when Jack and his mama left the house. I think Tom was rough on that boy. He always struck me as an unreliable character."

"Yeah." I wasn't sure what I could tell Grandma without breaking Jack's confidence. "I think you're right."

"Well, you can't fix that, Danny. You can't turn back the clock."

"I know." It all seemed terribly sad. Jack and his mom, Jack and me. Nothing working out like it should. "He scares me a little, that's all. Like he doesn't worry about things he should, or doesn't care about things the rest of us do." I thought about it as I spoke. "It isn't that I feel sorry for him, exactly. I just wish life could be different."

"No sense wishing for something that will never be," Grandma said, unexpectedly stern. "You take what life gives you and you do something good with it."

Grandma did that sometimes. When you wanted answers, she forgot the question. When you wanted sympathy, she'd tell you to quit feeling sorry for yourself.

I knew better than to argue. "Sure, Grandma. Whatever you say."

CHAPTER 24

I TOOK the city bus to school on Monday. Grandma had a cold, and her arthritis made it harder to get going in the morning now that it was cold and damp all the time. I made her promise the night before that she'd call Mrs. Burker if she needed anything. I hated not being around to help her myself.

Meanwhile, I had my own problems to worry about. I spent the bus ride looking at the people around me, wondering if I was being followed. The guy with the dingy brown hat pulled low over his eyes—could he be after me? What about the woman with the flowered dress? Was that really a purse she was carrying? Was there something inside—maybe a gun?

The bus dropped me off at the parking lot about twenty minutes early. The lot was dark, and as far as I could tell, empty. I knew other people would start to arrive in a few minutes, but for now at least, I was alone. I stood there for a minute, shivering in the cold morning air. Then I kicked the gravel for a while and worried about seeing Jack and Cam. That didn't do my nerves any good, so then I worried about my algebra homework. Finally I decided I needed something to distract me from what was to come.

I walked over to the misshapen tree at the far end of the parking lot and studied the limbs closest to the ground. Clumps of dead brown leaves hung from the end of the branches, rustling softly as a breeze passed through them. With a quick check to make sure I was still alone, I dropped my backpack, rubbed my hands together, and focused on a single large leaf.

Seconds later, my body was tingling and the leaf was winging its way to the ground. I stared up, and a second leaf sailed down beside the first.

Next I looked up at the branch. It was thin and swayed gently under a load of dead leaves. I focused on it, and with a satisfying crack, it snapped at the juncture with a larger branch, hung at a crazy angle for a moment, then fell straight to the ground in front of me.

I stared down with a now-familiar mix of triumph and fear. I still didn't understand the power, but I was coming closer. After two days of practice I had learned to summon that familiar tingle whenever I wanted it. I was becoming more adept at reading the tangle of forces around me, though I didn't know yet precisely what they were. I assumed at least some of what I was feeling was gravity—the gravity of the sun and the moon, and the gravity of the earth. So far, all I could do was nudge those forces, alter their balance as they acted on objects around me. But I wondered what would happen if I unraveled them, or accidentally set them permanently in some alternative direction. I didn't think I had the ability to do that, but what if I did and just didn't know it yet?

The more I thought about it, the more nervous I became. We'd learned last year in my social studies class that the atomic bomb worked by splitting some of the bonds in an atom. I didn't remember exactly which ones, but I recalled that the bomb only represented a tiny fraction of the energy that could be released. If I severed some of those bonds, I could blow us all to kingdom come. That possibility alone convinced me to try harder to understand what I was doing, and made me desperate for someone to talk to about it.

My only option for that, of course, was Jack.

Or was it? Now that I knew about Jack, I couldn't help but wonder again what was really going on at Delcroix. Because it was difficult to believe that it was just coincidence that the two of us, with our strange powers, had ended up at the same school.

Then again, we were different from the other kids at Delcroix. Esther and Hennie had incredible gifts, but they were right there, out in the open. Everybody knew about them. Jack and I weren't like that. We didn't have gifts like the other students'.

But we're the ones Mr. Judan and Cam personally recruited. Why is that?

The familiar crunch of tires on gravel interrupted my thoughts. I spun around, hoping whoever was in the car hadn't seen me playing with the leaves. They were still far enough away that I doubted they could see the sticks at my feet, let alone notice a few leaves dancing to the ground.

That car was the first in the series now turning in from the highway. The time for games was over. I meandered toward the center of the lot and let the crowd surround me.

Esther arrived about five minutes later. She found me with uncanny speed, and ran over, her chest and backpack bouncing in an uneven rhythm. "Why didn't you call me this weekend?" she called out when she was still twenty feet away. "We were supposed to talk about Hennie and Yashir!"

"I had too much homework. Grandma didn't want me to call anyone until I finished it."

Esther stopped in front of me, her hair a foaming cloud of black around her head. "That's okay, but we have got to get you a cell phone so we can text each other, at least." She must have seen me looking at her hair, because she gestured toward it and grimaced. "I combed it. It's like a nervous tic or something."

We both laughed, and I tried not to think about how embarrassing it was to be the only kid in the entire school without a cell. Esther dropped her backpack next to mine and scanned the parking lot. "Have you seen Hennie?"

"Not yet."

I wondered if I should broach the topic now, or wait until later. I realized I should probably wait, but I was practically bursting. We only had one phone in the house, and the cord didn't stretch to my room, or I would have called her over the weekend and asked. I just didn't want Grandma listening in on my conversation.

"Esther, have you really kissed a lot of boys?"

"Well," she said casually, still looking around the lot, "not a lot, but a few. Why?" She turned and gave me a sharp look. "Does this have something to do with Cam? Did he kiss you or something?"

"No, no!" I raised my hands in protest. "Definitely not. I was just curious, because, well, because I haven't. And I'm just wondering. About kissing, I mean. In case it comes up in the future." I sounded like an idiot, babbling nervously as her steely eyes seemed to pierce right through me.

"Sure, right." She rolled her eyes. "Okay, the truth is that it's a little weird at first, but totally fun. You just wait. You'll see."

"What if you weren't sure if you liked someone or not, and then you kissed him?" I realized this was a very risky question to ask, because it would subject me to further interrogation down the road. But if anyone knew the answer, it would be Esther. "Could you tell if you were meant to be together? By kissing him, I mean?"

This had been driving me crazy all weekend. If I was meant to be with Cam, why had I liked kissing Jack? I knew Jack wasn't right for me, and I knew I couldn't be the girl-friend he needed, yet I'd still made out with him in my back-yard. Why? I could blame it on the power, which always left me a little giddy and overwhelmed, or on the fact that it was my first kiss and I was curious to finally see what all the fuss was about. But in the end it came back to me, kissing Jack of my own free will.

"Oh! Well, you know, I'm not really sure." She frowned, as if surprised by this apparent hole in her encyclopedia of knowledge. "I'm not sure you always have to like someone to like kissing them. But when you do like them, it's amazing. Like when I kissed Sam Hopkins for the first time. Wow." Her face got all dreamy. "I thought I was in heaven."

"Heaven, huh?"

Her description made me feel a little better. I wouldn't call what had happened in my backyard heaven. I'd enjoyed it, but there had been an edge of discomfort to the whole experience—like I knew it wasn't quite right.

It would be much, *much* better if Cam kissed me. Heaven, probably.

Not that that seemed like a serious possibility. We'd been hanging out for weeks, and he'd never made a move on me—and he'd had plenty of opportunities. If Cam did like me as more than just a friend, he had a funny way of showing it.

"Are you positive you aren't asking this question for a reason?" She narrowed her eyes. "Are you absolutely positive?"

"Oh, look." I pointed across the lot, hoping to distract her. I wasn't sure I could be a very convincing liar, especially if I had to repeat what I'd said to Hennie. She'd see through me in an instant. "Isn't that Hennie's car?"

"Yep, that looks like her." She shook her finger at me. "But don't think I'm going to forget about our little conversation."

"Okay, okay." This friend thing was a double-edged sword. It was nice to be able to ask these sorts of questions, but it also meant you couldn't keep secrets. Or at least you couldn't keep secrets about things like boys.

Hennie arrived, looking gorgeous as usual in a jean miniskirt and rose-colored shirt. Esther just had to tell her exactly what I had asked. Hearing the question retold made me squirm with embarrassment. Hennie looked at me with her usual deep, gentle gaze, and I had the feeling she already knew exactly why I had asked it.

But she didn't say anything about Jack or Cam. Instead she said, "I don't have nearly as much experience as Esther with boys. But last year at camp, Walter Maitland and I made out, and I'd had a crush on him forever."

"Walt Maitland?" Esther interrupted. "Are you kidding?"

"He's a lot cuter than when you knew him," Hennie said. "He plays football now. Anyway, I was going to say that Walt turned out to be a complete jerk. But he was so cute, I didn't even care. All I knew at the time was that I was finally kissing the guy I'd liked forever."

"And . . . ?" I prompted.

"Yeah, and . . . ?" Esther said. "I can't believe you've never told me this story before."

"And he was a great kisser," she pronounced with a grin. "I loved it."

Esther and I both groaned.

"So you're telling me exactly the opposite of what Esther said?" I asked.

"Not necessarily. I'm just saying he definitely wasn't the guy for me, but I still wanted to be with him for a little while."

"Basically there's nothing either of you can tell me," I said.

"Pretty much," Esther said.

"Thanks for clearing that up."

"Any time." Esther giggled.

A familiar black car with a dent in the side squealed into the parking lot. At the same time, the Silver Bullet arrived at the far side of the iron fence. Jack got out of the car, sunglasses shading his eyes, even though the sun had barely come up. He looked tougher than usual, with a leather jacket open at the neck and a pair of black jeans hanging low around his hips.

"How does a freshman get to drive, anyway?" Esther asked, nibbling her lip shrewdly as she watched him amble across the lot.

"He's got a fake license," I said without thinking, and then gave myself an inward kick. He probably hadn't meant for me to pass that information along.

"Oh." Esther's eyes widened.

Hennie's eyes narrowed, and she glanced back and forth between us. You could practically see the wheels turning in her brain, and I wondered if she was hearing that second voice she'd told us about in the library. Luckily for me, though, she was kind enough to not to say anything then and there.

Esther and Hennie weren't the only ones who'd spotted Jack. I noticed at least a dozen other heads turning, Allie's among them. This inspired a jolt of something—jealousy? Pride? I'd be lying if I didn't admit that part of me wanted everyone to know he had kissed me, that I had attracted the attention of someone good-looking and dangerous. But the bigger part felt a sense of regret. Watching him now with slightly more clinical eyes than I had before, I felt more certain than ever that I'd made the right decision.

The heavy iron gate retracted, and the metallic voice blared loud enough to be heard across the parking lot. "Caution, the gates are opening! Caution, the gates are opening!"

The Silver Bullet pulled through slowly and ground to a stop. Allie ran over to walk with Jack the rest of the way to the bus. Just before they passed out of view, he pushed up his sunglasses and swept his gaze around the lot. He could have been looking for anything, but I knew he was looking for me. He stopped a second later, his eyes locked on mine.

I jerked my gaze away.

"Jeez, Dancia, he looks pissed," Esther said in a hushed voice. "What did you do?"

I shivered, unable to keep from looking back at him. His silvery glare lasted only a minute before he dropped the glasses back down onto his nose. Then he turned to Allie, and they moved out of sight.

"It's hard to explain," I said, defeated. Jack had been my only chance for a friend who understood what it was like to have psychic powers. I should never have kissed him. I should have pushed him away from the start. Then maybe he wouldn't have gotten so angry at me, so hurt.

"You had to turn him down, didn't you?" Hennie said quietly.

I nodded. Hennie patted my arm, and Esther clucked sympathetically in the background.

"Whatever," I said, breaking the spell. "It's over. We should get on the bus."

We had gotten about halfway across the parking lot before Hennie realized she had left her backpack on the ground where we had been standing. We watched as she ran back to get it.

"Isn't that Yashir?" Esther said as a familiar dreadlocked form got out of a car across the lot.

"Yeah." I waved.

Yashir started toward us, on a path directly in line with Hennie. I could tell the moment she noticed him, because she slowed down and her back got really straight. She looked at her feet and then seemed to deliberately pick up her head.

"She's going to talk to him," I whispered to Esther. "She's really going to do it."

Yashir noticed Hennie at the same time. He said something to her, but they were too far away for me to hear what it was. From his smile a moment later, I assume Hennie answered him.

They were having an actual conversation.

Esther squeezed my arm. "This is *huge*," she said. We watched as they exchanged words, still walking toward each other. That was when Esther gasped in horror. "Dancia, look at Hennie's backpack. She's headed right for it!"

Sweet, clumsy Hennie was having her first conversation with the boy of her dreams, and she was on a collision course with her gigantic leather backpack. If she tripped now, she'd never recover from the embarrassment.

I thought quickly. "Esther, is that Chris? With a girl?" I pointed in the opposite direction at a boy in line to get on the bus. I hoped it wasn't really Chris, the guy Esther liked, because he had his arm slung around the shoulders of a blonde named Liz, from the cross-country team.

"What?" Esther spun around.

The moment she looked away, I focused on the backpack and marshaled the familiar tingle of energy. I poked at the forces acting on it, like I had at the tree branch, but that only made it lurch up a few inches and then drop back into place. Desperately, knowing I had only a few seconds, I imagined pushing down on one side of it, like a tiddledywink, and amazingly enough, it worked. Clumsily, the sturdy bag jumped a few inches to the left, landing just out of Hennie's path. Luckily, Yashir and Hennie were too focused on each other to notice the backpack's odd behavior.

"That's not Chris," Esther proclaimed, turning back to see Hennie standing next to Yashir, still talking. She grinned. "Oh, thank goodness she didn't trip. I thought she was a goner."

A warm feeling spread through me. "Yeah, thank goodness."

Jack didn't say a word to me for the next few days, and I tried not to show how hurt I was. It seemed crazy, because we'd only known each other a couple of months, but I'd come to rely on him even more than I had known. Without Jack to talk to, my classes dragged on endlessly, my homework was impossible, I had no idea what music to listen to, and Catherine's taunts and jabs were too much to bear.

By Thursday I was a wreck. Though I should have been thrilled that I'd found a way to use my power and not have it hurt someone, dealing with Jack's anger took away all the joy. Meanwhile, I barely talked to Cam. On Monday he told me he would be busy all week with a couple of big projects. I still looked for him every day at lunch and was absurdly disappointed when he wasn't there.

I suppose it was because of what had happened with Jack, I don't know, but I was desperate to talk to Cam. It wasn't like we were best friends, but I missed him and the little walks we used to take, and the time we climbed up that tree together in the woods. Sometimes when he passed me in the hall and waved, I felt like he was someone I had seen in a movie but didn't really know.

That made me feel even worse, like I had hurt Jack for a dream that would never come true.

Finally, after an endless morning of Jack glaring at me and teachers complaining about homework assignments I hadn't finished, I hurried down to the cafeteria. Standing at the entrance to the lunchroom, I tried to look like I was checking out the menu options instead of pathetically trying to locate Cam in the crowd.

My breath caught when, out of the corner of my eye, I saw Cam wave at me as he headed toward his usual table, Anna to his right. I tried to look surprised, as if I hadn't noticed him. He motioned for me to follow them. Anna smiled and repeated Cam's gesture, and then made a point of draping one arm over his, as if he was her property.

She was always like that. I'm not sure if she was jealous, precisely, but she certainly let me know that I was not going to get between her and Cam.

As I maneuvered my way around the masses, Catherine gave me her usual contemptuous sneer, from a table with a bunch of other Button-downs. Hennie waved at me as she collected her dessert. I didn't see Jack, but that wasn't unusual.

When I got to their table, Cam and Anna were sitting down, and he'd started to dig into a plateful of spaghetti and meatballs. He swallowed a mouthful in a hurry, and wiped his face clean.

"How's it going?" he said. "Seems like I haven't see you in forever."

"Yeah. I guess you've been busy." I regretted the words as soon as I said them. The last thing I wanted was to sound like I was whining about him not paying enough attention to me.

"I know. It's totally my fault and I'm really sorry about it. I'll make it up to you, I promise." Cam sounded eager to talk to me. So eager, in fact, that it made me suspicious. He changed positions to face me more directly, which meant Anna had to move her arm. She shot me a private glare and then put her hands in her lap.

Jack's words burned in my ears, and I had to force a friendly smile, even to Cam.

The sensation of someone watching crawled up my spine. I took a quick look around. Sure enough, Jack had appeared at the entrance to the lunchroom, and he was staring right at us.

"You should pull up a chair," Cam commanded. "We can make room."

"No, that's okay." It could have been the distaste directed my way from Anna, or perhaps Jack's voice ringing in my ears, but either way, the thought of sitting next to Cam had lost a bit of its magic. I nodded toward Esther, who was in line for lunch. "I told my friends I'd sit with them."

"We're your friends too," he protested.

Are you? I wanted to ask. Are you really? Instead I said, "I know, but I promised. We're going to compare our World Civ homework."

Anna sidled up closer to Cam and purred, "Dancia, do you still want to go for a run with me? Coach had to cancel practice today, so we could run together this afternoon."

I'd been putting off running with Anna ever since Cam had suggested it. By this point I'd used up every excuse I could imagine. The idea of being alone with her was almost as nauseating as eating with her, but I managed a fake smile. "Gosh, Anna, that is *so* nice of you. Thanks. I'd love to."

"Looking forward to it," she replied sweetly.

I had the feeling that Anna and I understood each other, and that our workout would be anything but fun.

"I guess I'll see you later, Cam." I started to walk away. He jumped up and followed me a few feet from the table.

"Don't let Anna intimidate you," he said softly. "Truth is, she's been a little weird since we broke up last summer. I should tell her to back off, but I don't have the heart to hurt her feelings. Know what I mean?"

His eyes pleaded with me. He looked sincere, but I wasn't convinced, and I guess I must have shown it.

He put a hand on my arm, and I jumped, struck as always by the way his touch made me want to melt onto the floor. "You have study hall sixth period, don't you? I've got my ethics seminar fifth and sixth period. We're starting independent study tomorrow, so I can go to the library if I want. I could tell Mrs. Langdon you're helping with my project, and we could hang out together."

I hesitated. Cam had the power to make my insides go squishy and my mind draw a blank, but that also meant he would have the power to turn me into a blubbering idiot if he turned out to be a fake. My heart warred with my head for a minute, but my heart prevailed. How could I turn down my dream?

"All right. I guess I could use a little time in the library."

He flashed his million-dollar smile. "I'll come get you."

I swallowed hard and made my way on unsteady feet to where I had seen Esther, not even noticing when Jack sprang up and headed in my direction. He caught up with me a few tables later.

"So, did you tell Prince Charming what you were doing last Friday?" he asked.

I tried not to react to the enmity in his voice. "Don't be like this, Jack."

Can't we just be friends, Jack? Please, please, please?

"I found something interesting this morning. Thought you might want to take a look."

I sighed and turned to face him. "What is it?"

"A little something I came across in your boyfriend's room. Something that might make you think twice before you keep letting him follow you around." He held up a piece of white paper that looked like a form someone had started filling in.

"What were you doing in his room?" I gaped at him, astonished, though I suppose I shouldn't have been. "Did you break in? That's illegal."

"I didn't break anything, and I reassembled the door before I left. They'll never suspect. But I thought you deserved to know the truth."

"What makes you so sure you know what the truth is?"

"I have good instincts," he said, his lips pressed together in a hard line. I was momentarily distracted by remembering what it felt like to have those lips on mine, but snapped back to attention when Jack pointed to the paper. "Take a look. It's about you. That's not illegal, is it? To steal something about yourself? Or someone you care about? Or thought cared about you?"

I snatched the paper out of his hand. Sure enough, at the top of the page it read, "Candidate: Dancia Lewis." Below that it said, "Watcher: Cam Sanders." There was a space for the date, and then the next line read, "Record any contact you had with the candidate today." There was some space for a response, and someone had written in blue blocky letters, "Met candidate on the bus and at lunch."

My hand started shaking.

"This isn't funny, Jack," I said, my voice quavering. "You made this up, didn't you."

"Why would I do that?"

"To make your point about Cam. To make me feel like crap."

"Keep reading. You tell me if I would make this up." He pointed halfway down the page to a new question that read, "Note any concerns you have about the candidate here, and your recommendations for addressing those concerns." In the same neat handwriting it said in response, "Candidate appears to be spending a great deal of time with Candidate Landry. (Concern about this alternative candidate noted on previous reports.) Will try to encourage candidate to keep her distance from Landry. Will attempt to build stronger relationship with candidate to allow for better surveillance."

The taste of acid filled my mouth.

"Don't look now," Jack whispered, leaning toward my ear, "but your Watcher is watching. I don't think he likes seeing me so close to you. I wonder what he'll put in his report tonight."

229

I grabbed the paper out of his hand. "You are a horrible person. If this is for real, I don't blame Cam for writing this about you."

Unable to think clearly, I started for the lunchroom door, my only desire to get as far as possible from Jack and Cam and everyone at Delcroix. But then I saw Cam stand up and amble toward one doorway, and Trevor make his way to the other. They moved casually but purposefully. It was like watching a movie.

They were guarding the exits so they could follow me if I left the room.

I couldn't be sure the paper was real, I reminded myself. Jack was not above making up something like this. Maybe it was coincidence, the way Cam and Trevor were now positioning themselves by the doors. Maybe there was a reasonable explanation for all of it. Like a science fair project or something.

I told myself to stay calm. I looked around and saw Esther and Hennie sitting at a table near the back of the room. I turned on my heels and headed in their direction.

I had no idea what was happening, or if Cam and Trevor were really watching. But if they were, I wasn't going to let them see me cry.

CHAPTER 25

I WADDED up the paper and shoved it into my back pocket. Then I pasted on a bright smile and joined Esther and Hennie at their table.

"What's going on? You look really pale—are you sick?" Hennie said immediately.

"This is my normal unhealthy skin color," I joked.

Esther pulled out the chair next to her, her eyes narrow. "What happened with Cam? Weren't you eating with him?"

"I told him I wanted to sit with my friends."

Hennie gazed intently at me. I knew she was listening to that "second voice," and had to use all my willpower to keep the fake smile pinned across my face.

"You said you'd rather sit with us than with him? That's crazy," she said.

"Why? He's not that great, you know. And I can't stand Anna." I collapsed into the chair and put my hands in my lap so they wouldn't see them trembling. Cam and Trevor disappeared from view, and I wondered if they were lurking somewhere in the halls, waiting for me to exit the cafeteria and go to class.

"Now I *know* there's something wrong with you," Esther

declared. "Not that great? He's amazing. He's like a dream man."

I winced. "Can we change the subject? I don't really want to talk about Cam right now."

"I'm sorry." Hennie put a hand on my shoulder. "Is there anything we can do?"

I choked back a fresh wave of tears. I will not cry, I will not cry, I chanted to myself. "No, it's not a big deal."

Not a big deal unless Cam was actually some sort of a hired stalker who was only pretending he liked me because someone at Delcroix said he had to.

"If he was mean to you, he's in big trouble." Esther made a fist and slammed it menacingly into her open palm.

"Yeah," Hennie agreed. "We'll take him down for you, Dancia. No problem."

The image of delicate, fragile Hennie whacking Cam in the kneecaps with a baseball bat leaped to my mind, and I started to giggle. It was one of those giggles that verges on complete hysteria, but at least part of it was genuine. Esther joined in, and then Hennie. I laughed so hard, tears ran down my cheeks.

Once we had control of ourselves, Hennie said, "Seriously, Dancia. We'd do anything for you. That's what friends are for, you know."

I nodded and gazed at them gratefully through a watery haze. "Yeah, absolutely. That's what friends are for."

Ten minutes later I choked down the remainder of my garden burger, said good-bye to Esther and Hennie, and went to my locker to retrieve my books for fifth period— English I. The halls were filled with slamming doors, laughter, and shouting. I felt like I was in a reality show, and any second someone would come by to interview me about my experience at Delcroix. "Everyone's really nice," I would confide. "We're just like any other high school kids." And everyone watching would roll their eyes because they would know the truth, that we weren't the least bit like other kids.

I was the first one to class, so I watched everyone file into the room. I imagined which of them might be candidates, like me. Or were we all candidates? I could already see the Watcher reports for Esther and Hennie: *Candidates assimilating well. No concerns to note, other than association with Candidate Lewis. Will continue to monitor closely.*

Who were the other Watchers anyway? Was Trevor one? He showed up at Ethics every now and then. Mr. Fritz said he was working on a special project, but now I wondered if the notes he was taking were about us, not Mr. Fritz's lectures. Come to think of it, Jack had complained weeks ago that Trevor was practically a fixture on their side of the residence hall, and even though it was almost Thanksgiving, he was still counting us every day at lunch.

My thoughts were driving me back to the edge of hysteria, so I tried to distract myself by opening up my backpack and arranging my notebook and pen carefully on the desk. The only problem was, I'd doodled Cam's name into the notebook over and over again, and so looking at it, of course, made me think of him.

Could he really betray me like that? I didn't necessarily believe he liked me, but I'd never imagined he didn't even want to be my friend, that hanging out with me was nothing more than his job. Fortunately, *that* depressing thought was interrupted by the start of the lecture.

"Thank you all for coming to class on time. Now, we're going to jump right into the politics of fifteenth-century England. Can any of you tell me what you learned this weekend about that time period?"

After receiving a few halfhearted responses, our teacher, Mr. Phillips, began to drone from the front of the room. We were starting our first Shakespeare play, and it wasn't even fun Shakespeare, like *Romeo and Juliet*. It was boring Shakespeare—*Henry V*. Which meant that we had to learn about the history of the time, the politics, and Henry's crazy partying days before he'd assumed the crown. This might have been fascinating to the fifteen-year-old boys in the class, but it left me cold.

The lump of paper in my back pocket kept nudging me, making me squirm on my seat. Didn't I owe it to Cam to keep my mind open? Give him the opportunity to explain himself? If I lost his friendship because I'd believed Jack over him, and it turned out Jack was lying, I'd regret it forever.

But then there was Delcroix and all the strange things that had happened since I'd started here. The men following Jack and me, the fact that we both felt a shock when we shook Cam's hand, Jack's powers, the odd construction of the third floor . . . the list was too long to ignore.

As much as I wanted it to, this mystery wasn't going away. And unfortunately, I made a lousy Nancy Drew. But I couldn't sit there in my seat and pretend nothing was going on. I had to know the truth, and that meant I needed to talk to Cam.

"Mr. Phillips, I'm not feeling very well. Can I go to the bathroom?"

He cleared his throat, his train of thought clearly interrupted by my question. "What's that? Not feeling well? Should I call the nurse?"

"No, no." I made my way toward his desk through a maze of backpacks and legs, and whispered close to his face. "It's a girl thing. I'll need to go to my locker first, if that's okay."

This was a foolproof way to prevent a male teacher from inquiring too deeply into your intentions. He immediately flushed a dark purple color and grabbed a hall pass from his desk. "Of course," he whispered back. "Take your time."

I left my bag there and sprinted up the stairs to the third floor.

At the start of school I would have ignored the paper, ignored Jack, and slunk into a hole where I wouldn't have caused too much trouble. The thought of confronting someone and admitting the truth about my power would have been impossible—particularly to a guy on whom I had a gargantuan crush. But something in me had changed since I'd started at Delcroix. Something that made me refuse to put my tail between my legs.

I had a power that could make extraordinary things happen. I needed to learn to control it. I knew that now. It wasn't evil and neither was I. It was time to stop acting like I was.

I was through with secrets. It was time for the truth.

The third floor felt strangely still, as if a heavy hand were weighing on the air. Most of the doors were closed, and when I walked by I could see small groups of students inside, either playing instruments, watching a teacher write notes on a whiteboard, or singing in small groups around a piano.

I reached the far end and turned down the hall where Jack thought there was a secret passage. I had thought the ethics seminars met in those rooms, but as I peered through the tiny windows in the doors, I saw they were all empty.

Shoot. I dug my nails into my palm and blew out an annoyed breath. Cam had said something about his ethics seminar doing independent studies, but I thought they were starting tomorrow. I thought they'd be here today. Frustrated,

I slipped into a classroom and stared at the back wall, gnawing on a hangnail while I tried to figure out my next step.

I might be able to catch Cam after school, but then he'd be going to play soccer, and other guys would be around. We'd never be able to talk in private. Then I had practice, and then there was dinner, and then study hours. I'd have to wait until tomorrow.

I turned to leave, but a tug of curiosity stopped me a few feet from the door. Shaking my head, I paced the distance from the front to back wall. Thirty paces. Just like Jack had measured. What did it mean?

I was standing there staring at the back wall when I heard the voices. They were muffled, but the closer I got to the wall, the clearer they became. I realized the sound was coming from behind the wall—exactly where Jack had thought a secret passage might lie. At first I strained to make out the voices while facing the hall, so I could run if I saw anyone approaching. But as the murmuring continued and I started to catch scattered words, I abandoned caution and pressed my ear against the wall.

The voices varied in volume, as if people were walking around. The conversation sounded heated, possibly an argument. When I realized one of the speakers was Cam, I felt a surge of adrenaline so strong I had to lean against the wall to keep my balance.

". . . really like her . . . not what a Watcher does . . ." I strained to hear the rest, but only scattered words were audible.

"Sometimes a Watcher needs to be a little more creative," a low, persuasive voice rolled out. I immediately realized it was Mr. Judan. You couldn't mistake that deep soothing bass rumble.

He faded, and all I could hear was a sound like a train in the distance. Then he came closer, and I could make out words again. "He's the most powerful candidate we've identified in decades, except, perhaps, for Dancia herself."

Powerful? Me?

"If they were to go rogue together, the entire country could be in danger," Mr. Judan continued.

"I don't . . ." Cam's voice trailed off again.

Cam, speak up! I wanted to scream. But his voice simply didn't carry like Mr. Judan's. "Agree he's a danger . . . doing my best to keep them apart . . ."

"No excuses." Mr. Judan's voice cut through Cam's higher-pitched murmur. "They went home together Friday. You must see that that doesn't happen again. I don't care what you have to do. You took an oath, my boy, to defend Delcroix and the rest of the world from those who would use their gifts for selfish or dangerous ends. This is when you make good on that oath."

There was a long silence.

Finally Cam said, "Don't worry, I won't let you down."

I heard footsteps and picked my head up abruptly. It suddenly occurred to me that I had no idea how they got behind the wall, and that I could be standing right in their path. Tiptoeing as quickly and quietly as my sneakers would allow, I made my way back to the door, then ran down the hall all the way back to English, my head buzzing.

Obviously, Jack was right. Something unbelievable was going on at Delcroix, and Cam was knee-deep in it.

"Ah, Dancia. I was just about to send someone to find you." Mr. Phillips sighed with relief when I marched back into the classroom.

I plopped the hall pass down on his desk. "No need. I'm

back." It had only been ten minutes. Ten minutes, but my life had changed completely.

"Are you ready to run?" Anna laced her shoes into a double knot and straightened her ponytail. It was a rare sunny November day, with delicate beams of light filtering through the canopy of fir trees.

"Today was supposed to be a long run for me, so I'll probably do about ten miles. But you should feel free to stop before that." Anna adjusted the waistband on her tiny black-and-pink running tights, which neatly exposed her perfectly toned stomach. She had a matching bra-top to go with the tights.

I was wearing my old Danville Central Hospital T-shirt and cotton sweatpants.

"Fine with me." It would have been nice for my ego to pretend I could keep up with Anna, but there was just no way. When she started running she was like some kind of machine. She'd just run and run, and never even seem to get tired.

She started at a leisurely pace for the first hundred yards or so. The trail was wide enough for two, and we stayed side by side, even though I was dying to drop behind so I wouldn't have to look at her. We dipped down a small incline and then up an embankment on the other side. This seemed to be a marker for Anna, because she shot off like someone had fired a starting pistol.

I struggled to catch up, breathing hard even though we had just begun.

"I guess you're pretty into Cam, huh?" she said.

I wiped the beads of sweat already forming on my brow. "What's that?" I gulped some air. "He's a good friend, I guess."

Or not. I didn't really know *what* he was anymore. Just like I didn't know what to think about Mr. Judan, or anyone else at this stupid school. Anna was probably setting me up for something too.

She snorted. "Friend? Hmph." We zigzagged around a fallen log and a muddy spot in the trail. Anna neatly avoided both. A branch poked my ankle, and I splashed mud on my shirt.

"What's that supposed to mean?" I forced out between pants.

Anna slowed her insane pace a hair, even though she hadn't yet broken a sweat. "I don't know how to tell you this, but I would stay away from him if you don't want to get your heart broken."

I couldn't believe it—first Jack, now Anna lecturing me about Cam? I sucked in a desperate lungful of air, trying to concentrate on what Anna was saying while keeping from tripping over my own sneakers.

"He's a little out of my league," I said. "I never thought we were more than friends."

Anna nodded. We ran in silence for minute, and then she said, "So, what's the deal with you and Jack?"

I stopped dead still in the trail for a moment. "Jack?" I sputtered.

In a matter of seconds, all I could see was Anna's back disappearing into the dense foliage. I ran hard to catch her; I think she might have slowed down a fraction to let me do so, but it was hard to tell.

"He's a friend, that's all," I called, still a few feet behind. "Why?" She didn't answer, so I ran faster until we were side by side again. My lungs burned, and a cramp had started under my ribs. "Why does everyone want to talk about Jack?" I cried in frustration.

"I was just wondering. He is awfully cute." She wove delicately around a stump and a narrow section of trail. "I guess if he was my friend, I'd be keeping my eye out for him."

"What? What do you mean?" Something in her tone sent a chill down my back.

"I just mean not everyone around here likes him as much as you do. You might want to tell him that."

The trail turned and crossed out of the woods to flank the playing fields. A small group of guys chased a soccer ball, while a group of girls and guys tossed a Frisbee.

Anna stopped, and I almost plowed into her back. She rested her arms on top of her head and stared at the soccer players. I realized one of them must be Cam. A second later he broke away from the pack long enough to wave at us.

I didn't wave back. I hung down over my knees and tried desperately to catch my breath. He rejoined the game.

"Jerk," Anna muttered.

We started running again, this time in silence.

As I settled into my stride, I tried to interpret Anna's strange warning. Cam's animosity toward Jack was hardly a secret, but was she suggesting Cam might be capable of hurting him? That was hard to believe. More likely, Anna was so bitter about being dumped that she was now spinning stories about Cam. Or maybe she was hoping I'd rush to Jack's defense, and that would turn Cam against me.

It was all pretty far-fetched, but the worst part was, whatever code she was speaking, I didn't get the feeling she was lying.

"Why are you telling me this?" I summoned the nerve to ask. "You don't even like me."

Anna checked her watch. "Not everything's about you, Dancia."

With that she shook her ponytail and effortlessly length-ened her stride. I stopped on the trail and watched as she sped away from me, her brown hair swinging behind her like a flag.

CHAPTER 26

I SUFFERED through my usual evening of studying, ignoring Catherine, and pretending I fit in with twenty-five other clueless freshmen who had no absolutely idea what was going on behind the walls of their fancy private school. Just before lights-out, a fight broke out in the bathroom when Cara accused Hannah of stealing her razor. Hannah, in turn, accused Cara of using her hair spray. Sides were taken and tears ensued. Parties sent emissaries back and forth between rooms. Hennie got involved to negotiate a truce and soothe hurt feelings.

Catherine gave them all dirty looks and went back to our room and slammed the door. For once I was relieved to be able to follow her and go straight to bed. I had enough real drama in my life. I didn't need the manufactured kind.

Cam wasn't at lunch the next day, so I sat with Esther and Hennie. I purposely put my back to the doors of the cafeteria so I couldn't watch to see if he'd come in. My friends seemed to know something was up, and didn't mention Cam once. Esther had a short story due in her creative writing class, and Hennie had a vocabulary quiz in Hindi, so they didn't have time to pay much attention to me anyway. I bit my fingernails, poked at my taco salad, and refused to even look at Jack. As far as I could tell, he was ignoring me too.

I barely heard a word Mr. Phillips said during English; I just stared at the clock and counted the minutes until I could run to study hall. Cam had said he would come get me then. Even with Anna's odd warning ringing in my ears, I still wanted desperately to see him, all the while dreading the moment I would look into his eyes and know how he really felt.

Though I was convinced he would deny everything, I had decided to confront Cam about the "Watcher report." I just couldn't give up on him completely. Part of me still believed there was a way out of this, an explanation for the whole awful mess. The paper lay tucked into my back pocket, wrinkled from where I'd wadded it up the day before.

I started to panic the moment he entered the room. That wavy hair tickling the edges of his ears, those broad shoulders, and the smile that seemed to work even on teachers. It all had a magical effect, and I suddenly couldn't imagine even suggesting that he was involved in anything so ugly as what the paper might suggest.

He handed my teacher, Mrs. Westerly, an official-looking yellow sheet, and she beckoned for me to approach her desk.

"Dancia, Cameron has requested that you assist in his seminar project. I don't normally allow freshmen to opt out of study hall so early in the year, but he has personally vouched for you." She glared at me over the top of her glasses.

Mrs. Westerly liked to think of herself as being tough.

"Now, you may go to the library," she continued in a stern voice, "but nowhere else. Understood?"

"Okay." I gulped.

Cam gave me an encouraging *Don't worry about it, I'll take care of everything* look. "Thank you, Mrs. Westerly," he said.

"I'm holding you responsible, Cameron," she warned.

"I understand."

I went back to my desk to grab my books, and a few of the girls in the class gave me jealous looks. It was a good thing I had given up on my fade-into-the-background plan. All the time I'd been spending with Cam had made me a bit of a celebrity among the freshman girls. Even Allie had asked me a week or two ago whether we were going out.

Cam's arm brushed against mine as I walked out the door, and he gave me a little wink. My confusion deepened. Could he really be this good an actor? How could he be so sweet, and so devious?

"How was your run with Anna?" he asked. "I saw you guys yesterday, by the practice field. You looked like you were working hard. I hope everything went okay?" He took his time with the words, as if making sure he said precisely the right thing.

I considered my response just as carefully. Anna was one of Cam's best friends, and his ex-girlfriend. I wouldn't do myself any favors being catty about her. "It was . . . challenging. She's very fast. And serious about what she does."

We walked passed the trophies and plaques on the wall by the front door. I stopped in front of a picture of a team of runners. Each person held out a silver medal. Anna was standing in front of the group. She had a grim smile on her face, as if she were trying hard to look happy.

"You know, that's at last year's state championships. She was pissed they only got second," Cam looked at the picture with a mix of admiration and something else—regret? Was he sorry that he had broken up with Anna?

"I get the feeling she can be a bit competitive." I lingered, shifting between watching Cam and studying the picture. I wished for something in his body language that would tell me how he felt about her.

"Now that's an understatement." Cam pointed to the stairs. "We should go. I'll get in all kinds of trouble if we get caught in the hall."

I took one last look at Anna's face and followed Cam up the stairs. We passed the front desk and wound around the stacks. The library extended through several connected rooms, and Cam seemed to know where he was going. I kept my mouth shut and followed, trying to ignore the curious gazes I felt directed our way.

We maneuvered around study cubes hidden at the ends of shelves, and around dark corners of the library I didn't even know existed. Finally, Cam led us through a set of double doors to a dim, windowless room, where one fluorescent light flickered overhead.

We sat down at the only desk in the room, and Cam pulled his chair beside me. He cleared his throat. "I have something I want to talk to you about—" he started to say, but I interrupted him.

"I have something I need to say first." Somewhere in my tortured mind, it occurred to me that if I didn't say something quick, he would turn up the charm and I would end up drooling and mindless, unable to do anything but sit at his feet like an obedient lap dog.

I took a deep breath and steeled myself for confrontation. I pulled the crinkled paper out of my back pocket and spread it out on the table in front of us. "What's this, Cam? What's a Watcher?"

He leaned forward to examine the paper, and his eyes widened. His cheeks went white, then red. "Where did you . . . How did you get that?"

Jack hadn't made it up. My last bit of hope dissolved. "I don't think that matters. I just want to know what it means."

"Jesus, Dancia. You shouldn't have this." His voice was barely above a whisper.

Pain, sharp and sudden, laced through my heart. "It's about me, isn't it? Don't I have a right to know if I'm being watched?"

"Did Landry give you that?" He slammed his hand down on the paper. "I knew I felt a disturbance in my room yesterday. He must have broken in while I was grabbing breakfast."

"It doesn't matter where I got it, Cam," I said flatly. "I want to know what it means."

"It's for your own good," he said, through pinched lips. "For everyone's good."

"Delcroix isn't just a private school, is it? What else is going on here? Is this some government thing?"

He shook his head. "No, of course not. Look, it's not what it seems. It's nothing bad. Honestly."

I waited for him to explain, but he just kept staring at the page, his shoulders tight, his foot tapping the ground rapidly as if he were waging some internal battle. I waged my own battle, fighting the desire to collapse with the pain—the sheer heartache of having all my insecurities proven horribly, completely true—and the desire to punch Cam right across his perfectly square jaw. Finally I grabbed my backpack and stood up.

"Listen, if you're not going to tell me what's going on, I'll find out myself. At least I know why you've been so nice to me. From now on I won't let myself fall for it." I started to walk away, but he caught my arm.

"Dancia, it's not that I don't want to tell you. But I can't." His eyes pleaded with me. "And I do like you. I like you a lot. That's why this is all such a mess. You've got to believe me."

I tried to shake off his arm, but he held on tighter. "Cam." My voice broke. "Don't make a fool out of me. Please."

He pulled me gently back down into my chair, taking my hand in his. Reluctantly, I set my backpack on the floor and let our eyes meet.

He will not turn my brain to pea soup, I chanted to myself.

"I do have to watch you," he said, his gaze even softer than usual—almost tender. "But I would have done it anyway. What I said to you that day I got the message from my dad was true—you're a real friend, Dancia. Someone special."

"You've got friends, Cam," I said. "You don't need me."

"But you're different from other girls I know. You're more"—he fumbled for the word—"more real. Like you don't pretend to be something you're not."

I laughed sourly. "You have no idea how wrong you are. I've been pretending all my life. I guess of all people, my Watcher should know that."

"You may have hidden your gift," he said, "and you had every reason to do that. But you've never hidden yourself. You've always been Dancia—tough and funny, absolutely determined, and a fierce protector for those who need you. I admire that a lot. I admire *you*. You've got to believe me."

How did he manage to keep getting my hopes up when I knew at the end of the day he was just going to crush them?

"Look, things are all messed up right now because of

247

this." He let go of my hand and gestured toward the Watcher report. "But I seriously like you, Dancia." For the first time since I'd met him, he seemed hesitant. "In fact, the main reason I haven't tried to be anything more than just friends was because of the whole Watcher thing. I didn't want to get those things mixed up. You're too important to me." He pushed his chair back from the desk. "I'm sure you're pissed at me. I understand that. But there's more to us than this paper. I just hope you can believe me."

My heart turned to a puddle of mush, along with what was left of my anger, but somehow I managed to find my voice. "I don't understand what's going on here. How can I believe a word you say when you won't tell me the truth?"

He sighed and ran his fingers through his hair, scattering the ends around his face. "If I tell you, I'll have to tell Mr. Judan," he said under his breath, looking around as if expecting Judan to materialize right there in front of us. "He's supposed to be the one to make the decision on whether to tell candidates about the program." Cam picked up the Watcher report and glared at the paper as if it were responsible for all his troubles.

Just when the silence had become too much, he continued, "This is really big, Dancia. Really important. If I tell you, you can't tell anyone else. I'm serious. No one. Are you sure you want to know the truth?" The intensity radiated from him in waves. He was almost trembling in his concern.

I paused. "I can't tell anyone? Even my grandma?" It occurred to me that if my powers were real, and there was a whole school dedicated to kids like me, maybe I could finally tell Grandma the truth.

"No." His eyes were suddenly hard and sharp. "It's for her own good. Once you know about Delcroix, you could be in danger yourself. It's not something to take lightly. And Jack can never know. It would be incredibly dangerous. You have to promise me that."

I thought about Anna's crazy warning—about someone being out to get Jack—but things were moving so quickly, I was too dazed and overwhelmed to ask more questions. All I knew was that I was finally going to learn the truth.

"I promise."

He stood up abruptly. "There's no going back now, you understand?"

If he was trying to scare me, he was doing a good job. "Sure," I said, trying not to let him see how terrified I was.

Slowly, he walked over to the doors that led back into the main library, closed them with a soft click, and turned a lock under the handle. The fluorescent light gave everything in the room a greenish-gray glow.

Cam's face became ghostly. "Follow me."

CHAPTER 27

WE WALKED to the far corner of the room, where the flickering light cast long shadows on the books. Cam reached up to the top of a metal shelving unit, moved a book aside, and punched a series of buttons on a hidden keypad. A soft whirring sound began high overhead, and the row of books on the wall to our left creaked softly.

"It only stays open for a second," he said. "You'll have to squeeze in right after me. Don't let yourself fall behind."

As if spinning on some giant axis, the bookcase revolved about twenty degrees to the left; just enough for Cam to turn sideways and slip inside. As soon as I crossed the threshold, the whirring started again, and the bookcase swung back into place.

For a second, it was pitch black. I fought the desire to scream like a girl in a bad horror movie, until the absurdity of it all—a secret passageway behind a bookcase? You've got to be kidding me!—brought a smile to my face. A light turned on overhead, revealing a narrow corridor illuminated by glowing white lightbulbs. Cold air clung to sterile gray walls.

"Where are we?" I whispered, the smile fading. Something about the place made me feel like I was in a prison. Or a should-have-been-closed mental institution.

"Behind the library. We go up a flight of stairs to get to the other library. That's what I need to show you."

He didn't sound like he wanted to chat, so I shut my mouth and followed him up a circular staircase with a cold metal railing and industrial-plastic steps.

Lights turned on above us as we climbed. Cam reached the top and disappeared from view. I gripped the chilly railing tightly, my legs shaking so badly I feared I would do something horrifically embarrassing, like trip and smash my face into the steps above.

We passed through a hole in the ceiling, my head emerging step by step as what had been the ceiling turned into the floor. That was when I got my first look at Cam's big secret.

It was another library. A small, narrow one, with books along one wall and deep window wells on the other, the windows covered by pieces of plywood. Everything was gray and a little dingy, as if the cleaning crew didn't get back here often enough. I got to the top of the stairs and walked slowly to the first shelf, tilting my head to read the titles.

The Science of Levitation
Using Your Talent for Shape-changing
Unlocking the Power: Turning Mass to Energy in Everyday Objects
A New State: Altering States of Matter Through Chemistry

"Delcroix isn't just a school for geniuses," Cam said flatly. "That's part of what we do here, but only part. More important, we look for people like you, Dancia. People with special talents."

I gulped. "What do you mean, like me?"

"Your power," he said. "If you want to talk truth, here it is.

251

We've known about your secret for some time. We recruited you because of it."

I should have expected it by this point, but somehow hearing him say it out loud made me dizzy. I swayed toward the wall behind me.

Cam grabbed me around the waist and set me in a window well. "Put your head between your knees," he commanded.

I dutifully obeyed, feeling like a complete idiot, peeking out to see his chest only inches away. When the world stopped spinning, I lifted my head. "I think I'll be okay."

He gave me a half smile. "Sorry about that. I didn't mean to completely freak you out. I guess it's a bit of a shock, huh?"

"A bit."

"I felt the same way when they told me."

We sat for a minute in silence. I stared at the rows of books on the wall. Many looked old, with cracked leather bindings and gold edges to the pages. Others were relatively new, but all had been extensively used. Nothing on the shelves looked untouched.

My anger dissolved into something more like relief. As weird as it all was, a weight was lifting from my shoulders. I didn't have to pretend anymore.

"You knew about me all along?"

"Well, not exactly. We knew someone in Danville was using a Level Three Talent, but you only used it sporadically and somehow without attracting much attention. Most people can't get to Level Three without training, and we usually hear about those that do. You were harder to identify than most. It wasn't until the incident at the hospital that we could trace it all back to you."

I leaned back against the window. "A Level Three Talent?

What's that? How did you know someone was using one?"

He began to pace as he spoke, and I had the sense this was a speech he had given before. "Everyone at Delcroix— actually, everyone in the world—has a talent. Most talents are basic everyday stuff. They can be as simple as being a good cook or having a knack for throwing great parties. Those are Level One Talents. Level Two gets you noticed. Those are your geniuses, your computer hackers—the type we recruit for Delcroix. Level Twos are people like your friend Hennie, who can read people so well it's like she's reading their mind, or Esther, whose impersonations are incredible. Some Level Twos stay there, some can be trained to go even higher. If Hennie takes her talent to the next level, she'll actually be able to read minds. Esther could learn to shape-shift. You're a Level Three. Someone who can use her mind to do extraor- dinary things."

"Esther could shape-shift?" I thought about how she said her pants got looser sometimes when she pretended to be someone. Maybe she was already a Level Three Talent and they just didn't know it. "Can you tell me how it works?" I whispered, both excited and terrified to finally learn about my power. "What it is I'm doing?"

He shook his head. "Not until we experiment with you a little. You know, ask you to do certain things and observe the results. But my guess is that you're playing with some of the forces of nature, perhaps with gravity. Everyone's talent is a little different, but they fall into some general catego- ries. Earth Talents, like yours, can manipulate the chemical and physical forces of the earth. Life Talents have extraor- dinary powers to understand, persuade, and communicate with people and animals. Somatic Talents have extraordi- nary bodily powers—Trevor, for example, can see through

253

walls. I have a Life Talent for recognizing other talents. I feel a resonance when someone nearby uses their power. It's hard to describe, almost like a vibration. And I felt that resonance over the past few years probably every time you used your power."

Forces of nature. Gravity. That sounded right.

"Can a person have more than one talent?" After all, Jack had said he felt something when I used my power, sort of like what Cam described, but Jack could also change the form of things.

"Yes, but usually one talent is more powerful than the others. I'm a Level Three for recognition, Level Two for persuasion. It's why people always vote for me to be class president. I could probably use my persuasion to be a really good politician, but not much else. But if it was my primary talent, I could learn to control people's minds. Mr. Judan's a Level Three for persuasion."

I shivered. I knew there was something spooky about Mr. Judan. "Is there a Level Four?"

He stopped pacing. "After Level Three, it gets messy. There have been reports in the past of Level Fours, but there aren't any around today, so we can't be sure. But you're already a strong Level Three, and you haven't even been trained."

"How does it work? Your recognition thing, I mean."

"The first time I touch a Level Three Talent, I get a vibration. I think you may have felt it when we first shook hands."

I nodded. "It felt like a shock. I always wondered about that."

"Normally, you wouldn't even feel it. It's a . . . meeting of energies." He shrugged helplessly. "I don't know quite how to describe it. We typically don't even try to identify Level Threes until midway through freshman year, and the candidate doesn't even know what's happened. But with you and with Jack, things were different from the start. When I touched you it was a hundred times stronger than anything I'd ever felt before. You jumped a mile. Mr. Judan even saw it. That's when we knew how powerful you were, and how important it was to get you into Delcroix."

"Why don't you tell the"—I fumbled over the word— "candidates . . . what Delcroix's really all about?"

"We can't go around training just anyone to use these kinds of powers. What if they were to use them for the wrong purposes? Can you imagine how dangerous that could be? We make them take the pledge to get into Delcroix, but we can't stop there."

I nodded. He looked so grave, so serious, that I got a little scared. If I could put someone into a coma, and I didn't even know what I was doing, think about what I could do with a little training.

Cam continued his explanation. "Before we start formal training, we subject candidates to significant stresses and challenges, and we investigate their reactions. We cannot risk training someone who will use their powers for evil. So we watch and wait. That's why we do the wall and other group experiences. At the beginning of sophomore or junior year we invite those students who show they can be trusted to join the program."

He approached my seat in the window well and put a hand next to my knee. Then he leaned forward until I could feel his breath on my face. There was so much information coming at me, I could barely take it all in, but at that moment, all I could think about was Cam saying that the reason he hadn't tried to be more than friends was because of the Watcher thing.

It was enough to make me dizzy all over again.

"Throughout all of it, we have a network of Watchers monitoring the progress of each candidate. Some are teachers, like Mr. Fritz, who watch candidates in the classroom. Most are other students, like me and Trevor and Anna. We each get assigned a handful of candidates, and we find ways to spend time with them. We participate in activities with our candidates, offer to help with homework, and observe them in the dining hall. Although each of us is assigned specific students to watch, we work together closely so we don't make anyone uncomfortable. For example, Anna might keep an eye on you during cross-country, while I might be there for you at lunch."

I swallowed hard. "So someone's watching me all the time? Pretending to be my friend and then taking notes about the things I say or do?"

"You're making it sound worse than it is. Most candidates don't know about their talent, but they do know they're different. They've often been ostracized or bullied for the very gifts that we want to encourage. They need extra attention. We're giving them that attention. We don't watch because we want to hurt anyone. We watch because we care about our candidates. We want to be there for them. And if they start going down the wrong path, we need to know that too."

I wasn't entirely convinced, but Cam's face was so open and sincere, it was hard to doubt that he believed what he was saying. "Does everyone have a Watcher?"

"Not exactly. The teachers, advisers, and team leaders

do some reporting on every freshman. Technically, you're all candidates. But the reality is that most people never get past Level Two. Only a handful of candidates will be brought into the program, and we usually know who those people are before school even starts. Those are the ones who are given an individual Watcher."

"Are you watching Jack?" I had to ask, even though his very name felt like taboo.

"We all watch Jack," Cam said grimly. "We know too much about him not to. But officially he's assigned to Trevor."

My gaze darted around, meeting his and then pushing back, like the wrong end of a magnet bumping against another. "Okay. So what's the program?"

"Different things for different people. There's basic lessons, learning more about how talents work, the forces that they utilize, that sort of thing. After that you specialize. For me, it's learning how to read the vibrations I feel, how to identify more about a candidate than simply whether they have a Level Three Talent or not. They think maybe I can learn to tell from the time I recruit someone whether they can be trusted in the program. You'll learn about the forces you can control, and make sure you know exactly what you're doing so your talent doesn't end up hurting anyone."

That made me shudder. I had hurt people. For years, I had hurt people every time I used my talent. Did Cam know that? What would he think of me if he ever found out?

"What happens to the ones who aren't asked to join the program?" I said.

He turned around and rested his back against the edge of the windowsill, staring forward as he ran his fingers through his hair. "Most of them never figure out what they could have been. They go through Delcroix, get trained in a lesser talent, and go on with their lives. The ones that do figure it out, well, that's why the program exists in the first place. To protect the rest of the world from the ones who would do harm."

I looked down at my hands. "And you think I could do that? Help protect people?"

Cam reached over and laced our fingers together. My hand appeared small and white, almost fragile next to his. "We don't really know what you're capable of, Dancia. But when you're upset, even the air around you sparkles. That day in Mr. Fritz's class, when you had the trip-to-the-moon activity, you did something that felt like an earthquake. I practically busted down the door of the girls' bathroom, I was so worried about you. Mr. Fritz had to call me off and get your friend Allie in to check on you instead."

A part of me melted into the window well. Cam had been worried about me.

He smiled and turned back toward me. The corners of his eyes crinkled, and my stomach fluttered. "There's extraordinary power in you. We just have to find a way—carefully—to unleash it."

I don't know what might have happened then, because the sound of feet tromping up the circular staircase broke the silence. A head emerged from the floor below, then another. First Trevor, then Anna, then two other people I vaguely recognized from the lunch table.

"Holy shit, Cam. What's going on?" Trevor demanded.

Anna's eyes bugged out. She looked at Cam, then me, then our hands still knitted together, her face growing whiter by the second.

Cam straightened but didn't let go of my hand. "I thought you guys were going to the woods today."

"It started raining." Trevor ran up the last few steps and threw up his hands in disbelief. "Jesus, Cam, I know you like her, but have you lost your mind?" He glared at both of us, his eyes blazing. Normally I would have been terrified, but his wrath seemed reserved primarily for Cam. "We watch and protect, Cam. This isn't protecting. This just exposes her to more danger."

Cam's hand tightened on mine. Stupid as it was, that tiny piece of confirmation from Trevor meant more to me than almost anything Cam had said. Besides, it was oddly comforting to think that Trevor—scary Trevor—was looking out for me. If I hadn't been completely freaked out by the group of them staring at me, I think I would have smiled.

"You don't understand," Cam said, shooting me a quick look. "She figured it out herself. Most of it, anyway. I was just filling in a few details. Not that it really matters, because we all know it's just a matter of time before she's up here with us. And I would stand for her. Right now if necessary."

"How could you stand for her?" Anna demanded. "You barely know her. And what about Jack? She's attached to him. I know it."

Cam's mouth set in a hard line. "I'm her recruiter and her Watcher. I know. Besides, you've heard her history. She's already shown how she'll use her talent. And trust me, Landry isn't a problem."

Clearly, "stand for her" meant something important, which was pretty cool. Still, it pissed me off to have Anna and Cam discussing Jack and me. I wondered how many times they'd done that since school started, and got even madder. Watching me for a few months at school didn't mean they knew me—or Jack, for that matter. They didn't know how he helped me when Catherine was so mean I almost lost it.

They didn't know how we studied together and explored the school together.

They didn't know how terrified he was of being followed.

And what did Cam mean when he said that Jack wasn't a problem?

I hated to do it, but I pulled my hand free from Cam and jumped off the windowsill. "I should go," I muttered, and started to make my way around the group.

Anna put her hands on her hips and glared, though I couldn't tell if she was directing her anger more at Cam or at me.

Trevor raised a chilly eyebrow. "Dancia, whether you like it or not, Cam's just made you one of us. Leaving won't change that."

Cam walked over and stood at my side. "Trevor's right. You're part of a new team now. For better or worse."

From the other end of the hall, an unmistakable voice boomed. "Cameron! What's going on here!?"

Mr. Judan had arrived.

CHAPTER 28

"DELCROIX IS affiliated with two other training programs in the United States, and several others worldwide. Most of the teachers here, though not all, are familiar with our true mission: to develop extraordinary talents and see that they are put in service to the good of humanity."

I squirmed in the lush velvet armchair Mr. Judan had directed me toward upon entering his office, wishing I could pace the floor like Cam. The large windowless room was surprisingly opulent, with elegant brass lamps, an antique-looking loveseat, and portraits of men wearing old-fashioned suits and neckties, and women in high-necked lacy gowns.

"Principal Solom and I are also members of the Governing Council, which oversees the activities of Level Three and Level Four Talents across the globe. The Governing Council sends our talents to help in cases of natural disasters, wars, and other extremely dangerous situations. Although we do not show our face publicly, you can rest assured that were it not for the council, over the past few years, India and Pakistan would have set off a nuclear holocaust, thieves would have raided a chemical weapons plant here in Washington, and a little germ known as Ebola would have led to the deaths of thousands, perhaps millions, on the East Coast. We do these things by direct intervention and by preemptive attack; our Watchers allow us to monitor the activities of dangerous people and ensure their plans never come to fruition. In fact, the Watchers—a program I initiated, by the way—are the council's most important weapon in preventing harm to the people we protect."

"You mean there are grown-up Watchers? Watchers outside of Delcroix?" I asked.

A look of pure self-satisfaction crossed his face. "Watchers are the cornerstone of our new security program. Some very motivated students, like Cameron, begin training to become Watchers while they are in school. Others train after they graduate. Either way, they must complete an exhaustive course of education in everything from foreign policy to martial arts. When they are done they will be able to operate in any country, in any situation. Their goal, quite simply, is to ensure that their targets do not endanger the lives of those around them. Of course, it's always a struggle to find and train enough qualified Watchers to keep track of all the dangerous people in the world. Watchers must be flexible, be able to go anywhere, and deal with any emergency." I looked at Cam, imagining him as a cross between Superman and James Bond. He lowered his eyes but smiled, as if he were both pleased and embarrassed by Mr. Judan's words. "They monitor everyone from political dictators to your friend Jack Landry, and must be ready to react to any situation."

I pictured Jack, running from Sunglasses Guy that day before school had even begun, and recoiled. "Wait a minute, you were watching Jack before he came to Delcroix? What's wrong with Jack? He's not a dangerous person. Why were you watching him?"

Mr. Judan sat behind a dark oak desk. He tapped a

pencil gently against one hand as he spoke. "Watchers follow known threats and young people who have been identified as having potential Level Three Talents. We've been following Jack Landry since his father accused his four-year-old son of threatening to choke him with invisible chains. Reports like that are usually dismissed by the police, but we tend to take them seriously. We've known him to use his talent repeatedly since then."

Somewhere between Trevor's appearance on the steps leading to the secret library and the booming sound of Mr. Judan's voice, I had begun to sweat, and now a tiny trickle slipped from my temple down my cheek.

When had they started following me?

"But his dad is a horrible man. You can't blame him for trying to defend himself," I insisted.

"Jack has led a difficult life, that's true. But that life changed him, and something inside turned from the good. We brought him to Delcroix because we had to see if he could be channeled safely. But now we're certain he cannot."

"You barely know him," I cried. "How can you be sure?"

Cam and Mr. Judan exchanged significant looks. Cam knelt down in front of my chair. "Jack's done a lot of things he probably hasn't told you about, Dancia. He's a member of a gang—a serious one. We don't think he's done anything illegal since he's been in Danville, but it's only a matter of time. He's dangerous. Not only to himself, but also to people around him."

No he's not! I wanted to scream. He's a good person inside, I know he is! But I kept my mouth shut. I didn't doubt Jack was capable of breaking the law. He'd told me he'd stolen cars. I just knew there was more to him than that.

"I was willing to give him a chance," Mr. Judan interjected, "but things have gotten much more serious. Early this morning Jack broke into the program library and stole two books."

"How do you know it was him?"

"We don't know for sure," Cam admitted, "but there's traces of him all over the library. I could feel it."

"The books that Jack stole contain information he could use to unlock his talent," Mr. Judan continued. "We must get those books back. We've already searched his house but didn't find them. We think he may have hidden them somewhere."

Mr. Judan stared at me with one eyebrow slightly raised. I drew back against the chair. He seemed to be asking me a question. "What?" I whispered.

"Dancia, I can't say I approve of Cameron having made the decision to bring you here"—he reserved a little frown for Cam—"but we knew having you and Jack together at Delcroix in the same year would cause some . . . complications." He enunciated the word as if it left a sour taste in his mouth.

I bristled at the implication that either Jack or I had done something wrong. "If you don't like having me here, I'll leave."

A tiny, humorless smile crossed his lips. "I don't think so."

I breathed an inward sigh of relief. As bizarre as everything seemed, and as weird and unsettling as Mr. Judan and the whole Watcher thing was, I desperately wanted to stay at Delcroix and be a part of the program. They believed talents like mine could be used to protect people. It was all I had ever dreamed of—for my power to be useful and to keep people from harm. I wouldn't have to hide and be guilty. I could be proud of who I was and what I did.

"But we do have expectations of our students," he said. "And now that you'll be joining the program, you're going to be a part of something far bigger and far more important than anything you've ever known."

His eyes bored into mine. I glanced away nervously, briefly catching Cam's stare, which was just as intent. They wanted something from me. And I had a bad feeling I knew what it was.

"What do you mean?"

"Jack must be stopped."

There, it had been said.

"Are you going to kill him or something?" I blurted out.

Mr. Judan's eyes were cold. "Our job is to watch, and to do everything in our power to make sure those with talents don't hurt other people. Right now that means getting those books from Jack before he learns something dangerous."

Acutely aware that he hadn't answered my question, I said, "Jack and I aren't talking right now. I have no idea where he might have hidden your books."

"Surely you could find a way to speak with him. If you could convince him to bring the books back quickly, we wouldn't need to worry quite as much."

"Look," I said flatly, "Jack's got this thing about being watched. It makes him crazy. He knows you've been following him, and he hates it. If he does have the books, I can't imagine what I could possibly say to him that would make him want to give them back."

Mr. Judan steepled his fingers together and rested his chin on them. He stared at me for a minute, then opened a red ledger on his desk and started making some notations in it.

Without looking up, in an almost casual voice, he said,

"You seem to have strong feelings for Jack. That's understandable. We even anticipated that might happen. But I need to have those books back by tomorrow morning. Any later than that, and I'll have to assume the worst. We only have a few Watchers in town right now, but there are more on the way. What happens next is really up to you."

Cam headed back down the circular staircase at a quick but controlled pace. I followed, with considerably less grace.

"Where are we going?" I demanded.

"We're going to Jack's house. Mr. Judan and some of the others have already searched it and can't tell where he might have hidden the books, but you might see something we didn't."

"Don't I get any say about it? Maybe I don't want to go hunt down Jack like he's some kind of criminal. The whole Watcher thing is a little creepy, don't you think?"

Cam spun around, something like hurt appearing in his voice. "We aren't creepy, all right? It's a job. A really important job. And if you care about Jack, you'll help us get those books back before the other Watchers get into town. If you think I'm bad, wait until you see the professionals. Jack has the potential to affect hundreds, maybe thousands of lives. They aren't going to just let this go."

I immediately regretted what I had said. I'd forgotten that Cam was training to be one of them.

Was one of them.

"What will they . . ." I wanted to ask *what will they do with Jack?* but I wasn't sure that Cam could answer that question. Or that I wanted him to.

I stayed quiet after that. Part of me was terrified by Mr.

Judan and everything Delcroix now seemed to represent. But the other part rippled with excitement. A chance to learn to use my power—this time for good. A chance to be on a new team, as Cam had put it. They all seemed so sure of themselves. Like they had the answers. It would be so nice not to have to worry about the answers for a change.

Besides, they'd given me a chance to help Jack, and maybe, in some small way, I could make up for all the hurt I'd caused him.

We retraced our steps down the long gray hallway. When we reached the end of the corridor, Cam pushed a button on the wall, and a tiny screen appeared, showing the room in the library where I had confronted him about the Watcher Report. It was empty, and the doors were still closed. He pushed the button again, and the wall creaked open.

Cam slipped through the slim opening, and I followed, catching my shirt on a fake book and briefly panicking that I would be squashed like a bug when the wall swung closed. Luckily, my hands stopped trembling long enough to pull myself free. Cam didn't look left or right as he strolled through the library. We avoided the front door and went down a narrow flight of stairs I hadn't known was there, then passed through a hallway to a heavy gray fire door. We went through that and down another hallway before reaching a black door without windows or any identifying marks.

Cam extracted from his pocket a silver key ring with a hook on it that looked like a bottle opener. He stuck it into the door and turned the handle. We passed through, and the air immediately got colder and damper. A small light illuminated a box of switches on the wall to our left, but otherwise everything was dark and still.

"Where are we?" My voice echoed, and my imagination filled in the shape of the room—tall and cavernous, with a ceiling of rock. Kind of like the Batcave.

"Parking garage. Where they keep the Silver Bullet and a few other vehicles," Cam said. He hit a number of switches, and huge overhead lights flooded the space. My imagination proved mostly accurate. We were in a large open room with two buses, a black Mercedes, and a tan Buick. The image of Jack's face, white and pinched with anger when he realized we were being followed, leaped to my mind. Cam opened a box on the wall and grabbed a key, then unlocked the door of the Mercedes.

"Let's go," he called over his shoulder as he sank into the driver's seat.

I slid down into the smooth leather with the knowledge that I had now truly entered an alternate universe. "I thought the Silver Bullet was the only vehicle that could get past the gate."

"It is. We take a different route."

The car roared to life and we headed into a dark tunnel, our headlights illuminating the blacktop below. We climbed a steep hill and then stopped when we reached a steel grate lit on the far side by hazy yellow sunlight. Cam leaned over and pushed a button on a device that looked like an intercom. A voice boomed out, "Who's there?"

"It's Cam Sanders, Pete. On official business for Mr. Judan. I've got Dancia Lewis with me. She will be assisting in an official investigation."

The voice came back, a trifle apologetic. "Sorry, Cam. You know what happened this morning. We're on lockdown. No one goes out. Even you."

"We don't have time for this. Call Mr. Judan," Cam barked.

Cam tapped impatiently on the wheel as we waited. I remembered Jack talking about the gates, and how they would be used to keep us in.

Everything he had said about Delcroix, from the gates to being followed, had been true. But Jack hadn't known that it was all for the good. That they only wanted to protect people.

The voice crackled through the speaker. "He gave the okay. Be careful out there."

The thick crosshatched gate opened, and Cam hit the accelerator so hard, my ponytail slammed against the headrest. We pulled out onto a gravel road I didn't recognize. It led to Highway 78, a little farther down from the parking lot. Thick bushes grew up along either side of the road, partially shielding it from the highway.

We cruised the streets, me worrying endlessly about Jack and the Watchers, Cam looking grim and determined. I kept shooting him glances out of the corner of my eye, and despite the magnitude of everything that was happening, I still got a little jolt of pure pleasure every time I did. Let me tell you, there is nothing sexier than a guy driving a black Mercedes.

We eventually pulled into the driveway of an old bungalow not far from my house. Cam pushed open the front door, which wasn't even locked. Whoever lived there was either dirt-poor or just didn't care. Maybe a little of both. Inside, the house was littered with beer bottles, pizza boxes, and piles of mail and papers. Dishes were stacked in the sink and on the counter, and a few flies were buzzing over a dirty table.

"This is it." Cam said. "You take a look, see if anything tips you off."

I picked my way past the trash to the two bedrooms in back. One was fairly neat, with a stack of papers on the dresser. Jack's room. I tiptoed hesitantly inside, feeling horrible. What was I doing? Had I become a sort of Watcher? Could it possibly be right to spy on Jack? I reminded myself that this was for his own good. We had to find him and the stolen books before Mr. Judan, or Jack, did something drastic.

I gingerly opened the dresser drawers and found a few clothes and books, but nothing remarkable. By the mirror I saw a picture tucked under some papers. I pushed the pile aside and pulled out the photograph.

It was me, looking away from the camera. I was wearing an old ball cap and my usual summer outfit of T-shirt and shorts.

"Holy crap," I breathed.

Cam saw what I was looking at and sighed. "He started following you a couple of weeks before school started. That's one of the reasons I warned you to keep away from him. I was always nervous about inviting him to Delcroix, but Mr. Judan couldn't be budged. I think he hoped he could be the one to train Jack."

I clutched the photo tightly. He must have started following me after I crashed Sunglasses Guy's car, after he'd felt me use my power. The picture raised more questions than answers. What exactly did I mean to Jack? I knew when I pushed him away, after we'd kissed, that he'd been hurt. But how deeply?

Could I be the reason he stole the books?

And then I knew where Jack had gone. He hadn't come here, to this horrible house.

He'd gone to find me.

My grip on the picture tightened until it folded down the center. I dropped it and began rubbing my hands together nervously.

Reluctantly, I turned to Cam. "I think I may have an idea where to look."

CHAPTER 29

WE DROVE straight to my house. I had no idea why the Delcroix guys wouldn't have looked there yet, but I could have sworn that's where Jack would be hiding. As soon as we pulled up, I jumped out of the car and ran up the path, hoping to get to the door before Cam did. Maybe some part of me even hoped to have a second alone with Jack before he was caught.

He was sitting at the table with Grandma, drinking soda from a glass. He didn't look surprised when Cam and I burst through the door.

"Goodness, what's the hurry, Danny?" Grandma scolded. She straightened in her chair when she saw Cam behind me. "Oh my, did they let everyone out of school early today? Who's that with you?"

Even in his haste, Cam nodded politely. "I'm Cameron, the student recruiter. I came by with Mr. Judan this summer."

Grandma shot me a quick look. "Oh, Cameron, of course! How nice to see you again." She pushed back her chair. "Can I get you something? A soda or some juice?"

Cam gave her one of his melting smiles. "No, thanks," he said. "But that's very kind of you to offer."

"Grandma, we need to talk to Jack alone." I looked around, but unfortunately, there weren't a lot of places to do that. "We'll all go outside, if you don't mind."

A worried frown knitted her forehead. "Is everything okay?"

"Sure," Jack interjected. He slouched in his chair like he didn't have a care in the world. "I imagine they have a few questions for me."

Damn it, Jack, I wanted to scream at him. *Take this seriously!* He wasn't looking at me, just tracing a finger along the side of his glass. Water pooled under his touch and then slid down to the table.

"Well, tell me if I can do anything," Grandma said.

Cam had said I couldn't tell Grandma about Delcroix, for her own good. He'd said that the knowledge was danger-ous. My throat went dry as I thought about Grandma being threatened because of me—because of something I was, or something I knew. For some reason this made it easier to be pissed at Jack. He didn't have a grandma to worry about. The only one Jack worried about was Jack.

"We will." I practically hauled Jack out of the chair and pushed both guys toward the back door. From the back, Jack looked much smaller than Cam. They were so differ-ent: Cam's broad shoulders bristling with repressed energy, Jack's thin body in an affected slouch. I followed them out to the backyard, trying not to look at the cans that lay on either side of the stump, where they had fallen only a week before.

"So, what's this all about?" Jack asked. He shoved his hands deep in his pockets and leaned against the house. "Are we planning for the big school dance? Did you want to invite me to be on the decorating committee?"

"Where are the books, Landry?" Cam demanded.

"My, oh my," Jack said mildly. "You're awfully agitated, Cameron. What books?"

"The books," Cam spat out. "You know what I mean."

"I have no idea what you're talking about."

I glared at him. "This is serious, Jack. Tell us where the books are, or you're going to be in huge trouble."

Jack looked at me with mock horror. "Trouble? Me? Now that would be something new. Besides, I don't have the books anymore. And since when is it 'us,' anyway? Did you join the Delcroix party while I wasn't looking? Or should I say, while I was turning those bastards around in circles, spending hours creating false trails just to get a few minutes alone with Grandma?"

"Please, Jack," I implored. "We don't have much time. Please tell us the truth. Don't let them be right about you. You could still change their minds. You could show them who you really are."

He flipped his hair back from his forehead and laughed. It was a hard, ugly sound that made me cringe. "Their minds were made up when I was four, just like everyone else in this town. Besides, I won't be around long enough to care. I'm through with Delcroix, Danny. I just came over to say goodbye to Grandma, and talk to you."

"You're not going anywhere," Cam said flatly. "Even as we speak, every Watcher in the state is converging on Danville. You might have fooled them for a little while, but they'll be back. You might as well give up."

I cringed. It sounded so cruel when Cam said it that way. I looked at the driveway, wondering when they would appear.

"I've been hiding all my life," Jack scoffed. "Your Watchers aren't as good as you think they are." He turned to me, and through the teasing and the lounging and the air of false confidence, I could see the fear in his eyes, and it made me want to cry. "I thought I'd give you a chance to come with me. We make a pretty good team. I thought maybe once you figured out the truth about him and all the others up there at that so-called school, you would realize that."

"I can't go with you, Jack," I said. "You know that."

"Why? Because of Grandma? We'll keep in touch, send her some letters. She'll be fine." His voice took on a note of urgency. "You can't let them run your life. They'll never let you go anywhere, do anything ever again without being watched."

"We don't watch people in the program," Cam cut in.

"Sure you don't," Jack said. "And we're supposed to believe that because you've been so honest until now?"

"You can believe what you want," Cam said. "It doesn't really matter, Jack. Dancia wants to use her powers for good. You know that. She doesn't want to be like you."

"And I suppose she does want to be like you?" Jack snarled, his lean body snapping to life. Jack threw a punch at Cam so fast I barely knew what happened. Caught by surprise, Cam's head snapped back as Jack's fist connected with his jaw. He stumbled a few feet.

"You don't want to do this," Cam warned. "I can make things much worse for you."

An invisible force slammed Cam's head from one side to the other. He grunted, and blood appeared in the corner of his mouth.

"Jack, stop!" I yelled. My voice seemed to echo across the backyard. I looked at the house, half expecting to see Grandma appear at the kitchen window. But there was no sign of her, and for once I was grateful for her lousy hearing.

I tried to push my way between Jack and Cam, but a wall of air stopped me from getting closer. When Jack had used the wall on me before, it had been barely visible, only a faint ripple of light outlining its edges. This wall had a yellowish cast, and it swayed like a curtain when Cam caught Jack under the jaw with a punch.

"I'm not going to let you people follow me, do you understand?" The whites of Jack's eyes gleamed, and at that moment he looked exactly like the man in the hospital.

I looked frantically around the yard but saw nothing I could use to join the fight. Jack was using his power on Cam, who didn't have any way to fight back other than with brute strength. Still, Cam managed to land a few punches, one that left Jack's nose bloody.

"You're a child, Jack," Cam taunted. "Don't you see? You don't have the experience or the training to use your power this way. You'll run out of juice in a few minutes, and then it will be just the two of us." He landed a hard punch on the side of Jack's face, and Jack stumbled backward, the wall dissolving as his eyes fluttered open and closed.

Jack stopped and swayed for a moment, then shook his head and glared at Cam. The wall disappeared. "Fine. You want an even fight?"

He took a step forward and swung a fist that caught Cam in the gut and left him gasping for air. But Cam returned it with an uppercut that sent Jack staggering back several feet.

As it had so many times before, rational thought seemed to fade, and all I knew was that I had to help. The power rushed through me, leaving me full and tingling with energy that I wasn't sure how to use. I looked around frantically.

The only things I saw were the cans I hadn't cleaned up from the week before, so I sent them careening along the ground toward the two guys. They had to move quickly to avoid being tripped or whacked in the ankles. The distraction forced them to stop trying to kill each other long enough for me to yell, "Cut it out, Jack! If you don't have the books, they won't do anything to you."

They froze, as if they had forgotten I was there.

Jack looked at me, panting, his eyes full of pain. "You don't understand. The books were just an excuse. They've been planning this for years."

Cam shook his head and wiped a smear of blood from his mouth. "You had a chance at Delcroix. But you blew it."

"Cam, can I talk to Jack for a minute?" I said.

"About what?" he asked suspiciously.

"I just need to talk to him. Please?"

Cam stared at me, his jaw set. "For a minute, that's it."

Jack grabbed my hand and pulled me aside. "Come away with me, Danny," he pleaded, his voice low so that Cam couldn't hear. "I'll tell you about what I read. It wasn't much, but it was enough. We're powerful enough together to take care of ourselves."

A little part of my heart died at his admission. "Jack, what were you thinking? Didn't you know they'd come after you?"

"I couldn't stand watching them lie to you. You needed to know the truth."

"Oh, Jack." My chin began to tremble. I reached out and touched his arm. "I do know the truth. You've been both right and wrong. Please, let them teach you, let them train you. They want to help people. That's what this is all about."

"You call this helping?" He gestured toward Cam, raising

his voice. "Were those Watchers helping when they let my dad beat up my mom? If everyone was so worried about me, why didn't they help me before now?"

I stopped and looked at Cam.

He straightened defensively. "Watchers don't get involved that way. If we got involved, people would find out what we do, and we can't have that. The program relies on secrecy."

I didn't particularly like that answer, but for now it had to suffice.

Jack's mouth tightened. He looked between me and Cam. "This is really about him, isn't it? You think Prince Charming is going to ride away with you on his white horse. Well that's not how it really works." He threw off my hand. "He's no better than I am."

"I know that." I also knew that beneath the anger and defensiveness, Jack cared about me, cared with an intensity I didn't fully understand. But I didn't care back, not the way he wanted—or needed.

"I need to stay at Delcroix, Jack," I said. "I need to know what my powers can really do, and I don't want to learn by accident, when I hurt someone, or a lot of someones. We can do incredible things, Jack. Don't you want to learn about it?"

"We could learn from each other," he said, a note of desperation in his voice.

"No. I don't want to hide anymore. Don't you see? I'm finally coming clean. Running away isn't for me anymore. I've been fighting my nature all my life, and I'm sick of it." A shiver ran through me as I spoke, and I realized the truth of my words. "I want to be able to use the power when people need me and I'm not scared to take the responsibility. You're the one who taught me that, Jack. All those years, I had myself convinced I had no control over it, just because I didn't want to admit that I had made those choices. You showed me the truth." I took his hand again, held it between mine. "You are a good person, Jack. I know you are, regardless of what anyone else might say."

Jack turned to the house, his jaw set and trembling. "I can't let them watch me," he said, pleading with me. "You understand, don't you?"

I closed my eyes and took a deep breath, and then let it out slowly. I did understand.

I turned to Cam. "Can't we let him go? He said he doesn't have the books."

Cam's eyes widened. "Let him go? Are you crazy? I know for a fact that he took the books! I felt it in the library!"

"He's not a bad person," I pleaded, avoiding the issue. "There's good in him, I know it. You can't bring him back to Delcroix. Who knows what they'll do to him there?"

"They'll watch him," Cam said defensively. "It isn't like they'll torture him or something."

"Do you really believe that?" I asked softly.

I had my answer in the way he avoided my gaze.

"Cam, I know what they told you about him, but can't you feel the good in Jack? You're his recruiter. You know he's not as bad as they seem to think."

It was a calculated risk. Cam could have felt precisely the opposite. He opened his mouth to speak, then closed it again, his jaw clenched. The air around us grew heavy as Cam considered my plea.

Then something incredible happened—even as I watched, the hard lines of his shoulders softened, drooped. As though he had reached an internal conclusion that he didn't want to make.

Jack looked from me to Cam, assessing, calculating.

"Please, Cam," I said. "For me."

"He's dangerous," Cam insisted, though his voice was less sure than it had been a moment ago. "How can you let a person like this go free?"

"Because what they want to do to him isn't right," I said. "Jack's a human being. You can't pretend otherwise and treat him in the same way the program has for all these years. And it will only get worse now. You know that."

Cam didn't respond.

That was when we heard the roar of a car headed our way. Jack's body tensed, and Cam sighed. "They're here. I figured it wouldn't be long."

I ran to the edge of the yard and peered over the fence. A car hurtled toward us from a few blocks away.

"I've got to do something," I said, turning toward Cam and pleading with my eyes for him to understand.

He hesitated. As I watched the car approach, one of the windows rolled down, and something appeared. Something that caught a glint of sunlight. Something metallic.

"Oh my God, that's a gun," I gasped.

Cam and Jack ran to my side. The three of us stood there leaning over the fence to watch the approaching car.

I poked Cam in the ribs. Hard.

"Cam. *Gun*. You said they were just going to watch him," I whispered, more urgently this time. It was one thing to believe the Watchers were capable of killing Jack. It was another to see the proof of it, pointed our way.

Cam didn't move, his eyes pinned on the car.

Jack stood frozen, his gaze darting frantically between me and the car. His mouth fell open, and the whistle of his breath—fast, like a trapped animal—was faintly audible.

No one seemed able to move. As the car reached the corner of my block, I realized if anyone was going to save Jack, it would have to be me.

I took a deep breath and focused on the tingle of power still coursing through me. Then I deliberately stared at the car. With a nudge to the forces holding it in place, I knocked the gun from the Watcher's hand. It hit the ground and skittered across the asphalt.

The hand withdrew for just a second before another gun appeared in its place. A face half covered with mirrored sunglasses emerged from the window. I shuddered, recognizing the man I had seen following Jack what seemed like a lifetime ago.

I knew I needed to do something more drastic, so I pushed a finger toward the windshield of the car, as if I were the weight of the sky pressing down on the glass, and it shattered, sending thousands of pieces flying in every direction. The car swerved but kept coming.

They were two houses away.

Sweat beading on my forehead, I studied a telephone pole and tugged it to the ground. A shower of sparks flew from the power lines overhead as it fell. The car—which I could now see was the familiar tan Buick—swerved violently left and right to avoid the falling pole, but didn't stop.

I was a second behind, too slow, too late. I could see the gun more clearly as they approached. That was when I heard our front door open.

"Good Lord, what's going on?" Grandma's voice was almost lost in the roar of the car and the hissing electrical lines.

Grandma. My heart almost stopped. What if they hurt Grandma?

I narrowed my eyes. I had never used my power for a sustained time like this, and my body felt heavy, my head a weight on my shoulders that was difficult to control. But now they were messing with something sacred. Someone I would do anything to protect.

I had vowed days ago not to break any bonds that might inadvertently set off another Hiroshima, so I flailed for a moment, unsure what to do next to stop the progress of that oncoming car and its horrible cargo. I looked up for a second, as if searching for inspiration from the heavens, and my eyes caught the corner of Mount Rainier, its flat top hidden by a thick cover of clouds.

That was it. I needed help from something bigger than me. I focused on the street, this time studying the forces underneath, the cauldron under the pavement. I had never thought to look there before, and I recoiled at the forces I saw, surging and pulsing like hot lava. Aware that I could be doing something horribly dangerous, I held out one hand, opened my fist, and then squeezed, as if I could bring something from far below up to the surface.

I heard a low rumble, felt a vibration in my shoes, and then the earth yawned. A sinkhole appeared directly in front of my house. The Buick's brakes squealed as the driver tried to avoid the hole, but it was too late. It plunged into the ground, the front of the car and its occupants swallowed beneath the street.

For a second, everything went absolutely still. Puffy white smoke billowed from the back of the car, which now pointed at a sixty degree angle to the sky. Then a car alarm started down the block, and life resumed. Voices emerged from the hole—angry voices, cursing the car and demanding to know what had happened.

Across the street a door opened. Mr. James, an old man who always seemed to be wearing a bathrobe, emerged from his house. A second later, a woman appeared from the house next to his. They looked at the car, gasped, and ran back inside, I suppose to get a phone.

Cam, his face pasty, shot me a disbelieving look. "We are going to get in so much trouble for this," he whispered under his breath.

"I couldn't let them kill him," I said, half pleading, half defiant. "And I wouldn't let them hurt Grandma."

Cam swung around to face Jack. "If you're attacked, just focus on your shield," he said quickly. "Don't let them distract you. They can't fight your talent directly, but they will know the second you relax it."

"Do you have a car?" I asked Jack, looking back and forth between him and the gigantic hole in the middle of the street. I pictured the driver climbing out, gun drawn, and had to fight to remain calm.

Jack nodded, the panic retreating from his eyes, replaced by a sad, hard defiance. "Around the block. I didn't want them to see it out front."

I nodded. He knew what he was doing. He had been hiding a long time. "You'd better go. It won't take them long to get out of that hole."

He wiped a drop of blood from his nose and turned his back deliberately on the street. "Are you sure you won't come?"

"I'm sure."

Without another word he ran and jumped the back fence.

I wondered if I would ever see him again.

By the time Cam and I got to the street, the wail of a siren could be heard in the distance and the two Watchers were climbing out of the car. One took off running down the block. The other pulled out a phone and started barking something into it.

Grandma stood by the house, looking around anxiously. I ran over and gave her a hug.

"Thank goodness you're okay," she said, patting me on the back. She peered over my shoulder as we separated. "Where's Jack?"

I swallowed the lump in my throat. "He had to go."

Grandma studied my face and then Cam's, before nodding gravely, as if she understood.

"I should get back to school," Cam said. He passed a quick, silent message to the Watcher on the phone. Then he leaned over and pressed a quick kiss on my cheek, got into the Mercedes, and drove away.

If Grandma thought it was odd that he disappeared so quickly, she never said so, though she did raise her eyebrows when he kissed me. I must have turned red, because she chuckled and said, "About time."

"We're just friends," I spluttered, barely able to breathe as the feeling of his lips on my skin rippled through my body.

"Of course," she replied. "What did you think I meant?"

The electric company arrived not long after the fire truck, police car, and ambulance. They had to bring a crane to extract the car from the twenty-foot hole. A geologist said an underground pool of water must have collected down there, causing the sinkhole and undermining the stability of the telephone pole.

I stood there for a long time, looking at the street and marveling at what I had done.

It was Grandma's regular Friday bingo night, so I spent the rest of the evening alone, reliving the whole crazy afternoon and wondering what had finally convinced Cam to let Jack go. Had he done it for me, or had it been the sight of the gun that changed his mind? Over and over, I relived the moment where he kissed my cheek, and replayed in my mind the way Trevor had said, "*I know you like her . . .*"

He must care for me, I told myself. He must.

When I lay down in bed that night, something sharp poked at my head. I reached under my pillow and found two books. Instantly I understood why Jack had come to my house. He had never expected me to come with him. Maybe he had hoped that I would, but he had been through too much in his life to expect it.

He had come because he wanted to show me the truth about Delcroix before he left.

I turned on my light and stared at the books, awed by the damage they had done. They were slim, leather-bound volumes with soft covers, the leather so smooth in places it reflected the light with a yellow glow. One was titled *An Introduction to Earth Talents*. The other was *A History of the Governing Council*.

Not wanting to touch them, let alone read anything between their covers, I wrapped them in a pillowcase and slid them into my backpack. Jack hadn't lied. He didn't have the books. He had given them to me.

CHAPTER 30

GRANDMA DROPPED me off at the Delcroix parking lot on Monday. It was the last week of school before Thanksgiving, and as I stepped out of the car, the cold rain that had been falling unexpectedly turned soft and white. I waved as Grandma drove away, and then looked up at the sky. Through the glow of the streetlight, white flakes drifted down toward me. For a moment I let the childlike thrill of seeing snow overwhelm the anxiety and fear I'd been fighting all weekend.

The mix of snow and rain fell for a few minutes before turning to freezing rain. I wondered if Grandma would make it home without rear-ending someone. As if in perfect time with my thoughts, a gray sedan pulled into the parking lot and slid a few feet on the slick asphalt. A chauffeur jumped out and opened the back door. Catherine emerged with her navy coat belted tightly around her waist.

For the first time as I watched her, pity outweighed my hatred. In her own way, Catherine was just as much of a freak as I was, and she didn't really have parents to help her any more than I did. In all the time we'd been at school, she'd never gotten a visit from her mom or dad, who were in D.C. most of the time, and they had a chauffeur bring her to and from school each weekend, just so she could go to their empty house and stay with a nanny. At least I had Grandma.

As the parking lot filled, I had to tell myself to stop hoping that Jack might suddenly appear. He was gone. I almost wondered if he'd ever really been here.

My backpack felt heavy on my shoulders, the weight a painful reminder of the load I carried. The school looked the same way it had the week before, but everything had a new meaning. The wrought-iron gates loomed against the muddy brown lawn like a living presence, huge arms surrounding the school in a tight embrace. I pictured the library, the tunnel Cam and I had driven through, and wondered how many other secrets lay inside the innocent-looking, red brick structure.

I wanted to be happy. I should have been happy. After all, just three days before I'd learned the truth about my power, found people who could teach me to use it, and the boy I'd dreamed about for months said he liked me. He'd held my hand and looked at me like I was more than just a friend. But looming above everything was an inescapable fact: Jack was gone, and a part of me had gone with him. I couldn't pretend anymore that there were easy answers, or that burying my head in the sand would make my problems go away. And I was fairly certain that from here on out, life was only going to get more complicated.

It wasn't long before the people I knew best started to arrive. Allie got there first, her ponytail bobbing. I watched Hector jump down from the cab of a four-by-four, and Marika kissed her mom as she waved good-bye.

They were thinking about homework and teachers and what they would wear to the dance in a couple of weeks. I had to worry about whether I'd set off a nuclear reaction the next time I played around with the forces of nature, and whether I'd done the right thing by coming back to Delcroix instead of running away with Jack.

I mean, I knew I wanted to be with Cam, and I knew I wanted to use my powers to do good, but how did I know that would really happen at Delcroix? Everyone here seemed to think Jack was a horrible, dangerous person; so much so, they seemed willing to kill him. I couldn't quite fathom that. It was wrong to kill someone just because you thought he *might* be dangerous, particularly if you had never really understood him in the first place.

And then there was all the trouble I had created for Cam. He'd looked so worried when he'd driven away on Friday. I had no idea what he planned to tell Mr. Judan, but I felt sick when I imagined the trouble he might be in because of me. I wasn't supposed to know what Delcroix was all about for another year, so it wasn't like there were other freshmen I could talk to about what had happened. And Anna still didn't like me—or maybe she liked me even less now that I knew the truth.

It would have helped if I'd talked to Cam over the weekend. I'm sure he was too busy dealing with the mess I'd created to stop by. I didn't even know if they would have let him leave school to see me. But it would have been nice to hear his voice or see him smile. To know that he cared about me.

Just when I'd almost convinced myself to run back home and hide under my covers, Esther arrived. When she saw me, she squealed and ran over like we'd been separated for months.

"I called you ten times this weekend and no one ever picked up. Enough is enough!" Proudly, she held out a little cardboard box with a picture of a cell phone on the top. "Now don't be all weird and say you can't accept it, because it's really for my convenience, not yours. And we only pre-paid two hundred minutes, but you're so responsible, you'll probably make it last till New Year's."

I stared at the box, and a little fountain started somewhere behind my eyes. Two big tears slid down my cheeks. "There was an accident on my street," I said, my voice shaky. "Our phone went out."

I tried to look away, but Esther just gave me one of those embarrassingly huge hugs and stared me right in the face.

"Well, we were worried about you," she said. "You looked really upset last week, and then when we didn't see you Friday after school . . ." She gave me another squeeze and then released me. "Hennie and I decided we needed some way to get a hold of you."

Hennie ran up, her long hair flowing in perfect waves down her back. She stumbled over her shoelace and grabbed my arm to steady herself. "Did you already give it to her?" She scowled at Esther. "I wanted to be here when you gave it to her!"

"This is really nice," I said, looking back and forth between them. "I don't know what I'd do without you two."

Hennie hugged me, less fiercely than Esther but with no less emotion. "For some reason I had this feeling you might have left school for good. But you wouldn't do that, would you? Without talking to us?"

I shook my head and wiped my face dry. "No way. I'd miss you guys way too much. Besides, who would pay my cell phone bill if I left?"

We all laughed and hugged again, and a weight that

had been hanging on my heart dissolved. "So what's up with Yashir?" I asked Hennie. "Weren't you going to call him this weekend?"

"I bet she chickened out," Esther said.

Hennie stuck out her tongue. "Just goes to show you don't know everything."

"No way!" Esther said. "You seriously called him? And talked to him?"

"I'm not sure what else you'd do on the phone," Hennie said smugly.

"And . . . ?" I said.

She looked around as if to make sure we weren't going to be overheard, and then whispered, "I think he likes me."

Esther threw her hands in the air. "It's a miracle! She finally figured it out!"

"We talked for an hour," she said dreamily. "And I couldn't have done it without you two." She gave each of us a quick hug.

"No problem," I said, hugging her back. "Now, any chance you want to do my World Civ paper for me?"

As soon as we got to school I went straight to Mr. Judan's office and handed him the books. He just nodded and said thank you. Like he had expected me to come back with them all along.

Crowds of students were streaming up and down the hallway when I emerged. Trevor passed me as I paused in the doorway. He raised his eyebrows in question.

"I brought them back," I said defensively.

He turned his steely gaze to the wall of Mr. Judan's office, and then turned back to me. "I never doubted you would. I just didn't think it was right to ask."

I started to reply, but the words died in my throat as a tall, chestnut-haired figure approached behind him. Cam looked tired, dark circles under his eyes, and his hair was messed up in back. There was a purple bruise over one of his eyes and a Band-Aid on his jaw. He always looked so put together, it was hard not to gape at his disheveled appearance.

"We've got a couple of minutes before class," he said. "Can I talk to you?"

His face was dark and serious, and I had the sudden fear that he was going to tell me we had both been expelled, and I'd have to go to Danville High School after all.

I nodded and followed him across the hall to the nurse's office. The door was ajar; the nurse stood a few doors down, chatting with one of the teachers. When she turned to yell something at a kid running down the stairs, Cam and I snuck in and pushed the door closed behind us.

It was a small space, just a desk and a bed. When the door clicked shut, I felt the walls close in around us.

Cam and I were alone.

"How are you?" he asked.

I forced a lighthearted tone. "I'm fine. There's a big sinkhole in front of my house, and the phone company said it would be a few days before they could replace the pole that collapsed, but other than that, it was a pretty boring weekend."

He flashed a smile, and for a second the old Cam twinkled in his eyes. But then this new, sober Cam reappeared, and he began to pace by the door. "I felt terrible running out on you like that. I figured I had to get back as soon as I could. I wanted to explain what happened to Mr. Judan in person."

"What did you say?"

"I told him that we found Jack, and he and I fought, but he got away," he said.

"Was he pissed about the sinkhole?" I asked.

Cam shook his head. "I told him you were the one who found Jack. I guess that was enough. He didn't ask about what happened to your street."

I felt a rush of gratitude for Mr. Judan. "That was lucky."

"We spent the rest of the weekend looking for Jack," Cam continued. "But Jack was right. He really does know how to hide."

I nodded, saddened that Cam had been forced to lie. It didn't sit well with him—that was obvious. "Are you okay with that?"

"I don't know." He looked at me, his dark eyes tormented. "I just keep wondering . . . did we do the right thing? What if he does something terrible, or hurts someone?"

"Oh, Cam, I'm not sure." I struggled to find the words to explain how I felt, and why I thought it was worth the risk to let Jack go. "I guess I didn't really have a choice. Jack is a person. He made me laugh. He cared about me. There was good in him, I know it. I couldn't give up on that."

Jack was powerful, even I could see that. He could be dangerous. There might even have been a little evil in him. But isn't that true of all of us?

Cam sighed. "I know. I couldn't have let him go if I didn't believe that. I just hope the good is stronger than the bad."

He was quiet, and I thought about what Grandma had said a long time ago, that sometimes you'll only know that you've taken the wrong path because something inside you will feel twisted. Giving up Jack to the Watchers would have been wrong. When he looked at me Friday afternoon, and I saw those men headed in our direction, I knew it. I felt it in my heart.

In the hallway the bell rang for first period. I adjusted my backpack. "I guess we should get to class."

Cam nodded and held out his hand. "Dancia?"

I dropped my eyes. "Yeah?"

Gently, he pulled me toward him. When we were only inches apart, I looked up. His mouth hovered above mine, his eyes tender. "I'm glad you stayed," he whispered.

And then he leaned down and brought his lips to mine. The kiss started out soft and light, like the brush of a summer breeze, and I melted into it. He pulled me against him, safe and warm. Our arms intertwined, and where my kiss with Jack had been sudden, jolting—even a little frightening—this kiss was simply . . . heaven. Our lips fit together perfectly. I didn't have to think about what to do next.

And for the first time in my life, I knew I was right where I belonged.

Dimly, I heard a bell ring. We parted and I rocked back on my heels. He stared at me with a crooked smile.

I smiled back. "Me too."

ACKNOWLEDGMENTS

So many people have supported me through this journey, it's hard to know where to start. I learned an incredible amount about the craft and business of writing from my RWA friends, especially the Romance Bandits and Rose City Romance Writers. Thank you for all your wisdom, love, and support.

I couldn't have written about Delcroix Academy without an incredible high school where there were fantastic teachers to inspire me. Thanks to the faculty and staff at City Honors High School, especially Mr. Duggan, who told me a long time ago to just keep writing.

Thanks so much to the entire team at Disney-Hyperion, who have amazed me with their skill and talent. A huge thank you also goes to Tamar Rydzinski, who pulled this manuscript from the slush pile and turned a dream into a reality, and Emily Sylvan Kim, agent extraordinaire.

Finally, I'd like to say thank you to my entire family, who for some crazy reason seemed to take it as a given that someday I'd get my name on the cover of a book. Most importantly, my love goes out to my mom and dad—two incredible people who never stopped loving and believing in me. Thank you.

FALL DOWN,
LAUGHING

DAVID L. LANDER

WITH LEE MONTGOMERY

Jeremy P. Tarcher
a member of Penguin Putnam Inc.

FALL DOWN, LAUGHING

LAUGHING

●●●●●●●●●●●●

HOW SQUIGGY CAUGHT MULTIPLE SCLEROSIS AND DIDN'T TELL NOBODY

Most Tarcher/Putnam books are available at special quantity discounts for bulk purchases for sales promotions, premiums, fund-raising, and educational needs. Special books or book excerpts also can be created to fit specific needs. For details, write Putnam Special Markets, 375 Hudson Street, New York, NY 10014.

Jeremy P. Tarcher/Putnam
a member of
Penguin Putnam Inc.
375 Hudson Street
New York, NY 10014
www.penguinputnam.com

Library of Congress Cataloging-in-Publication Data

Lander, David L., date.
    Fall down, laughing: how Squiggy caught multiple sclerosis and didn't tell nobody/David L. Lander.
        p.   cm.
    ISBN 1-58542-052-2
    1. Lander, David, L. date—Health.   2. Multiple sclerosis—Patients—United States—Biography.   3. Comedians—United States—Biography.   I. Title.
    RC377.L36   2000   00-032576
    362.1´96834´0092—dc21
    [B]

Printed in the United States of America

1   3   5   7   9   10   8   6   4   2

This book is printed on acid-free paper. ♾

Book design by Amanda Dewey

ACKNOWLEDGMENTS

◉

First and foremost thanks go to my family, Kathy and Natalie, for enduring the trials of bookmaking. My brother, Bob Landau, for being on the other end of the phone. Freddie and Corrina for their support through the years and two of my favorite mothers-in-law, Edie Fellows and Polly Bergen. Thanks to the Willner family for taking me in when no one else would.

To the folks at *Laverne & Shirley*, Penny Marshall, Garry Marshall, and Cindy Williams. A special thanks go to Michael McKean who, along with Lenny, has stood by me for decades. Joe Safety, a good friend who always cared and was always there. Also thanks to Steve Levine, George Gerdes, Peter Elbling, Harry Shearer, Rich Garon, Dara Jaramillo, Don Hartack, and the 4:30 Club.

Big thanks go to Harriet Sternberg who helps me manage my life. Without her, I couldn't find my way out of a paper bag.

Tom Sherak and his family who extended a gracious hand at a critical time. The National Multiple Sclerosis Society whose work changes my life everyday. Special thanks go to Arney Rosenblat and Leon Lebuffe.

Physicians who have helped me keep vertical, balanced, and informed include Drs. David Kipper, Mitch Freedman, Ted Phillips, Larry Jacobs, Lorraine Purino and Frederick Munschaeur.

Grateful acknowledgment of the folks at Biogen and Spectrum who work hard to pass the good word of

Avonex, especially Lisa Easley, Mike Bonney, Jeff McLaughlin, and Tom Norton.

To our couples group that banded together for four years; to share, support, and care for each other.

And finally thanks to the bookmaking crew. Tom Greenberg, who helped pull and keep it together. Thanks to Frank Weimann and Thea Lander. Wendy Hubbert and Allison Sobel for their hard work. A special thanks to Lee Montgomery for listening and to Bonnie McCourt for word processing and the afternoon serenade of Charlie Chaplin lore.

To Kathy for keeping me honest
and Natalie for just keeping me

CONTENTS
◉

FOREWORD

●

S. Mitchell Freedman, M.D.

I first met David Lander in Norfolk, Virginia, at the
annual meeting of the Hampton Roads Chapter of the
National Multiple Sclerosis Society. The gentleman
who had invited me to speak at the meeting figured
he could easily entice me to drive from Raleigh to
Norfolk on a Saturday by revealing that David Lander
would be the keynote speaker. Breathless excitement

in his voice at his end of the phone conversation was greeted by deafening silence at my end.

"Who's David Lander?" I sheepishly asked.

"Oh, come on. You know, *Squiggy*, from *Laverne & Shirley!*"

Refrains of "Schliemel, Schlemazel" rang in my head. Would Lenny be there, too? I wondered.

"That's nice. Why is he speaking? Does someone in his family have MS?"

"No, *he* has MS."

"Squiggy has MS?"

"No, dummy, *David Lander* has MS."

I agreed to come to Norfolk, but frankly thought little more about David. Sure, it would be fun to see Squiggy in person; everybody likes to meet TV stars. But I was much more interested in getting to know the other invited speaker, Dr Heidi Crayton, the director of the Multiple Sclerosis Center at Georgetown University Medical Center. A colleague and I had just opened the Triangle Multiple Sclerosis Center in the Raleigh Durham area, so I was eager to make contact with such a nationally known MS authority.

Little did I know what I was in for.

Dr. Crayton gave an interesting, though unconventional, talk on helping patients deal more effectively with their neurologists. Then she started discussing what drives neurologists crazy about patients. She was letting out trade secrets to beat the band! When it was my turn, I spoke about the workings of MS, answered questions about available treatments, and speculated about the future of research in the field.

Lunch was served. David, Heidi, and I exchanged a few pleasantries, and then he made his way to the dais—not without some difficulty.

I stirred my coffee and fiddled with my dessert, hoping his talk wouldn't be too long. I looked at my watch, trying to gauge how quickly I could get David's autograph and leave. After all, it was a four-hour drive back to Raleigh.

And then he started speaking. Slowly, at first. The microphone didn't really work, and his voice didn't carry. The podium was awkwardly placed. He shuffled his notes. How could a TV star be so nervous? What was going on?

"Hi, my name is David. I have MS." Then followed a story just like the hundreds I had heard before in my office. There was no trace of Squiggy in David's voice as quietly, deliberately, and patiently, he told of his experiences with multiple sclerosis from his diagnosis to the present. Before I realized it, I had put down my coffee spoon and shoved aside the dessert plate. Little was David aware that as he directed his remarks to those in the room with MS, he was also inexorably pulling me, as a neurologist, into the world of the disease in a way I had never experienced before.

There is an old saying in medicine that has been passed down from professors to medical students: "When all else fails, try listening to the patient." David made me listen. He challenged me that day in Norfolk, and now with this book, to listen carefully. His gentle and often self-deprecating humor spoke volumes about the frightening and complicated experiences he had in the course of coming to grips with this mysterious disease.

What is multiple sclerosis? What is this illness that turned David Lander's world upside down and that has disrupted the lives of well over other 300,000 people in the United States alone? MS is a disease of the central nervous system (that is to say, a disease of the brain and the spinal cord) characterized by *inflammation, demyelination,* and *axonal loss.*

Early on in the disease, there is a poorly understood inflammatory reaction that appears and recedes in multiple different areas of the nervous system. This inflammation can smolder along unbeknownst to the patient for years, but over time it becomes associated with a breakdown or disruption of myelin, the insulation that covers the nerves. These dual processes of *inflammation* and *demyelination* eventually manifest themselves clinically in a myriad of ways. For most patients, numbness or visual loss herald the onset of MS. For others, dizziness, weakness, loss of bladder control, clumsiness, or even slurred speech can be the clinical beginnings of MS. For a rare few, *"falling down, laughing"* is the start of this curious disease.

The diagnosis of MS can be rather straightforward for some patients. The medical history and the neurologic abnormalities may point immediately to MS. Often, however, the early symptoms are either ignored by the patient, misdiagnosed by the physician, or erroneously dismissed by all as being psychosomatic. For such individuals, arriving at the correct diagnosis can be an exasperating and even demeaning experience. David Lander describes this frustrating process poignantly, insightfully, and humorously. Patients will readily identify with David's ordeal. Rarely has the patient perspective been so articulately laid out. Physicians, particularly neurologists, have much to learn from David.

MS characteristically strikes young adults between the ages of eighteen and fifty. Women are more frequently affected than men. Although cases of MS have been described throughout the entire world, there is a distinctly higher incidence in cooler climates both above and below the equator. Such an observation has led many to implicate an environmental or infectious agent as the cause of MS. Clearly, MS runs in families about 3 to 5 percent of the time, which suggests to others a genetic component to the illness. Undoubtedly, both genetic and environmental factors are at play.

Perhaps what makes multiple sclerosis so unusual is the unpredictability and seeming capriciousness of its clinical course. In some patients, the neurologic symptoms come and go randomly. These patients are said to have *relapsing-remitting MS*. In a disturbingly large number of patients, the relapsing-remitting course changes over time so that symptoms appear and stay. The disease is then categorized as *secondary progressive MS*. A small number of patients have *primary progressive MS*, in which no remissions ever occur. In those patients with both primary and secondary progressive MS, it is thought that the inflammation and demyelination have lead to irreversible nerve damage (or *axonal loss*), causing permanent disability.

Patients have often described the course of their MS to me as a roller-coaster ride. They never know what to expect from this maddening illness. Symptoms appear for no obvious reason. Symptoms recede with just as little sense. David describes what this is like while trying to work in the heady world of Tinsel Town, but his experiences parallel those of all patients facing life's daily challenges in the presence of MS. Obviously most don't have to perform for Penny Marshall or Arnold Schwarzenegger, but they do have to face their mother-in-law or their boss or their best friend or their colleagues who all are looking at them with raised eyebrows, wondering what is the matter.

While research has deepened our understanding of MS, there is still much to be learned about this disease. As recently as ten years ago, MS was regarded for all intents and purposes as untreatable. Advances in neuroimmunology and neuropharmacology have brought us immunomodulatory therapy. This treatment of the inflammatory component of MS has given new hope to patients and has encouraged neurologists to approach MS with more intensity. The presently available medications are not without problems, however, since they all must be given by injection. David's description of his adjustment to the idea of injectable medication made me realize I had to spend a bit more time with my patients when proposing this type of therapy.

David has thrown a new light on MS by sharing with us the way this particular illness has changed his life and career.

Physicians, with their well-intentioned zeal to let patients know we are up to date on the latest advances in the understanding of MS, sometimes get a bit too "clinical" and impersonal. More than one patient has endured my rattling off of endless statistics about MS. Their eyes glaze over while they wait uncomplainingly to tell me what is *really* important to them in their lives. David speaks for all patients and compels us as physicians to listen. Certainly, patients want their physicians to be knowledgeable, but they also want us not to lose sight of them as complicated people living complicated lives.

After David's remarks in Norfolk, the two of us chatted over coffee.

"Doc, I'll let you in on a little secret."

Wow, Hollywood gossip! I thought.

"*I* don't have MS. *Squiggy* has MS."

There is a bit of Squiggy in us all. Whether it is actually David's alter ego who has MS matters not, because it is David Lander himself who has humanized and demystified MS with *Falling Down, Laughing.* David reminds patients with MS that they are not alone. His spirit of good humor can embolden many of those struggling with multiple sclerosis to renew their optimism and restore their hope for a brighter future.

INTRODUCTION

Lenny and the Squigtones

Until last May, I was best known as Squiggy on the TV sitcom *Laverne & Shirley*. But then I told *People* magazine and anyone else who would listen that for the last fifteen years I've had multiple sclerosis. During my silent years, between 1984 and 1999, I continued working in Hollywood while hiding the symptoms of my illness. I did voice-overs for various cartoons and animated feature films, played supporting roles in a dozen movies and was a regular on a handful of television series, including *On the Air, Twin Peaks,* and *Pacific Blue.*

In my real life, I somehow managed to stay married to the same wonderful woman for twenty-one years. Today, we live in a suburb outside of Los Angeles with our seventeen-year-old daughter who has never known her father without MS.

At the time of my diagnosis, I had just turned thirty-six and was coming off seven years on *Laverne & Shirley*. I was five years into my marriage with Kathy Fields; our daughter, Natalie, had just had her first birthday. The biggest problems of the moment were actor problems, not real-life problems. I was trying to break out of being typecast as Squiggy, a role I loved, but one I needed to move beyond. Before that, I had had a ten-year history as a writer and actor who did comedy on radio, television, and in clubs. I was confident of my future, and was beginning to branch out. I was developing a new television series, writing a film script for MGM, and performing supporting roles in a few major films.

Like everyone with MS, there were clues that something was wrong with me but nothing added up as remarkable. Symptoms appeared and disappeared as if by magic; slowly, little by little, inch by inch. I would step in holes that were not there, trip on cracks in the sidewalk, or watch a drink slip through my hands twice in one night without feeling it leave my fingertips.

It seemed like my body was out of sync, like a badly dubbed Hercules picture. I could no longer trust it to follow the simplest instructions. On some days, crossing streets and climbing curbs became a challenge. On other days I would be okay. I knew something wasn't right, I just didn't know what it was called, if it was serious, or if it would ever go away.

On the days my body didn't listen, I told myself it was just one of those days, I didn't know what "one of those days" meant; nothing hurt, my body just wasn't working like it should. Then, without warning, I'd feel normal again. It was like living on a fault line. I knew a quake was coming, but I didn't know when it would erupt or how big the quake would be.

Nothing made sense. I had begun to doubt my experience of what was happening. I thought maybe I had become a hypochondriac, or just losing my mind.

The National Multiple Sclerosis Society estimates there are approximately one-third of a million Americans (350,000) living with MS today. There are 2.5 million people with MS worldwide. Over two hundred new cases are diagnosed weekly in the United States, making a total of 10,000 new cases each year.

Although extensive research continues, no one understands the cause of multiple sclerosis. One theory is that it is caused by a virus, and may have a genetic predisposition. But the frightening truth is, MS can strike anyone any time. It is the most common diagnosis of a neurological disorder in young adults between the ages of twenty and fifty, and is slightly more prevalent in women, who comprise two-thirds of all cases in America. Additionally, it appears that people who grow up in temperate climates (with seasons) have a greater risk of developing the illness than those who grow up near the equator. For example, MS is ten times more common in Denver than in New Orleans, and fifty times more common than in Mexico City.

Multiple sclerosis destroys a vital part of the nervous system. Scientists believe that certain immune cells attack the myelin sheath, a protective coating surrounding nerve fibers, which acts as an insulating material for the impulses that travel from what are known as "thinking" cells in the brain to other cells in the brain and spinal cord. When myelin is destroyed, it's replaced by scar tissue that gives MS its Latin name, meaning "many scars." The scars block or short-circuit nerve messages, so body functions become uncontrolled. Symptoms, ranging from severe to mild, depend on the type of MS and the locations of the damage.

A small percentage of people with MS have so much difficulty controlling their movement that they are confined to a wheelchair. For others, only balance and coordination are affected, and simple activities like walking can become difficult. Some people with MS have problems speaking or swallowing. Others have problems with vision, fatigue, weakness, stiffness, dizziness, vertigo, numbing, and tingling. MS is a disease that by its nature is wildly unpredictable; how it strikes, who it strikes, and how it progresses, can differ as dramatically as night and day.

Most people have seen the frightening images that often accompany the media's vision of the disease. Total paralysis, the inability to speak, or being confined to a wheelchair are all images splashed in films, television movies, and magazines. When I was diagnosed, the only cases I knew were *these* cases; the *worst* cases I had seen on telethons, public service announcements, and in fund-raising literature, all avenues that tend to focus on the most crippling aspects of the disease. All I could think of was, *Would that be me in a year? Would I become completely paralyzed? What future did my family and I have?* I mean, how many roles are there for a thirty-six-year-old Jew in a wheelchair?

A diagnosis of MS is devastating, there's no doubt about it. But my hope is that by telling my story, many will see that life does not end for people like us. Over the last few years, promising new drugs have been developed that are helping people carry on with "normal" and productive lives in ways that were never before possible.

In sharing my experiences and those of my family and supporters, my goal is to help raise awareness of these new options and to serve as a positive example of someone who continues to live, work, and laugh despite having MS. When I went public with my illness and began work as a goodwill ambassador for the Multiple Sclerosis Society, listening to the experiences of others helped me begin to heal in unimaginable ways. Now I'm hoping that I will help others do the same.

This book is dedicated to everyone who is living with a debilitating chronic disease like MS, and to the family and friends who support them. You are not alone. As someone told me when I first went public, "Welcome to the club."

HOW I GOT TO BE A KID:

GROWING UP TO BE AN ACTOR

My childhood in the Bronx

In the beginning I was just a boy with a dream: I wanted to be a cowboy. I had a great collection of toy guns that I found endlessly entertaining. I couldn't imagine living without them, so at the age of six I devised an elegant solution. I would make a career of it. So when people asked, "What do you want to be when you grow up?" I'd answer, "I want to be a gunslinger."

Looking back, I have no idea why my parents weren't alarmed. They somehow knew I didn't have what it took to be a professional gunslinger. Gunslingers were humorless and I was funny. Cowboys were serious, I was not—I had too many interests and was too easygoing as a kid. Besides, cowboys ride broncs, but they don't live in the Bronx.

Beyond a love of toy guns I knew a couple of things about myself. Number one, I loved the theater. Number two, I hated the Yankees, and still do. Number three, the Pittsburgh Pirates were my team: a life-long decision made when I was four. I liked the way the team's name sounded, though I had no idea where Pittsburgh was, and the only pirates I knew sang Gilbert and Sullivan. My brother Bobby told me they were the worst team in baseball. It was true. That year, in 1952, they lost 120 ball games out of 154. He said by the time you know what's going on they'll have to be better.

I was born David Landau on June 22 in 1947 in Brooklyn, New York, delivered by my mother's brother-in-law Uncle Jack Liswood, whose wife, Aunt Rebecca, was also my pediatrician. My parents, Saul and Stella, and my older brother and I made our home in the North Bronx in a four-room apartment in a six-story apartment building. I remember an enormous front yard with two large hedges that created a beautiful path to run through. For many years an old farm stood across the street, though it appeared to be a tiny farm of nothing, maybe a total of two chickens. The people who lived there were blond and blue-eyed and looked like no one I knew (everyone around me was Jewish or Italian). The farmers left by the time I was eight or nine, when their home was torn down and replaced by apartment buildings housing more Jews and Italians. At the time I figured everyone in the world belonged to these two groups—even President Eisenhower.

Both my mother and father taught school in the New York public school system. Mom taught science in junior high school, and Dad was the chairman for the math department at James Monroe High School. Besides being teachers, my parents were nuts about the arts—especially the theater.

Broadway Theater was thriving in the 1950s and 1960s in New York—with forty shows running at any given time. With tickets priced between $2 and $6, the middle class could afford to go to shows on a regular basis. For my parents, who had seen the original production of *Oklahoma!* for 55 cents, "regular" meant "as often as possible." They trundled into town on the subway at least once a week, often seeing the same play twice—first together, then later with Bobby and me.

My parents, Saul and Stella Landau,
on their honeymoon in 1937

For my father, the thrill of the theater began long before a play actually came to town. He scanned newspapers for any theater news. His favorite column was *News of the Rialto* in the Sunday theater section of the *New York Times*. If he found something interesting (as he often did when reading about legendary collaborations that produced musicals like *My Fair Lady* and *West Side Story*), he'd sit at his desk in the living room and write the producers long, beautiful, hand-written letters requesting tickets. The game was to order tickets before the first advertisement appeared in order to get seats in the first five center rows (my mother was hard of hearing).

Beyond that, *when* my father saw a show and *where he sat* was a great source of pride, particularly when dealing with the most popular shows which, once opened, would be sold out for months in advance. Dad was proud of the fact that he saw *My Fair Lady* twice in the first year of its run—the first time within the first week of opening and then again with Bobby and me six weeks later.

Dad fell in love with theater after seeing his first play, the Marx Brother's *The Cocoanuts* at the New Amsterdam Theater on Forty-second Street. He was only fifteen, and he had just arrived in New York from Poland. One show was all it took to hook him. After that, theater became a part of life.

As a young man, Dad worked as a social director for a Jewish adult camp in the Catskills. In those days, summer camps were a big deal for New Yorkers, especially for young people looking for husbands and wives. My father loved to put on plays, but because he couldn't afford to buy the scripts, he had to go and watch a show and copy down as much of the dialogue and stage direction as he could. He'd then stage the plays at camp, casting himself in the lead.

Despite Dad's passion for theater, he seemed content as a teacher. Though he had friends who became successful actors, he never expressed regret at his own amateur status. Years before, a friend tried to talk Dad into going to Hollywood with him to attempt a professional career, but Dad refused.

"Why didn't you go?" I asked him.

"Show business didn't give me security, and I loved math," Dad said.

In his eyes, teaching was an honor and an important profession. When I was flunking math in the sixth grade, he was heartsick because he believed my teachers were not doing their job. When I said, "Hey, Dad, did it ever occur to you that I might be stupid?" It was the only time he ever raised his hand to me, as if the thought of striking me had crossed his mind.

My father was a proud man, and remained an avid theatergoer until the day he died. Even in retirement, he'd happily drive twenty miles to see a high school production of *Death of a Salesman*.

My mother often remarked that I had inherited my father's sense of humor.

"You're almost as funny as your dad," she'd say. "Nah!" Dad would answer, "Funnier."

"You're a natural," he'd add. "Don't stop this. You don't discourage this."

Bobby and I would spend our summers at camp in upstate New York. For a few years, my father was the drama counselor and my mother was the nature counselor. Dad would put on three or four plays a summer, and my brother and I acted in them. My first part was Dopey in *Snow White and the Seven Dwarfs* when I was four and a half. My role as Dopey didn't sit well. "Dopey?" I asked. "Dad, why did you cast me as Dopey? He has no lines."

"You want lines, you have to learn how to read."

With my father's strong encouragement, by the age of ten I gave up my dream of a gunslinger or athlete for the life of an actor. But my love for theater had a tough competitor in television, particularly the Sid Ceasar and Phil Silvers shows. I had also heard about a school in New York City that trained actors, called the High School of the Performing Arts. A school where one could study acting? I couldn't believe my ears. I wanted to go there!

At age fourteen I auditioned and got in.

On the first day of school, I met a boy named Rich Greenberg and we had lunch at the Automat. I was nonplussed about what I had seen so far: It was not impressive.

"It seems to me that no one here knows anything about the theater," I said.

Incredulous, Rich peered at me from over his sandwich. "You want to be an actor?"

Rich Greenberg had no intention of acting. He lived nearby, and the school was convenient. This was typical of those days. Though Performing Arts had phenomenal dance and music departments, the drama department seemed to be a place where young men went when they didn't know where else to go. My favorite play at the time was *How to Succeed in Business Without Really Trying*. I saw it on Broadway twenty-four times. Each time, I envisioned myself in the part of Finch played by Robert Morse. In fact, I've often wondered if I willed myself to be short, knowing I could not possibly grow any taller than Bobby Morse and still play that part.

Standing room was one cheap way to see a lot of theater. The other was second-acting, sneaking into theaters after intermission. Almost every Wednesday, my best friend, Steve Ryan, and I would wear suits to school. In those days people dressed up when they went to the theater. At three o'clock, when classes were over, we could catch the last half of any matinee. We mingled in the crowd during intermission and then snuck into the theater looking for an empty cluster of seats, careful to choose a spot where the ushers wouldn't notice us.

I did this so often and became so confident of my strategy that I even took a date to *Star Spangled Girl*. We went to the library and read the first act and then snuck into the theater to watch the second act.

Performing Arts was located in the heart of Manhattan's Theater District at Forty-Sixth Street and Sixth Avenue. I'd take the subway to and from our Bronx home and every Wednesday during the spring of my senior year, I'd buy *Variety* to accompany me on my rides. I liked to look in casting news to see if there were any open calls for actors not in the union, Equity. I eventually found an open call for a male lead between eighteen and twenty-five for a role in a summer stock production of *Enter Laughing*. Auditions were held at the Henry Miller Theater only a few blocks from school. I had seen the Broadway production of the same play several times and knew I could do it. Since the auditions were held in the afternoon, I had to cut my acting class. The teacher, Mike Howard, was always telling us what bullshit Performing Arts' rules were, so even though I knew students were not allowed to audition for a professional theater company until after their graduation, I didn't think it would be a problem since the show wouldn't open until after graduation.

When I showed up at the open call, there must've been over two hundred people in the theater. The stage manager came on to the stage and said, "Thank you for coming. Everyone over twenty-five can go home now." I was stunned to see three-quarters of the actors get up and leave, but excited to survive the first cut of my first professional audition.

Two cuts later, I was still in the running.

I didn't get the part.

To make matters even worse, I got busted for cutting classes to audition for the part I didn't get. Mike Howard was pissed.

"Rules are rules," he said, "and we can't have separate rules for you." Without mentioning my name, he had the class vote on whether I should be allowed to graduate. The class voted twenty-three to two, in favor of my getting a diploma. I'd love to find those two kids who voted against me. I'm sure now I could get them to change their minds.

During the audition process, I had met another would-be actor with my same last name. He told me he had been thinking of changing his name from Danny Landau to David Landau, but he was an Equity member and Equity wouldn't let two David Landaus in the union. Innocently I told him I'm not in the union. Years later, when I was cast in my first Equity job, I was told I couldn't use it.

Eventually it came back to me; that little sneak, the Danny Landau I had met auditioning for *Enter Laughing*, had gone ahead and changed his name to David!

"How about if I use my middle initial?"

"Nope," Equity said. "It's got to be a different name."

I called my Dad and together we chose the name Lander. We had thought about Landers, but when I was talking to Equity they said, "Landers. Are you related to Ann Landers?"

I didn't want to be asked that for the rest of my life. As it turned out, it didn't matter. *S* or no *S*, Lander is a name people instinctively want to hang an *s* on. When Kathy and I were married, even the invitations read: "Landers."

Performing Arts continued to punish me for that audition. I wasn't allowed to perform in the Final Projects for the Graduating Class, a performance that was open to parents and friends. Instead, they made me a "drape technician," so all I had to show my parents was twenty-two scenes of my technique pulling curtains—hand over hand. (I didn't screw up a single one.)

My last few months at Performing Arts were particularly ridiculous in other ways as well. In one of the final plays, *Stage Door*, I came on in the second act, and because the audience was full of my friends from summer camp, the whole place applauded. The chairman of the drama department, Dr. Dyke (no kidding, that was her *real* name, but in those days I didn't get the joke) was a tall woman—Janet Reno-kind-of-sexy. She had the most peculiar habit of inhaling loudly almost with a snort, and had a haughty stance as if she was forever looking down at the rest of the world from over her glasses. When I came offstage she pulled me forcibly by the ear. "You are making a mockery of this production," she snarled.

I thought, *Whoa lady, It's not like I was smoking in the boys' room. It was just my fans.*

By then, I had been already accepted at Carnegie Tech (now Carnegie Mellon University). In fact, I was the only one from Performing Arts who had been accepted.

On our first day of orientation, Earl Gistor, the head of the Drama Department, gathered the freshmen together in the Studio Theater to tell us how hard it was to stay in the program. Each year students needed to be invited back, he said, and to make his point he asked that we take a look on our right—I was on the aisle—and to the left, because these students wouldn't be asked back. I looked to the aisle on my right. I looked to my left where there was an empty seat. I tried moving down a few seats so I'd at least have someone on my left, but he saw me coming and ran away.

Unlike Performing Arts, everyone here wanted to be an actor, and most were incredibly talented. A few days after our arrival, I met my good friend and fellow "dramat" Michael McKean. To this day we don't agree on how. In any event, when we did meet, we hit it off right away.

Every night we got together in my dorm room in Boss Hall, which we called "The Malt Shop" in honor of Rick and David Nelson's malt shop on *Ozzie and Harriet*. There we hung out, smoking and doing routines that we first knew as "Lenny and Anthony"— which eventually became what the world knew as Lenny and Squiggy.

These characters were loosely based on two guys each of us had known from home. Michael's Lenny was Polish, from Sea Cliff on Long Island. Anthony

was Italian and from the Bronx. First, we began performing Lenny and Anthony for our fellow students in
what we called DL (Dave Landau) shows. We then
continued them informally for friends only. We performed in living rooms from Pittsburgh to New York,
and then finally Los Angeles, where our informal
shtick hit the stage in 1975.

"If you spent as much time on your acting as you
do on these two stupid guys, you'd be a lot better off,"
one of our drama teachers told us. I knew it was true,
but I couldn't help myself. It was too much fun. By the
time we hit prime time as Lenny and Squiggy, we
knew these characters so well, I swear every time I
slipped into character I could feel my IQ shrinking.

An old adage in the theater that is pounded into
acting students is: do not intellectualize. With Lenny
and Squiggy, such a feat would be impossible. These
two were *that* dumb. And when we did the characters,
so were we.

Some fifteen years later, Carnegie Tech, now
Carnegie Mellon University, honored Michael and me
as distinguished alumni. We were flattered, but
slightly perplexed. After all, neither of us had gradu-
ated. In our dual speech, we reminisced about how

our four undergraduate years had seemed to go by in ten months. Only then did the school realize that we had both left after our first year! The school wanted us to speak to all the drama classes, but we refused. How could we possibly say anything wise to a sophomore when we ourselves had left college as freshmen?

The kids we did speak to asked all sorts of questions: how to find an agent; when did you get your first break; and so forth. One student asked whether it was true an actor could succeed on talent alone, or did you really need to know someone?

"Talent is the only thing that will give you your big break," I blustered. "If you have talent it really doesn't matter who you know."

"Well," the kid continued, "how did you get your big break on *Laverne & Shirley?*"

"Oh, I knew Penny Marshall."

In the middle of my second semester at Carnegie, I went to New York to audition for New York University's new School of the Arts. Within a week, I was accepted. NYU's program, run by a former professor of Carnegie's drama department, had none of Carnegie's academic restrictions. There were no grade levels like freshman or senior, just groups. As your skills progressed, you'd move into new groups. Plus, classes didn't begin until one P.M. At Carnegie I'd had to slip into tights to do movement classes at six A.M. Thankfully, those days were over.

NYU was located in the East Village, which, in 1966, in New York was a great place to be. This was when the great Yiddish theater—the Village Theater on Second Avenue—became Fillmore East, home of some of the greatest rock performances in history.

I moved into a one-room flat on Third Street and Avenue A, where I owned a bed, a hi-fi, a TV, and that was about it. In addition to taking acting classes, I did a lot of creative writing.

I got my first paid writing job through a friend I'd known at Tech, named Bob Boris. Bob lived on the Upper West Side and was working for Benton Boles, a big advertising agency. Bob had met a press agent, Bernie Bennett, who worked in the same building and needed a joke writer for his clients. From the very beginning I didn't entirely trust Bernie, maybe because of his name. It was just too on the button for a press agent; it sounded fake. Thinking about it now, it probably was.

"I want you to meet him," Bob told me. "He needs someone funny to write one-liners. You can do that, can't ya?"

One-liners, why not?

Bernie didn't have an office really, it was more of

a box—a cubicle with a desk and a typewriter, none of which looked used. He told me he had a lot of big clients—from movie stars to restaurant owners—and in order to get their names mentioned in the gossip columns, he needed funny one-liners that could be quoted as having been said. There were three big columns at the time, including Leonard Lyons and Earl Wilson, both in the *New York Post;* and the jackpot, "Dreamstreet," Bob Sylvestri's column of nothing but one-liners that ran every Friday in the *Daily News.*

If Bernie could get some good jokes with his client's name attached into Sylvestri's column, it would be worth eighty cents a line to me. At thirty lines, that would be $25 a week. The columns came out on Fridays, so Bernie had to get them in by Thursday. My deadline was typically Wednesday at four, which meant that more often than not I'd spend my Wednesday afternoons in English class writing one-liners.

Class was held in a huge auditorium. I'd sit in the back, pull out a joke pad, and begin jotting down joke after joke. I couldn't live with myself if I only had six measly lines to deliver, I'd write as many as I could. I'd end each one with a consonant. If it didn't make sense, at least it would read funny.

When I delivered the lines to Bernie he would quickly go down the list and read them out loud, tapping the paper with a pencil. "Funny," he said nodding, tapping.

"Funny. Funny." *Tap.* "Funny, not funny, funny, funny."

A hulk of a man, a little greasy, Bernie would stop and look at me. "I don't get it."

"Funny. Funny. Not funny. Funny. You know, if I were you . . . I'd take this line . . ."

And I'd look at him. "It's your line. You can do whatever you want. You can build a house on it for all I care."

One afternoon before I was supposed to meet Bernie, I was working madly, scribbling jokes in class, jotting down everything I could think of that came into my head: *There's a new item on the market. It combines the topless dress and the miniskirt. It's called a belt.* That joke was so topical I think four or five people might have used it before I did.

While I was busy working away, my professor stopped in the middle of his lecture and pointed at me.

ME? No! I thought. He must be pointing at someone else. But then everyone in the class began pointing.

"Get up, man," somebody said. "He's pointing at you."

"Yes, you, young man," the professor said. "Up."

I sheepishly rose, covering up my joke pad as best I could. I was about to be humiliated, I knew it.

"This boy," my teacher said, "is the only one in this auditorium who has taken copious notes throughout my lecture."

I smiled, thinking, *Please do not make me read my notes.*

"It's all right," he said. "You may sit down now," he said. "I just wanted to use you as an example of someone who comes to class to learn."

He beamed a big, old job-well-done smile, and when I smiled back, I wondered if he would be interested in my belt joke.

As it turned out, the belt joke was a hit. It appeared in Sylvestri's column that Friday, and was attributed to one of Bernie's clients who was French and owned a steak house in the Upper East Side of Manhattan. I was so excited I showed all my friends. Bob gave me a hard time. "How would you feel, D. L., if other guys were getting laid on your one-liners?" he laughed. "I mean, imagine if some beautiful blonde walked up to this French guy in a restaurant and said, 'I read your belt joke. It was brilliant. Take me.' "

During this time, McKean and I were still doing shtick. While I was at NYU, he was living with his parents on Long Island and working as a stock boy for Abraham & Strauss. He'd come into the city on weekends and we'd mess around with Lenny and Anthony. We had no plans; we just tripped around the city, doing shtick and having fun.

It was on one of those trips that I decided I'd had enough of New York. Michael and I were walking in the rain and I caught my reflection in a shop window. I looked like hell. My hair and clothes were soaked. We slipped into the men's room at the Edison Hotel to dry our hair under the hand dryers and I tipped my head upside down, I thought, *This is it. Man, I'm sick of this shit.* I've got to get out of this town.

I left New York for Los Angeles in June. I had studied acting for five years now. I was tired of going to school. I wanted to try the acting biz in the real world, so I took my life savings and packed the contents of my apartment into a big black suitcase. I first flew to Pittsburgh to say good-bye to some buddies at Tech. A funny guy named Albert Einstein (Albert Brooks) gave me the number of a good friend of his, a guy named Rob Reiner. "Look him up," Albert told me. "You'll love him."

I stuffed Reiner's number in my suitcase with endless other numbers that I planned to call in search of a place to stay. I had cousins in Long Beach, but the last people I wanted to bunk with were my relatives. This was the Summer of Love. Staying with family would have been a bummer.

I spent my first hour in L.A. in a phone booth. All the numbers I had were either out of service or wrong, so I reluctantly called the cousins. A half-hour later, my younger cousin, David Willner, drove up and saved my ass.

I remember the relief I felt when I saw him. It was about six o'clock on a warm L.A. evening when we drove out of the airport. I relaxed in the passenger seat and looked out the windows—sunshine and palm trees everywhere, and on the radio, Vin Scully was calling the Dodger-Cardinal game. *I can't believe I did it*, I thought. *Man, I am in L.A.!*

TWO

ENTER LAUGHING, SORT OF:

THE ADVENTURES OF LENNY AND SQUIGGY

When I first arrived in Hollywood

I arrived in Los Angeles on June 8, 1967, with four hundred bucks and a dream. Because I had no place to live, I alternated between sleeping at my cousins in Long Beach and on friends' floors in the city. Some floors were very famous, like the Venice commune where Jim Morrison of the Doors lived. I never met the great man. He was always asleep, but one morning, two of his groupies made me a breakfast of spaghetti over easy and freshly squeezed beer.

One of the few telephone numbers that worked when I first arrived belonged to Albert Brooks's friend Rob Reiner. Rob and I decided to meet at a coffee shop in Westwood and became fast friends and writing partners. While we wrote our first script, he invited me to stay in the attic of his parents' Beverly Hills home. I remember my first trip up the stairway. I saw more Emmys strewn about than I've ever seen since. At the time, Rob's father, Carl Reiner, was among the best and the brightest writers and actors of TV's golden age. He also created *The Dick Van Dyke Show* and as a writer and actor for *Your Show of Shows* and *Caesar's Hour*. He was also the author of the book, *Enter Laughing*, the basis for the play, which marked my first professional audition. What's it about? A Jewish kid from the Bronx who dreams of a career as a stage actor. It wasn't that different from my own dream when growing up in the Bronx, but by 1967, at the age of twenty, my dream was to get a job.

Fortunately, one of Rob's and my first scripts opened the door to a staff-writing job on the TV special *Romp!* a laugh-in variety show geared toward the young hip set. It starred Ryan O'Neil and Michele Lee, and was produced by a guy named Al Burton. Burton had made his career organizing Teenage Fairs in cow towns around the country and was now making a transition to television. *Romp!* was to be a big hit with the hope that Burton would be the world's next Dick Clark. Like we needed another one.

The first week, Reiner and I were excited about the hip, funny sketches we wrote that we thought would go over well with Burton. But by the second week, it was clear he didn't agree. Burton brought in a couple of writers who he thought were even hipper than us. They were so hip they changed all our material. Rob wanted to take his name off the credits. I didn't. I never before had my name on any credits.

In the end, both our names were left on, but Rob was right. The show was panned by *Variety* in a review that read, "Among the untalented writing staff are Rob Reiner and David Lander." I was sitting at the famous Schwab's drugstore counter when I read it. Beside me syndicated gossip columnist Sydney Skolsky worked on his column "This is Hollywood" as he did every week. I turned and smiled sheepishly as I folded my paper and shrunk into my seat. I couldn't believe it. The new writers had cut everything we had done, and yet *we* were panned.

Rob and I continued working together as writers and as actors. He directed me in a one-act play called *The Exposure of Raymond Splotros*. We got mixed reviews. But whenever Rob was lauded, I was panned—

and vice versa. One of the finest reviews of Rob from the early days was one of my worst. I can't say I'm thrilled by the knowledge that Rob still keeps it, handsomely framed and displayed prominently, in his office at Castle Rock Entertainment.

By the summer of 1968, Albert Brooks had arrived from Tech and he became part of our crowd. The three of us often got together to talk about how much better off show business would be if we were in charge. One afternoon at the Old World Café on Sunset Boulevard, the waitress came to take our order, and Reiner told her, "I'll take the Belgian waffle. It's so light. It's like eating a cloud."

Brooks, who wanted something healthier, ordered an organic salad.

When the food came, Reiner continued his goof. He bit into his waffle. "It's like eating a cloud." He then looked at Albert's salad in horror and recoiled. "I am eating a cloud and you are eating dirt," he scowled.

"Sky above, mud below," I laughed.

I wasn't eating anything but orange juice and crackers. My number had come up in the draft and I didn't want to go. The starvation strategy worked: As a result of a subsistence diet and plenty of walking (I had no car), I had lost forty pounds since coming to L.A. I had gotten down to 120 lbs, and my scrawny physique spared me an all-expenses-paid tour of Vietnam.

My first apartment was at Pico and Sepulveda Boulevard under the San Diego Freeway. I had rented it with a friend and actor, Peter Jason. On the day we moved in I noticed what sounded like a loud, constant *whoosh—whoosh—whoosh*.

"What's that?" I asked the landlord.

He looked at me as if I was the first person who had ever asked him that.

"Oh, that's the freeway."

"Well, does it ever stop?

"No, it's a freeway," he said. "You'll hear that all the time."

"Well, how am I going to be able to sleep?"

He hesitated.

"Just pretend it's the ocean," he said. "People move out to Malibu and pay a lot more money than you to hear that sound."

"Well, if the sound of the ocean keeps me up when I have enough money to move to Malibu, I'll just pretend it's the freeway."

"Yeah," he said. "You do that, kid."

I had to laugh. It was one of those classic *only in LA* lines that would resonate for years.

● One of my first nonacting jobs was answering other people's phones on an answering service called Sunset Dial. This was a company unlike any other because all the operators were male. "Women like to have a male voice answer the phone," the owner told me. "It discourages unwanted suitors. And wake up calls are better coming from a male. Women find it somehow . . . comforting."

The owner, a former actor who had played mostly cowboy roles, was flexible. Should I have an audition or get an acting job, he assured me that my place at the service would be secure. The Dial was located on the second floor of a walk-up on Gardner Street just off Sunset Boulevard in Hollywood. We'd open at six A.M. every day but Sunday and I'd work until about seven in the evening. There were usually two of us working the board, which provided a direct line into our client's home phone. Most days I sat around waiting for the phone to ring, always knowing it would be for someone else. I'd give actresses and models their messages or tell them, "All clear." We had one client who called religiously three times a day for messages.

Three times a day I would tell him, "All clear." It was always all clear except when his bill was due at the end of the month. When he called, I told him he had one message (at last). It was from us telling him that his bill was due.

At about that time there was a new radio show on KRLA, a satirical newscast called the *Credibility Gap*

that was getting a lot of attention. In the late sixties, politics made great fodder for satire. One of the Dial's clients, a singer, an actress, and all-around wonderful person named Sally Smaller, sometimes worked for them. I always looked forward to giving Sally her messages. She seemed to laugh at everything I had to say.

One afternoon, she asked if I knew how to write comedy, and if I could do voices, "What do you mean, do I do voices?" I said. "Of course I do voices."

Apparently two of the *Gap* cast members had come down with the flu and they were looking for someone with a comedy background to come in for an on-the-air audition. It paid $60 a day, the same amount I made in a week at the Sunset Dial.

KRLA, a 50,000-watt station in Pasadena, was located on the property of the huge Huntington Sheraton Hotel. I had no car, so Rob chauffered me and joined me on the show. He ended up staying all day, writing and performing along with me and the other cast members.

When we walked into a big office, it looked like your average newsroom packed with desks, typewriters, AP and UPI wire services. In the corner sat Harry Shearer, a slim and intense guy with shoulder-length hair. He held up a piece of yellow copy from the newswire and asked, "You want to do something on this?"

Within an hour we came up with a sketch and that day, Harry, Rob, and I wrote and performed three shows. Lew Irwin, the news director, liked our work and hired me on the spot. The following day I met the other members of the *Gap*: Richard Beebe, a veteran radio newsman who had come down with the flu; actor Bob Goodwin, and singer-songwriter Len Chandler.

After a few months Chandler and Goodwin would leave the show, so to my mind it was always Richard, Harry, and I who made up the *Credibility Gap*. Beebe had been on KRLA the longest. He was a seasoned radio newsman with a booming basso voice. We'd typically do a straight version of a news story first and then satirize it. This was 1969, the height of the Vietnam War when Richard Nixon, Spiro Agnew, and Henry Kissinger were constantly in the news. On our show, Shearer played Nixon, Beebe played Agnew, and I played Kissinger.

We performed our sketches upstairs in a studio, usually only with five minutes to spare. Because this was news and had to be up to the minute, the deadline was sometimes cut so close to the bone that we'd be recording the end of the show as the beginning of the show was going on the air. It got so close once, we were throwing tapes over the balcony from our recording studio on the third floor to the news studio on the second.

About a year later, Michael McKean joined us. I had been after him for the whole time, calling him every week. He was still in New York at NYU. "C'mon out to L.A.," I'd say. "It's a good time. I can get you work on the radio writing shtick three times a day."

McKean eventually showed up and found me

Michael and Harry and me during
the Credibility Gap *period*

firmly ensconced in L.A.—and married. Two months after I started at the *Gap*, my roommate Jim had gone home to Oregon and asked me to watch out for his girlfriend, Thea. I did. Thea and I knew each other for all of four days before we went to Las Vegas and got married. Surprisingly, the marriage lasted seven years to the day. On our seventh anniversary, Thea and I looked at each other and knew it was over.

About two years after I began at the *Gap*, we were all fired from KRLA. The station had been running a promo to find out which disc jockeys were the most popular. No one had bargained for the thousand pieces of *Credibility Gap* fan mail. But after the show, listeners would apparently turn the dial to another station. Trying to catch listeners off guard, the station decided that instead of three ten-minute shows, they would do ten three-minute shows. That way, I guess the reasoning went, listeners would have to listen longer. Each show was to air twenty-seven minutes after the hour, but because this was the time before digital watches, it was nearly impossible for people to find us. To make matters worse, the advertising department had placed a huge advertisement in the *Los Angeles Times*, listing the wrong time for the show.

Around this same time we did a sketch based on

Vice President Spiro Agnew's visit to a hospital in Vietnam. What caught our attention during the pep talk he gave to the wounded soldiers there was his comment, "Though none of you will ever lead a normal life again, I envy you because you will always have your honor."

That line was better than any line that we could ever write. So we had our own Agnew, played by Richard Beebe, say the exact same thing on the air. Little did we suspect that forty miles away, a conservative carpenter in very conservative Orange County sat in his car messing with the dial. He had happened to hear Beebe's Agnew by accident. He had never heard of the *Credibility Gap*, but he had heard of Agnew and thought the *Credibility Gap*—whoever we were—had made the vice president of the United States sound insensitive and stupid. He called the station and happened to catch the ear of the station manager, Larry Webb.

Webb ordered us up to his office, where not one of us had ever before set foot.

"Before that show airs again," he told us, "I want you to rerecord it, but this time make Agnew sound smarter."

"Those were Agnew's words, not ours," Harry said.

"I don't care."

"But we can't change the news," Richard said.

"Do it," he said.

We didn't.

A month or two later, we were gone.

When the *Los Angeles Times* did a story on our dismissal, Webb said, "We had to let them go. The times are just too serious for satire."

He might not have known it, but Webb's statement was eerily similar to a comment made by Paul Joseph Goebbels, Hitler's propaganda minister, when he shut down all the cabarets in Berlin just before the Nazis marched into Poland.

Within a few months, we were hired on at an FM underground station called KPPC. This was radio like it ought to be. The disc jockeys played nothing but album cuts of incredible rock and roll, and we were free to do up to thirty minutes of show each day sandwiched between long cuts of music. We thrived on the freedom here: some shows ran five minutes; others went for a full half-hour. It depended on what the sketch called for and what the news was that day.

In 1971 the Pirates won the World Series and in an unrelated move, the station ownership changed and everyone was fired. Les Carter, KPPC's manager, once asked me if I preferred to keep my job or have the Pirates win the World Series.

"Pirates," I said. "I can always get a job, but I don't know if the Bucs will ever win the WORLD Series again."

◉ Shortly after leaving KPPC, the *Gap* hit the stage with Michael McKean joining us full-time. We made three albums: *Woodschtick* in 1973 for Capitol Records and *A Great Gift Idea* for Warner Reprise in 1974. Each album brought us on tour where we opened for a lot of folk and rock and roll acts. We'd

Listening to "Woodschtick"
with Harry Shearer, 1973

play clubs and colleges—sometimes in cafeterias and, every once in a great while, a real theater or auditorium. We played at New York's Bottomline, opening for Bill Cobbom who had six tons of drums bolted to the stage. Though we were completely jazzed to be playing New York, when we saw the stage—or what was left of it—our four hearts collectively sank. The only place we could do our act was the stage-right corner, which was so small, we couldn't all fit on the stage at the same time. This stage business had been a real pain in the ass. A year before on the Capitol tour, we had played, of all things, a *rack-jobbers* convention in a ball room in Tuscon. By show time they had yet to order a stage. When we talked to the guy who booked us, he bowed his head and uttered one of the more famous lines used in the film *Spinal Tap*, "This is my fault. Well, kick my ass. Kick my ass."

A high point of the *Credibility Gap* occurred when Bob Shane, the talent coordinator for *The Johnny Carson Show*, saw one of our performances at the University of California at Irvine. He approached us after the show to say how much he loved our work: "Johnny has got to see this." We set up a date at the *Tonight Show* studios at NBC in Burbank.

Carson and his producer Freddy Decordova roared with laughter when they saw our sketch. But it was a satire of Polish folk humor, which would cause a ruckus with the Polish community. *The Tonight Show* could never get away with it. Could we come up with something else?

Shane suggested another sketch: *The Danny Wade Show* in which I play Danny, a small-time talk show host in Cleveland, who was interviewing Batman and Superman about how they were planning on fighting drugs in their upcoming comic books. The sketch ran about twelve minutes. When we did a run-through for Carson's technical crew, we had to shorten it to five minutes, cutting out all the jokes. Bob Shane assured us that no one would see this; it was only for the cameras. After we finished, Bob met us backstage. He was ashen, stricken. "The worst has happened," he told us. "Johnny saw the run-through and hated it. You've been cut from the show."

"But you told us this could never happen!" I said.

"It just did."

I distinctly remember the sound of throwing the garbage can against the mirror of my dressing room. It was rubber, so it didn't crash but rather made this pathetic rubber *squish-squish bump.*

Not too long before the *Credibility Gap* ended, Michael and I brought Lenny and Anthony together again. Up until then, we had limited our audience to only friends, but Harry encouraged us to bring Lenny and Anthony to the stage. The boys went over like gangbusters. We were thrilled. We thought maybe there was a future for these guys after all.

The Saturday after Thanksgiving in 1975, the *Gap* was performing at the Improv when Rob Reiner called me to say that his wife, Penny Marshall, and he were throwing a party to celebrate the sale of Penny's new show, *Laverne & Shirley* to ABC. There was no pilot for *Laverne & Shirley*. Penny and Cindy Williams had recently done a guest appearance on *Happy Days* as two loose women, and ABC's president Fred Silverman thought they would do well with their own show. They were given the slot at 8:30 on Tuesdays following *Happy Days*.

I had to leave the party around nine to get back into Hollywood to perform with the *Gap*, and as I was walking out the door, Penny asked me if I would return with Michael and perform Lenny and Anthony. They would make perfect last-ditch dates for Laverne and Shirley, she thought, but Rob and Penny had been big fans of Lenny and Anthony; nobody on the writing staff had ever seen them. The plan was for Michael and me to come back after our show. Most of the writers would be there, as well as Garry Marshall, one of the producers and Penny's brother.

McKean was reluctant. "I'm not going. I don't know any of those people."

"C'mon," I urged him, "your wife is pregnant and you have six dollars in the bank. If we can get our guys on TV just once, we qualify for maximum unemployment!"

After our performance with the *Gap*, Michael and I drove over the hill to Penny and Rob's house in Studio City. In the car, we agreed not to bring out Lenny and Anthony unless it felt right. The last thing we wanted was to be pushy. But as soon as we got there, Rob looked over to us and said, "So? You gonna do Lenny and Anthony?"

A hush fell over the crowd. The house was packed. Michael and I launched into this routine we had never done before or since: Lenny and Anthony at the Domestic Trades School in New York, learning how to be butlers. Lenny and Anthony had to do a homework assignment dramatizing the exchange between a butler and the master of the house. Lenny was the butler and Anthony was the master of the house. Lenny was the butler and Anthony was the master of the house, only they couldn't agree on anything. So besides being really stupid, they were disagreeable and swore a lot.

I don't remember if we did five minutes or a half

an hour, but it went over great. The next day I got a call from Garry Marshall. "Everyone thinks you guys were terrific last night with these two guys. But can they be funny and *clean?*"

"I don't know," I said. "We've never done them clean."

The following week, we were hired as apprentice writers. We were going to learn the sitcom business, and our teacher was the great Garry Marshall. What this meant was we got $300 a week under the table and no credit. By the end of the season, we were told, Garry would give us the chance to write a script. After that we could join Writers Guild of America (WGA) and get paid like real writers.

Laverne & Shirley was slated to shoot the following week. In the meantime, we watched how *Happy Days* was done.

The goal was to write and act what we wrote, which sounds simple but wasn't. We were involved in a complicated writing hierarchy: the script was written by one guy and then rewritten by about twelve others. Different scenes were assigned to different writers. In the morning, everyone disappeared. By the end of the day, they'd show up again with their scenes. At that point, Garry, who was the producer but should have been called the head writer, would put it all together. The next day, the actors would read the script in the morning and have it on its feet by the afternoon when it would be tightened and sweetened, and often rewritten all over again. The following day, the actors would return and rehearse while the writers would watch, adding jokes and tightening. Finally, everyone but the actors—writers, producers, secretaries, and the dialogue coaches—would order dinner and go through the script again. Usually those with the loudest voices would get their jokes in as a secretary frantically tried to get everything down to redo the script for the next morning. Each rewrite was in a different color—white, light blue, pink, and then finally bright yellow. The process would begin on a Monday and end on Friday, the night of filming.

The creators of the characters and the show, Lowell Ganz and Mark Rothman, were both in their late twenties. Lowell was skinny and intense but worked his ass off, and though we didn't always agree I always respected his ability and passion. Rothman, on the other hand, was a very large man who had little to say, except when it was time to order dinner.

Michael and I understood that our first task was to rewrite a scene between Laverne and Shirley. This was strange: we had worked together for seven years, but had never written women's dialogue for any part we were not performing ourselves. One afternoon, Garry came to our office to see what we had come up with. He was less than amused by our work.

"No! No! No!" he said. "You're not supposed to be writing the girls. Put in those two funny guys you do, Lenny and Marvin."

"Marvin?" I said. "You mean Anthony?"

"No, not Anthony," Gary said. "We have too many Italians on the show."

So Anthony—at least his name—was history. I didn't like the name Marvin, so we had to come up with a better idea. Anthony had a cousin he talked about named "Squiggy," but Squiggy was also Italian. Since the show was set in Milwaukee, which had a huge German population, we figured we could make Squiggy German. Thus Anthony Faziliano became Andrew Squiggman, or Squiggy for short.

We wrote the boys into the first scene of the first script, and everyone loved them. They asked us to write the characters into the second act. From what we had seen the act was going to take place in Laverne and Shirley's apartment, but we couldn't figure out a way to get Lenny and Squiggy inside. That's when McKean suggested a soon-to-be-famous joke: a way to get Squiggy into a room without having to knock.

In the scene, Shirley is fretting that she will never meet Mr. Right.

"Don't worry, Shirl," Laverne says. "One day your Prince Charming could walk right through that door."

The door bursts open, and Squiggy says, "Hello."

Gary loved it. "It's your trademark," he said referring to J. J. Walker's trademark on the show *Good Times*. "It's your own DIN-O-MITE."

After the first show aired, I heard from college friends I hadn't heard from in years. They were blown away to see our old friends from the Malt Shop Days on TV, but they wished we hadn't cleaned them up for television. I guess they had never heard of the FCC.

The show was number one its first week and went on to be the highest-rated show on TV in its first two seasons. Six weeks after the first show, Garry Marshall called Michael and me into his office. We were convinced Garry was going to ask us to leave, but instead he told us that ABC president Fred Silverman had called. "He thinks those guys are doing a different play than Laverne and Shirley," Garry said. "Fred wants to see their play."

So Garry hired us to write a presentation script to be used to evaluate the show potential before doing a pilot. But first, Michael and I felt that a few other things had to happen. Michael and I were only apprentice writers; we had yet to garner any of the perks of actors or writers of a hit TV show. We were not allowed to drive on the lot, we shared a dressing room, and we were being paid only a measly sum as writers, plus the day player fee for actors. A lot had to change before we would agree to spend our time writing another script.

We said no for two weeks; then finally Garry put me on the phone with Fred Silverman. "Take it or leave it," Silverman said. "Now or never."

Everything we wanted then magically appeared. The following morning when Michael and I arrived at the studio, we drove to our new parking spot on the lot and saw a sign that said, WELCOME TO FORT DIX. The studio was dressed up as a fort crawling with extras marching on maneuvers on a set of army barracks. Lenny and Squiggy were in the army, which, incidentally was the name of the show—not a great title, but that's what they wanted. Everyone at Paramount was very excited, but when ABC didn't pick up the show, all the people who thought we were so brilliant no longer answered our calls.

A week later, we were back as supporting actors on a big hit TV show. And once again, I was successful in staying out of the army.

*Kathy and me at our wedding
with Penny Marshall and Rob Reiner*

Not too soon after this, I reconnected with a friend, Kathy Fields, who was hired to shoot publicity photographs of the show for ABC. I had known Kathy for years. She was friendly with my then ex-wife, Thea, as well as many mutual friends. When she was on the set, somehow, we were able to renew our friendship and over time, it grew into a loving relationship. We began dating. We had been friends for so long, it was immediately a comfortable and loving relationship.

Kathy had great insight into the film and television

business after growing up in the center of the industry. Her father, Freddie Fields, was a super agent who made countless contributions to the film industry. (Does Creative Management [CMA/ICM] or film packaging ring a bell?) Kathy had leads in important films like *Johnny Got His Gun* and *The Happy Ending*, but ultimately opted to work behind the scenes as a still photographer. Her wisdom and support was unparalled by anyone or anything I had ever known, and after living together for a year and knowing each other for nine, we married in March 1979. The Bucs won the World Series that year, and dedicated the year to us. Talk about a good omen! A few years later, our daughter, Natalie, was born. Ten weeks premature at two pounds thirteen ounces, her arm was barely larger than a Bic lighter. She was perfect. Her hand was as big as my thumb nail, but she had all five fingers and what looked like little tear drops for finger nails. She was beautiful.

THREE

SQUIGGY CATCHES MS:

THE ONSLAUGHT BEGINS

Portland, 1980

There's something irresistible about Buffalo in February. This is what Michael and I must have been thinking when we accepted the invitation to help raise money for a multiple sclerosis telethon in upstate New York.

As television celebrities, that's what we did: special appearances on talk shows, auto shows, and telethons. Penny Marshall and Cindy Williams's special engagements as Laverne and Shirley were considerably more upscale. While they waved from a float at the Macy's Thanksgiving Day Parade, Lenny and Squiggy did an auto show in Cleveland, signing autographs from the back of a truck. And while Penny and Cindy sunned themselves in Palm Springs, we froze our asses off in Buffalo.

I knew next to nothing about MS. I also didn't understand how telethons worked. So, before we went on the air, I spent some time with neurologist Dr. Larry Jacobs, the MS Telethon director and one of the world's leading authorities on MS. "Why would anyone give money to MS if they already gave to Jerry's disease on Labor Day?" I asked him.

"Anyone can get this one," Jacobs said without missing a beat. "People are born with muscular dystrophy, but anyone can wake up with multiple sclerosis. All it takes is a trauma to the nervous system. You can hit your head on the lid of your car trunk and wake up the next day unable to walk."

So there was my pitch. At two in the morning, I stood in front of TV cameras and told whoever was awake in Buffalo, New York, what Dr. Jacobs had told me—that MS was an equal-opportunity destroyer and that it could hit any of us anytime.

I struck a chord.

Despite the early morning hour, the telethon's phones began to ring. Little did I know that same chord would sound again five years later. Just my luck. This time it was for me.

The year was 1983. A year or so after *Laverne &
Shirley*, I began to notice small, strange physical problems: numb fingers and limbs, vertigo, and difficulty
with balance. I had a hard time running. In the months
from winter to spring, symptoms appeared and disappeared, and I slowly began to understand that there
might be something really wrong with me. But still I
denied it. I thought that whatever was happening was
not serious. Just pretend it's the ocean, I told myself.
Just pretend the staggering exhaustion of seventeen
hours on a set was from a wild weekend with a friend.

While playing an assistant choreographer on *The
Love Boat*, there was one scene in which I had to walk
down the boat deck behind my boss, played by Ben
Vereen, an old friend from Performing Arts. I found
myself having difficulty keeping up with Ben and hitting the mark in time to say my line. We kept cutting
and retaking the shot. The director was growing very
irritated, but for some reason my legs would not move
fast enough. In a fit of frustration, I finally said, "What
difference does it make if I hit the mark? The laugh
machine will get the joke."

The AD went ballistic. "I don't know how you did
it over at L and S, but here we take our comedy very
seriously."

That was the funniest thing he said all day.

That winter I flew to Mexico to co-star in *Conan the Destroyer* with De Laurentis Films, directed by Richard Fleischer and starring Arnold Schwarzenegger, Wilt Chamberlain, and Grace Jones. For those of you who don't know the film, don't worry: It was far from memorable. But as a sequel to the original *Conan the Barbarian*, I crossed my fingers, and said yes. After eight years in television, I was eager to break into film. Up until this point I had worked on only *Used Cars* and *1941*, and both had been good experiences. Fleischer was a respectable director. (His father, Max Fleischer, had created *Popeye*—and he had told me they wanted to make this *Conan* funnier.

By the time I accepted the role of Conan's funny sidekick, Malek, it was December 1983, and Kathy and I and Natalie, who was eight months old, flew to Mexico City for the few months of shooting. By then, Kathy had worked on many very big films including *Towering Inferno*, and John Huston's *The Man Who Would Be King*, so she understood the perils of on-location living. But she and the baby still wanted to be with me. Rehearsals began in Mexico City where I brushed up on horseback riding and sword-and-dagger fighting (skills I could probably use later in life) and

Kathy looked for a house. We then went our separate ways. I flew north to Juárez and Kathy and the baby flew home to pack up and rejoin me in a few weeks when the shoot resumed.

A two-hour plane ride from Mexico City, Juárez is a run-down crossing town just over the border from El Paso, Texas. De Laurentis put the cast and crew up at a cut-rate hotel in the center of town, which boasted a few cafés and a disco. There was a mall in El Paso, and some evenings the cast and crew would go across the border for dinner and a movie. The hotel was packed with the staff for two De Laurentis movies. David Lynch was in town reshooting *Dune*. Most of the principal photography had been done, but because the film wasn't working, Lynch was shooting more footage. As *Dune* went more and more over budget, De Laurentis began to compensate by cutting scenes from our movie and replacing them with dialogue.

The shooting location was two hours from our hotel. Getting there was often its own adventure, especially when traveling with Wilt Chamberlain and Arnold Schwarzenegger. Once, when the *federales* stopped our van, Wilt raised a hand as if to say I'll take care of this. He climbed out and towered over the Mexican cops who circled around him. "Señor Chamberlain," they said. "Oh, Señor Wilt, so big."

Unfortunately, from the very beginning the director Richard Fleischer and I did not see eye to eye. One of the first scenes we shot was with Arnold and me both on horseback. Arnold would say a line. Then I'd say a line. Back and forth we went until I said the joke; a put-down of my character. We did this several times. Remember, we're on horseback being followed by a camera truck. But because there are no mufflers in all of Mexico, we're shouting our lines over the roaring motorboat sounds of the muffler.

"Why are you shouting your lines? You're right next to him!" Fleischer screamed.

"Because he can't hear me and I can't hear him," I screamed back at him.

"What?!"

We go back and forth screaming, and then I'd suggest we switch lines.

"You know what might be funny is if Arnold said the joke. That way, it establishes the kind of relationship these guys have."

Fleischer and Arnold both loved the idea and we shot the scene that way.

The following day I was waiting in the lobby with Wilt, when Fleischer walked toward me. He was an older man in his mid-sixties and walked with a cane.

He looked at me with a newfound disrespect. "You blew that joke."

"What do you mean?" I asked him.

"It doesn't work when Arnold says it," he said.

"That shouldn't be too big of a problem," I said. "Didn't you shoot it both ways?"

He had, but he was furious that I'd been the one to make the suggestion.

Things grew worse. One night at dinner, Grace Jones and I began running our lines together. Grace was very hot at the time of the making of this film. She's incredibly exotic-looking, but when she opened her mouth she sounded like a girl who grew up in Brooklyn. As we ran lines back and forth, I suggested she use her native Jamaican accent. When she did, she sounded so sexy. She was very excited about it, but Fleischer hit the roof.

"Who are you to play director?" he yelled.

Strike Two.

The thunderous and inevitable conclusion was reached a few days later. I was sick with what I thought was the flu, but I continued to work. Arnold and I were playing a desert scene, in which I have a bag of jewels and the army is quickly approaching from behind. Arnold takes out a huge sword, and I begin stuffing the jewels in my mouth and swallowing them. The problem was, what was in the bag was whatever jewels the prop man could find. They were rusty old brooches that still had the pins on them. Holding them in my mouth for too long could make me even sicker, and there was no way to swallow them—no matter what.

"What we do when I put them in my mouth?" I asked Fleischer. "Do I make the motion and sound of swallowing and then you cut back so I can take them out of my mouth to say the line?"

"Oh no," he said, "You just keep them in your mouth."

So I did. I stuffed all the jewels in my mouth and sat there. He then he asked that I take a jewel out and hold it up so a ray of the sun shoots through the jewel and onto my forehead. Great. It would be very cinematic, but all the jewels had a metal backing so there was no way for the light to go through the metal and onto my head.

All the while Fleischer kept yelling, "No! No! No!" and the soundman was complaining about hearing the jewels rattling against my teeth. It was a disaster. "I hear David's teeth rattling," he said.

"Well, Richard," Arnold strutted around. "Next

time you hire an actor maybe you should have him read the lines before you give him the job."

Thanks, Arnold.

There was no winning, and I was growing sicker and sicker. I had developed a strange weakness in my legs and the next day I had a very high fever. I went out to the location and we shot a scene in which Fleischer made me lie in the mud as my double stood idly by. The following morning the producer, Ed Pressman, a nice enough fellow, got a doctor to give me some huge, green horse pill and we drove up to the location. I was very wobbly. Fleischer and Pressman whispered to each other and I was sent back to the hotel. I slept for a day and a half only to be awoken by my manager, Herbie Nannas, who was screaming all the way from Los Angeles.

"What are you doing?" Herbie screamed.

"What do you mean, Herbie?" I said.

"They're saying you're drunk."

"I'm sick."

"They're saying you're drunk," he screamed. "And they fired you.

I lay in bed trying to register what was happening.

"I'm getting the next plane out of here," I said.

"No, you're not. I told Raffaela De Laurentis that

at least she should have the decency to fire you personally. You have to wait for her to show up."

By the time I returned to the States, there was significant weakness in my legs. The best way to describe it was a jelly leg—as if one leg was drunk and the other sober. It came and went, but each time I experienced that type of weakness, I began to lose self-confidence. In our house in Hollywood Hills, I remember looking down the stairs and feeling dizzy. At the time, the only thing I knew about vertigo was the Alfred Hitchcock movie. It didn't make sense. I thought I needed to be higher up to have vertigo. Here I was getting vertigo standing on top of a stair landing.

⬤ When I left Mexico, I tried to go to the gym every day. Arnold had told me it was good practice to do three or four sets of exercise weights every day. To warm up, I ran. I loved to run, but I started to realize I wasn't going very fast and I wasn't getting anywhere. After three or four steps I would lose my balance and fall over. I couldn't go any more than four or five feet. That's when I said to myself, *Wait a minute, something is wrong.* But before my thinking went any further, I reasoned it must have been the aftereffects of the flu, or that maybe after being fired I was depressed.

I stopped going to the gym.

March is the season for baseball spring training, and Kathy and I would go to Florida every year to see my mother in West Palm Beach and watch the ball games. One night I felt weak and the next day after driving across the state to see the Pirates play, I was on my way to the press box up a long rickety staircase and I couldn't walk. I looked up the stairs and knew I didn't have an ounce of strength in my legs.

McKenzie Field is a cozy old ballpark where the Bucs train. Each row of seats was up a step and between each step, there was a space where I could see the ground. I imagined I would fall right through.

After the game, the weakness went away and we returned to Los Angeles in April. I was scheduled to appear at a celebrity benefit run by a longtime writing partner and friend, Peter Elbling, for the National Committee for an Effective Congress. While rehearsing a very simple dance number, Howard Hessman from WKRP turned to me and said, "I can see that dancing is not your strong suit."

"You're right, it isn't," I said. "I guess I'm just clumsy."

The choreography involved a very simple left foot down and right foot cross over, but I couldn't manage it. Later that week, the night of the show, I arrived early and parked in the lot behind the Wiltern Theater. When I got out of the car, my leg buckled, and I collapsed.

"Damn it! What is that?"

I knew I could not walk up the four steps that led to the stage door. So instead I went around to the front. I was scheduled to go onstage and perform a character I do called Dave Sportz, but I wasn't sure I would be able to make it to the center of the stage. An hour later, I felt better, though I was frightened I would collapse again. I'll never forget that feeling. I was backstage when the lights went down and suddenly I had to go to my place. The desk looked like it was two miles away. When I finally got to my chair, I dropped into it with huge feeling of relief. I couldn't believe I had made it. And then, *boom!* The lights came up.

I immediately launched into my speech, with a clipped Walter Winchell delivery. "This is Dave Sports Speaking of Sports Today's Dave Sportz Speaking of Sportz Spotlight falls on . . ." The scene was in full gear, but my mind was circling a different world. I was preoccupied with wondering how I was going to get up and walk backstage when the lights went out. Then my mind raced from the curtain call to the dance number.

The day of my first big fall, Easter 1983

Somehow I made it offstage, but the curtain call was a different story. Buck Henry stood to my left. I looked at him. "Hold me up, will ya? I may fall over into the orchestra pit." He must have thought I was joking, because all he did was laugh. But I didn't fall.

Later that week, Kathy, Natalie and I were at my father-in-law's annual Easter bash. I had just bundled one-year-old Natalie into my arms and was walking back to the house. But as I passed the pool, my legs buckled as if someone had hit me at the back of the knees with a baseball bat. *Bam.* I fell to the ground, holding Nat like a football I didn't want to fumble.

Everyone ran over to make sure the baby was okay. Ursula Andress was there and she removed Natalie from my arms. "Oh David," she said, "I've had the same thing with my ankle."

She wasn't the only one. "I know what you're going through," somebody said.

"I've had that," someone else offered. "My ankle was pulled." This and that. This was a hamstring I had. Pinched nerve. Everybody had an explanation for my fall.

But I knew I hadn't tripped on anything, and I knew it wasn't an ankle. I knew what a twisted ankle felt like and I knew *this* didn't feel like *that*. This felt like nothing I had ever felt before.

Knowing what I know now, I could see how this disease worked. Right before my fall I'd been on edge, because a TV producer at the party had just told me that *Laverne & Shirley* was turning out to be a failure in syndication. He seemed thrilled. Like a jerk, I believed him. While I have no medical proof, I think that the insecurity I felt after our conversation showed in my body.

With MS, after every exacerbation, you learn, *Well, I can't trust that anymore.* You read the National MS Society pamphlets after you're first diagnosed, and you feel worse than you did before: *If you think* this is bad, wait until a month from now when you lose your sight and your speech. The worst MS symptom I heard about was through third baseman Wade Bogg's sister who had MS. We had met at a golf tournament Wade hosted to benefit MS research. Bogg's sister told me she woke up one morning and couldn't swallow. To this day, that remains one of my scariest thoughts.

Later that spring, I was appearing on *Hollywood Squares*. It was a Saturday afternoon, and the Dodger game was on the TV in my dressing room. Right before it was my turn to be introduced I watched Vincent Price run across the stage and thought I would follow doing the same. I started to trot, but my legs had no interest in cooperating. Then, after my introduction, I looked at the ladder leading up to my box in the middle of the *Hollywood Squares*, and I didn't know if I could make it. I refused to come down throughout the taping of all five shows because I was pretty sure I wouldn't be able to climb back up. When we broke for lunch, I had it sent up to my square. You might say I ordered square service.

A few days later I had an audition in Hollywood on Sunset and Doheny, a place I had been many times. I parked in a garage nearby. When I got out in the street though, I couldn't get down off the curb. I could imagine lifting my foot but that's as far as I got. My

foot just wouldn't work. By this time, I had completely lost faith in my legs. I didn't trust them to be
able to step off a curb without buckling.

I looked across the street and I saw another curb.
That was the first time I ever used those handicap
ramps for wheelchairs. It never occurred to me that I
was handicapped. I just hoped it would all go away
again tomorrow. I questioned what was happening to
me, but I had no desire to find answers. I kept shoving
whatever it was aside. Maybe it's all in my head, I
thought.

While most of my odd symptoms would come
and then suddenly float away around this time, I began
to feel a numbness in my hands and legs, like my limbs
had fallen asleep. Usually you'll hit the hand or foot a
couple of times and it wakes up, but no matter what
I did, I had no feeling—just an appendage attached to
me. Once, when I woke up and my left arm felt like it
was dead, I remember looking at my arm thinking,
Now, what is that? Why is this thing here? I couldn't
move my arm, it just dangled. There was no pain, but
I couldn't feel a thing. I kept hitting my arm: *Wake up,
wake up man!* A few days or weeks later, that same

feeling went into my legs. I got out of bed one morning, I just went *splat*.

I found myself sprawled on the bedroom floor, and I tried to crawl to the bathroom and couldn't move. I began to cry in frustration: "I just can't get my legs to work," I screamed at Kathy. Terrified, she ran to my side and held me in her arms crying. She tried to help me to my feet and I could tell by her face, this was serious. I had been hiding many of my symptoms from her because I didn't want her to worry. But now we both knew I had to stop messing around and see a neurologist right away.

The following afternoon, I had the feeling back in my legs, and I felt good enough to drive myself to an appointment with a neurologist. As I watched the doctor test my reflexes and sensations with various instruments, I knew I was failing his evaluations. I watched, but couldn't feel the quarter he moved up and down the sole of my foot. He ran an instrument that looked like a pizza cutter up and down my spine, but I had no idea it was touching me until he said so.

The neurologist told me that what I had was probably one of two things—a tumor on my spine or MS. Either way, he said, it didn't look like walking would be in my future for long. I couldn't believe what I heard: "We need to admit you to Cedars to do a spinal tap," he said. "I have a hunch it could be MS."

Several things were going through my mind. This was horrible news. *Tumors. MS.* And, strangely enough, *There goes the ball game.* The Phillies were in town that night but I would be in the hospital.

I called Kathy and tried to tell her about the doctor's suspicions, but I couldn't get the words out of my mouth. I broke down.

"There's good news and bad news," I finally said. "The bad news is if it's a tumor, they'll try to remove it. I'll never walk again, and chances are I'll be dead in a few years. The good news is, if it's MS I'll never walk again, but I'll live."

I hung up the phone and thought, *You call that living?*

WHAT KIND OF HOSPITAL IS THIS?:
FINDING OUT WHAT'S WRONG

Our first publicity shoot, "the Simon and Garfunkel pose"

When I was still emerging from a fog of anesthesia, Kathy and the neurologist stood as unsteady blurs at my bedside and delivered the news. *"You have multiple sclerosis."* The words sounded strange. I repeated them silently. It was unlikely that I would be able to walk again, the doctor said, and if I did, it wouldn't be for long. High doses of steroids might help in the short term. But in the end, the only thing I could count on was that the disease would progress. I would get worse.

My legs lay still, completely numb from the spinal tap. The information the doctor had just given me was not sinking in. It hovered in the air, separate and incomprehensible. Worst-case scenarios circled. In my mind's eye, I saw Lionel Barrymore in *It's a Wonderful Life* and Raymond Burr in *Ironside*, both in wheelchairs and hooked up to iron lungs. I turned away from the doctor and looked out the window of my room, located in a wing of private rooms on the top floor of one of the towers at Cedars Sinai Hospital. I could see only blue sky and the silhouette of another hospital tower. The doctor droned on about all the horrible things I would look forward to and I thought, *Talk about bedside manner. Frankly, Doctor, I am not impressed.*

Later that afternoon, an Associated Press reporter called from the hospital lobby to find out why I was in the hospital. I tried to convince him that in fact *he* was in the hospital and I was downstairs but to no avail. He then asked what was really on his mind— Did I know anything about Andy Kaufman?

"What about him?" I asked.

"He just died in the room next door."

"Of what?" I asked. "Andy was a little crazy but he didn't do drugs or anything that would make him die."

Later that night, my general practitioner, Dr Kipper, stopped by for a visit. He had also been Andy

Kaufman's doctor, and he told me Andy *had* died earlier in the day in the room next door.

I looked at Kipper and thought, *What kind of hospital is this? I have MS and Andy Kaufman is dead?* It was all too strange. I didn't understand. "Andy was crazy," I told Kipper, "but you don't die of crazy."

"No you don't," Kipper agreed. "You die of cancer."

Cedars Sinai was crawling with reporters hunting for information about Kaufman. They and everyone else in the hospital seemed stunned. My friends came in and out of my room shaking their heads about the news. Like the rest of the world, none of us had known Andy was sick.

And I had my own problems. I could empathize with Kaufman's reticence. After all, I, too, was in the hospital with a potentially life-threatening disease, and I was lying to everyone in sight about it.

When friends Michael McKean, Harry Shearer, and my writing partners, Peter Elbling and Garry Goodrow visited, I told them it was a bad disk. I remember looking at Peter and Garry one afternoon. We had spent the last month working on a pilot script for my new show. "Hey, fellas," I wanted to ask them, "how do you think it would play if my character was in a wheelchair?"

For the five days I was in the hospital, it seemed as though every time I turned on the television all I saw were actors running. (Since when did actors run everywhere?) I saw them jogging on beautiful beaches, sprint in hot pursuit of a bad guy, chase after their dog in the park on a crisp autumn day. No one seemed to walk from place to place anymore—let alone get *wheeled* around.

Everyone bought my bad-disk story, though Shearer did not believe the truthful news of Kaufman's death. Like many, he was convinced that Andy was alive and well, and the death was feigned—one of Kaufman's wild pranks. "No," I told Harry. "It's not, it's real. He's really dead."

Laverne & Shirley and *Taxi* were both filmed on the Paramount lot, just a few stages apart. So while Andy and I were far from great friends, we chatted on occasion. I ran into him and his agent, George Shapiro, one afternoon when visiting a friend on the *Taxi* stage. Andy was upset about working in television and worried about what was happening to his character, Foreign Man, now known as Latka. I understood where he was coming from. We had both hit the big time, but playing a supporting role in a TV sitcom had not been in either of our plans. "We bring comic relief to situation comedies," I said. "That's what we do. Latka is the Lenny and Squiggy of *Taxi*."

"That's right," Andy said. He turned toward George, who was sitting on the other side of the room. "Did you hear that, George? That's it."

By the middle of my first night in the hospital, I was able to walk again. I had called for the nurse and when she didn't come, I pulled myself out of bed and walked to the bathroom. I was amazed! Twelve hours of intravenous Prednisone were miraculous. By the following day, I felt almost normal. I could still walk, and my legs felt strong enough that if I didn't know better, I could have sworn it was all a bad dream. Of course, I could never forget the truth. But the steroids worked so well that it was easy to imagine I might have miraculously gotten better. I kept reminding myself that what I had was incurable, but it was tough to keep fooling myself when Dr. Kipper kept saying that he had never seen such a fast recovery.

That's how it works in the wonderful world of MS—an illness that affects everyone differently. The only typical experience of most people with MS is what's known as an exacerbation or attack. Anything can set one off, including heat, stress, physical or emotional trauma, or any infection like a cold. But scientists maintain what's most notable about MS flare-ups are their unpredictable nature. Sometimes, an exacerbation can be caused by nothing at all.

After each flare-up, though, the progress of the disease can worsen. The cells attack the nerve myelin and sometimes the damage is extensive; other times

My family at the time of my diagnosis

it's not. When I have flare-ups, my legs buckle and I fall down. I often have other symptoms—weakness that leads to drop foot—the inability to lift my foot high enough to prevent tripping when walking—balance disorientation, and numbing of my hands and feet—I am so far a lucky guy: after each flare-up I have recovered without losing too much mobility.

While today I accept the unpredictability of living with flare-ups, in the beginning, I had no idea what to expect. Nobody else did, either. The professionals in my life took on the roles of good doc, bad doc. My first neurologist focused on the worst-case scenario by telling me I would not be able to walk. Kipper focused on the best-case scenario by insisting that flare-ups might be infrequent. Neither turned out to be right, but of the two, all my bets were on Kipper. He bucked me up at a critical time. I thought that maybe the worst had happened and maybe I could go on and live with a disease like MS. Maybe I would be one of those people who had this terrible experience and would never have it again? They even had a name for it. "Singular sclerosis." That's what I wanted: in and out sclerosis.

This was where I placed my focus—on a happy ending. I didn't want people comparing me to anyone else they knew who had been laid low by MS. Whoever they had in mind, it wasn't going to be me! I needed to believe that I was going to be one of the lucky ones, and for a while, I was.

When I got out of the hospital, I continued on steroids for four months. At first I was given very high doses intravenously which were followed by a tapering oral dose. I remember going to Peter Elbling's house to finish writing a pilot, and downing huge handfuls of prednisone pills. This was my wonder drug. As long as I took it, my MS was controlled.

But high doses of steroids have their downside and as time went on, I developed a love/hate relationship with the drug. I'd go around euphoric and smiling. Then an hour later, I'd get mad at a busy signal on the phone. I was impossible to live with. On steroids, intense feelings of well-being are followed by impatience, restlessness, and anger. *But I need it!* At times, I hated myself for becoming dependent on the prednisone. I lost patience with my family. I lost patience with life. Emotionally, it rocked me. And physically it made my skin break out and my face puff up. I grew sad and bloated, but the drug worked miracles. When I was on it, I could do whatever I wanted and whatever was asked of me.

Despite my good reaction to steroid therapy, my first neurologist had said that it would only be a matter of time before other symptoms would arise. Based on the location of the sclerosis, he outlined future possible symptoms in great detail: dizziness and vertigo; mood swings; loss of hand dexterity; coordination difficulties and muscle stiffness and weakness; speech and voice impediments; memory loss and drop foot. His words haunted me, and I spent my idle time asking myself the same question—how much longer would I be able to walk? And as much as I wanted to believe that I was destined to have a miracle recovery from MS, by the time I was diagnosed, I had already had several exacerbations. I didn't know what they were then; I just knew that I fell down a lot. My legs would grow weak, as if someone had taken the air out of my tires, and when I was tired, I often lost my balance.

Once I understood what these episodes were, I figured out that I could always tell what was going on with my MS by looking at my pants. At any given time, I could walk to my closet and find four pairs with a hole in the right knee. *That was at the ballpark and that one over there was in June on the stairs.* Falling down happened so often that when I felt myself begin to lose my balance, I would yell, "Excuse me." *Thud.* "Damn, there goes another pair of pants."

I learned that I could count on being able to trust

about 500 feet in each leg before I ran into problems with weakness or drop foot. Sometimes I could go for thousands of steps, but generally I couldn't trust any more than that number before asking for trouble.

Working in film, this was a real problem. When you do a scene where you're walking and talking to someone, you walk about thirty feet. Then it's "Cut, OK, let's go back, we're having trouble with Camera A," and you go back and do it again and again. By the time they yell, "Print it!" you're walking a little lop-sided and they're saying, "What's with the limp?"

Knowing I had to think fast, I'd say something brilliant, like, "What limp?"

I also had to learn how to deal with having to pee a lot. That was another MS-related problem. I lost bladder control. I could always feel when I had to go to the bathroom, I just didn't have much time to get to where I needed to be. It wasn't a huge deal; it just required organization and planning—not one of my strong suits. During the first two years after diagnosis, I don't know how many times I peed in my pants while I was driving home from an audition. There I'd be driving along the freeway on a nice sunny afternoon and I'd think, *Uh oh. Oh no!* and begin madly looking around to pull the car over or get off on an exit. There'd usually be a song on the oldies station like, "Oh listen to the pounding rain! Rain. Rain. Rain." And there'd be no way to get off the freeway. What could I do? I knew that I had to pee and I knew there was nothing I could do about it but stop the car and climb out. If that wasn't possible, well, it just wasn't. I could see the headlines, "David Lander, known for his role as Squiggy on *Laverne & Shirley*, stopped traffic today on the Ventura Freeway and hurled himself over the barrier holding onto what appeared to be a small sausage . . ."

Once I was driving back to my house in Calabasas from the ballpark with a friend, a writer, who was pretty much into himself.

"We better pull over," I said.

"Why?" he asked. He was busy chatting away about something.

"Well, I have to pee."

"Oh, hold it in. You'll be home soon."

"No, no, no," I said as I pounded on the car door. "I really have to pee. STOP THIS CAR AND GET ME OUT!"

"This is a joke, right?" he asked. "Shtick?"

"No, you idiot, this is no joke!" I screamed. "Stop the car!"

And then he stopped the car. The door flew open while I was pulling my fly down. I didn't care who saw. I couldn't care less. I had to pee and that was it.

The problem was especially awkward when I worked on the stage. I never lost control, but I always wondered what would happen if I did. Imagine the reviews. *"Mr. Lander's performance was a real pissa!"*

Losing control of such basic activities caused me to lose confidence not only in my body's ability to do as my mind commanded, but in my ability to *do* anything. I began to distrust my instincts. Conquering fear and depression became my biggest battle. I found out that I no longer wore my heart on my sleeve, but on my whole body. Anything could trigger feelings of being overwhelmed that could translate into a symptom. Something as simple as "Gee, I hate that haircut," or "I saw you in that show. It stunk!" If somebody hurt my feelings, I could no longer contain my response. My deepest feelings began to express themselves in how I walked or talked.

I was on the end of a physical and emotional yo-yo. On a good day, I would think, *Well, I'm gonna do okay even if I don't beat it.* On a bad day, I thought, *Watch yourself, your handicap may be showing.*

FIVE

◉

DIAGNOSE AND ADIOS:

THE LIMITS OF MEDICINE

Dave Lander: Pittsburgh Pirates Infielder

In the years since I've been diagnosed, I've come to know multiple sclerosis as a disease that promises nothing and never breaks that promise. The only way I've learned to live with it has been by learning to live without the things I've taken for granted. But it's a slow process, and I dearly miss the things I can no longer do—like running. I used to love to run. I had been a pretty good broken-field runner when I played football in junior high school. But after MS, I knew in my heart that I wouldn't be able to run again. This hasn't stopped me from trying, though. From time to time, I still use running as a measuring stick to evaluate my physical progress. It seems like a particularly poignant metaphor for my inability to deal with my illness: no matter how hard I try I can never get very far without hearing that awful sound: *Thud!*

Early on, my first and best defense was lying. I lied to everyone. And not only that, I lived the lie. I almost convinced myself that there was nothing wrong with me. When I was well enough to keep up a charade of health, denial helped me feel as strong as I was pretending to be. Feeling isolated and alone, Kathy felt it was important to have a support system. We discussed telling a few family members and friends. I was okay with that as long as they weren't in show business. Well, that ruled out about 99 percent! No one from *Laverne & Shirley* or the *Credibility Gap* was told, not even one of my best friends in the world. Michael McKean wouldn't know until ten years after my diagnosis.

The only problem with denial, of course, is that the truth always lurks in the background, ready to circle back to bite you in the ass. The fact was, even in the early stages of the disease I battled typical MS symptoms. On bad days, I felt weak and struggled with drop foot. To compensate, I sometimes walked with a limp. I had problems with balance, and I often felt hopeless because there seemed to be nothing that medicine could do to help me.

At the time of my diagnosis, the prevailing MS wisdom was, "You don't beat it; you can't even treat it." Another catchy phrase among the medical community was "diagnose and adios." In those days, doctors recommended what was termed "symptomatic" treatment: counseling, physical, occupational and speech therapy, pain medicine, and other agents that simply helped alleviate the symptoms without addressing the underlying physiological problem. Fifteen years ago, the immunological treatments that hold such great promise today were almost nonexistent, except for steroids used to moderate symptoms during exacerbations.

What a difference a decade makes!

This may sound odd, but there has never been a better time to have MS. Most people who are diagnosed today have the option of one of the new immunological therapies known as the "ABC drugs"—Avonex, Betaseron, and Copaxone—which can reduce the frequency and severity of relapses and may help stall the progression of the disease.

These drugs operate on a whole new level. They don't relieve symptoms, but instead impact the actual demyelination process to limit future exacerbations. Betaseron and Avonex are forms of interferon beta, a substance made by the immune system. Copaxone mimics a component of human myelin and acts as a decoy for the MS cells that attack nerve tissue. Intravenous corticosteroids, known as supersonic anti-inflammatory agents, are also used today to shorten the duration of exacerbations and improve their overall outcome.

Remember, though, that when I was diagnosed, there was nothing available but steroids and bad news. Along with a prescription for prednisone, the doctors recommended small tips for making my life with MS a little more manageable. "Get mild exercise and avoid heat at all costs," they said. "Avoid hot baths. No saunas. No sunbathing. Whatever you do," I was told, "keep your body cool. This will reduce symptoms and help avert future exacerbations." My doctor told me of one patient who took this advice so seriously, he would come home from work every day and fill a tub with ice cubes. "How do you fill a tub with ice cubes?" I wondered at the time. I had an ice-cube machine in my refrigerator, but I thought, *If I have to keep taking buckets of ice and pouring them into the tub I'll be doing that for an hour—up and down the stairs from the ice machine to the tub—and by then who knows what shape I'll be in?*

Nevertheless, I was listening to all these gems of advice. And so I began requesting a shower in my dressing room whenever I did a TV show or movie so I could stand under the cold water to cool my body in between takes. The MS made my body groggy, like it hadn't woken up with the rest of me. The cold water was like throwing water on my face when I was sleepy. It felt great. If my leg dragged or I had strange sensations in my fingertips, I would stand under a cold shower and almost instantly liven up.

At first I was fanatical about cold showers. A few years later, a doctor informed me that warm showers were okay. Heat didn't cause the disease to progress, he told me; rather it heightened symptoms making you feel as though the disease is progressing.

The recommendation to get regular exercise was ironic, I thought, for someone with a disease that made exercise so difficult. I began going to a rehab program to work with a trainer. I also rode a stationary bike for about twenty minutes a day and recorded the details of my exercise program in a daily journal. All this effort paid off: I made visible progress building strength in my arms and legs and improving overall coordination, all of which made me feel much stronger. One afternoon I even pulled out my running litmus test. I got maybe ten steps before I bit the dust. Run. Run. Run. *Thud!* The story of my life!

The bottom line is, having MS is no fun and my

early years were some of the hardest. Coming to terms with the diagnosis was difficult, to say the least. Doing so while living in the spotlight of the film and television industry made it close to impossible—especially when trying to work and keep it a secret. But I never gave up. I kept at it. I had good days and bad days. At one time or another I tried almost everything to keep my life as normal as possible, and while at it, tried to have a laugh or two along the way.

One of the side effects of being on prednisone was that it made my face blow up like a balloon. Seeing myself in movies and television shows after a long steroid regime was like watching the Night of the Living Fat Heads—terrifying. I looked like the Pillsbury Dough Boy, with more chins than the Chinatown telephone book. (Remember, in the days before we all became so politically correct I got paid eighty cents for that line!) The steroids were the only treatment option I knew, but the putty face had to go. Since the facial weight gain from steroids has nothing to do with what you eat, liposuction was the only thing I could think of. Everything was fine until I noticed that the plastic surgeon had taken more off one side than the other. My face was lopsided! "Hey, doc," I said, "It looks like I left half my face on another neck. Even me out!"

He did, thank God. And later I found, if I waited a few weeks after a major course of steroids the bloat would disappear by itself.

Because the medical community offered so little that could be done, I began to explore anything that might help me with MS—no matter how cockamamy. For years I've taken shots of megadoses of Vitamin C and B12 which really seem to help keep my immune system strong. Other therapeutic strategies, though, have not proven to be effective. For example, I was struck by inspiration after seeing a *60 Minutes* special on the toxicity of mercury dental fillings. One of the patients featured was a Florida woman with severe MS, who had believed that there was a correlation between MS and mercury toxicity. She had her dentist replace all her mercury fillings with gold. After the procedure, *60 Minutes* showed her out and about, walking. Previously confined to a wheelchair, now she was even dancing for the cameras.

I went, "Wow!" The next morning I called Dr. Kipper.

"I don't know," he said, "I haven't read anything about this, and there's nothing in the AMA magazines. But I don't see how it can hurt you so, if you feel it will help you, try it."

Then I phoned my dentist. "You're about the twentieth call I've gotten today," he complained. "Why does *60 Minutes* put this crap on?"

"Can you or can't you?" I asked.

Though it took hours to painstakingly pull out all my mercury fillings and replace them with gold, in the end it was all for naught. I kept waiting to be overtaken by the urge and ability to dance, but it never happened. I did try hard to smile wider after the procedure—my mouth had gone up $600 in value.

I had also heard that acupuncture might help with various MS symptoms, from spastic muscles to bladder control. The procedure was pleasant enough, I found. In fact, I kind of liked it—but it never accomplished anything I could feel or see. If you think about it, the whole thing just didn't make a lot of sense. Slip a needle in and, lo and behold, it will help your kidneys?

I tried acupressure, too, and Chinese herbs. But all they did was put me in a bad mood, winding me up and giving me a stomach ache. Psychic healers? You bet. One of them sprinkled me with a "fairy dust," which I immediately forgot about. Later, I took a shower and watched the magic go down the drain.

I also tried medication to help with my bladder.

The only problem was the drugs stopped me from peeing. I wouldn't pee all day, which seemed contrary to every health principle I had ever heard of. After a week or so, I quit that, too.

Then, on the recommendation of my neurologist who was interested the mind-body connection, I explored the benefits of transcendental meditation. Every morning and evening, I dutifully repeated my mantra, "Erring, erring, erring." I know you're not supposed to give a mantra away, but this one bears repeating: erring? Like herring?

"It sounds so negative," I told Kathy, "it's like I'm making a mistake. Why can't I get something positive like 'base hit or home run'?"

As much as I disliked my mantra, it did fit my current state of mind. Every time I repeated it, a little voice would say, you got that right.

Some friends recommended that I try Yoga and Tai Chi to build strength and flexibility. In my first, and last, Tai Chi class, I stood on one leg, pushed my arm out, and fell flat on my face. (How do you say *SPLAT* in Chinese?) Yoga was a little better—at least I started out on the floor. But both classes were packed full of strangers who were much better at it than me, and I felt very self-conscious. My classmates all recognized me as Squiggy, and I wasn't ready yet to have my secret known. So I signed a few autographs and quit.

After a few years of chasing a cure, I settled down and decided to let a cure search for me. Thankfully, the disease was in a sleepy remission. I experienced some symptoms but very few major flare-ups. My biggest problem was feeling depressed because work was really slow in coming. Everywhere I looked I thought, *Here's another fine MS you're in.* But then on March 29, 1994, the day after my daughter Natalie's eleventh birthday, life threw me another curve.

The pain began while I was riding my Exercycle. It was not anything I had ever felt before, and so I got off my bike that had begun to resemble the lack of momentum of my life—peddling, peddling, peddling, but never getting anywhere.

I walked up the stairs to my bedroom, pain squeezing up my left arm. I flashed on that scene in *Superman* when Clark Kent's father clutched his arm, put his hand on his chest above his heart, and dropped dead. That's what was happening to me, I realized. I was having a heart attack—and I wasn't even being paid scale. Feeling dizzy, I sat on the bed and placed my head between my legs. Just as I was about to kiss my ass good-bye, I heard someone come into the room. "Dad?" Natalie said. "Are you okay?"

———

I was taken by ambulance to Cedars Sinai Hospital and admitted for a six-hour angioplasty. Though the small artery that had caused the heart attack couldn't be reopened, thankfully it could be shut off and rerouted with no problem.

A week later, I was sent to a rehab program. I left early the very first day because I was depressed. I was just sick of being sick. At age forty-eight, I felt there was something pathetic about a middle-aged actor with MS having a heart attack. I shouldn't be hospitalized and in therapy for another decade, tops, I figured. Yet here I was, a walking disease: MS, kidney stones, high blood pressure, and now a heart attack.

But the truth is, even before this latest illness, I had been plagued with black thoughts. Part of me had given up. I was miserable in my life and in my career, I was drinking too much, and I had let MS get the better of me.

On the day of my heart attack, Kathy had written in her journal: "It's so hard to watch someone you love struggle and feel pain, especially when you know he feels unsure of himself. Today I felt so badly for David and for us . . ."

A few days after I came home, she wrote: ". . .

David gets stronger every day. He confessed to me that prior to his heart attack, he had been feeling like he was ready to give up. But he now seems to have a renewed appreciation for life. All the tension that has been culminating over the past few years peaked with David's heart attack. It can only turn around now."

Could I say that a heart attack was the best thing that ever happened to me? Well, kind of. It was a blessing in disguise.

I returned to rehab after a few weeks of feeling sorry for myself. My fellow patients, who were much older than me, were all actors, too, some of whom I grew up watching on Broadway. They were a great group, very supportive. We did a lot of joking and great storytelling, and we all watched each other's progress, and rooted each other on.

When I was told that my program would include twenty to thirty minutes on a treadmill, I explained to my physical therapist that it would be impossible because a treadmill could be too dangerous for someone with MS.

"I could lose my balance and get sucked under the tread belt," I insisted.

Equally stubborn, he insisted I give it a try.

With diet and exercise, I lost twenty pounds by the end of July. My heart was strong, my attitude was

One of the 12 characters I played in the film Family Reunion, shortly after my heart attack. I weighed 127 lbs.

stronger: I had licked the I-can't disease that had followed me around for the last ten years. I now felt that there was more I could do for myself if I only gave it a chance—I just needed to step up to the plate and start swinging.

When I got home, one of the first things I did was change the message on my answering machine. I hadn't heard from my agent for two months, so I crafted a recording that said, "Leave a message but if you're my agent, you're fired."

My agent's response was, "David, you are a very small man in a very small suit."

He got that right, though. I laughed when I heard it. I couldn't decide if I should have felt offended or well fitted, but either way it felt great to be able to finally get rid of him.

The summer after my heart attack, I took my family to Washington, D.C., to give Natalie a tour of the nation's capital. One afternoon I took a train to meet up with a friend who hosted a sports-talk radio show from Camden Yards in Baltimore. I would also get to see the Orioles and the Indians play a twilight doubleheader that night.

I decided to walk the fifteen minutes through the park to the train station because it was a beautiful day, but I hadn't even gotten down the historic steps of the Capitol Building when I began to lose my balance. I kept going, though. Once in the park, I took one path, then another, until I realized that fifteen minutes had passed and I could no longer see the train station. I panicked. My legs went wobbly and I fell to the ground. My glasses flew off. "Calm down," I told myself sternly. I collected my glasses, pulled together what was left of myself, and ventured forward. Or at least I think it was forward.

My panic was causing me to feel even more disoriented and imbalanced than usual, and another ten minutes passed before I reached the exit of the park. A couple of well-dressed tourists approached me just in time to offer a hand as I fell flat on the street.

"Hey," they asked, "are you who we think you are?"

"No," I said. "Not today."

They helped me hail a cab, which dropped me off on the wrong side of Union Station. I had fifteen minutes left to cross over two traffic islands, reach the entrance, and make my train.

I waddled, I wobbled, I stumbled, praying that no one else would recognize me. I could see the headline: "Drunk Squiggy Escapes by Train."

Once in the station, I realized that I had to get from Track 1 to Track 16 in two minutes. I began to run but knew it was no use. In fact, it was a joke. I flagged down a redcap, who loaded me on his luggage cart.

"Hey!" he yelled. "Stop the train! I've got a cripple here!"

A conductor helped me stumble to my seat. Sitting down was a huge relief and within a half hour, I felt so much better, I got up and walked to the club car to get a drink. The conductor shot me a disgusted look and said, "Why are you posing as a cripple just to catch the train?"

He reached for something in his back pocket and I thought he was about to radio for security to throw me off the train. Instead, he pulled out a notebook. "Hey, Squiggy," he asked suddenly, smiling, "Can I get your autograph?"

This walk in the park has haunted me for years as a symbol of my inner conflict. My secrecy and deception created a huge dilemma: How could I ask for help when I refused to acknowledge I was sick? Looking back now, I find it very sad that, at the time, being humiliated seemed preferable to being sick. My veneer was cracking, though. My family and I had become extremely isolated because of the decisions I had made, and my strong front was breaking down as my disease marched on. A few months later, while driving to the post office to mail a letter, I spotted the mail truck in our neighborhood. Waving my letter, I climbed out of my car and began running toward the mailman. The truck disappeared around the corner though, and I tripped on a crack in the sidewalk and landed smack on my head. My glasses broke, I hit my nose and began bleeding profusely from a cut in my forehead. Eventually, an ice cream truck tinkling out, of all things, "London Bridge is falling down," delivered me to our doorstep, where a shocked Kathy awaited. Of course all this took place in plain view of my neighbors, who began to ask questions that Kathy, no longer willing or able to lie, began to answer truthfully.

A few weeks later, on the way back from the ball-park, I hit a boat that was parked on the side of the road. (It was the boat's fault!) I wasn't hurt, but the trauma pushed my MS further into full-scale exacerbation. As it was marked by a time of many falls, I don't remember much of it, but Kathy wrote about the days leading up to the hospital. "It was about 11:30 when I got the call from the police that his car had flipped three times on Topanga after getting caught on a boat trailer that was sticking out into the road. After seeing his car upside down, I couldn't believe he walked away uninjured, let alone alive."

The next few days I began to fall. Kathy would not let me drive, so a friend took me to a game at Dodger Stadium where I had a really bad spill. That night, Kathy began to scour the town for a neurologist. We had recently moved to the area, and had no contacts. One of them, a Dr. Perino, returned her calls and had me admitted to the motion picture hospital. When he asked me if I'd considered taking a new drug called Betaseron, Dr. Perino changed my life.

I had heard of this medication a few years before, after seeing a newspaper headline: "Cure for MS Believed Found."

Of course I had immediately called Dr. Kipper, who'd never heard of it. "Beta-blockers?" he asked. "They won't help you!"

No wonder he wasn't familiar with Betaseron; at the time it was still in clinical trials. In order to take part in the trial, your illness had to fulfill a number of criteria and then you had to take part in a lottery. I had been told that my symptoms weren't severe enough, and taking the drug experimentally would be a waste of time.

It was also expensive and I wasn't certain my insurance would cover it. I was still hesitant to let SAG know I had MS.

But now, only a few years later, Dr. Perino was telling me that not only would Betaseron help me, I could make a strong case with my insurance company. "You need to approach SAG with the truth," she said. "They're there to protect you. That's is why you've paid into the insurance program for all these years."

I was tired and plum out of excuses. I couldn't say my symptoms didn't warrant giving it a try. I couldn't say, "I can't afford it." So I went on Betaseron, which really helped, and two years later, I switched to Avonex, which still really helps.

Though the "ABCs" all operate a little differently, they have all radically changed the face of MS. In clinical studies, patients taking Betaseron, approved in 1993, showed fewer nerve lesions formed than patients on placebos. Avonex showed similar properties but had the added benefit of reducing the risk for progression of the disease by 37 percent.

Right away, when I began taking the Betaseron, I noticed the upside and the downside. On the one hand, I didn't get as many flare-ups. As many people with MS agree, it's not what you feel so much as what you don't feel that becomes important. On the other hand, I had to inject myself under the skin every other day. Though the needles bothered me, I soon grew accustomed to the injections. Knowing there was something that could actually help stall my illness, I felt empowered. I felt more confident each time I took a shot.

Treating my illness also helped me begin the process of dismantling years of denial. Who knew that a simple procedure of mixing a solution into a syringe could have such great consequences?

THE LEADER: "SMARTASS"

SIX

THE YEARS OF FALLING DANGEROUSLY:

COVERING UP

My character in Who Framed Roger Rabbit

A few years ago my agent sent me out on an audition for the lead in a new television pilot. The part was as a former TV star turned Hollywood landlord. It seemed like a good part for me, but when I showed up at Warner Brothers, I was nervous. Healthwise, I wasn't having a good day. I felt stiff and my balance seemed a little wobbly. Even after working for fifteen years while keeping my secret, I still worried that MS would show.

The receptionist recognized me. "Hey, Squiggy," she said.

I sat down across from her and thought, well, at

least I don't have to worry about being typecast. Her phone rang.

"The landlord?" she asked. "No. No, we've already filled that." Slightly annoyed, she hung up the phone with a tsk, tsk.

"Has the part already been offered to someone?" I asked her.

"No, it's open," she said. "It's just . . . that was Richard Pryor's manager. I don't know what he's thinking. Richard has MS. Can you believe that?"

"No," I shook my head. I couldn't believe it. The Great Richard Pryor wanted to work. The nerve! What could he possibly be thinking?

Remembering that story, I have no questions about why I kept MS a secret for sixteen years. As crazy as the concept sounded to this receptionist, I shared Richard Pryor's sentiment: I, too, wanted to keep working. And it's funny. Over the years I have revisited the idea of going public, but every time I considered speaking up, I'd meet up with someone like this receptionist who would remind me again. So my motto regarding MS became: When in doubt, keep it to yourself. In the world of MS and movies, denial was absolutely the best policy.

Hollywood is not a place to be sick. Not then. Not now. Not ever. Even as the issue *du jour* is batted around by the news media, as more celebrities go public with illness, one cannot help noticing the lengths we travel to spin a problem into a certain light. The sad truth of the matter is that Hollywood reflects the philosophies of our culture. Here, as everywhere, the tiniest human frailty is open to being inflated, dramatized, misinterpreted, misunderstood. A simple cold mentioned on the news at noon can be pneumonia on Entertainment Tonight by five. A mole is stage-five cancer. Few people are able to understand a mysterious disease like MS, and it's unlikely you would find them listed in any show biz directory. As one Miramax executive, recently quoted by my agent, said, "David Lander? Oh him! Well, he's on death's door with MS." If there was any dying going on, it was dying of chronic dumbness.

It's an unfortunate fact that show business, like many industries, does not have the time or inclination to accommodate illness. Huge sums of money go into the making of pictures, and the companies that insure motion pictures require actors to pass physicals as protection against any problem that could cause expensive charges or delays. In fact, while few executives would admit as much, it is not unusual for an actor to be denied a role because of a health problem. At the age of thirty-eight, when I had a routine physical as part of my work on *Conan*, a renowned insurance doctor who worked for the studios had made a big deal about my blood pressure. I shuddered to think what he would have done if he knew I had MS.

Another little-known fact of the acting business is the system for Screen Actors Guild's (SAG) health insurance, the Producer's Pension and Health Plan (PPHP). Essentially, all actors have to work at least sixty days a year or have $10,000 of earnings to qualify to receive health care insurance. I was scared to death that MS would make it impossible to find work and I would lose my family's health coverage. Then what? My residuals were sometimes less than the stamp that sent them.

Soon after my diagnosis, Kathy had already begun exploring careers outside film and television. She had entered real-estate school and was teaching art in private schools to prepare for the possibility that I might not be able to continue to work. Even so, I didn't want to risk losing our health insurance.

When I walked out of the hospital in May of 1984, I was a different person from the David Lander who'd gone in. Quite honestly, my attitude sucked. Before MS, I was at the top of my career. After? I didn't know if I could get or keep a job. I had always been pretty outspoken in creative situations. But after my diagnosis, I was just not as strong emotionally. Isolated by my secret, my nerves were frayed—literally and figuratively. I had lost my confidence as a person and an actor. Up until MS, I'd been very vocal. If I had a good suggestion for improving a piece of dialogue or a scene, I'd let people know, but after MS, I seldom dared to open my mouth. And while the MS wasn't always active, it was always with me.

So how did I manage to hide my illness while working in the movies?

Ironically, I didn't learn to act for nothing.

Early on, as I tried to to deal with the special challenges of my disability, I often thought of the adage of the famous acting teacher, Stella Adler, who said: Every character should have a secret; something nobody knows but you. Of course, I thought my own secret qualified under this principle. Unlike other actors, I no longer had to invent a secret for my characters. For every part I played, I had a secret: MS.

The question then became: How could I keep it to myself?

If you watch a blind person move around a room he knows, he does so effortlessly, following walls and furniture with fingers, moving through difficult areas using memory and the strategic placement of a hand. Negotiating surroundings in the world of MS is very similar. When I'm experiencing the usual MS symptoms, it's as if my body cannot see. If my body does not physically know an area, I cannot always trust the ability we usually take for granted of getting through a room without losing my balance, tripping, or falling flat on my face.

Unfortunately, by virtue of the business of acting, unless one is in the same play every night, each job requires negotiating new surroundings. For me and MS, that meant I had to get to know a set or an exterior scene before I could feel confident.

Any normal actor would simply look at the script and the set and that would be that. But for me, the simplest movement had to be rehearsed like a stunt. I had to walk the set. I had to practice handling the simplest of props. I had to know the area I'd be working in to be able to move about it confidently. If there were stairs, I had to climb up and down them. I had to rehearse every physical maneuver to feel confident of my ability to get the job done. Since I didn't want anyone to know I had MS, I had to somehow accomplish these rehearsals in private.

In *Highway to Heaven*, a show produced and directed by Michael Landon, I would sneak onto the set at lunch in order to rehearse the physical part of my role. I was playing a ne'er-do-well who lived in a huge mansion who walked down a big staircase. When I took a look at the set, I knew that every time I finished the take, I would have to walk back up the stairs. With all that up and down, I was afraid I would run into trouble. So I snuck onstage and tested myself walking up and down the stairs. Initially, I would list to one side because of my balance problems. I also had to look down to keep my footing—but my character would never keep his eyes glued to the ground while walking downstairs. A waitress had once told me the best way she could balance was if she focused on something straight in front of her, so that's what I did. I focused on something off the set and, keeping my eyes on it, prayed I wouldn't topple down the staircase. I didn't.

Many years later when I worked on the soap opera *The Bold and the Beautiful* I wouldn't have the same luck. This time I was walking down the stairs in front of the famous house featured in the Hitchcock film *Psycho* on the back lot of Universal Studios. The stairs were no problem, but when I reached for the railing for balance, I held onto a gargoyle that was not attached to anything. Whoops! Down I went in a splendid dive, ending with a crash.

One of my biggest challenges working with MS was not only anticipating the unpredictability of sets, but the mysterious nature of the comings and goings of the disease. I never knew how I would feel from day to day or hour to hour. I could never count on being strong. The type of uncertainty this created was a breeding ground for ritual and odd habits. For example, I tend to not only feel more confident about a role when I'm comfortable with my surroundings, but oddly enough, when I'm familiar with my shoes. I've known from the beginning that I would need special shoes to get me around without a limp.

At some points I discovered that I walked well in a shoe called Rockports. So I began wearing them to every audition and every acting job. They seemed to make an important difference to my confidence and my sense of well-being—so important, in fact, that if I didn't have them on, I wasn't sure I could do the job. Imagine my horror when on one of the first gigs I played after my diagnosis, the *New Love, American Style*, the wardrobe girl couldn't find black Rockports in my size. She opted for Dexters. I was beside myself, but what could I do? As convinced as I was that I wouldn't be able to walk well, I couldn't make a big deal about my shoes without coming dangerously close to revealing the real reason for my footwear preference.

The part I was playing was an unscrupulous agent who was trying to get laid, and though it involved more sitting then walking, I wanted my strut across the set to be strong. So before the show, I tried out the Dexters out in the privacy of my dressing room, walking around in circles to make sure I would do okay. They worked out fine! The Dexters seemed to offer the same support as the Rockports, and not once during that shoot did anyone question my gait. Of course, the Dexters became my new shoe of choice. I wore them on every show I did for years until they were finally lost somewhere on location, ten years later on *Pacific Blue.*

Initially, when I was learning to work with MS, every TV show and motion picture would present a new challenge. I was new to both the denial game and MS game. Since I could never predict what would happen once I accepted a role, in some instances, I was asked to do the impossible and I succeeded. In other situations, though, I didn't even have the courage to try.

In the film *The Man with One Red Shoe*, I purposely threw the audition so I didn't have to face my fear of what I could no longer do. The summer I was diagnosed, producer Victor Drai approached me about a part in this movie he thought I'd be perfect for. As an actor, I knew he was right. The problem was that the role entailed riding a bicycle around town for the duration of the entire film. I've been told no one can forget riding a bike, but while I might have been able to do it before and even after my diagnosis, I didn't know for sure if I could trust my ability now. What if I fell off the bike while we were shooting? What if I couldn't get back on? What if I could but fell off again? Would they fire me? Would they know?

I was terrified of finding out about one more thing I couldn't manage.

When I auditioned, the director, Stan Dragoti, sensed I hadn't given it a good shot. "Would you like to try it again?" he asked.

"No," I said. A part of me knew I had given up on myself, but I still felt relieved. I had blown the audition—yet that was exactly what I wanted. I didn't have the strength or coordination to fight the disease, keep the secret, *and* ride the friggin' bike.

A few days later, my agent called and told me I lost

the part to Jim Belushi. "They really screwed you on this," he said. "You deserved it."

I pretended to agree with him while I thought, *Thank God.*

Surprisingly, I was wanted for another part in which the only strenuous thing I had to do was have 100 gallons of water blown in my face on a sewer set. I was to play a CIA agent ordered to bug Tom Hanks' apartment. The CIA boss (Dabney Coleman) was apparently convinced that Hanks had some secret document he'd flushed down the toilet. My character was ordered to climb through a manhole to search the city's sewer system for the missing papers.

It was about 100 degrees that day on location in Washington, D.C., and my costume was a yellow rubber suit with oversized black boots. I looked stupid, but the scene was simple enough. I was to be pulled out of an undercover ambulance and lowered down a manhole.

Remember Dr. Anderman's advice to stay out of hot climates and wear loose-fitting cotton clothing? Considering the stress of 100-degree heat and rubber suit on my old MS body, I was frankly amazed that my symptoms didn't worsen. In fact, when I watch this film today, my astonishment continues. Inside the rubber suit I was dying, but outside I was acting. It was re-markable. At the time, I remember thinking, *I can do this!*

It was not easy to keep my mouth shut and not ask for a slower pace, especially when one of my fellow actors was insisting on special treatment.

The night before the shoot, he had experienced numbness in his fingertips. When he showed up the following morning, we learned that he had been diag-nosed with Berger's disease.

He refused to leave his trailer and so Drai and Dragoti began handling him with kid gloves. As my colleague stayed in his trailer negotiating terms, I sat on the sidewalk, sweating in my rubber suit. When he finally came out to do a scene, he held his hands aloft to keep the blood flowing to his fingertips. Mean-while, I pulled off one of my rubber boots and poured out a pint of sweat. I was fading fast, but I was not giv-ing in.

It was decided that we would shoot this other actor's close-ups first. He then would be excused while we did mine. I wish I could have said, "Berger's disease? Oh yeah? I outrank you. I have multiple scle-rosis. They should be shooting my close-up first."

But the bottom line was that I was afraid to make a

similar scene. As I watched this guy dance around with his fingers in the air, I admired his honesty and courage. He was doing something I didn't feel I could do.

A few weeks later, the shoot moved to L.A. I was feeling pretty good about myself; we were now in the fifth week of shooting and there were still no problems. One afternoon, however, Lou Pitt—who had been my agent at ICM—watched me walk onto the set.

"Say, what's with the limp?" he said. "Why are you walking funny?"

At the time I didn't realize that I had a limp, or even if I did, I certainly didn't think it showed. A little later, when I made my entrance into a scene, I had to climb three steps to get there within a certain amount of time. It was one of the most awkward moves I've ever seen myself make.

"Is that supposed to be a joke?" the assistant director asked me.

"Not if you didn't get it," I answered.

And so that was the way I dealt with it. I pretended. Sometimes it worked, sometimes it didn't.

In one case, many years later, I was able to incorporate my limp into a comedic shuffle when I played an Eastern European television director named Valdia

Gotech for a David Lynch sitcom called *On the Air.* Lynch loved it.

"Wow," he said, "you even walk foreign!"

My character also spoke gibberish—no easy feat even for the healthy. Mark Frost and David Lynch wrote this strange, vowel-inverted language. Every evening I ran lines with Kathy and we were both amazed that it was more easily memorized than English. Another thing about MS is that it sometimes affects the area of the brain that controls speech and memory. Not for me! I had every line letter-imperfect, just as it was written.

Because of the fact that I was always acting with a secret, before accepting a part I would first read the script and decide what I could and could not physically do. Sometimes I read stuff that I knew wouldn't be possible. I often still took the part and tried to find a way to do it once I arrived on the set. But no matter what, running was one thing that seemed utterly far-fetched. If a scene called for my character to run, I would request a double. "I was in a terrible car accident," I'd tell the producers, "and I screwed up my back a little so I have difficulty moving quickly." They would almost always be understanding. There was never any problem finding someone about my height with more hair, who'd run anywhere for money.

Sometimes in the movie business, though, things change at the last minute, allowing no time to make excuses. This is what happened on a film called *Betrayal of the Dove*, a project I did with Harvey Korman that missed theaters and went straight to video

One night before shooting began, the director called me at home. "You know that cute little scene in the coffee shop?" he asked. "It's too damn stagnant. You're just sitting there having coffee, for Christ's sakes."

"Yeah, well, what's wrong with that? I have to tell Harvey who I think the murderer is. What better way to do it than over coffee?"

"But there's no action."

"Well, that all depends how I sit there. I can do a lot of body language sitting down. And when I make my point, I'll stand. Think of how dramatic that will be."

By this time, I had lost the director. "Jogging," he interrupted.

"What?" My stomach fell to the ground.

"You'll do the scene jogging. You'll tell Harvey who the murderer is. While trying to keep up with him, running around the track. He'll be in a jogging suit, and you'll be in a three-piece suit running right next to him. It'll be hilarious."

Hilarious? It might be funny for him maybe, but what about me? I hadn't run in ten years.

"Why don't you bring a gun and shoot me?" I suggested. "It'll save time."

The following morning, I arrived at the location with an enormous sense of dread. It was ridiculous, I knew, but I couldn't think of any option but to carry on. If I fell down, I'd think of something on the spot, I figured. Or I'd pretend it was a new injury.

Fortunately, however, things never came to that. Harvey's jogging suit was made out of some shiny space-age material and every time he moved, it made a crinkly sound. It was impossible to go more than a few steps without the fabric cracking and screwing up the sound, so we'd jog a little and then stop. Jog a little more and then stop again. We eventually finished the scene sitting on the grass in the middle of the track. By the end of the day, I was ecstatic. I couldn't believe it. I ran. I did!

When I look back on my career, it's a wonder I got fired as rarely as I did. I could almost always talk myself out of trouble, but even so, I was constantly afraid that my illness was going to be found out and I would be dismissed from a show. On a stage play called *The Nerd*, my fears came true.

I was hired when the show was in its ninth month at the Drury Lane Theater in Chicago. I was to take the lead when the show moved to the suburban Oakbrook Terrace Theater in a few weeks. The producer, Howard Platt, an actor I had met while driving a telephone in an AT&T commercial, had hired me to lend some star name recognition to the new production. The plan was to rehearse for a month and then move the production, but the problem was, no one in the production could rehearse with me. Equity rules forbade it. The only actors I was allowed to work with were the understudies.

There was a lot of physical shtick in the play including a bit where I jumped on and off a couch with a paper bag over my head. A week before the scheduled opening, Platt came to my hotel and said if he didn't see progress soon, they would have to seriously consider letting me go.

I was crestfallen. "I know I can be great in this part," I told him. "But you need to give me a chance to work with the other actors."

Having skipped the usual months of general rehearsals, two days later we went straight to technical rehearsal, complete with light and sound cues and props. My character had to use seventy-eight props, none of which I had worked with until that moment. Tech rehearsals are tough anyhow, but without having the opportunity to have a dry run with the rest of the cast, it was like acting uphill.

Acting uphill with multiple sclerosis.

The rehearsal was a disaster, but somehow I survived it. Afterward, the producers ran backstage. I couldn't read their faces, but felt in my bones that whatever they had to say, it wasn't good. And it wasn't. They had come to tell me that my mother had suffered a heart attack. By the time I got back to the hotel, there was another message—from my mother saying, "Stay in Chicago. I'll be just fine. Good luck on opening night."

I tracked down the producers to let them know my mom was okay, and I wouldn't have to leave the show to be with her, but their reaction wasn't exactly what I expected. Instead of being excited, they told me that they had already hired another actor. "It's your drinking problem," one of them said. "We think it would be better if you got some help."

I was actually relieved the producers thought I was an alcoholic.

After my mother suffered another heart attack, I left Chicago for West Palm Beach and on what would've been my opening night I spent the last few hours of my mother's life by her bed side. Following her funeral I returned to Chicago to collect my clothes.

A few years later, after I began taking Betaseron and then Avonex, my condition improved slightly but I still had symptoms that made it difficult at times to predict what I would be capable or not capable of doing. In some cases, my worst fears came true on a few shows I did in the late nineties, like *Nash Bridges*, and *L.A. Heat*, where as hard as I tried I just could not keep up the charade. In *L.A. Heat*, I played an accountant who ran everywhere. I ran through bullets. I ran after cars. It was ridiculous. My double did most of the running, except once when I somehow—don't ask me how—did the running. The director was impatient and asked that I run a little faster. Well, I did and fell flat on my face. The same thing happened in *Nash Bridges*. My character ran everywhere. In one scene, when I was thrown through a plate glass window, I had to get up and run, avoiding pushcarts as I went.

Run. Run. Run. *Bang. Splat.* Pushcart hits the Dave. Head hits the pavement. Everyone thought I was dead.

⬤ Even though I was still getting work, I felt that my career was slowly taking a nose dive. A few friends began asking me what was going on, and though I never set out to disclose my secret, I was tired of lying and so I would usually ended up blurting the truth. Once, when I was complaining to Harry Shearer about being treated poorly by Lorne Michaels of *Saturday Night Live*, Harry asked me, "Why do you want to work on a show like that?"

"Because I have to, Harry," I replied. "I can hardly work anymore. I have MS, okay? I don't know when I'm ever going to get a job."

Not long after that, I told Michael McKean. We had been writing something together about Lenny and Squiggy, and Michael was giving me a pep talk.

"You know, you could be producing TV shows," he said. "You're wasting away. I don't know why it is you're not working more. Maybe your agents have been lousy, maybe it's bad luck, but you should be doing . . ."

He stopped and looked at the stationary bicycle in

the corner of my office. "By the way, how's your back?"

"Oh, it never was a back, Michael. It's multiple sclerosis."

And that was it. No one understood why I kept my illness secret from Michael, of all people, but the truth is, I never singled anyone out. I singled everybody out. Michael happened to fall into the "everybody" category.

The reason I did this is that I didn't want pity, or even sympathy, from anyone. If I was going to fail or succeed in my career and in life, I always wanted to do it on my own terms. I never wanted to suspect that I was being given special treatment or opportunities because I was sick. I also never wanted to put Michael in a position where he'd have to make excuses for me. If he didn't have information about my illness, he wouldn't have to defend me. He'd never have to say, "Well, you can say anything you want about the guy, but he's had some tough breaks. He's got multiple sclerosis."

In the past year, as I have traveled around the country speaking on behalf of the National MS Society to others who have this illness, I've learned that my feelings are quite common. People with a physical challenge don't want pity or sympathy from anyone. If we're going to fail or succeed in our careers, and in life, we want to do it on our own terms.

My friends and family at first had a hard time understanding why I was being so stubborn about accepting help or even well-wishes. But as I've been traveling around the country in recent months, speaking to others who have chronic illness, I've learned that this is not unusual.

THE TRUTH COMES OUT:

FALLING OUT OF THE CLOSET

With longtime friend Penny Marshall at the Dinner of Champions

It was early evening in February of 1999 when Penny Marshall called me and asked the big question, the one I had spent the last fifteen years avoiding.

"David," she asked, "are you fighting MS?"

My stomach felt like it had dropped through the floor. How did she know? I never told her. I never told anyone! I walked from the family room to the dining room to move away from the sounds of the television, as my mind raced frenetically: *Who snitched?*

I tried to connect who knew what. With the exception of Michael I hadn't told anyone on the cast of *Laverne & Shirley.* He had promised not to breathe a word, and I knew him well enough to know that he wouldn't blow that for me.

I sat on the edge of a chair at the head of the table and looked through the windows to the outside. It was dark, and I could only see my own reflection and the glassy shadows of the room behind me.

"It depends on what you mean by 'fighting,' " I finally replied to Penny. "If fighting means hiding, then I guess I am. Who wants to know?"

"Tom Sherak asked me if it was true," Penny said.

"Tom Sherak? Does he have it?"

"No, his daughter, Melissa, does. Every year he manages a big fundraiser—the Dinner of Champions for the National MS Society."

"It sounds like an eating contest."

"It's a fund-raiser, and he wants to honor you there."

What for? I thought. The only thing I had ever done for MS was get it and keep it a secret.

"Will you talk to him?" Penny asked.

"I don't know if I want to go public yet."

⦿ "Well," Penny said, "it's not until September. You have seven months to think about it. Besides, you'd really enjoy meeting him. Tom is one of the nicest guy in show business."

"Really? What does he do?"

"He runs Twentieth Century-Fox."

When I hung up the phone, I felt pulled in a million different directions. I was honored that anyone would think of me as a champion. But, on the other hand, I had mixed feelings about telling the world I had MS. Of all the scenarios I had imagined for going public with my illness, I had never dreamed of doing it in front of a bunch of industry bigwigs eating chicken.

Kathy and Natalie shared my initial reaction: How did these people find out? Since we'd spent so much time and energy to hide my MS, the fact that Penny Marshall had called out of the blue was curious at best. We weren't able to tie it together that night, but we later traced the leak to one of our neighbors. The son of the people who'd seen me take a nose dive in my attempt to mail a letter was very friendly with Melissa Sherak.

When I asked Kathy what she ultimately thought I should do, she took all of thirty seconds to make up her mind. "Go for it," she said. She, too, was exhausted from carrying this load of an uncertain future, and a decision to go public was at least a decision toward some sort of a resolution. Over the years she had been a pillar of strength and I knew I couldn't make a move like this unless it was what she and Natalie wanted. This involved their lives, too. The next day, Kathy reported Natalie's response, and that said it all. "She cried with relief," Kathy told me, "and said how great it will be not to have to make excuses for Dad anymore."

The three of us talked a lot about what might happen, and while there were many decisions to be made, the bottom line was I had their support for taking part in the Dinner of Champions. In the end, we all felt telling the truth would be a great relief. I also began to think about how my coming out might put me in a position to help other people with MS.

⬤ Even though I was leaning toward coming clean, I hadn't yet made a definite decision. Kathy saw it as a gift to move forward, but my big fear about going public was that all I'd end up with was an article in *People* magazine and, if I was lucky, a Movie of the Week.

And then what?

There were millions of questions circling in my head, and any answers I could come up with were not inspiring.

What did I have to gain?

Nothing.

What did I have to lose?

Everything.

Much as I wanted to believe it would be different, in my heart of hearts I was pretty certain that once show biz knew the truth it would mean the end of my career as an actor.

◉ The day after I talked with Penny, Tom Sherak called and suggested we get together for lunch. His voice was so warm, and his manner so open and friendly that I thought Penny might be right. Maybe he *was* the nicest guy in show business. In any event he was determined to win me over—without pushing me away.

"I just want to make sure you know where I'm coming from before you make your decision," he said.

I was tempted to say it would be better if you told me where you were going so I wouldn't miss lunch, but I didn't. Instead, I agreed to meet him at the Fox studios executive dining room.

When I hung up the phone I felt excited. Excited about what exactly, I didn't know.

It was odd timing that I had a meeting at Warner Brothers with my old writing partner, Peter Elbling, on the same day that I was to make this crucial decision about going public with MS. Elbling is an old friend whom I had met in the late seventies when he was writing for *Laverne & Shirley*. Shortly after my diagnosis Elbling and I had begun to write a script called *Squeezeplay*, which we were now trying to bring to Warner. *Squeezeplay* had been optioned many times over the years, but it had never been made.

Whatever happened in the meeting with Warner I knew would be moot by the end of the day after I had met with Sherak. Trying to keep my mind on the task at hand was no easy job. I talked scripts, but all I could think about was multiple sclerosis.

It was a strong day for me healthwise so I had no trouble getting up Warner's old Hollywood-style rickety stairs. At the top, Peter and I met with a smiling producer who, though he had no money for an option, was very excited about shopping *Squeezeplay* around. Again.

By this time, Peter and I had rewritten the script at

least fourteen times and had lost our initial wide-eyed enthusiasm. In fact, we had grown a bit cynical. "Sure, sure. Whatever. Yeah. Thanks, bye."

"Do you think we'll ever hear from him again?"

"Nah!" Peter said.

Climbing into our separate cars, as we had done millions of times before, we drove off toward our equally uncertain futures.

I had an hour or so to kill until lunch, so I drove over the Hollywood Hills from Burbank and around my old haunts up Sunset Boulevard. Never in my wildest dreams had I believed my life as an actor might end like this. As fertile as my imagination was, even I could have never dreamed up MS for a future. But that's what my life had become about—MS. Up until this moment, it had been all about hiding. If I decided to tell the truth now, I'd have to negotiate a whole new relationship to my life, my family, myself, my profession, and my disease.

As I pulled into the Fox lot, I still had no sense of what my decision would be. I was still torn, plus I was afraid that admitting I had MS in public would be giving up in some way. My deepest fear was that the more I admitted I was sick, the sicker I might become. Denial was safe, like a warm coat. It was a way of coping that was comfortable and familiar. The idea of letting go, though, was scary.

I parked on the lot in handicapped parking—the first time I had ever done that at a studio! I'll always remember the moment when I placed the special permit in full view on the dashboard of my car.

It had only been the year before that I allowed myself to use a cane in public to help with a limp caused by drop foot. That, too, I had fought bitterly. Kathy talked me into it based on two lines of reasoning: one, I would look distinguished and two, a cane could become my trademark, like Squiggy's hello.

Rationalizing that not all people who use canes have MS (and just think how comically Charlie Chaplin used one!) I gave it a try. Kathy had bought me one of those three-piece gizmos that you could unscrew and put in a pocket or under the seat so it would be less conspicuous. The first time I used it, we had gone to the movies. We settled into the last row, and I unscrewed the pieces and placed them under the seat in front of me. Five minutes into the film I heard a strange rattling, and noticed a ruckus in the row ahead of us. People were standing almost as if they were doing a wave like you see in at the ballpark. But this was no spontaneous rooting section. I realized they were retrieving sections of my new cane.

The Stage 15 parking lot was a bit of a walk to the Fox dining room but I was still feeling that it was a good walking day. Physically I was strong, confident, and focused. I could clearly visualize getting from point A to point B, so I was better equipped to actually make it without incident.

Sherak's secretary escorted me to a table in the center of the dining room, where I was met by Tom Sherak, his daughter Melissa, a few other Fox executives, and Leon Le Buffe, president of the Southern California chapter of the National Multiple Sclerosis Society. I'd never seen so many people so happy to see me. For a group of strangers, they were phenomenally supportive. In response, I felt free to be myself—MS and all.

During lunch I told Le Buffe that if we had met last year, I wouldn't have spoken a word to him. In response, Sherak gave me a curious grin. "I don't understand why you kept this a secret, David. Who were you hiding from?"

"People like you."

Everyone laughed.

Tom's daughter, Melissa, seemed to understand my uncertainty and insecurity. The instant rapport between us was startling.

Our conversation was geared toward taking a new angle on life. The Dinner of Champions was a step toward taking a new job: helping to raise money for medical research while increasing public awareness of the devastating effects of MS. This dinner was one of the MS Society's biggest fund-raisers. The year before, 1998, it had raised $2 million, and the sponsors were hoping to do better this year. (They raised $3.1 million in 1999!)

"Last year we had Annette," Sherak said, "and she was so beautiful. The year before we had Richard Pryor—he was brilliant."

Someone else said. "You'll be just fine."

Wait a minute, I thought. *I don't want to be just fine.* "What happens if you find someone with MS who's more famous than me between now and dinner?" I asked. "Will they get the award and I'll get an honorable mention and a table in the back?"

By the end of lunch, I had decided to tell the world I had MS. I felt so supported that I couldn't imagine another time or situation that would be any more compassionate.

Now that I was going public I felt it was important to actually do something for MS, so that when they gave me the award, I would have actually done something to earn it.

Tom suggested my serving on the board of directors for the Multiple Sclerosis Society of Southern California. It sounded interesting, so about a month after our lunch, I found myself walking into the MSSSC boardroom. After fifteen years of keeping quiet, I was now ready to spread the word about MS to help erase the stigma that comes with it—as with any debilitating illness. I felt excited and good about myself in a way I hadn't in years. Coming out had been very good to me so far!

The board was made up of about twelve members, all of whom seemed to have firsthand experience with MS. A few had the disease, but most were family or friends of those who did. Tom introduced me, and I told the board my history with the disease—even getting a few laughs in the right places. When I walked out of the boardroom, Tom gave me an approving smile. I knew I had taken another step toward redefining myself as a performer.

The next step in the process was to find a good publicist to orchestrate my announcement. Being in the center of the world of show biz, Sherak had a few recommendations.

How to best spin the story of a once-famous television actor's coming out with a chronic, usually degenerative disease? The key was to downplay the disease, up-play the secret, emphasize the tragedy, the drama, the triumph.

Ah, Hollywood.

My account ended up being handled by Dick Guttman and Beverly Magid of Guttman Associates in Beverly Hills. They understood exactly what I was afraid of, publicitywise. I didn't want to find out about me in the *National Enquirer* or *The Globe*.

What about *People*? Beverly suggested.

People sounded fine. In fact, they had been calling over the last few months, wanting to do a story about my scouting for the Anaheim Angels. I never followed up on it because I had been informally scouting for the team for years and it never seemed like that big of a deal.

◉ We agreed to give *People* the exclusive right to break my tragic secret to the public in May. But at the last minute my story was postponed for a few weeks because of the Columbine tragedy. I'll never forget the night before the May issue of *People* was to hit newsstands. I was no longer going out in the world as an actor playing a part. I felt I was stepping out as a role model for others suffering from MS. I was speaking for people like me with different jobs but similar problems: Lawyers, doctors, teachers, and bricklayers, all of us with one simple goal—let's see if we can get through this day without falling down.

Once my story hit the newsstands, the reaction was overwhelming. For the first time, I truly felt that I was not alone. Hundreds of people contacted me via the Internet and through the mail. One man revealed that he had been keeping his MS a secret for twenty-five years. Everyone, it seemed, was congratulating me on my courage to come forward.

My home phone rang off the hook: ABC, CBS, NBC, CNBC, CNN, and *20/20*. The media response was phenomenal. I spent a few weeks doing interviews: *Entertainment Tonight. Access Hollywood. Good Morning America.* After all these years of hiding, it was a relief to be finally talking.

In only five hours of television and one disease, I saw myself transformed from comic actor to comic genius. Watching the news the day the *People* article broke, in a weird way I felt I was looking at my own obituary. I kept seeing myself in the newscasts in the past tense. There I was as Squiggy. Then the producers would dub in some serious music, and when it stopped an announcer would say, somberly,

"MS—that's what he's got, that's what he's hid, that's what he's fighting, that's what's made him famous again."

Wow, I thought. What a career move. I should have done this years ago.

But as the media spun and everyone wished me well and praised my courage, show biz shrugged. As I had feared, Hollywood welcomed me and my news with closed arms and a total silence. I received exactly zero calls or notes from the people I had worked with without revealing my disability. What did they think of me for deceiving them? Were they pissed off? I wondered if anyone who had ever fired me in the past felt any remorse now that they knew I was trying to hide MS.

If they did, I never knew it.

A little more than a month after I came out in *People*, I was to play my first stage role as an actor with MS. I had been asked to play a mute king in a production of *Once Upon a Mattress*.

The stage felt very safe because I had spent a great deal of time rehearsing. I knew where I was supposed to walk, and I knew where I was supposed to sit. But I was concerned about the location of my throne, which was set atop six steps—which I would have to *run* up. In the past I would have kept my apprehen-

Natalie and me in my
Once Upon a Mattress *costume*

sion to myself, but in my new life of full disclosure, I shared my worries with the producer. He had the stagehands take some extra precautions, and also warned my fellow actors: "Just be prepared to catch him if he goes flying," the producer said with a smile.

Perhaps the best part of the show was the large number of people with MS in the audience who applauded my every move: Every step I took, every wench I goosed, every sprint up the stairs to my throne, was a triumph not only for me but for everyone with MS.

Months later, Kathy, Natalie, and I dressed up in our evening finery, climbed into a limousine, and headed off for the Dinner of Champions. Moments before, Tom Sherak had called to congratulate me on my courage. "Your life is never going to be the same," he said.

At last the night had come for the dinner that had sparked my splendid new journey. My publicist met the three of us at the entrance to the Century Plaza Hotel, and we headed toward the grand ballroom—and a phalanx of television cameras and a sea of bobbing heads with microphones. Walking down the long line of news cameras, we stopped at each for thirty seconds—ABC, NBC, CBS, CNN, FOX.

The questions were all the same.

"Aren't you glad you came out?"

"What's it like hiding such a horrible disease?"

Getting through the line of press took about twenty minutes and, while I had been walking fine up until that point, I was getting tired and beginning to feel a pain in the base of my spine. I needed to sit down and recharge. I thought briefly about what might happen if I fell, and it occurred to me that right now I was walking for many others besides myself. I wanted to show the world a different face of MS. We're not cripples. Just watch me walk!

Finding the way to our table, I found myself checking the setup. As I had so many times over the last fifteen years while preparing for a part, before the other guests filed in to take their seats I rehearsed walking from the table to the stairs to the stage.

When we sat down, Kathy took my hand and smiled. We had made it. From now on there was no secret.

In the back of our minds, though, even on this triumphant evening, the same question remained: *Where do we go from here?*

◉

EIGHT

THE MAGICAL MSTERY TOUR:

A NEW LIFE

Kathy, Natalie, and me

If I wrote a movie about my life, I would change the end to reveal that I faked the disease in order to jump-start a stalled acting career. The irony is, of course, I wouldn't be considered for the lead role because I have MS. I can see it now: a handful of actors read for the film, but each arrives at the audition with his own idea of how to portray MS. Kevin Pollack wears a body cast. Nicholas Cage shows up in a wheel chair. Jim Carrey sports a perfect Squiggy spit curl and drags a leg. Directly behind him is Kevin Spacey pushing a walker.

That's where my imaginary scenario begins to go

haywire. A producer calls and reports the following at breakneck speed: Rodney Dangerfield is set to play my dad, and although Marion Ross has accepted the role of my mother, she may be "too Jewish." Jason Alexander's been offered to play the part of my brother, but only if the casting director gets one of those guys from *Friends*. My daughter, Natalie, will read for Kathy before we were married and Cindy Williams will play Kathy of today only if she doesn't play herself during our *Laverne & Shirley* days. Michael McKean will play Michael McKean—if we can't get Jeff Daniels to do it. Emilio Estevez will write the adaption, but wants to change the disease to something more cinematic like epilepsy. My early life in the Bronx will be shot in Australia, but the Hollywood stuff will be done in Toronto. And just yesterday Garry Marshall agreed to direct, but only if Richard Gere will play him.

We all have public personas, but for me embracing my outer life as an actor with MS has been a reflection of the very private process of accepting the disease itself. I was slow to do both, but going public acted as a catalyst that made me feel more free to process what was happening to me physically. Having MS forced me to redefine who I was beyond the film industry, and it also made me face that living with a chronic, progressive disease isn't anything like it might be in the movies. There's no script for my mind or body to faithfully follow; the people around me are real individuals whose reactions to me and MS I can't always control or direct, and whether or not I like the way things appear to be going, I can't call the writer of my life story and request that the end be changed.

Following the heady successful years on *Laverne & Shirley*, my acting career stopped and started. It never quite reached those heights again and I'll never know why. I know MS affected my life, but I don't really understand how it apparently affected my ability to act. Did I lose my edge as an actor because of the disease? Maybe. Was I somehow not as expressive or insightful? I don't know. What I do know is that by not embracing the truth of what was happening for so long, I lost faith in my ability because I wasn't comfortable enough with who I was to be able to play someone else with conviction.

When I went public, on the other hand, if someone at an audition asked why I was limping, finally I could say it was because I have MS. This was a major step. There were so many times I had to say, *"Oh, I slammed my foot in the car door." "Oh, it's gout." "Oh, it's lumbago,"* that it was such a relief to stop making excuses and speak the truth. As a result, I was much more confident and comfortable at auditions. If my MS came up, it was mentioned only in the kindest of ways. So my experience of working changed dramatically. Since I no longer had anything to hide, I stopped watching myself. I felt more comfortable in my skin and as a result took more risks with my self and my characters.

Going public entailed a complete reversal of the coping tactics and personal beliefs that had kept me going while I was keeping my illness secret. Hiding had demonstrated my complete lack of faith in the people of the film and television, but coming out was a 100-degree about-face. It was an action that demonstrated utter faith. Most of my professional peers reciprocated with kindness and sensitivity, continuing to refer work my way, requesting my presence and participation in benefits and special-award dinners that are often so part of life as an actor. And since going public, I've received no more or fewer calls for acting jobs. Now, each time I am hired to work, I believe my example is an inspiration for anyone who lives with a handicap.

While my colleagues have been nothing but open-minded and understanding about my MS, I know it's sometimes difficult for them to cope with feeling of discomfort concerning the disease. I've noticed some people avoid the topic like the plague. Others have the opposite response. And want to talk about nothing else. And then there are those who seem sincerely shocked to see me in public, as if they are amazed I am still alive. There is no right way to react to people with MS, and I cannot criticize anyone for his or her reactions. If things were reversed I don't know how I would react—especially if I heard that a friend or peer had kept his illness a secret from me for fifteen years. I've often thought about the appropriate response when you learn a colleague is fighting a disease like MS. Do you avoid the topic? Do you congratulate him on the courage they've shown? Do you feel sorry for the person? Do you honor him at another Dinner of Champions? Or do you ask him how he is?

These days some people are careful to ask about my health. I never mind when people ask me how I'm feeling, as long as I feel they really care about my well-being. But I have to say, there are those who wear compassionate smiles while asking, "How have you been," but their tone is a little exasperated. What they really want to know, I'm afraid, is *How have you really been? Walking for much longer?*

I generally respond with an innocuous "fine" but

what I want to say is, "The way you asked the question, I don't think I can live down to your expectations."

The reactions of my closest friends and colleagues have been diverse. I ran into Rob Reiner at a birthday party right after the Dinner of Champions. "How ya doin'?" he said. "I read about that thing in *People*. You look great."

"That thing," Rob had said, referring to MS. Sometimes it's very hard for people to say the words.

To this day, some of my good friends would rather chop off their arms than talk about MS. Others have treated my public pronouncement like a wedding invitation. *How come you didn't tell me earlier? I thought we were good friends.* As for me, I wanted to be treated just like anyone else. Anyone with a handicap shares that impossible sentiment because as much as we'd like to believe it isn't true, it is. When you're handicapped, you are different.

Squiggy fans have been incredibly supportive. While I was walking in a ballpark recently, a group of teenage boys yelled from the bleachers, "Go, Squiggy, go!"

"Where?" I shrugged.

I also get positive feedback from the baseball community. One sports reporter complimented me for my courage, saying, "Mr. Lander, you have balls of steel."

I wanted to say, "Oh, maybe *that's* what gave me MS instead of those fillings!" but all I did say was, "No wonder I've had such trouble at airports."

The more open I've become, the more clearly I see how my celebrity can help others living with the disease. After I appeared on *Good Morning America* last year, more than 1,000 people immediately joined me for a chat on the ABC Web site. Shortly after the show, the National Multiple Sclerosis Society set up a meeting to talk about my new role as a goodwill ambassador for them. I knew I could make a difference: people who live with MS are hungry to talk about their experiences and to hear what others are going through. As an ambassador, the society wanted me to share what it had been like for me to hide my illness and then come forward to honestly share what treatments had worked for me and what hadn't, to talk about how my family had been affected by what I was going through, and to offer suggestions for coping with MS on a personal and professional level.

I was happy to do this—but I just can't talk about

MS without using at least a little humor. So in my first day on the job as Goodwill Ambassador, I immediately poked fun at the title. "I can handle being an ambassador to a disease," I told the audience I was speaking to. "But where am I supposed to draw the line? It seems like every ten seconds, I have to welcome someone else in."

Being a shticktician with MS has opened up for me a whole new world of comedy. It's my own patented brand of not stand-up, but fall-down comedy.

"Good afternoon," I told one audience. "I'd like to take this time to welcome you to my disease. I can get you a room next to the myelin sheath with a view of an incredible shrinking brain!"

As Goodwill Ambassador, the National MS Society has asked me to travel all across the country—a job I'm happy to do because it puts me in touch with people whose lives I can truly relate to. In the fall of 1999, for example, I embarked upon a nine-city two-week national tour. My doctors were stunned by the pace I was able to sustain, but the truth is the more grueling the schedule, the better I felt. I had spent so many years not talking, and now all I wanted to do was talk to make up for lost time. I would do seven radio, two newspapers, and at least one *Good-morning-wherever-you-are* television interview in each city—a schedule that I considered a personal test of strength and will. I passed with flying colors: the fact that I could go on TV or radio and continue to *stand*, never mind be funny, while in an upright position was invigorating.

Being known as "that guy who used to be Squiggy" has allowed me to put a human face on multiple sclerosis. By telling my story, I've helped others share theirs. With MS, you're not working with the same deck that everyone else has been dealt. It is a difficult and almost impossible disease to live with. Daily life is full of dirty tricks and low blows, but my new role as ambassador has made me feel part of a larger mission.

These days on my tours for the MS Society, I often speak at what I call MS Festivals—professional conferences attended by biotechnological and pharmaceutical companies, as well as neurological specialists. Some of the world's top medical minds are working toward finding a cure for MS and I'm usually paired with one of them during my speaking engagements. Typically, the doctor will speak first, discussing new treatment approaches and promising avenues of research. I then follow with the story of MS and me. At

The MS Walk

my first festival, I remember how odd it felt to look out into an audience of 200 people like me, I felt very much at home. Imagine being a Pirates fan at Shea Stadium. In New York, I was an outsider, but if you go to Pittsburgh, you're surrounded by thousands of people and we're all rooting for the Pirates. That's how I felt, looking at my audience of fellow MSers that first morning.

What I enjoy most at these conventions is telling stories and switching the narrator from "me" to "us."

There's no disease as unpredictable or terrifying as MS, and having it can be lonely. When I see other people's strength in their spirit and in the light in their eyes, it gives me strength, too.

Now, when I stand up in front of an audience I know that the people I'm speaking to are the only ones who really understand what we're going through. It's not as much fun when I make speeches to fund-raising people who don't have MS. The jokes don't work as well because the audience can't laugh at the same stuff MS folks can. People without MS aren't sure it's politically correct to laugh at jokes about the handicapped, whereas when I play an MS event and trip while walking to the stage, people with MS murmur, "Yeah, I know what's that like." When I get to the podium, I'll say something like, "Since people with multiple sclerosis fall down so much, it's a great disease for people who like to be lazy. It's like having a degree in clumsiness: when you fall down, onlookers will say, "Oh, that's okay. He has MS. He's supposed to fall. It's his kind of normal. In fact, I hear that people with MS actually like falling down—since they're so good at it."

⬤ In my new role of offering help to others, my life as an actor, specifically as Squiggy, has made all the difference as to what I've been able to accomplish. I prepare my speeches the way I've prepared for many film, stage, or television roles. If I know I'm going on at a certain time, I'll plan ahead when to eat so I'll be at my physical best. Afterward, I evaluate my performance, and always try to make it better. If I expected five laughs and only received three, I try to figure out where I blew the joke.

I know that to some extent, I have been labelled and typecast by both my most prominent roles in life—as Squiggy and now as a spokesperson for MS. Someone recently asked me if I minded being predominantly known for being Squiggy—if I would have traded a few years at the top of my game as that character for many years as an actor playing many other parts. I thought about it, and realized how grateful I am for Squiggy. Being Squiggy has enabled me to help change the popular opinion of MS. If not for him, very few people would truly care if I had MS. Squiggy is so much of a popular icon that he can make a difference—which maybe David L. Lander couldn't.

Squiggy helps me reach children whose parents have MS. It's a difficult disease for kids to understand, but when they find out that Squiggy is coming to town and has MS just like their mom or dad, they see that MS hits everyone. As Penny Marshall once said, "If Squiggy can get it, anyone can."

In the middle of my 1999 MS tour, I went to Vancouver to play Squiggy in a movie. I was watching dailies one afternoon when I realized I wasn't half as excited about acting in this film as I was about speaking about MS.

Meeting and talking to other people in similar circumstances has helped me feel that I'm not alone. I know that all the roads I travel in my thinking, others travel, too. I recently met a woman with MS whose husband was converting their home to accommodate her physical needs in the event her disease progressed. For the time being, she was very strong and mobile, but this couple was already planning on changing their lifestyle to accommodate her illness. This has always been the last thing I've wanted: I've always believed that if the disease worsened I'd maintain my current lifestyle but just go a little slower. When this woman talked about her life and her plans, though, I began to see realities in my own life that I still tend to try to avoid—in spite of everything I've learned about honesty. Like many who have MS, despite my progress, I don't always look at reality straight on; I tend to see the frets slightly askew.

 What I've gained by interacting with the MS community is immeasurable. Though I wish it was under different circumstances, I've met great people: patients, neurologists, devoted volunteers, and family members who work with regional MS societies. I've been constantly amazed by the enthusiasm of all these folks; their spirit is contagious and their hope drives me forward.

During the fifteen years in which I was living a lie, I was very lonely. But once I committed to the truth, my life was enriched in unimaginable ways. I know I will continue going on the road as long as the MS Society wants me to, even if I am in a wheelchair, because that is what life's all about for me. I am here. I can still think, even in a wheelchair. I can still talk and laugh and exchange ideas. What fulfills me these days is reaching out and having people reach back.

On bad days, no matter how I feel physically, if I'm scheduled for an appearance or a job, I go. On the day I was supposed to appear at an award dinner with Garry Marshall at the Playboy Mansion, I had suffered a pretty bad fall earlier in the day, and I spent quite a bit of time on the floor trying to get up. By the time I was finally able to stand, I was bruised, battered, and exhausted. I wanted very much to climb into bed and turn on a baseball game, but instead I pulled on my pants, tucked in my shirt, and went to the dinner, hoping like hell I wouldn't fall down again.

I certainly had a great excuse for staying home, but I didn't want to use it. There were too many people at the dinner who'd be thrilled to see me standing, and thanks to my work for the MS Society, there are too many people out there in the world who are counting on me to set an example. The best contribution I can make to society is to show people I am still living and working with all my might within the limit of this disease.

Every week, two hundred people are newly diagnosed with multiple sclerosis. I want them to have the opportunity to watch someone walk across a stage fifteen years after his own diagnosis. I don't want to let others down; I don't want to let *me* down. I want to give us all hope.

UP THE DOWN RAMP:
THE OCCUPATION OF BEING ME

My old character performing Dave Sportz at Dodger Stadium

When talking to my caseworker at the Motion Picture and Television Hospital recently, I thought of an interview I saw once on *The Jack Paar Show*. Paar smiled at the great Oscar Levant, a musician and actor known for his wit and wry commentary, and asked him what he did for exercise.

"I get up each morning," Levant said, "and fall down a flight of stairs."

My sentiments exactly.

My caseworker had just asked me an equally ridiculous question, one I had no desire to answer. "What exactly do you see in your future?" she asked.

Lots of ramps, a one-story house, a wheelchair, and another book?

I was in the hospital because I'd just suffered a series of exacerbations that were particularly stubborn. I was working very hard on a variety of projects—including this book—and, as my doctors are fond of telling me, "MS and stress are bad for each other." But despite this physical setback, I still wasn't prepared for a question about my plans for the future. Thinking about the possibility of getting sicker was something I wanted to avoid for as long as possible.

"What do you mean, what do I see in my future?" I asked her, cagily trying to buy time and maybe distract her altogether.

"What about acting?"

"Do you see yourself lecturing or acting a few years down the road? Do you want to retire?"

"Well, I'll always act," I said, "but playing myself might be my greatest role."

When I was asked as a kid what I wanted to do for a living when I grew up, I remember answering the question by saying that there was a great job for me out there, it just hadn't been invented yet. The *Credibility Gap* turned out to be that job. *Laverne & Shirley* was that job. Neither had existed before I walked in, but rather were invented after I arrived on the scene.

I didn't mention this to the social worker, but I saw it as sure as the nose on my face. All my life I had traveled the path of invention, making it up as I went along.

When the caseworker left me, I crawled out of bed and sat in a chair, careful not to disturb the intravenous line in my arm leading to yet another megadose of steroids. The truth was, I had been flip with her because the king of making-it-up-as-you-go-along didn't want to think too far into the future. In actual fact, I had never felt so crippled in my life as the past few weeks, and this time I was beginning to worry that I might not bounce back.

My only hope was that MS would remain true to its unpredictable, come-and-go, up-and-down nature. If nobody could have predicted that I was down now, who's to guarantee that I wouldn't take a sudden turn for the better next week or the week after? If you're wondering what "up" of "up-and-down" is, it's simply walking. From my point of view, as long as I'm mobile, I'm a lucky man. This latest exacerbation, though, was giving me no opportunity to avoid the topic of what happens when the disease progresses.

For those diagnosed with the form of MS that I have, it's a disease that can grow progressively worse. Physicians are careful not to make predictions about their patients' futures, but they will characterize them according to several prognostic classifications. My MS is called "relapse remitting." The next worse kind of MS to have is called "primary progressive," typified by consistent and steady worsening of symptoms without the typical pattern of relapse and recovery. "Secondary progressive" indicates a similar pattern of a downward turn that is similar to "primary progressive" but occurs later in the disease.

Relapse remitting is what 70 percent of the MS population is initially diagnosed with. If you have to have MS, this is considered the best form to have. Its course is clearly defined by relapses, which are followed by partial or complete recovery. The medication I'm on, Avonex, has been very effective at stopping exacerbations from happening as frequently; otherwise the disease would progress faster. Luckily when my past flare-ups have occurred, my health has so far always returned. Each time, though, my sense of normal has fallen to a little lower than it was before.

Since my original diagnosis, my condition has come to be labelled "secondary progressive." This is fairly common: Fifty percent of MS patients originally diagnosed with relapse-remitting MS are diagnosed with secondary progressive within ten years of their initial diagnosis. It's also standard for people diagnosed with this type of MS to experience, as I did, an initial period of relapse remitting followed by a steady worsening disease course—with or without the characteristics typical of relapse-remitting like flare-ups, remissions, or plateaus.

Even though my old friend Dr. Jacobs has confirmed my updated diagnosis, I really don't want to believe it. I've always convinced myself that I have a mild case of MS; that my MS is the "good" MS and won't progress to wheelchair status.

But this current period of my life could be the toughest yet. These days, what I want to believe continues to come smack up against what's actually going on. The latest series of exacerbations I've been experiencing could be simply a reoccurrence of others I've had over the years, but I don't know that. Each time the disease presents itself in this fashion, I have no idea what lies on the other side—although Kathy is quick to remind me that over the years my exacerbations have been just as difficult, with serious clusters happening at about the same time of year every three years.

Nevertheless, I am not always soothed. When your body is not cooperating with your mind, it's frightening to not know if you'll ever recover the physical ground you seem to be losing. After these exacerbations pass, there's no guarantee I will come back to my previous—or in fact, *any*—level of functioning.

So my present mission is to prepare myself for the possibility of increasing disability. This is hands down the scariest part of MS. I've denied the disease; I've worked with it; I've embraced it. And now I have to face up to the possible reality of living with a more advanced stage of it when truthfully I'd much prefer to be looking at the reality of crossing my legs whenever I feel like it.

When Kathy recently asked what I thought about the future of my MS, I couldn't resist a joke. "I'd like to see it in Pittsburgh," I told her, "in time for the opening of the Pirates' new ballpark in 2001."

Just as physical balance has been a key challenge in my life for the past sixteen years, it looks like one of the things I'm going to have to continue to work on is mental balance—achieving a state of mind that's prepared but hopeful. Being hopeful is critical to my peace of mind; but being prepared is just as critical for my family's well-being. It appears that the harder I try to avoid the reality of the disease's progression, the more difficult it becomes for my family to cope with it. The less I take responsibility for my illness, the more the burden falls on them. It's already forced those I love to carry an unusually heavy load: during times of exacerbations, my wife and daughter find their lives turned inside out. When I'm experiencing a rough time with MS, it's difficult for them to leave me alone for fear I'll fall down the stairs and no one will be there to pick me up. Because my balance can be temporarily affected, during these tough periods I often need to be driven to places I ordinarily would have walked or driven myself to: auditions, meetings, the post office, and other errands. I also cannot help out as much around the house, so the pressure of keeping our home from disintegrating around us falls on them. This has not been easy for my family, nor is it now, as Kathy continues to build her career as a marriage and family counselor, and seventeen-year-old Natalie prepares to apply to college.

In the interest of full honesty, I have complicated matters by not making preparations to deal with my illness when it worsens. I haven't moved my office to the first floor of our house or looked into purchasing a new one-story home because I've always felt climbing up and down stairs has been good for me and has kept me strong. I haven't wanted to install handrails in the shower because I didn't want to feel "handicapped." I didn't want to widen doorways because I didn't like to imagine myself confined to a wheelchair, or rely on a cane or walker.

Though this is a strategy shared by some, my latest exacerbation has forced me to question my logic. One recent weekday morning, I lost my balance in the shower and fell. I didn't have the strength to pull myself back up and I had no handrails to grab onto anyway. I would have called Kathy for help but she was well into one of her twelve-hour workdays. I would have preferred not to ask Natalie to help in such a situation, but that didn't matter since she was at school.

It ended up taking me well over an hour to crawl out of the tub. Every inanimate object in the bathroom had ganged up on me. Whatever I grabbed either fell off or turned in my hand. I tried the shower handle but ended up turning on the hot water. Yikes! When I was finally able to get on my hands and knees, I crawled for a while in search of something steady on which I could pull myself up. I tried a bureau but ended up slamming my fingers into the drawer. I fell down. I got up. Two steps later, I landed with a *thunk*. I didn't have the strength to roll over. The noises I made were the worst; the slapping of wet flesh and the banging of bone like little car crashes. Then finally, when I crawled into my office to grab my walker, it tipped over on me and collapsed.

It was difficult to accept, but that was a moment of truth. The shower incident was one in a series of an increasing number of signals indicating that my over-all physical condition was changing and I might have to face up to some unpleasant facts. My episodes were coming and going, but not disappearing as quickly or completely as they used to. At the end of a bad day—which might include a fall just like the one in the shower—I would feel hung over, stiff and exhausted. I had lingering fatigue and balance problems and worsening pain and weakness.

The shower incident was only one of many episodes over a two-month full-scale, up-and-down fiasco with MS, during which I was scheduled to travel to Washington to take part in the Society's annual Issues and Empowerment conference, which would culminate with participants making over 800 visits on the Hill to advocate for legislation to improve the life of people with MS and other disabilities. The legislation included Medicare coverage of self-injectable MS drugs. Afterward, I was supposed to speak to a Biotech Trade Association in Boston, a consortium of neurologists and biotechnology firms that meets annually to discuss issues and treatments concerning a myriad of neurological disorders, including MS. Biogen is the maker of the drug I'm currently on, Avonex, and I was asked to speak about the great things it had done for me.

The day I was to leave for Washington, I took a nasty fall in my office. And this time when I fell, my family fell with me. Kathy and Natalie were unable to lift me to my feet, and since they couldn't just leave me on the floor, we were all trapped inside for the afternoon. No matter how hard I tried to get up, my head always led to the ground. My balance had taken a holiday. The only time I felt strength was when I would try to do something—for example, try to pull myself up again—and the part of my body not being used would fight back as if my arms and legs were members of opposing wrestling teams.

"Maybe you should smear me with Vasoline and just slide me down the stairs," I suggested at one point—an attempt at humor that Kathy didn't think was funny. Natalie managed to break a weak smile, though, and went next door to find a neighbor who could help us. Together, the three of them put me into the car to the hospital. Though they had to carry me down the stairs, at the end of our fifteen-minute drive to the Motion Picture and Television Hospital, I was able to get out of the car and walk into the hospital completely unaided. Sometimes, the disease is like having a car that makes a very alarming and suspicious *ping-ping-ping* noise for weeks, until the next minute you bring it into a service station for a checkup, and the engine just purrs like a kitten.

Since I was in the hospital, there was no way I could travel to Washington, but still I never let go of the idea of going. *Even if I can't make it the first night,* I reasoned, *I can still get there the following day. Who cares if the doctors and my family are dead set against me leaving the hospital? Who cares if the National Multiple Sclerosis Society told me to stay home and take care of myself?*

Lying in bed, I worried endlessly about all the things I was missing: the speeches, interviews, and meetings. As if this wasn't enough to keep me awake, I was on massive doses of intravenous steroids to help blindside the MS. Since one of the major side effects of steroids is sleeplessness, it's no wonder that in the middle of the night, I found myself turning on the television. What should pop on the screen but an early episode of *Laverne & Shirley* in which Squiggy, as usual, barges through the door of Laverne and Shirley's apartment. I was mesmerized watching my formerly very young and mobile self, knowing he was me. I studied the way he walked, ran, and jumped, fell down, stood up, and brushed himself off. Such agility and mobility! Suddenly I had an eerie feeling of *déjà vu*. At the height of my *Laverne & Shirley* days, I often wondered where I would be in twenty years watching an old rerun. I never imagined my future would look like this.

The hospital released me the following morning but later that afternoon, as I gathered my belongings to fly to Washington (better late than never), I took another fall. Kathy and Natalie had to practically carry me down the stairs go back to the hospital.

Though I realized there was now no way to make it to D.C., I kept my eye on Boston for the following day. Everybody told me not to go: the doctors, my wife, and even the MS Society. But the more they said no, the more determined I became. I was not going to bail out and later look back and say, "What a shame I didn't take a five-hour plane flight to where I was supposed to be."

In my mind, it was critical to work *through* MS instead of not working *because* of it. The challenges were becoming bigger every day, and every time I achieved something in spite of my disease it gave me a great sense of accomplishment. Lying in the hospital, I could not accept that this was the end of my story. *This can't be the end*, I kept telling myself, *This can't be how it's going to be for the rest of my life.*

If I didn't keep this commitment now and make

the trip to Boston, I felt that I could never again be confident of being able to physically keep doing the things my mind was set on. So I called a travel agent, bought an airplane ticket, and arranged for a limousine service to pick me up from the hospital at six A.M.

Look out, Boston, here I come!

I couldn't walk worth a damn, so for the first time in my life I asked for wheelchair assistance. In the old days, when I was asked I always waved it off. Not for me, thank you very much. I'd long ago accepted the fact that I couldn't run, but say good-bye to walking and accept a wheelchair? Never.

This time, though, I said, "You bet."

As I was being wheeled through the airport, I felt like a big Squiggy float in the Macy's Thanksgiving parade. I was bloated and had gained weight from the steroids. My face felt as big as the moon. I'm surprised anyone recognized me, but even in that condition people were staring at me as if they did.

In the end, I was in Boston for just twenty-four hours, but they were some of the most important in my life. I had gone knowing full well that I was having great difficulty walking and that I could no longer fool myself into thinking, *Yes, I have MS, but I have a good version, so I'll never have to get into a wheelchair.* Using a wheelchair in the airport broke some kind of mental barrier I'd been carrying around for years. If the Biotech people gave me a wheelchair, I decided I'd take it instead of waving it off as usual.

I thought I had come clean the year before, but until that moment I had been back to my hiding tricks. *No more*, I made a pact with myself. As it happened, a wheelchair followed me around for the whole day of the consortium, but I never used it because I didn't feel I needed to. I now know that it's a delicate balance: having the wisdom to use a chair when I don't need it, and the guts to use it when I do.

On the flight back to L.A., we flew through three time zones and I watched the sunset over and over. I thought about what I used to say when the reruns of *Laverne & Shirley* were beginning to be shown all over the world: *The sun never sets on Laverne & Shirley.*

A week later, the National Multiple Sclerosis Society sponsored a walk in Los Angeles and asked the cast of *Laverne & Shirley* to make an appearance to support the cause. It turned out not to be a good day for me: I had mixed up some of my medication and taken a sleeping pill instead of a blood-pressure pill. I was unsteady on my feet, but I was there along with my family, Cindy Williams, Michael McKean, Penny Marshall, Betty Garrett, and Garry Marshall.

It wasn't exactly the way I saw a reunion, I have to

admit. Because of the medication mix-up, I ended up watching it all later on *Entertainment Tonight* from a hospital bed. But it was fun seeing the gang again, and a wonderful reminder about how much they all mean to me. Plus, Cindy later told me that I gave a helluva speech and got great laughs.

Me with the Pittsburg Pirates: John Candelaria (#45), Larry Demery (#44), Dan Giusti (#31), and Bob Moose (#38)

So here I am back in the hospital for the umpteenth time after confronting another hard dose of the reality of MS. How would I answer the caseworker's question now, after spending some time looking at the world while sitting in a wheelchair? How does my view of the future look? Well, it ain't so bad from here. If the worst happens, it happens. In the meantime, I am on the mend.

A week after the MS walk, I was doing laps around Dodger Stadium to welcome in the new baseball season, and as of this writing, I am still going strong. But as everyone with MS knows, there is no predicting.

I know, however, that whatever happens, MS can't take it all. I will always have my heart and soul, my wit and wisdom. Wherever the chips may fall, if I fall with them I will make it a point to do so gracefully—and laughing.

ABOUT THE AUTHOR
◉

Best known for his portrayal of the character
"Squiggy" on the sitcom *Laverne & Shirley* (1976–
1983), David L. Lander has appeared in feature films,
including *Who Framed Roger Rabbit*, *A League of Their
Own*, and *Scary Movie*. He has guest-starred on more
than thirty television shows, including *Mad About You*,
Twin Peaks, and *Pacific Blue*. A lifelong baseball fan, he

is a scout for the Anaheim Angels and part owner of the Portland Beavers, a Minor League ballclub. In addition to his active film and television career, Lander is the Goodwill Ambassador for the National MS Society. He lives in Los Angeles.

Lee Montgomery is a writer and editor who divides her time between Portland, Oregon, and Topanga, California. She is the editor of anthologies *Absolute Disaster* and *Transgressions* as well as numerous other books.

Permissions

Photo on page 1 Kathy Fields Lander

Photo on page 9 by Saul Landau

Photo on page 14 unknown

Photo on page 33 by Thea Lander

Photo on page 41 by Thea Lander